79

... with her family. She ... full-time writer. She is the author of ...ot ('a richly evocative novel ... com-...mmersed in the colours, scents, sounds and ambience ...medieval life' *Historical Novel Review*) and *Of Love and War*.

The Loving Cup

Vanessa Alexander

headline

First published in Great Britain in 2001
by HEADLINE BOOK PUBLISHING

First published in paperback in 2002
by HEADLINE BOOK PUBLISHING

A HEADLINE paperback

10 9 8 7 6 5 4 3 2 1

ISBN 0 7472 6679 4

Typeset by Palimpsest Book Production Limited,
Polmont, Stirlingshire

Printed and bound in Great Britain by
Mackays of Chatham plc, Chatham, Kent

HEADLINE BOOK PUBLISHING
A division of Hodder Headline
338 Euston Road
London NW1 3BH

www.headline.co.uk
www.hodderheadline.com

To Jane Morpeth, my editor.
Many thanks and good wishes.

Historical Foreword

In 1649 Charles I stepped through the door of his Banqueting Hall onto the execution platform outside Whitehall Palace. His death marked the end of the Civil War between King and Parliament and led to the rule of Oliver Cromwell. For eleven years after that, England was ruled by a Protectorate, but the death of Cromwell and the collapse of the dour regime he had imposed on the country brought about the restoration of Charles II.

Charles, a witty and astute prince who had spent most of his exile in France, returned to England determined to rule and thoroughly enjoy himself. The great lords in Parliament were suspicious from the first of his pro-Catholic and very pro-French leanings. Matters were not helped by Charles's marriage to Catherine Braganza of Portugal, nor by his brother, James Duke of York, openly proclaiming his Catholic sympathies. Nevertheless, the true bone of contention was not so much religion as politics: who would govern the country? The Opposition in the House of Commons and House of Lords suspected Charles of manoeuvring to secure massive loans from the French King so as to be able to rule without Parliament.

In 1678, the Opposition, led by the Earl of Shaftesbury and his Green Ribbon faction, decided to bring matters to a head and check Charles's ambitions once and for all. The monarch, however, proved too wily to trap, neatly evading issues and problems. Accordingly, Shaftesbury turned to rogues like Titus Oates and William Bedloe, to spin a tale and weave a web which would ensnare a King . . .

Prologue

Catgut Alley, Farringdon Ward

October 1678

I passed you the loving cup,
I filled it to the brim.
My life, my soul, my desires, my heart!
My dear Samuel, all my days are thinking of you!
Without your love, there is no life!
Your very breath, your very being
Replaces the heart which used to pound within me.
I cannot live without you. I cannot love without you.
You are my dawn and my morning,
My noon, my dusk, my evening.
I am yours.
We meet in the dark and the dark becomes sun.
The sun becomes dark without you.
Your smile is the light of my life.
Your words the life of my soul.
Our love is hidden yet like the seed in winter,
In earth's warm, dark womb, it gathers strength.
I wait for the day it breaks the hardened, frost-trapped
    ground.

I cannot live without your presence.
I cannot love without your presence.
I can only live, by the beat of your heart,
The new life you have given me.
We play our parts, like actors on the stage.
We must take care that care itself does not spoil our love.
Clumsy words but, in the passion of the night or the
Cold of dawn, my love still runs true.

Josiah-Praise-the-Lord Stanker read these lines, chapped lips moving slowly, in the light of a lantern horn slung on the dirty post of the Cuckold's Apron inn in Catgut Alley. Josiah had seen better days. He had lost his wig and, some said, his wits with it. In these dark days, Josiah was a professional beggar, sneak-thief, the occasional dabbler in pamphlets and broadsides. Indeed, a veritable Autolycus, a snapper-up of mere trifles. Josiah-Praise-the-Lord Stanker had once been a preacher, a soldier in Cromwell's new Model Army. He had worn the quilted jerkin, the breastplate of the Lord Protector. Steel helmet on his head and the sword of righteousness in his hand, Josiah had slaughtered the enemies of the Lord, the Amalekites and the priests of Baal. Now, the Lord had withdrawn His hand, for Charles Stuart had come home. 'The Tall, Dark Boy' with his thick, black wig, Moorish face and those devilish loving lips which seemed to be pressed more often against a whore's tits than mouthing the words of Holy Writ.

Josiah had truly fallen low in the world. He had just eaten a dish of eels and downed a blackjack of ale and come out to relieve himself by the alley wall, when he heard the quick clip-clop of boots, echoing loud across the wailing of cats and the raucous bawling of a doxy further down. Slinking into the shadows, he had drawn his wicked little dagger. The figure passed, and for the briefest moment, Josiah had glimpsed the soft, broad-brimmed hat with its scarlet plume, the black vizard over the eyes, muffler drawn up, the heavy cloak, the riding boots and, above all, the embroidered sword's scabbard slapping against velvet-clad legs. Josiah had swiftly slipped the dagger away. For all he knew, this could be a roaring boy, a fighting man; certainly not some pullet ready to be plucked, or a drunken merchant with his fat paunch bubbly with ale and his purse full of coins.

'A penny, sir,' Josiah whined, creeping out of the shadows, calloused hand extended, shuffling his feet to emphasise his limp.

Scarlet Plume had whirled round, hand going to the hilt of his sword. Josiah was aware of bright eyes gleaming behind the mask, the soft, delicate skin of the lower face. The gloved fingers were long; the way they beat a small tattoo on the hilt of the sword meant Scarlet Plume was well used to the sudden draw, the poised stance, the savage thrust and parry of the professional swordsman.

'I didn't mean to a-fear you, sir.' Josiah stepped forward. 'But I am starving, belly clenched to my backbone it is. Fought for the King I did, at Marston Moor, God bless him!'

Stanker noticed how Scarlet Plume's eyes were no longer fierce, lips parted in a smile. He quietly praised his own sagacity. This fellow was a Cavalier, a courtier, Frenchified and dandified.

'God bless His Majesty!' Josiah added.

'Aye, sir.' The voice was soft, low. 'And God bless our Queen.'

Stanker caught the foreign accent, just the roll of the 'r', a slight lilt. Spanish?

'And God bless the true religion,' Josiah offered, then bit

his lip. Had he gone too far? The hands moved. Suddenly a coin flipped in the air.

'And God bless you too, Josiah-Praise-the-Lord Stanker!'

The former preacher caught the coin and stood, mouth gaping, as Scarlet Plume strode off up the alleyway. How did the fellow know him? And then Josiah had seen it, lying on the ground, a small scroll of parchment. He'd plucked this up and taken it over to the lantern light to peruse.

When he had finished reading, Josiah slid down the wall, the parchment clasped tightly in his hand next to the coin. He felt both cold and old. How long since he had felt a woman's arms around him? A sweet voice murmuring endearments in his ear? What had he known but the anger of God and the lack of love amongst his fellows? Josiah's mind went back down the memory of the years, lighted with what? The glow of campfires? The weak flames of tallow candles in a thousand tavern rooms or the raging fires as houses and cities burnt amidst the screams and wretched cries of women and children? No more the glories of Marston Moor, the thundering cavalry charge, the clear certainty that God's will was manifest. Oliver Cromwell, the Lord Protector, was twenty years in his grave, or had been, until Charles Stuart had dug him up, hung Cromwell's corpse from the Common Gallows and spiked his head over Westminster Hall. Josiah had gone down to see it and stared up in absolute horror. Despite the ravages of the grave, and the washing given to the severed head in brine and cumin by the executioner, Stanker had been able to make out the features of a man he had once regarded as 'the Lord's Anointed'.

Stanker closed his eyes and wept. He wished he had gone after Scarlet Plume and handed back this love poem. Asked him about the love of his life, asked him how a man could make any woman such a passionate object of longing and desire. Then Stanker's head came up.

'But that's wrong!' he whispered. 'By the Lord, that's wrong!'

Scrambling to his feet, he went back to the lantern; his dirty fingers unrolled the parchment, eyes hungrily searching the words.

'Where is it now? What was it?' he mumbled.

Ah, there, he had found it. The poem was to someone called *Samuel*. But that was ridiculous! Scarlet Plume was a man! Was the well-dressed stranger one of those bum boys, then? A sodomite?

'Ah, what is the world coming to?' Stanker mumbled through rotting teeth.

A vague suspicion occurred. Surely Scarlet Plume *was* a man? And yet . . . He remembered the long fingers, the melodious voice, those eyes, the beautiful skin round the mouth and chin, lips full and red. Was it a man – or a pretty boy? Or even some young woman disguised as a man? Stanker could well believe it. The recent fashions, the flared petticoat-breeches, the ribbons and the wigs were all worn by the Cavaliers – men pretending to be women. Had the opposite now happened, women pretending to be men? Josiah rolled the parchment up. He was glad he had met Scarlet Plume. This poem could go in his moth-eaten wallet. He glanced at the coin in his palm and gasped in astonishment. He had expected a penny but it was a silver coin. Josiah looked up at the narrow strip of sky between the overhanging houses. The stars in the frosty heavens winked like icicles.

'Thank You, Lord,' Josiah whispered. 'For my good fortune.'

Stanker scratched the side of his unshaven cheek, one finger tracing the scar. At any other time, with such bounty in his hand, he would have headed like a ferret down a hole, back into the warm glow of the tavern. However, despite the ale he had drunk, Stanker was still curious. Who was Scarlet Plume? How would she or he know him? Stanker opened his mouth and, with his tongue, in a favourite gesture, counted his remaining teeth – 'the yellow stumps' as he called them. Then he sniffed: was that a smell of burning? Dear God, not again! Stanker had a fear of fire. He would never forget that night, twelve years ago, when he had fled as God's fire had raged through the city. But, no, it was only smoke from a cookshop.

Somewhere down the alleyway, the same noisy prostitute screamed as a customer took her violently. Stanker was aware of the mist curling in from the river: one of those hideous London smogs which came creeping in like the very gas of Hell. He'd go into the tavern, he decided, spend the night roistering, drink Scarlet Plume's health and ponder more upon this mystery.

Scarlet Plume had by now reached the Duke's Theatre, hastening towards the welcoming glow of light issuing from its doors which were flung open to the cobbled street. The usual crowd had gathered, thronging into their seats. Scarlet Plume was not opposed, bustling forward, swaggering, cloak thrown back, fingers tapping the sword hilt, eyes watching the crowd. The jilts, strumpets, whores and doxies were out in force tonight. Some were quite pretty, others, with their shabby wigs and white, painted faces, more desperate than alluring. Ballad-singers and storytellers swarmed about trying to sell greasy hand-bills. One, more enterprising than the rest, lounged against a pillar just within the doorway, shouting for customers to visit 'Mr Taverner's Curiosities in Fleet Street'.

'I tell you, sirs, gentle ladies. A picture of an elephant who will drink nothing but wine! A Moor all stuffed with straw, his hair and beard as white as snow! The asp which bit sweet Cleopatra's breast! The sling and stone which brought down the great Goliath!'

Scarlet Plume pushed on by. The shabby entrance hall was full of the good and the great, of people of every estate. Be-wigged, silken-clad courtiers, their beautiful brocaded suits decorated with ribbons, rubbed shoulders with portly merchants in their stained coats. The latter rested on walking-canes as they surveyed the throng and quietly told themselves they had only come to see what evils the theatre really held! The air was pungent with tobacco smoke, unwashed bodies, the cheap perfume from the ladies of the night and the bitter-sweet smell of oranges. The sellers of these, young girls and boys with trays fastened round their necks, voices strident, pushed people aside. No respector of status or station, they fought rivals off to sell their oranges before the play began. Garish hand-bills on the walls proclaimed that tonight's performance was Beaumont and Fletcher's *Women Pleased*.

'Excuse me, sir! Oh, sir, please excuse me!'

Scarlet Plume looked down. A small, silver-haired man with the soft, wrinkled face of a preacher, dressed in the dark garb of a clergyman, plucked at his sleeve, fingers moving to caress the backs of the brocaded gloves.

'Yes?' Scarlet Plume demanded.

'I have a good book for you to see, sir.'

'I have my own copy of the Bible,' Scarlet Plume retorted. 'Surely this is not the place for Holy Writ?'

'Oh no, sir.' The soft grey eyes seemed to fill with tears, lips puckered in a smile. 'I have a book full of pleasure.' He opened his cloak and pulled out a hand-bill and thrust it into Scarlet Plume's hand. 'I have this, sir, for your personal perusal, should you wish.'

Scarlet Plume read the hand-bill, and laughed out loud, a clear ringing sound which carried across the entrance hall.

'Why, sir, I apologise.' Scarlet Plume stepped back, sketched a bow and thrust the bill back into the man's hand. 'I thought you were a preacher. I have no desire to read the *Conversations of Octavia.*'

'You know the book, sir?' The voice still remained courteous though the face had lost its sanctimonious look.

'I know bawdy when I see it!' Scarlet Plume replied. 'Full of pictures, eh? Of young women in a number of postures?'

A simpering look confirmed this. Scarlet Plume's hand fell to the sword.

'Now, sir, take your dirt and disappear before I call the bailiff's men!'

The printer and seller of lewd tracts disappeared in the twinkling of an eye. Scarlet Plume looked round, searching for the Government men, the spies, the bully boys of the Green Ribbon Club, the mongrels and mastiffs of Shaftesbury's coven. But there were no faces to be recognised. No one peering from shadowy corners, just flushed, sweaty faces, wet lips and glittering eyes. A young bawd caught the searching glance and hurried over. She was garbed in a low-cut dress, breasts peeping out from her bodice, her face pasty-white and highly rouged, beauty spots on her cheeks.

'You are looking for something, sir?'

'We are always looking for something, madam.'

The bawd's hand went out to brush Scarlet Plume's breeches just beneath the belt.

'Madam!' Scarlet Plume admonished. 'Do not do that!'

'Why not?' The hand was withdrawn, the voice rose slightly.

'Because what I have there would surprise you.' Scarlet Plume's lips parted in a smile. 'And even if it didn't, it's not for you.'

The bawd made an obscene gesture and flounced away. Scarlet Plume pushed and shoved and entered the theatre. Ill-lit with smelly, tallow candles, the pit was packed with a noisy crowd. The stench was great. Scarlet Plume sniffed at the small perfumed sachet stitched into the lining of one brocaded glove and stared around. The boxes above the stage were full of the so-called better quality: men and women, most of them masked, shouting and screaming at each other. Some had brought bottles of sack. Others, having finished their oranges, were now pelting the pit with skins.

'Excuse me, sir, you are standing in my spot!'

Scarlet Plume turned. The young man who stood so threateningly was tall, slim-built, his face almost masked by the broad-brimmed hat he wore, its front tugged down to cover his eyes. His was a strong, sunburnt face with a laughing mouth, high cheekbones and slanted, mischievous green eyes. His nose was slightly crooked, a small scar high on his left cheek. He was dressed simply in a black coat, unbuttoned, to reveal a white cravat and a scarlet embroidered waistcoat. Scarlet Plume stepped back and looked the man up and down, taking in the high riding boots pulled up just under his knee, the blue sash round his waist, the quilted breeches and, above all, the broad leather swordbelt, a rapier sheathed on his left, a small dagger on his right.

'I did not know this was your spot, sir,' Scarlet Plume remarked.

'I paid good silver,' the stranger replied, hand resting on the hilt of his sword. 'Wellingbone the manager would take an oath that I paid good coin so my spot I'll take.'

9

'Shut up, you two cocks!' a voice bellowed from behind them. 'The play is about to begin.'

'Yes!' someone else bawled. 'Take your quarrel elsewhere. No swords here!'

Scarlet Plume sketched a bow, turned in the direction of the voices, tongue protruding, an insulting gesture which silenced any further objections.

'I will call you a liar, sir.' Scarlet Plume turned back to the stranger. 'You are a liar and a thief.'

'We'll call the Watch!' a voice shouted.

'We'd best leave. My name, sir,' the stranger bowed gallantly towards Scarlet Plume, 'is Samuel Atkins.'

'Is it truly?' Scarlet Plume whispered, taking a step forward, face only a few inches from Atkins. 'I take my words back, sir. You are not a liar but you *are* a thief. I believe you have stolen something from me.'

'And I shall not give it back.' Atkins's voice was low and cool. 'Do you understand? I shall never give back what is mine. It has always been mine, it is mine and it shall be mine!'

'Even if I begged you?' Scarlet Plume hissed.

'Even if you begged me.' Atkins's face drew closer. 'You could go down on your knees, you could draw your sword and place the point above my heart, I would still refuse to give way.'

'Are you so cruel?' Scarlet Plume taunted. 'Are you so hard of heart?'

'Not hard of heart,' Atkins replied, 'but resolute of soul. How can I return that which I cannot give up? How can I withdraw from something that is part of me?'

'What's this?' a voice shouted. 'I came to watch the play!'

One of the porters, aware of the growing confrontation,

shouldered his way through the crowd, shoving aside the ruffians and orange-sellers, slapping a thick cudgel from one hand to another.

'What's this? What's this?'

His words were drowned by the shrill blast of a trumpet, the signal for the First Act. The manager of the troupe was already on the stage, hands raised, begging for silence.

'We have a difference of opinion, sir.' Scarlet Plume turned. 'Over this spot. This gentleman claims Mr Wellingbone sold it to him but I know he sold it to me.'

'Well, you'd best see Mr Wellingbone himself, sirs,' the porter declared, pointing across the pit to a small side door. 'Go through there and up the stairs.'

Scarlet Plume and Atkins followed his directions. They left the noisy pit and went up a spiral, wooden staircase built into the side of the theatre: a draughty place of guttering lights and squeaking rats. On one occasion Atkins stopped in horror. An iron candelabra high in the wall had flickered out. At first he thought the holder was moving but then realised it was a large rat gnawing at the remains of the tallow. The creature didn't even scuttle away as they approached. At the top of one stairwell was a battered, yellow-painted door. Atkins felt along the ledge at the top, took down the key and opened it. Scarlet Plume followed him in. Atkins closed the door, turning the key in the lock, then grabbed Scarlet Plume by the arm, knocking off the broad-brimmed hat so the thick coiled hair fell down in tresses.

'Maria Eleanora!' he whispered.

He plucked off the black, white-edged mask and stared down at this woman who infatuated him, dominated his every thought, yet about whom he was deeply worried.

'You look sad, Atkins.' She glanced coyly up. 'I'll be sadder still if you don't kiss me.'

11

Samuel held her close and pressed his mouth against hers. Her lips tasted sweet, he could feel her tongue and warm breath, the crushed perfume she rubbed into her skin. His hands circled her slim waist. He released the silver chains of her heavy cloak and pressed his body against hers.

'How on earth can anyone see you as a man?'

Maria Eleanora laughed softly and pushed him away. 'Wellingbone has done us proud.'

She gestured sarcastically round the tawdry chamber: blue paper up on the windows against the flies, bare lime-washed walls. One had a baize cloth hung against it, depicting a very fat Venus being chased by an even plumper Cupid. A hooded candle flickered on the dresser. The dangerously weak-looking table, however, was covered with a clean white cloth and bore a pewter jug, two goblets and a dish wrapped in a linen napkin against the rats. On either side of the table were two high-backed stools and, in the corner, a small, four-sided cot bed.

'Wellingbone, hopeful as ever,' Atkins declared, following her gaze.

He stood back. Maria Eleanora, he thought, you are the most beautiful woman I have met. She had now taken off her cloak, to reveal the fashionable attire of a court buck, a dark-blue, velvet waistcoat fringed at the hip, its lapels falling down to just above the groin. Breeches of the same colour, tight-fitting, ribbons fastened below the knee, dark-brown calfskin boots. The doublet was open to reveal a pure white shirt, a band of the same colour round her lovely throat. The pendants hanging from her earlobes accentuated the black mass of untidy hair. Atkins would never forget her face: olive-skinned, oval, a perfectly formed nose above a laughing mouth and lips made to kiss. Her eyes were a strange dark-blue, the legacy of her English father.

'What are you staring at?'

Maria Eleanora struck a pose, like that of a court fop; one hand on her hip, the other above her head. She did a pirouette. The swordbelt clanked against her leg. She smiled apologetically, undid the belt and let it fall to the floor.

'Is that all you are taking off?' Atkins asked huskily.

The smile faded from Maria Eleanora's eyes.

'I am the Lady Maria Eleanora Gonzales Esqueba de Valeroma!'

'I know who you are.'

'I am a Catholic and a gentlewoman,' Maria Eleanora continued in a rush. 'Principal lady-in-waiting to Her Majesty Catherine of Braganza, wife of Charles II and Queen of England. More importantly,' her eyes flashed angrily, 'I am the lover of Samuel Atkins, clerk to the Secretary of State for the Navy, Mr Samuel Pepys of Derby House. I am not a whore, a bawd, a jilt or a prostitute. Of course, you have too much honour and regard for me to treat me as such.'

She went closer, put her arms round Atkins's neck, stood on tiptoe and kissed him on the lips, knocking his hat off with her hand. 'You English,' she sighed. 'Pretend to be so cold and righteous but, when you trap a lady in a closet or a chamber, you have more hands than a spider has legs.' She gazed up at him solemnly. 'On our wedding night, Samuel, as is right, not here in this dirty chamber. Only the Lord knows where Wellingbone is, with his watery eyes and slobbery mouth.'

'He can't hear us,' Atkins affirmed, putting his arms round her waist. 'I have checked this room myself. God help us, Maria, if He can. I'd be for Newgate and you'd be for disgrace.'

'Why?' Maria Eleanora's arms slid from his neck.

Atkins swallowed hard. He had served as an officer in the Navy, fought the Dutch in the Narrow Seas and he wasn't frightened of anything. Standing over six foot in his stockinged feet, Master Samuel Atkins in his dark fustian suit and plain linen shirt had no airs and graces. He wore a rapier and a dagger. He was frightened of no one, except Maria Eleanora in a temper. He scratched his head and looked at her from under his eyebrows.

'You have a long face, Mr Atkins.' Maria Eleanora turned sideways, glaring at him from the corner of her eye. 'A handsome face, a strong face and a firm jaw – but you're troubled?'

Samuel decided to break the confrontation. He took off his cloak, slung it over the bed and went and sat down on one of the table stools, gesturing at Maria Eleanora to join him. He loosened his collar and scratched at a bead of sweat.

'Downstairs . . .' he whispered across the table, filling a goblet. He paused as Maria Eleanora, throwing back her hair, gathered it at the nape. She made a quick sign of the cross before lifting the goblet in a toast. 'Downstairs . . .' Samuel repeated, heart sinking at the innocent look in her eyes. He would need plenty of wine to pluck up the courage to say his next words.

'Downstairs?' Maria Eleanora cocked her head as if listening to the faint sounds below. 'People are eating oranges, watching the play and sweating like pigs.'

'Some of them are wolves!'

'Oh no.' She shook her head. 'Surely, Samuel, not that path again.'

'You dress like a man.'

'That's the only way I can meet you. I've told you before, my father was an English merchant, a Catholic who fell in love with my mother and had the courage to pursue her. He fought five duels with her brothers, my uncles. My father wanted boys; instead he begot me and my three sisters.'

14

Samuel laughed.

'My father would never be frustrated,' she went on. 'We were dressed like boys. We were taught to ride like boys and duel like boys.'

'Do you like your disguise?'

'For a while I did. Have you ever worn a bodice and stays? Had your chest supported by a piece of steel you might fire from one of your cannons? Your waist tied so tight you can hardly breathe! And have you ever done embroidery, Samuel? Sat with a group of old women whose chatter would make you drive the needle through your brain?' She pushed back the stool and got restlessly to her feet. 'Have you ever tried to walk along cobbles on high heels until the pain in your neck makes you scream? Or listen to some dancing master who is really more interested in your page than he is in you?' She leaned across the table and kissed him swiftly on the tip of his nose. 'To be free, my dear Samuel, that is what my father taught us. Not to be men but to have a little part of our lives where we could run as free as the deer on a hill.'

'Some deer,' Samuel muttered. 'It's not the deer I'm worrying about but the wolves.'

Maria Eleanora stamped her foot. She went across, picked up her swordbelt and drew out her rapier. She brought it up in a salute of honour, the blade flat against her nose. Down it came, the tip towards him. She turned sideways, head slightly back, the other hand going up, fingers elegantly curled.

'On guard!'

Samuel watched, fascinated. Maria Eleanora moved like a dancer, her sword arm almost staying still, her supple wrist turning and twisting the rapier only a few inches from his face, a whirling arc of steel. No other sound except the slight shuffle of her feet, the quick intake of breath. She lowered the sword.

'Portugal has the best duelling masters. Even His Majesty, God bless him, has said the same.'

'Maria Eleanora!' Atkins got to his feet and plucked the sword from her hand. He held her fingers up and kissed each one. 'You are a fire-fly,' he murmured, rapt. 'My Portuguese fire-fly.'

'That doesn't sound very nice.'

'It's meant to.'

She was watching his eyes intently.

'Do you love me, Samuel Atkins?'

'I love you as much as I worry about you. I do not doubt your strength, your courage, your fire – or the power of your sword arm. In that matter,' he grinned, 'I would not go up against you. But that's not the way they come, my love. They are worse than rats. They skulk in alleyways with stiletto or pistol. Worse still, they hunt in packs.'

'I am safe,' she replied, re-sheathing her sword and returning to her seat. She pulled back the napkin and peered at the bread and cheese.

'It's fresh,' Atkins declared. 'Wellingbone is well paid. He knows I'll put a good word in for him.'

'So, he knows who you are?'

'He suspects I have friends in high places.'

'Like Mr Pepys?'

'Indeed. Mr Samuel Pepys, widower, Secretary for the Navy, close friend and confidant of the King's brother James, Duke of York, Lord High Admiral of England.'

'Is Mr Pepys worried about you?'

'He is very worried. He knows nothing of you,' Atkins continued in a rush, 'but he's greatly a-feared.'

'Of what?' Maria Eleanora picked up the knife, cut off a piece of cheese and popped it into her mouth. 'Of what, Samuel? Who are the "they" who skulk in alleyways?'

16

'There are men downstairs,' Atkins said slowly, 'who would attack, strip, ravish and kill you.' He tapped a pewter goblet. 'For one of these half-full. But they are only the dogs, not the masters; they can be hired by the dozen.'

'I have heard the rumours,' Maria Eleanora nodded, 'of plots and counter-plots. The Queen will not discuss them. She sits with her psalter or her embroidery or takes her dogs for a walk in the park.' The young woman's eyes grew tender.

'Do you love her?' Samuel asked.

'Catherine of Braganza,' Maria Eleanora declared, 'is small, plump and barren. She adores the King. She worships the very ground he treads on. When he turns and smiles, she becomes another woman yet he betrays her and is sorry for that betrayal. He comes to her chamber dressed like a gallant, civil and courteous in every gesture. He will sit and listen, take a glass of Madeira and then be off to his whores!'

Atkins's hand came up.

'No, they *are* whores,' Maria Eleanora continued, 'be they Nell Gwynn or the Duchess of Portsmouth. Nell I like, Portsmouth is an arrogant bitch. If she was a man I would kill her!'

'What have you heard?' Samuel declared.

'Oh, Atkins, don't play games!'

'You must be angry with me, you called me Atkins.'

'Atkins! Atkins! Atkins!' Maria Eleanora taunted back. 'Are you going to tell me, *Atkins*, what is wrong?'

'Very well.'

Samuel drained his goblet, refilled it and Maria Eleanora's. He cut some bread and cheese and chewed it thoughtfully. Maria Eleanora studied him over the rim of the goblet. She had never met a man like Atkins before. She was fascinated by him, this cross between an innocent boy and a fully grown man. Pleasant-faced but not strikingly handsome, his soft brown eyes reminded her of a pet doe her father had once kept in his park. He could be clumsy yet delicate, bluntspeaking but sensitive, generous-hearted and very courageous. Above all, he made her laugh. She had never met a man like Samuel Atkins for making her laugh. Just watching him now, a whole range of expressions passed over his face. Yet there was something else. Maria Eleanora's heart skipped a beat. Atkins was honest as the day was long. She had had her fill of fops and dandies, the sly-eyed courtiers with their wandering hands and lecherous remarks: about women being like mares, to be ridden as much as possible. She'd heard all their lying, blasphemous declarations of love when all they wanted was to lift her petticoats and treat her like a strumpet in a brothel before going off to compare notes with their friends. Maria Eleanora had met the like in both Portugal and London. Atkins was different.

Yet it was his very honesty which now made her fearful. Something was deeply troubling him, she could tell from a shift in his glance, a failure to hold her gaze; the way he kept drumming his fingers and staring towards the door. Maria Eleanora was aware of the growing fear in London, like an evil mist seeping through the city, curling its fingers round the royal palaces of Whitehall, St James and even the Queen's lonely mansion of Somerset Place. No wonder the King and his brother had fled to the calmer, more pleasant surroundings of horse racing at Newmarket . . .

Atkins cleared his throat and stared up at the ceiling. Now for a speech, Maria Eleanora thought.

'Samuel Atkins,' she demanded, lowering her goblet. 'Do you really love me?'

'More than life itself.'

His lover's hand went to the small pocket in her breeches. She cursed as she scrabbled about, a string of oaths which would have shocked Atkins if he had understood Portuguese.

'What's the matter?'

Maria Eleanora sprang to her feet, digging into the pockets of her waistcoat and the small wallet on her belt. She hurried across to her cloak and searched there.

'I wrote some lines for you, Samuel, and by the pig's udder . . .'

Samuel hid his smile. Maria Eleanora must have been listening to some of the servants talk at Somerset House.

'By the pig's udder, I have lost it! I'd wager a florin to a pound Josiah-Praise-the-Lord Stanker has picked it up!'

'Who?' Atkins exclaimed. Alarmed, he got to his feet.

'He's a beggar in the Farringdon Ward. He often comes to Somerset House looking for scraps.'

'A Government man?' Atkins declared. 'An agent of the Green Ribbon Club?'

'No, no, just a beggar I am sure, slightly crazed.'

Atkins grasped her by the arm and swung her round.

'What?' she exclaimed. 'Samuel, you are hurting.'

'Hell's teeth, Maria Eleanora, I love you dearly but you can be a fool! What have I always said? *Never put anything in writing.*'

'I will write what I want.' She struggled free. 'I know the danger, you've told me enough!'

Maria Eleanora stood nursing her forearm, her black hair now falling forward like a veil around her face.

'I am sorry,' Atkins muttered.

'You'll be sorrier if you don't tell me what's so pressing.'

Maria Eleanora returned to the table and picked up the goblet. She hid her unease; Atkins's face was very flushed.

'Tell me!' she ordered.

'Thirty years ago,' Samuel began, 'the present King's father stepped out of the Banqueting Hall at Whitehall, onto the scaffold, and lost his head. Civil War raged. Cromwell held power, then he died and our noble King Charles II, God bless him, returned to his own. You know the King better than I do. He's as shifty as he's tall. Treacherous as he's cynical. Merry of wit and glad of eye. Rumour has it that he's soft on the Papists, that he has a secret understanding with them. He's made matters worse,' Atkins shrugged apologetically, 'or better, if you prefer, by marrying a Catholic Portuguese Princess, your mistress, Catherine of Braganza. Even worse, he's allowed his brother James of York to embrace the Catholic faith. Charles had two ambitions; not to go on his travels again and to thoroughly enjoy himself. His pursuit of the ladies is legendary. No wonder they call him "Old Rowley", the "Merry Monarch" or, because of his dark looks, the "Black Boy".'

Samuel chuckled, then went on, 'Charles doesn't give a fig about religion and nor do his enemies – but they use it. They are led by that malicious, poison-filled dwarf, Anthony Ashley Cooper, Earl of Shaftesbury, who has gathered around him a group of London merchants and thuggish noblemen like Buckingham and that madcap, the Earl of Pembroke. They control the Whigs, the prominent party in Parliament. To put it bluntly, they want either to destroy Charles or bring him under their power. They want the King to proclaim his bastard son Monmouth as his successor and so exclude his brother, James of York, from ever succeeding to the throne.'

'I know all this,' Maria Eleanora intervened. 'The King has more bastards than leaves on a tree but no true heir.'

'Oh, it goes even deeper,' Atkins declared. 'Or so my master tells me. Shaftesbury and his whole damnable crew, the Green Ribbon Club, now meet regularly at the King's Head tavern in Fleet Street to plot and scheme.'

'But that's treason!' Maria Eleanora intervened.

'There are two types of treason, or so Master Pepys says. One against the King and the other against the kingdom. Shaftesbury hates James of York. He argues that no Catholic should become King.'

'But it's not about religion, is it?' Maria Eleanora asked.

'Of course not!' Atkins snapped. 'Shaftesbury couldn't give a damn. He wants power. He wants to be First Minister. He wants to control the Crown, Charles, the throne *and* the kingdom. He sees himself as our new Lord Protector. He dislikes the Catholics so much,' Atkins laughed contemptuously, 'he even takes bribes from a Catholic French King! Shaftesbury believes in nothing. He and the King have got a great deal in common. However, the London mob are fickle. Shaftesbury has sowed his seed well. One plot after another and they all have the same theme: Papists are in hiding – they plan the destruction of the King and the blowing up of Parliament. There's barrels of gunpowder under the Commons; the French navy stands off Sandwich; Spanish troops will land in Cornwall, and so on. The King and court will be murdered in their beds and London burnt to the ground.' He sighed long and deeply.

'But I have been with the King and Queen five years now, and I am what – twenty-three years old. *I* have heard such a hymn since I arrived in England,' Maria Eleanora objected.

'Ah!' Atkins pulled a face. 'Now the singing becomes stronger. A gentleman has turned up who rejoices in the name of Titus Oates.'

'I have heard of him.'

'So has everybody. He is aided and abetted by a crazed clergyman, Dr Israel Tonge. This self-proclaimed doctor, Oates maintains, has infiltrated different Catholic organisations and has learnt of a Great Plot against the King. He hints that Sir Edward Coleman, the Duke of York's former secretary, is conspiring with papists, both at home and abroad, to plot a revolution.' Atkins paused, staring down at the table.

'And?' Maria Eleanora prompted.

Atkins breathed in deeply.

'Coleman is a fool. He's a meddler. He has been warned by my master, Pepys himself, to be more prudent in his dealings.'

'And this Titus?'

'According to Mr Pepys, Oates is an arrant liar though, with Coleman, he has some leverage.'

Atkins got to his feet. He went across to the door, turned the key and opened it. The stairwell outside was empty, silent except for the squeaking of rats and the banging of some loose window further down. They were at least three storeys up but they could hear the racket from the theatre below. He closed the door, locked it and came back, clearly agitated.

'What my master suspects is this: Oates will whip up fury against the papists. His campaign has already begun. You've heard of Sir Edmund Godfrey?'

'Ah yes,' Maria Eleanora replied. 'A Justice of the Peace, a Magistrate well-known for his severity.'

'Well, Oates is now claiming that he will make a full deposition and revelation of his damnable plot to Sir Edmund Godfrey. In it, he may implicate the Queen.'

'This cannot be!'

'Oh yes it can, my little Portuguese, light of my life. Wickedness is rife in the city. Fear swirls everywhere. My master believes that it is only a matter of weeks, maybe even days, before that fear turns to terror. From the shadows the chanting has begun. Traitors here! Traitors there! Traitors under the bed! Traitors in the Tower! Traitors in the Navy! Traitors in the city! Traitors at court! Traitors in the Commons!' Atkins

22

paused, then said steadily, 'Shaftesbury and his coven wish to do terrible damage. They will strike at the King and his Queen, his Catholic brother and anyone else who comes into view.'

'Does that include me, Samuel?'

'Anybody.'

'But this Oates?'

'An ugly-faced man, broad of chin with a voice like an ass. He, or his plot, could be a threat to us.'

'Nonsense!' Maria Eleanora protested.

'No, listen!' he said urgently. 'You are Anglo-Portuguese, a Catholic and the Queen's lady-in-waiting. I am clerk to the Secretary of the Navy, who is a close friend of the Catholic Duke of York. You come to meet me disguised.'

'It's the only way,' she shrugged. 'You know that.'

'They'll put another cast to it.'

'Who's they?'

'Shaftesbury and his gang. The Green Ribboners, the roaring boys of the alleyways, the paid informers. They'll claim that we are spies.'

'But, Samuel, that's ridiculous. You were raised a Protestant – you told me that. Your loyalty is to the Crown and the Church. You take the sacrament every month.'

Samuel banged the table with his fist.

'Can't you see?' he almost shouted. 'They don't give a damn. They'll claim I am a secret Catholic and so is my master, whilst you are just a spy. Why else should a young woman dress like a man and slip through the dark streets of London on a wet October night? How long have we known each other?'

Atkins closed his eyes. Maria Eleanora was sitting rigid, her face pale, eyes dark pools.

'Two hundred and seventy-eight days, twenty-one hours and, I think, thirty minutes. I may be wrong about the

23

minutes. For every minute, Samuel Atkins, I have loved you intently. Do you remember the night we first met at the Earl of Danby's? My Lord Treasurer's soirée?' Maria Eleanora talked quickly, as if by the very volume of words she could stave off impending disaster. 'I saw you standing in the corner, your waistcoat buttoned up the wrong way, your stock all stained with wine.' She kept the tremor out of her voice. 'You were standing with your big hands hanging down, your brown hair tied behind you, eyes glaring out. I thought you were going to crush the goblet rather than drink from it. When I came over, do you remember?' She laughed abruptly. 'You shuffled your feet. I teased you. I thought you were doing a strange English dance. You spilt wine down my dress.'

Samuel smiled but wouldn't meet her gaze.

'And then you made matters worse by plucking up a napkin and dabbing at my breasts. Your great boots crushed one of my toes.'

Samuel started to laugh.

'Don't you realise, Atkins? I have never met a man so honest! I am a courtier born and bred. I sit with shadows. I talk to shadows. I listen to people talk to me and I wonder what mask they are wearing. They peel it off and another one lies beneath. There was no mask with you.'

'There never has been,' he declared. 'I am sorry about that evening.'

'I'm not. I'll remember it all the days of my life, as will my toes.' She laughed behind her hand. 'You went into a small closet and wrote a note of apology and the page boy gave it to the wrong lady.'

Samuel grinned as he recalled his discomfort at the very plump court lady who, thinking she had won Samuel's affection, came billowing across the floor like a man-of-war with all sails rigged. He'd spent an excruciating hour trying

24

to extricate himself and all the time staring at this vision of loveliness, 'the Portuguese', as one of his friends told him, standing so elegantly in a beautiful samite dress of dark Burgundy with its white ruffed lace collar. He couldn't take his eyes off her. The lovely face, the long neck with the silver chain and pendant around it; the way she stood, head slightly turned, trying to restrain the laughter whilst her dark eyes bubbled with mischief. She hadn't been at all put out by his clumsiness or the dark wine stain down her dress. Later on, she had told him that's why she had worn that colour, 'so a man like you would spill his wine over me'.

Atkins glanced quickly at her sitting on the stool, feet apart, black hair tumbling down. He loved that hair, so lustrous he wanted to dig his fingers into it, hold it close against his skin.

'Your hair was beautiful that night,' he whispered. 'Do you remember, it was all taken up? Kept in place by – what was it?'

'A net,' she replied sharply. 'With small pearls.'

'You wore pendants of the same in your ears.'

'More importantly,' Maria Eleanora snapped, 'is that I fell in love with you. I thought you fell in love with me.'

'I did,' Samuel told her hotly, his face coloured with anger. 'You misunderstand me.'

'Do I?' Maria Eleanora taunted. 'Or have you tired of me, Samuel Atkins? Is it because . . . ?' She gestured towards the bed.

'Oh, don't be stupid!' He turned away.

'If you are going to be angry with me, I shall go,' she declared. 'Look at me.'

'And if you are angry with me, Maria Eleanora, then speak truthfully. What would happen if the Watch broke in now, led by Shaftesbury's roaring boys?'

'We would tell them the truth. We would say we were

25

lovers and that one day, when the time is right, we will be married. We shall leave this fogbound island and go somewhere warm, where the sun always shines: a white-washed house in green fields above the sea. Do you remember, Atkins, we talked about that?'

Samuel got to his feet. He went to the narrow window, pulled back the shutters and stared out into the cold night. From the street below, a link boy shouted, 'Make way! Make way!' A carriage crashed by, wheels screeching on the cobbles, the clatter of hooves, the crack of a whip. From somewhere further down the alleyway a Bethlehem man, mad as a March hare, screamed obscenities at the moon. Samuel sighed and closed the shutters. He stared round this tawdry room. Maria Eleanora was sitting head down. He went across, knelt beside her, grasping her hand, rubbing her fingers between his.

'Maria Eleanora,' he said painfully, 'we cannot meet again. It is too dangerous.'

'For you?' Her head came up. 'Are you so timid, Samuel Atkins?' She glimpsed the hurt in those soft brown eyes and nipped his finger. 'I am sorry,' she apologised. 'But I do not understand.'

'I am not frightened for myself,' Samuel declared. 'I am an Englishman – I have nothing to fear. But you, Maria Eleanora, they can twist and turn. Bully boys waiting for you at the end of some alleyway: abduction, ravishment, planting treasonable letters on you.' He gestured at her male attire. 'Or just for dressing like that.'

'Is this the end?' she whispered. 'Is that what you are saying, Samuel? That we both leave this chamber and never meet again?'

Atkins was so stricken by the look on her face, he let go of her hand and got to his feet.

'I have always loved you,' he told her, 'and I will always love you, Maria Eleanora. I love you so much that I cannot keep placing you in this danger. Every time you leave Somerset Place your life is at risk.'

'We could get married,' she offered.

Samuel turned round. 'Maria Eleanora, that would make no difference. They don't care about you or me. We could walk off into the moonlight and they wouldn't give us a second glance. Do you think they want us dead or destroyed? No. It's not *us* they hunt. They want to use us, blackmail us, threaten us so that they can pull down your mistress the Queen and send my master to a traitor's death at Tyburn. We could walk out of this chamber and seek out some hedge parson . . .'

Maria Eleanora's head went down as it always did when she was in a temper.

'No, not a hedge priest!'

Samuel felt the anger welling within him.

'If we marry in one of your chapels before one of your priests, that's just what Shaftesbury and his gang will be waiting for. "See?" they'll scream. "There *is* a connection between Somerset Place and Master Pepys. Were these two love-birds their go-between?"'

'Charles is King . . .'

'So was his father. He still went to the block. Do you think they'd spare a Portuguese Queen who has failed to produce an heir?' Samuel shook his head. 'The King lives in a house of cards, my love. At a puff from one of that vicious crew, it could all come tumbling down.'

Maria Eleanora stared across the room, her heart breaking. She felt a deep sense of loss, much worse than when her father had died or when she had been chosen by the Queen to come to this shadowy, mist-filled place. She had known Samuel for months and his presence had transformed her life.

She was twenty-three years of age, not some giddy maid, some self-deluded mooncalf! She loved Samuel more than life itself. She was convinced it was a love which would last, not thriving on secrecy or shrouded assignations. She wanted an end to all that, to live with him as her husband all her life, free of fear, of deception, of threats.

'You know I speak the truth.' Samuel re-took his seat. 'I'll tell you, Maria Eleanora, what will happen. Shaftesbury is hoping, plotting for something to happen so as to fan the flames. After that it will merely be a matter of marking people down and taking them in. Already there have been arrests in the city, Catholics taken up and placed in Newgate. Of course, they are but the minnows; Shaftesbury's quarry is the greatest in the land.'

Maria Eleanora half-listened. On the one hand she rejected everything Atkins said but, on the other, she knew from different sources that he spoke the truth. There were whispers in the corner, secret comings and goings at night; ill-lit passageways and chambers along which passed muffled, cowled figures bearing messages – yet, what was all this to her? Despite the coldness of the paltry chamber she felt hot and flustered. Sweat coursed down her back.

'It will pass,' she whispered.

'If it passes,' Atkins agreed, 'then we shall meet again. But if it does not . . .' He allowed his words to hang in the air.

Maria Eleanora got to her feet and picked up her swordbelt and cloak; her eyes smarted, her lips trembled. The sadness shook her body like a sob. She breathed in deeply. I will not show it, she thought. Atkins had his back to her. She could tell from the movement of his head that he, too, was crying. She dressed slowly, swinging the cloak about her, picking up the hat, arranging her hair, pulling the brim down over her eyes.

'If I kissed you,' Samuel's voice was thick, 'I . . .'

'If I kissed you,' she replied, 'my heart would break. My only hope, Samuel, is that we shall meet again.'

The room had lost any warmth or colour. To Maria Eleanora it had become a prison cell, a place of division, of separation, of departure. A place which froze her heart and numbed her mind. She slipped on the gloves, her fingers ice-cold. She paused at a sound on the stairs. Atkins whirled round, his cheeks wet with tears. He stood for a while. The sound disappeared. He walked over and grasped her by the arms and stared down at her.

'Maria Eleanora, I will let you go on one condition. Tell me, say that you know I speak the truth.'

'You speak the truth.'

'Tell me that you love me.'

'There's no need. What will you do, Samuel?'

'I don't know.' He shook his head. 'When I was a boy we used to play a game; hunt each other through the woods. Now, it's no longer a game. Maria Eleanora, I am frightened for you, my master, your mistress. For anyone whose lives we touch.'

'You mentioned a game?'

'I am going back over the paths we have trodden,' he replied. 'I am going to hide our tracks. You must not come and see me. You must not write to me.'

His voice sounded so fierce and determined, Maria Eleanora found it difficult to breathe; her throat constricted as the sudden horror dawned on her.

'I am not in danger,' she whispered, 'am I? They don't suspect me! The hunters already have your scent, don't they, Samuel?' She grasped his hands. 'You haven't told me the full truth, have you? They are going to come for you and take you up. Pluck you out of my life like the assassins did my father.'

Samuel was becoming agitated now; he quietly cursed prolonging this meeting.

'You'd best go.' He took his hands away, put on his own cloak and hat and walked to the door.

'I want to see your face again,' Maria Eleanora declared.

He took off his hat and stood, back to the door, tears coursing down his face. Maria Eleanora felt as if she was going to faint. This man was such a poor liar! He told stories but none of it made sense except in one respect. The hunters were already closing in about him: that explained this meeting. He wanted to make sure that when he was taken up, seized in the dead of night, she would be safe.

'Don't say it. Don't speak any more, Maria Eleanora. I have done all that I can. I have said all that I may.'

And, not waiting for an answer, he turned, unlocked the door and stepped out into the stairwell. Cloaked, their hats pulled down over their foreheads, the two reached the bottom of the stairs and went out through a side door into the alleyway. Samuel recalled how he had left the candles burning. He shrugged; Wellingbone would have to look after that. Samuel felt threatened, tense.

'To the bottom of the alleyway,' he whispered and grasped her hand. They hurried into the darkness, boots slipping over the mud-strewn cobbles. The light at the end of the alleyway beckoned them on. Here and there a dog barked behind a wall or a cat caused the rats to squeal and bicker in the piles of refuse. The air was thick with the smell of saltpetre which had been laid out over the open sewer.

A shadow came out from a doorway but slunk back. Samuel's heart was beating faster, sweat coursed down his face. He was aware of Maria Eleanora's hand clenching his tightly. The alleyway seemed to stretch for eternity. They had to reach the bottom. Once they were gone from here they were safe, at least for tonight. Samuel groaned. Shadows thronged in the pool of light. Perhaps they were just revellers? A group of roisterers from a tavern? Maria Eleanora hadn't seen them. The line of shadows thinned out, blocking the alleyway completely. They stopped. Samuel stared round. There was no way back. Perhaps both entrances were blocked?

'Well, well, well!' a voice called.

The line of figures moved up the alleyway. Samuel could tell from their gait that these were not common footpads or a mob of young courtiers looking for mischief. These men moved purposefully; even by the poor light he could see cloaks being thrown back, heard the rasp as swords were drawn from their scabbards.

'Samuel,' Maria Eleanora murmured, letting go of his hand. 'We have no choice. Forgive my harsh words. Know that whatever happens, in life or death, I love you.'

Samuel, however, was now walking forward, drawing both sword and dagger. The line of figures stopped.

'I pray you, sirs,' Samuel kept his voice steady, 'we mean you no harm. Let us pass.'

'And you, sir,' came the mocking reply, 'we mean *you* no harm but we cannot let you pass.'

'Why is that?'

'We have business with you.'

'What business? I don't know you. I don't recognise your voice.'

Samuel stared hard. Five in all. He had faced worse odds on the foredeck of a Dutch man-of-war. It just depended who these men were, hired footpads or professional swordsmen? The leader in the centre was a skilled fighter. Samuel could tell that: the confident mockery in the man's voice, the way he stood slightly forward than the rest.

'I have no business with you, so why should my companion and I go with you?'

'There are those who wish to talk to you.'

'Then let my companion through,' Samuel retorted. 'And I shall go wherever you wish.'

'Never!' Maria Eleanora hissed in the dark.

'Master Atkins.' The voice was almost a drawl. 'We wish you and your companion to come with us. In fact, we would like to know who your companion is and why you must meet like cats in the night? Our masters . . .'

Samuel was surprised. One moment Maria Eleanora was standing slightly behind him, the next she was running forward lightly like a dancer over the cobbles. He cursed and threw his own cloak back. Even before he engaged, a scream rent the darkness. Maria Eleanora had drawn first blood. She flung her dagger at the leader whilst piercing the man next to him high in the shoulder. Blood bubbling out of his mouth, the man gasped and fell to his knees. The leader, made of sterner stuff, simply staggered back, sword slipping from his fingers. Maria Eleanora had already turned, and was engaging two more. Samuel attacked the fifth: their swords had hardly clashed when Atkins realised this was no professional duellist. The man jabbed with his sword but it was half-hearted. Samuel pressed his attack in a clash of steel and slither of boots. Another scream echoed through the alleyway. Samuel's attacker lost heart and fled, following his leader back to the mouth of the alleyway. Atkins looked to his left. A further assailant lay sprawled on the cobbles, body shaking and jerking. Maria Eleanora had forced the other up against the wall.

'Stand back!' Atkins shouted. 'Let him go!'

She did so. The man shaking his sword, more in fear than anger, backed away and, spinning on his heel, fled into the night.

Chapter One

Primrose Hill near St John's Wood in London

Thursday, 17 October

A dark, wet, windswept expanse, Primrose Hill was the
meeting place of lovers or those who liked to keep beyond the
eye of the law amidst the high-grown wasteland with copses of
woods, stagnant pools and the occasional huddled farmhouse.
From here the traveller could see the great conduit of Mary Le
Bow as well as the huge, soaring scaffold of Tyburn Gallows
placed in its prominent position on the Oxford road. At the
far side rose the White Horse Inn on the edge of a wood.
A welcoming place, the White Horse, with its sawdust floor,
dark comfortable wainscoting, hams and vegetables placed
in nets and pulled high below the rafters, well away from
marauding mice and rats.

John Walters, a blacksmith, and William Bramwell, a
baker, their tattered cloaks pulled fast about them, were
walking across the heath eager for the inn's warmth, a
tankard of ale and to toast their freezing toes and fingers
in the glow of the roaring fire. As they hurried past a black,
lifeless pool and glimpsed the hedged ditch which ran not
so far away, overgrown with bushes and thickets, the wind

whipped up the dead leaves and sent them whirling around their feet.

Bramwell saw the items first. He seized Walters's arm and pointed.

'Look ye at that, John!'

His companion did so. Peering through the dark, he glimpsed on the edge of the ditch, a pair of gloves, fringed, expensive-looking, and an embroidered empty sword scabbard. Walters was intent on picking them up but Bramwell was more cautious.

'Might belong to a gentleman or a soldier gone to relieve himself. Or,' he said with a wink, 'someone busy with a doxy. We'd best leave them, friend.'

When they reached the inn, John Rawson the tavern-master thought differently. He served his two visitors their ale and listened intently as the two customers sat on the high-backed settle near the hearth.

'There's been no one round here,' he declared. 'Come, show me!'

The three men went back out into the rain. It was about five o'clock in the evening, Rawson later recalled. They reached the ditch; the gloves and scabbard were still there. They also discovered a long, expensive walking-cane hidden in the grass. Rawson clambered into the ditch.

'Lord save us!'

The tavern-master pulled back the undergrowth to expose the corpse of a tall, lean man, dressed in black, lying on his face at the bottom of the ditch. Jutting out from under his right shoulder blade, at least six or seven inches of a sword. The corpse was slightly crooked, belly against the side of the ditch, knees on the ground, the feet slightly up, resting on some brambles. A little distance away lay the man's hat and periwig.

'Murder!' Bramwell whispered.

'Either that or suicide,' Rawson said heavily. 'It looks as if he's fallen on his sword.'

He turned the body and flinched at the bruise high on the face and the staring, popping, blood-filled eye.

'It's best to leave it,' Rawson decided, getting out of the ditch. 'We'll raise the hue and cry.'

They fetched the constable. Within the hour he'd arrived, struggling against rain-borne wind with a group of neighbours. Constable Brown clambered into the ditch and shook his head dolefully.

'Pray God it not be so,' he muttered, 'but I think it's Sir Edmund Godfrey the magistrate.'

He pressed his hand against the icy-cold skin of the face.

'We'd best take it out.'

They lifted the corpse. Brown had the gruesome task of removing the sword. It came out reluctantly with a glugging, popping sound. Under Brown's direction, the corpse was taken to the White Horse Inn and laid upon a table in the small parlour. Everyone crowded in, heavy boots rustling against the straw-strewn floor, cloaks and coats dripping with water as they peered at the corpse. They shook their heads and muttered, pointing to the fine wax droppings on the dead man's clothes. They noticed how the shoes, despite the wet weather, were clean and polished. His possessions included rings as well as a large sum of seven guineas; they also observed that his neckband or cravat was missing. The dead man's face looked as if he was a ghoul from a nightmare, eyes filled with blood, face and neck muscles stiffening.

'One thing I have noticed.' Brown, standing at the head of the corpse, waggled a finger. 'His sword's been driven through him – but can you see any blood on his clothes?'

By now the corpse had been definitely identified as Sir

Edmund Godfrey the Justice, the wood and coal merchant who lived on Hartshorn Lane near Westminster. Brown continued his examination. Pulling back the fine waistcoat, he undid the holland shirt beneath. This was loose and, when he pulled it back, everyone exclaimed in horror. A mass of black bruises covered the corpse from neck to stomach, whilst around his neck was a deep, gouged mark with a swelling under the left ear as if someone had tightened a tourniquet or garotte which had bitten deep into the skin; this had been tied so tightly the neck had snapped so the head hung loose. Brown noticed the sword punctures, one just beneath the heart, the other slightly below.

A rider galloped into the city to seek out Sir Edmund's brothers, Michael and Benjamin; the two men came sweeping into Rawson's parlour two hours later, their faces all tragic. They were joined by Henry Moore, Godfrey's old servant, dressed like a crow in black, spectacles on the end of his nose, hands and lips all a-quiver.

'We've found your brother,' Brown declared. 'Murdered on Primrose Hill!'

Chapter Two

Somerset Place

Friday, 18 October

Charles Stuart, King of England, lounged in his high-backed chair, elbows on its arm-rests: he did what he thought he was always best at, looking bored and sleepy. The King turned slightly, crossing his silk-garbed legs and staring down at the rosettes on one of his shoes. He was dressed in his best, a dark silk suit with an oyster-pink waistcoat, the white shirt beneath boasting a full lacy cravat. The King played with the tendrils of the thick luxurious wig which fell down to his shoulders. He kept his sallow, lined face impassive; only occasionally did the heavy-lidded eyes come up, the warm cynical look belie the rather drooping mouth. Charles hummed and hawed to himself and, leaning down, gently stroked one of his spaniels; a whole crowd of them lay round his chair fast asleep. Long-legged Charles liked nothing better than a brisk walk in the park, swinging his cane, whistling under his breath to send his dogs scampering. He'd then stand stock-still whilst he tried to count how many different trees, plants and flowers were in the Queen's gardens. He hadn't seen many. Darkness was falling now, and Charles was feeling distracted. He was only pretending to be languid and lazy whilst his busy mind teemed like a mill-stream. The King recognised that he was in danger. He felt like a fox which had given its pursuers a good run, but the bell-like howling of the hounds was drawing closer.

'Mangy mastiffs!' the King muttered.

He snapped his fingers and, escorted by his spaniels, returned to his wife's quarters. If anything the King was deeply concerned. He would have much preferred to watch his horses thunder across the grass at Newmarket or sit in his mistress's boudoir whilst Louise, Duchess of Portsmouth, frizzed her yellow curls and dressed for the evening. Charles plucked out his fob watch, snapped open the silver case and peered at the black hands.

'For the love of God!' he drawled over his shoulder at Henry Chiffinch, his diminutive house squire with his broad, open face, eagle-like nose and small, blackberry eyes. 'For the Lord's sake, Chiffinch!' he fretted. 'When will Her Majesty appear?'

'Why, Your Majesty, when Her Majesty is ready.'

Charles's face broke into a smile. He could count the number of people he trusted on one hand and still have two fingers to waggle in the faces of the likes of Lord Shaftesbury: Chiffinch was one of them. A man of infinite subtlety, Chiffinch carried the King's messages hither and thither; he always made sure His Majesty was comforted at night. If the Duchess of Portsmouth was in one of her moods then Chiffinch would hustle some other young lady of favour up the back stairs at Whitehall. Charles peered round the corner of the chair. Chiffinch was a diminutive Hercules with his broad shoulders and small, squat body; his hands were folded in front of his paunch like a vicar come to preach.

'And is my man here?'

'Oh yes, Your Majesty.'

Chiffinch glanced to his left, at the small secret closet where Charles's 'man' could sit, listen and see everything that happened. The King turned as a figure swept into the room, stopped at the end of the oval table and bowed.

'Your Majesty, my apologies. I am late but the streets are clogged and the taverns are busy.'

Charles beamed at Samuel Pepys, Secretary to the Navy, a man whom Charles knew to be addicted as himself to soft, perfumed flesh. Pepys, however, did not seem in amorous mood tonight; his plump face beneath the dark wig looked pale and anxious from lack of sleep. The slightly protuberant eyes brimmed with fear, the sensuous mouth was pulled tight into a line.

'Oh, for the love of God,' Charles said indulgently, 'sit down, man.' He pointed to the leather case Pepys carried. 'You are not foolish enough to be carrying papers, are you?'

'Your Majesty, I am just not foolish enough.'

Charles winked lazily at him and returned to his musings. He stared round the chamber. What a contrast, he thought, to the salon of Louise de Keroualle, Duchess of Portsmouth, with her white satin wallpaper, brilliantly embroidered tapestries, tables, chairs and dressers covered with her expensive clothes, furs, jewellery and cosmetic pots. Little dogs would race about, not to mention that filthy monkey which, dressed in the royal colours, climbed everywhere and left its droppings in the most injudicious places! Oh no, Catherine of Braganza was a marked contrast to Madame Portsmouth! This room looked, and smelt, like some parlour in a Spanish convent with its massive oaken furniture, heavy and black in the poor light. The tapestries were sombre as a nun's gown, all depicting worthy scenes from the Bible, except one – Suzannah being confronted by her false accusers in the presence of Daniel. Charles pulled a face. Even here the woman's beautiful body was hidden in drapes of muslin though he carefully examined one full, juicy, peeping breast. Behind him Chiffinch breathed noisily through his nose. One of his spaniels barked as it hunted rabbits in its dreams. Pepys, all fussy, had opened his leather case and stared down at it, muttering under his breath and clicking his tongue.

The doors at the far end of the chamber swung open. Pepys, followed by Charles, got to his feet. The King stepped on one of his spaniels which yelped and scuttled for safety as Catherine of Braganza made her stately entrance. Charles's heart skipped a beat. Poor Catherine! Dressed like any widow of Spain in her dark heavy dress, a veil of the same colour over her hair, her round face so homely yet those eyes, so full of gentle adoration. Charles loved her yet hated coming here. It would be better, he thought, if she reproached me. Acted as Louise did, screamed abuse or threw perfume pots. But not Catherine. She walked slowly up. Charles sketched the most elegant bow, took her hand, kissed the podgy fingers and, drawing her close, brushed Catherine's forehead with his lips.

'Madam, it is good to see you.'

'You lie.' Catherine's English was never very good.

Charles smiled and stared down at his wife's face, at her half-open lips, her jutting teeth which her enemies always ridiculed.

'You lie,' she repeated, her eyes crinkled in amusement.

Charles laughed and escorted her to the chair on his left. It was a common joke between them. The first English words Catherine had ever learnt were, 'You lie!' It made Charles laugh, yet it tugged at his heart for the Queen was right.

'Madam,' he whispered as he took his seat. 'I was born a rogue, I have lived my life as a rogue. And, but for the grace of God, I shall die as one.'

The Queen shook her head. 'You shall die loved by me, Charles. Anyone who dies, loved as you are, can never die alone.'

Tears pricked the King's eyes. He pulled out a mouchoir and waved it airily.

'For God's sake, Madam, you were so long in coming!'

He peered round her. Sir George Wakeman, the Queen's physician, stood, shoulders hunched, in the doorway.

'George!' the King bawled good-naturedly. 'Are you coming in or standing there to catch the draught?'

Wakeman bowed. He hurried up along the table as the guards closed and secured the doors behind him, and made to bow. Charles waved his fingers daintily.

'George, you are a physician. I try to keep such men from touching me. So, no bobbing and curtseying here, or kissing of hands. The night is young but I am not. Take your seat and let's begin.'

Wakeman, a silver wig framing a thin, anxious face, sat down opposite Pepys. His eyes searched the Secretary of the Navy's face as if he could read his thoughts and discover the purpose of this clandestine meeting during the hours of darkness. The King returned to examining the rosette on one of his red, high-heeled shoes. In truth he was waiting for Chiffinch, who was now scurrying around the room busy as a bee, ensuring windows were closed, drapes pulled, doors secured. He then brought candelabra and placed them along the shiny, walnut table. Sweet wine was served and a dish of comfits. The King lifted his cup and turned as if toasting the shadows which thronged this gloomy chamber.

'Well, what a pretty mess! What a pretty mess!' he began, glancing sideways at his Queen.

Catherine of Braganza sat silent and serene as one of the statues in her oak-panelled chapel. If only you knew, Charles thought. Every time he looked at her, Charles recalled the miscarriages, the stillborn children and the sheer desperation of this plain but courageous woman to bear him a living child, an heir. Wakeman sitting next to her, scratching the side of his face, had told them both the truth. Catherine would never bear a living child. Charles' head went down; this meant the crown would go to his brother, James of York. That was the root cause of this problem – the purpose of this meeting.

'Well, Master Pepys, what do we have?'

'A rising storm, Your Majesty. Shaftesbury and the Green Ribboners are out in force and the streets echo with a fury which will sweep the entire kingdom. Justice Godfrey is dead, done to death, murdered.'

'So,' the King drawled. 'The fire has begun and Shaftesbury is busy with the bellows. But what's the truth of it, eh?'

Pepys licked his lips.

'Sir Edmund Godfrey, Your Majesty, disappeared from his house last Saturday and was found late yesterday on Primrose Hill. According to the coroner, Sir Edmund had been strangled, probably with his own linen band which could not be found. His head had been twisted round so savagely the neck was broken. After death, someone had stamped on his chest, inflicting bruises from neck to stomach. He'd been dead about four or five days. The body was so stiff and rigid his clothes had to be cut off him. Two curious things: his shoes were very clean.'

'And secondly?' the King asked, ignoring his wife's gasp of horror.

'After he was killed, his own sword was thrust through his

body. The first attempt was unsuccessful, blocked by the ribs, but the second went clean through.'

Charles played with the ring on one of his fingers.

'How long had Godfrey been dead?'

'As I said, Your Majesty, four to five days.'

'And his shoes were clean?'

'Yes, Your Majesty.'

'So his corpse must have been taken to Primrose Hill?'

'Precisely, Your Majesty.'

'My lord,' Catherine broke in. 'I have heard the news but how does this involve us?'

'It doesn't,' the King told her. 'But if Shaftesbury has his way it will. Oh, by the by, Madam, your lady-in-waiting, Maria Eleanora? I glimpsed her as she came in. She looked pale-faced, red-eyed.'

Catherine hunched her plump shoulders.

'My lord,' she whispered, 'I do not know the cause. She does not eat or drink much, sits mournful as a ghost but will not tell me the reason for her sorrow.'

Charles leaned his head back against the chair. Maria Eleanora, he reflected, had the face of an angel. Charles often smiled and teased her, but went no further. He had promised himself that. He would never shame his wife to her face.

'Your Majesty,' Pepys said bleakly, 'this matter is serious. They claim Godfrey was killed by the papists and Newgate is filling with a line of suspects.'

'Who?' But Charles already knew the answer.

'Anyone with sympathy to the papist cause but, so far . . .'

'Just the little ones, eh?' the King interrupted.

'Just the little ones, Your Majesty.'

'Then we must let them have their way, Mr Pepys.'

'Must we, Your Majesty? They are talking of a new Guy Fawkes hiding beneath the Houses of Parliament, of a thousand powder kegs being brought up the Thames. Sentries prowl the streets. For God's sake, Your Majesty, they have cannon around Whitehall – barricades are going up, chains being dragged across the streets! They talk of fire balls being dropped on the city. The ballad-singers and street poets have never sold so many pamphlets. On the Strand they hanged a dog and cat because they belonged to a papist. The lords carry pocket pistols . . .'

Charles threw his head back and laughed.

'My, my, my!' He clapped his hands softly. 'And what does my Lord Shaftesbury say as he smokes his long clay pipe in the King's Head tavern? That the French and Spanish will come out of the soil or down from the clouds?'

Pepys shook his head. Because of his poor eyesight, he narrowed his watery eyes, glaring at the King who took nothing too seriously.

'I agree with Your Majesty that it is nothing more than childish nonsense, but Shaftesbury controls the streets of London. He hums a tune and soon the dance will begin.'

'Dance?' the King queried. 'Pray, Master Pepys, what dance is this?'

'The destruction of yourself, Your Majesty, of your house and of all who trust in you.'

Charles dug deep into his pocket and took out a small ivory fan; he snapped this open and wafted his hot face.

'Is it so serious?'

'Your Majesty, I tell you this. Within the month Shaftesbury will strike and strike hard.'

'At whom?'

Pepys bowed towards the Queen. Catherine of Braganza sat, eyes filled with horror.

'They would not dare,' she whispered.

'Your Majesty,' Pepys warned. 'They have already begun.'

Chapter Three

Samuel Atkins sat at his high desk, quill in hand, and stared fixedly at the ink-pot. Outside it was raining so he had shuttered the windows, making his small closet, what he grandly termed his 'office', in Derby House only more sombre. This was where Mr Pepys and his associates managed the King's ships; refurbishing old, constructing new, buying in stores, hiring men and seeing to a vast array of matters be it new ordnance and gunpowder from the arsenals or the price of biscuit and tack for the crews. Even here, the tang of the sea was strong. Indeed, this closet looked like a cabin with its hooded lamps, wax-splattered candle-stands, narrow windows and its few paltry items of dark, heavy furniture. The lamps were burning low.

Atkins looked down at the roster he had been studying, listing the crew of Her Majesty's ship, the *Glorious* now being prepared for sea at Tilbury. The clerk laughed softly to himself. He felt as if he was at sea. He steadied himself on the stool. He had drunk so much he felt as if the floor was swaying beneath him yet he had to be careful. Master Pepys was in a dreadful rage and Samuel was doing little to placate him.

'Every night!' Pepys had roared, standing in that small, narrow doorway. 'Every night you come back late! Samuel, what are you doing? You drink and you roister and yet you are not happy!'

Atkins balanced the quill between his fingers. Pepys was right: he was *not* happy. He recalled the events two weeks ago, that violent death-threatening attack at the end of the alleyway, the clash of sword, the slither of boots. He and Maria Eleanora had broken free, been allowed to pass unhindered but both had been frightened. Maria Eleanora hid it well but, when Atkins kissed her quickly goodnight, or was it goodbye, he could still feel her body trembling. She had begged to see him again, just once, but the attack had confirmed all of Atkins's fears. Whoever his assailants were, or whoever had sent them, they knew where he had gone, they had guessed correctly when he might leave and, above all, they wanted to question him.

But who were they? Atkins suspected Green Ribboners, sent by Shaftesbury or one of his lieutenants. But what did they want? Why should they be keen to question him? And, if he had gone, what would have happened? Would they have confined him in some dark chamber until he told them everything, but about what? He was only a humble clerk. Atkins swallowed hard and stared towards the door. His master Pepys, however, was a different kettle of fish. Did they hope Atkins would betray him? And, once they had the noose round Pepys's neck, would they use him as a lure to trap James, Duke of York? Over the last two weeks undoubtedly, his master's mood had become deeply enmeshed in the mire of despondency.

'I am in ill humour, Master Atkins,' Pepys had whispered the night before, standing in his nightshirt on the gallery of his house, one hand on the handle to his bedroom door. Pepys had stared, eyes brimming with tears, at a picture of his lovely wife Elizabeth who, when alive, had driven her husband to distraction. The Secretary of the Navy still adored her, even though Elizabeth had lain shrouded in her grave for many a year.

'I am in ill humour, Mr Atkins,' Pepys had repeated, 'and in such a dark hour,' his voice had grown harder, 'I need my servants to obey me, sir! Look at you!' Pepys had gestured at Atkins's wine-stained cravat. 'You smell like a brewery. You look as if you haven't eaten a decent meal whilst you are dead on your feet. I won't have it, sir. I will not have it!'

Pepys had stormed off into his bedroom. Atkins had crawled to his on the gallery above and sat staring through the window at the rain-soaked tiles, letting in the cold night air to clear the wine fumes as he listened to the patter of the rain. If Master Pepys was in ill humour, Atkins was broken-hearted. He missed Maria Eleanora more than he liked to admit. Every second of the day, her face was ever-present. Sometimes, when he closed his eyes, he could even believe he smelt her perfume or heard her voice. In crowded alleyways he'd turn quickly, thinking he had glimpsed those black curls, that sweet lovely face. It was all an illusion. Samuel would have loved to have written to her, begged a second meeting but he knew that he could be inviting her to another ambush, brutal kidnap or even murder. Samuel had immersed himself in his duties, but at night he'd roistered and feasted, spending every coin he owned, drowning his sorrows in cups of sack and blackjacks of ale.

Atkins straightened in the chair. The ladies of the night knew him well. He closed his eyes and tried to ignore the sea of guilt which threatened to engulf him. Cups of canary, round thighs, stocking-tops fastened with ribbons; the pretty faces of the doxies, white and painted, beauty spots, throats and wrists glittering with cheap jewellery. On weekdays it was bad enough, but on Saturday and Sunday, after the bells had chimed, Atkins had more freedom. The young clerk breathed out. He could hardly remember what he did. This ale-house or that tavern, seeking out friends, former officers only too

47

pleased to drink him under the table and carouse until the early hours. Where had he been? What had he done? One face he recalled, Captain Childs, a lean-visaged cove with narrow, glinting eyes and cheeks pitted with pox. He wore the tawdry finery of a spendthrift fop yet, even with his ale-dulled wits, Atkins recognised danger. Wherever he went, Captain Childs always appeared. Atkins liked him little enough. He had lent Childs money on occasion but, in his heart, he would always be wary of an officer who had surrendered his own ship.

Samuel felt in the pocket of his waistcoat and took out the small silver jewelled cross Maria Eleanora had given him. He just thanked God Master Pepys hadn't found that, an indication of papistry if there ever was one. Yet it was Atkins's link with his love. He rubbed it between his fingers as if that very action could summon her here. Was she angry with him? Did her heart ache like his? She had kept well away except for one letter. Atkins smiled and opened the lid of the desk. Balancing the papers on top, he unlocked the small metal coffer and took out the scroll one of Pepys's maids had given him on his return from revelry two nights earlier. He put the desk-lid down, smoothed out the parchment and, once again, mouthed the words scrawled there.

> *'Time will pass but my love shall not.*
> *The sky will crack but my love will not.*
> *The sea will dry but my love will not.*
> *The sun will turn to ice but my love will not.*
> *My love is and always shall be.'*

Atkins had recognised the hand as well as the little conceits Maria Eleanora used in writing out these rhymes, copying the wit of Rochester, Donne and the other poets. Samuel chewed on his lips as he wondered whether he should reply. But what if the note was not really from Maria Eleanora but a trap? Ever since the discovery of Godfrey's corpse, London had been engulfed by panic: a terror which had spread like a flame through the narrow alleyways and streets. The same refrain was on everyone's lips; all were singing the same hymn written by Shaftesbury and his gang. The hymn had now risen to a thunderous roar.

'Godfrey is foully murdered! Traitors are at large!'

The hysteria in London mounted every day. Companies of soldiers garrisoned the Tower, to guard the palaces and Government buildings. Cannon had been taken from ships in the royal dockyards to defend the main thoroughfares. Men, women and children now primed muskets in case the French or Spanish landed. The papists were said to be gathering in cellars, a vast, sinister underground army. Atkins didn't believe a word of it but he recognised the danger. Arrests took place every day. People were hauled off, clapped in irons and committed to the dungeons of Newgate, to be imprisoned in the pit. Here they were starved of food, revived with rough brandy and brought before the Lords' Committee, headed by Shaftesbury, to be questioned about the Great Plot. Titus Oates, with his broad jaw and braying voice, was now hailed as Saviour of the Nation. No one was free of his denunciations. Oates had the ear of no less a person than burly-faced Chief Justice William Scroggs. People whispered how there would be trials soon, whilst the hand-bills and posters screamed about the dangers threatening the nation, how these dangers could only be resolved on the gallows or quartering block at Tower Hill or Tyburn. Nobody was above suspicion. The King himself, it was whispered, was secretly a papist. Atkins's master, Pepys, had the truth of it.

'All this hysteria,' he'd muttered in this very office, 'is nothing but dirty froth on a filthy pond. Shaftesbury is just whipping up the hounds. The real hunt will begin one day soon.' Pepys, in fact, was frightened, very frightened. He trusted Atkins and confided in him. 'They'll strike at me,' he moaned. 'I know they will.'

Atkins had tried to soothe him but Pepys only became angrier.

'Yes, sir, they will. By God, sir, they most certainly will. And having a servant who wanders the streets at night does nothing to protect me!'

'But you have done no wrong, master,' Atkins protested. 'I see your correspondence, there is no evidence.'

'No evidence? Faugh!' Pepys had waved his hand. 'They can concoct evidence like a child makes up a riddle. Shaftesbury is not finished with me. God save us, he has yet to begin!'

Pepys had also discussed Godfrey's murder. Where had he been for five days, he wondered. And those strange bruises, the sword driven through him? Was it suicide? Was it murder? They had soon received their answer. Shaftesbury claimed it was both murder *and* treason. He had turned the King's Head tavern into the rallying point for all opposition to the King, and from there directed the printing presses, producing cheap hand-bills to inflame even further the mob's imagination.

Matters had reached their climax today with Godfrey's funeral in St Martin's-in-the-Fields. A vast crowd had visited the body in its oaken coffin and then escorted it, crowding round the pall-bearers, to be lain beneath the cold slab stones of the church. The mob had been out in force, heavy bells tolling across the city. Pepys had despatched Atkins to see what would happen. The church was packed: apprentices standing on pillars, every available place taken, squeezed up by the press of bodies. Shaftesbury's men were present, armed to the teeth, as if they expected the French and Spanish grand fleets to come sailing up the Thames firing cannon and laden with mercenary troops. Dr Lloyd, the eloquent but bombastic vicar of St Martin's, had been well primed. He had climbed into his high pulpit, escorted by two burly divines; these carried muskets and stood on either side of Lloyd in case his impassioned sermon was interrupted by some foreign assassin.

'Died Abner as a fool dieth!' Lloyd had thundered from the pulpit, squeezed between his two acolytes. Lloyd had rested on the lectern and surveyed his congregation with an eagle eye.

'Died Abner as a fool dieth!' he thundered again.

The congregation listened, in hushed silence, to Lloyd's bloodthirsty sermon in which he drew parallels between the Second Book of Samuel and Godfrey's murder. He even went so far as to claim that Godfrey's murder had been foretold by the Bible! On any other occasion Atkins, though a devout churchgoer, would have bellowed with laughter but the tension in that church, the seething anger, the hysterical terror were almost tangible. If the mob had found a papist dog or cat they would have torn it to pieces. Even so, one dark-visaged young man, his only fault being his colouring, was mistakenly taken for a Spaniard. He would have been beaten senseless in the graveyard if his friends had not intervened, screaming that he was 'nothing more than a coster-monger well known to us!'

Atkins had walked back through the drizzle to find Derby House deserted. He quietly prayed that Maria Eleanora would stay within doors and not dare to travel such dangerous streets. He stared down at the parchment and the love poem carefully inscribed there. Putting this aside, he took out a fresh piece of parchment, dipped his quill in the ink-pot and began to write his own.

I have loved you from the start
And I will love you to the finish.
I will love you because, without you, there is no life.
My heart is breaking, my soul aches,
My eyes are hungry for yours.
My touch for yours.
Your lips provide the wine of life,
Your smile the warmth.
Is there no release from this bleak winter?
Will you not come and thaw the frost in my soul?
I stand like a tree stripped of its finery.
A black relic of what I used to be, stark against the sky.

Atkins paused. Should he really write this? Would it entice Maria Eleanora to come and see him? He screwed the parchment up. He could tell no one about his love. His friends? They'd regard him with suspicion, mock him or, perhaps, even betray him.

'Would my friends betray me?' Atkins whispered at the ink-pot.

To be truthful, he had few friends and this was not the time to test them. Master Pepys would give him good advice but then break his head with a staff pole. And what would that advice be? Probably the very same he had given Maria Eleanora.

'How can I see you?' Atkins whispered through the darkness.

He could disguise himself! Despite his dry throat and aching limbs, the young man threw back his head and laughed at the prospect. What should he be? A strolling player? A beggarwoman? Where would he get the clothes? And Atkins was sharp enough to know that the Queen's residence at Somerset Place would be closely watched by the roaring boys from the Green Ribbon Club. Atkins had also heard strange tales. Weren't there stories that Godfrey had been seen near there before his death? Wild rumours declared that he had been dragged inside.

'No, no,' Atkins murmured.

He would have to be more careful. His head came up as he heard a sound in the passageway outside. Someone running. The door was flung open. A young boy, one of those Pepys used to send errands, came charging in, face all red and sweaty beneath the dirt, greasy hair spiked up.

'Master Atkins! Master Atkins, the soldiers are here! They are looking for you!'

Atkins heard the clatter. He jumped down off the high stool and pushed the boy to the door. He thrust him through, locked it then, running back to the desk, he picked up the love notes, the small crucifix and stared around. The footsteps outside grew heavier, followed by a banging on the door.

'Master Atkins! Master Samuel Atkins!' a voice roared.

'Captain, you may mind your manners, sir! This is Derby House!' roared back Pepys.

Atkins closed his eyes. Thank God for his master. He'd gain some time. He glimpsed the small fire-grate and, running over, he pushed the parchment and crucifix up into a small cleft high in the chimney-piece. There was just time to quickly wash his hands in the bowl of water provided and wipe his hands on the rough serge napkin. The pounding on the door had grown more insistent.

'Open the door! Open the door in the King's name!'

Atkins went across and turned the key. The door was flung open, sending him reeling across the room. He glimpsed his master's anxious face, framed by that thick curly wig, almost hidden by the sea of red serge coats and gleaming breastplates of the soldiers. They marched in, halberds lowered. Their captain, a young man with the lean, hungry face of a whippet under his black, broad-brimmed hat, came striding across, his sword drawn. He tapped Atkins lightly on the shoulder with a scroll of parchment.

'Master Samuel Atkins? I carry the King's commission. I also have Secretary of State Coventry's warrant for your arrest.'

'On what charge, sir?'

Pepys, jacket off, came striding into the room, swinging his silver-topped ash cane. He beat this noisily on the floor, chest thrust out.

'I object to this outrage!'

Pepys was at his most bombastic. Atkins caught his gaze. Pepys was warning him with his eyes to be careful.

'Do you have papers here?'

The captain, realising there was no present danger, re-sheathed his sword.

'Of course we have papers here!' Pepys snapped. 'This is Derby House, from where the King's men-of-war receive their orders against the *true* enemies of the realm!'

'There are enemies and there are enemies,' the captain retorted over his shoulder. 'Some are without and some within.'

'Do you have a warrant to search this house?' Pepys demanded.

'I have nothing but a warrant for the arrest of this man.' The captain poked Atkins in the chest.

'What are the charges?' Atkins burst out, trying to control his panic.

'You name it,' the captain drawled. 'It's all in the parchment: treason, murder.'

'Nonsense!' Atkins interrupted.

'Then, if it's nonsense,' the captain smirked, 'you can tell that to the Committee of the Lords sitting at Warrington House.'

'You mean Shaftesbury and his coven?' Atkins spat back.

'My Lord of Shaftesbury wishes to talk to you.' The captain stood back.

Atkins's throat went dry. There was something vaguely familiar about this soldier. Oh, he was dressed in the red and black jerkin of a King's officer, but he sported a green ribbon on his breast, and the way he moved, that mocking voice . . . Atkins took a step forward.

'Haven't we met before, sir? In an alleyway outside a theatre?'

The officer's head came back, a smooth, harsh face with twisted lips and cruel eyes. His right cheek was badly gouged by a duelling scar which ran down from the corner of his eye round to his chin.

'I don't think I've had the pleasure, sir.' The eyes were lying.

'What is this? What is this?' Pepys came bustling forward.

'You may collect your cloak and hat, sir,' the officer ordered.

The soldiers came forward, halberds still slightly lowered.

'I will come and do so quietly,' Atkins murmured.

He went across and took his cloak and hat from a peg on the wall. The officer snapped his fingers. Pepys thrust his way through the bodyguard, elbowing away hands, lifting halberds. He grasped Samuel's wrist, eyes pleading.

'Tell the truth, Samuel. Whatever happens, stand fast in the truth.' He leaned closer as if to kiss Atkins on the cheek but whispered quickly in his ear, 'If you go down, must you take me with you?'

The captain shouted an order; Pepys withdrew. One of the soldiers quickly searched the clerk for any hidden weapon then they left: crashing footsteps down the narrow passage-way, wide-eyed clerks, servants being thrust aside. Pepys called out something but Atkins didn't hear what he said. Across the stonepaved hallway they went, out into the cold night. Atkins tried to control his fear. The soldiers hemmed him around on every side. They marched quickly to the clatter of boots and clash of steel. Two link boys ran ahead of them carrying lantern horns. Atkins was aware of the houses jutting out, almost blocking the sky above him. People peering through shutters, faces in doorways, the warmth and glow from a tavern, the sound of a fiddle. He tried to compose himself. What could Shaftesbury, the powerful lord, want with the likes of him? When he stumbled and slipped on a piece of rubbish, one of the soldiers caught him by the arm.

'Steady, lad,' the voice whispered. 'You are not to be hurt, at least not yet.'

Atkins's world was now reduced to this, the crash of march-ing feet, the glint of steel morion helmets, the razor-sharp hal-berds slung over the guards' shoulders. He felt as if he wasn't there; he was in that chamber again with Maria Eleanora staring beseechingly at him. The fog came curling down the street, made worse by a sleety drizzle. A man shouted from an alleyway, and Atkins glanced up. A woman's pretty face was pressed against a casement window. For a moment, Samuel panicked. Was that Maria Eleanora? But then they were past. On one corner they had to pause; a moment of comedy as an old man lugubriously led a she-ass from door to door selling milk for children. Behind him trailed his wife, pulling a hand-cart, stacked high with cages of singing birds: larks and thrushes taken from the wilds of Hampstead. The soldiers shoved them aside and marched on.

The looming gate of Warrington House was illuminated by lantern horns and fiery cresset torches lashed to poles on either side of the entrance. An Abraham man, naked except for a loincloth, balanced a dish of burning coals on his matted hair. He came bounding up like some deranged prophet from the Bible.

'The wages of sin,' he boomed, 'are truly death! But did Abner die like a fool dieth? Does he mourn over David buried in Hebron? Lo, the skies are full of shooting stars!'

'Piss off!' one of the soldiers shouted, shoving him aside.

They led Samuel under the gateway and across a cobbled yard. Braziers glowed, people ran backwards and forwards carrying lantern horns. Grooms held horses, hooves scraping the ground ready for their riders, messengers who would go thundering out into the night bearing important proclamations from the Lords' Committee. The soldiers paused before the main doorway. The captain led Atkins, still flanked by a guard, up the steps into the porchway, along a corridor and up a broad, wooden staircase. Servants, bringing down trays of food, hastily stepped aside. Atkins smelt polish, faded flowers, sweat and, yes, something else, the stench of fear: his only thought was that Maria Eleanora must never be brought to a place like this. All around him were dark galleries, ill-lit stairwells, heavy oaken doors reinforced with bronze studs and guarded by mean-faced men who skulked in corners. There was no laughter, no music, no women, nothing soft or tender. The harsh, man-made, granite wall of conspiracy, treason and hideous death circled everything.

Atkins was aware of a long gallery. The captain paused before a door. He rapped lightly, it was pulled aside. A whispered conversation, then the door was flung wide open and the captain led Atkins and his escort into a long, barn-like room. The floor was stone-flagged, no carpets or rugs, not even rushes or sawdust. The walls were lime-washed, black heavy beams criss-crossed above him. He was aware of benches

57

down the side but his attention was taken by the long table on the raised dais at the far end. Five men sat there beneath a picture of the King framed in gold gilt. A brazier glowed at each end of the table, sconce torches flared on the walls either side of the painting. Candelabra, judiciously placed along the table, provided enough light without revealing the faces of those who sat in the shadows.

'My lord,' the captain called out. 'I bring you Samuel Atkins taken under warrant this day, the first of November 1678!'

'Then bring Mr Atkins forward.'

Samuel was given a push. He glared over his shoulder. The captain smirked back. By the time he had reached the dais a high, wooden-backed chair had been placed in front of it.

'You may sit down, Mr Atkins,' a voice drawled soft, but full of menace. 'You have met our redoubtable Captain Eastwell, he will stand behind you. There are others in the room but you need not worry about them.'

Atkins peered into the shadows behind these powerful lords. He saw a movement, the glint of silver and the glow of a clay pipe; more people sat, hidden deep in the shadows. The man in the great chair in the centre moved a candle. As he did so, Atkins was diverted by a figure sitting at the far end of the table, almost cloaked in the darkness. He now leaned forward into the light, a veritable grotesque; short and bloated, his fair woolly periwig framed a face the colour of dirty lead. Because of his huge broad jaw, his prim lips seemed to be the centre of his face. He was a monstrous toad of a man, with his stocky neck and jutting head, sunken eyes glaring at Atkins from under bushy eyebrows.

'The Lord be with you!' A long, nasal whine.

'And the Lord be with you, sir,' Atkins cheerily replied, determined not to show his fear.

'Do you recognise him?' the man in the centre asked.

Atkins kept his gaze on the grotesque who moved slightly forward; he was dressed in clerical garb.

'My Lord,' the toad whined. 'I know him not though he has the phizog of a papist and a traitor.'

'We will need more than that, won't we, Mr Atkins?'

Samuel turned to face the speaker. He had met him before. He had recognised the sharp, withered face beneath the fair wig, the heavy-lidded eyes, the cynical cast to his mouth. It was Anthony Ashley Cooper, first Earl of Shaftesbury, leader of the Opposition, garbed in his green silks, leading this committee by the nose wherever he wished it to go. Shaftesbury's eyes opened wide, head on one side as he studied Atkins.

'You know the rest, Mr Atkins? My Lord of Essex.' He gestured at the sour-faced man at the far end. 'My Lord of Buckingham.' A fat podgy man with double chins. 'My Lord Compton.' The grey-faced Bishop of London. 'And this,' Shaftesbury tapped the wrist of a huge, black-haired giant sitting on his right.

Atkins glanced at Fitzherbert, Earl of Pembroke, with his mad eyes, sallow gipsy face, hair and beard all tousled. The front of Pembroke's vest was wine-stained, flecks of food round his gaping mouth. Flushed on claret, his eyes glared ferociously at Atkins. He reminded the clerk of an angry sow.

'A most dangerous man,' Master Pepys had confided.

Atkins secretly agreed. Hadn't Pembroke faced a number of murder charges? The man should really be in Bedlam. If frustrated, he would ferociously attack with sword, dagger, any implement at hand.

'Yes, I do think you know everybody,' Shaftesbury murmured. He pulled the candelabra closer. 'Well, well, Mr Atkins.' He continued studying the clerk from head to toe.

'A fine young man – English-born, yes? And where do you lodge?' he continued, not waiting for an answer.

'With Mr Pepys in Seething Lane.'

'And where do you work?'

'With Mr Pepys in Derby House.'

'Are you a loyal subject, Mr Atkins?'

'Even more loyal than you, sir.'

Pembroke leaned forward as if to bellow a threat but Shaftesbury restrained him.

'Hush now,' he whispered. 'Well, Mr Atkins, do you have anything to tell this committee?'

'I would like to go home. I would like to know why I am here.'

'Ah, we'll come to that by and by. But, Mr Atkins, you very rarely go home, do you? You like visiting the playhouse, the taverns, secret chambers?' Shaftesbury raised one eyebrow.

'I meet my ladyfriends.'

'Anyone in particular?'

'Sir, a gentleman does not discuss his ladyfriends.'

Shaftesbury laughed softly.

'Pray, Mr Atkins,' the Bishop of London intervened. 'Do you know a Captain Childs?'

'Yes, my lord, for about two or three years.'

'Do you know, or believe, he has any reason to do you a prejudice?'

'Of course not. Nor have I ever given him any occasion to have any prejudice against me.'

'Did you ever,' Shaftesbury intervened, weasel-like, his fingers tapping the base of the candelabra, 'discuss with Captain Childs about the Plot?'

'What plot, sir?'

'A plot to overthrow the legitimate Government of this country.'

'Of course not!'

Atkins wiped his sweaty palms on the side of his thighs. This room had become cold, dangerous, the very cabinet of Hell. At the end of the table, Oates's great chin was almost pressed down into his chest. The others stared up at the beams, all except Shaftesbury and Pembroke. The ruffian Earl had his head down. Atkins suspected he was asleep. Shaftesbury, however, was as pert and lively as a stoat which had found its quarry.

'So, you know of no plot?' The words came softly.

'I have said as much.'

'Do you know of any lack of friendship between Mr Pepys, your master, and Sir Edmund Godfrey?'

'No, I do not.' Atkins half-rose. Then felt the tip of Eastwell's sword on the soft part of his neck just beneath the ear.

'Keep your seat,' Shaftesbury instructed. 'Tell the truth and you may yet save your life, Mr Atkins.'

Samuel's throat went dry. 'My life?'

'Did you ever discuss,' Shaftesbury insisted, 'Sir Edmund Godfrey with Mr Pepys?'

'No, I did not.'

'Do you know a man called Captain Bedloe?' Buckingham bellowed.

'I have never heard of him.'

'Call in the witness!' Shaftesbury spoke to the shadows behind him.

A door in the far corner opened. Atkins heard the clip-clop of high-heeled shoes and Captain Childs stepped through. He was fashionably dressed in a fine jacket over an embroidered waistcoat, well cut breeches with a green ribbon tied above the stockings, and red high-heeled shoes with silver buckles. He came swaggering into the pool of light behind Shaftesbury who simply snapped his fingers and pointed to a chair at the far end of the table next to Oates. Captain Childs took his seat, his thin, pinched features fully illuminated by the candle-light. The man was nervous, as shown by a constant licking of his lips, blinking of his eyes and a refusal to look in Atkins's direction.

'Do you know this man?' Shaftesbury asked.

'Why yes, sir,' Atkins replied. 'It's Captain Childs. I have eaten and drunk with him and lent him some money.'

'Captain Childs,' Shaftesbury demanded, 'do you remember Mr Atkins?'

Childs placed his hands on the table. 'Of course, as well as the conversation we had in the Lord's Chamber at Derby House. You told me how Sir Edmund Godfrey had vilified Master Pepys and that Master Pepys was bent on vengeance.'

'God and your conscience know,' Samuel retorted, 'that we had no such conversation! The only words we have had were about wine and your lack of money.'

'Come, come, Mr Atkins.' Shaftesbury's face was wreathed in smiles. He rubbed his hands together as if he already had Pepys and Atkins in the execution cart for Tyburn.

'Come, come, my lord,' Atkins mimicked. 'This is arrant nonsense.'

'But the captain has sworn this! I don't think he has the wit to invent such a tale.'

A low murmur of laughter greeted his words.

'Captain Childs knows a great deal about you, Mr Atkins.'

'Aye, and I know how he surrendered his ship to Algerian corsairs some two years ago.'

Captain Childs would have objected but Shaftesbury held his hand up, all smiles gone.

'What is this?' Shaftesbury muttered. 'What is this?'

'Captain Childs has not told you?' Atkins retorted gleefully.

'Ask him why he hasn't been given command of a ship for the last two years. He struck his colours . . .'

Pembroke turned, glaring down the table at the hapless captain who sat, head bowed, shuffling his feet.

'I don't think we need detain you any longer,' Shaftesbury declared coldly. 'Captain Childs, we no longer have need of you.'

'And I have no need of a coward!' Samuel's face flushed with anger.

He would have leapt to his feet but Eastwell restrained him. Captain Childs, realising discretion was the better part of valour, disappeared into the shadows behind the table. The door in the far corner closed sharply behind him.

'Come, come now.' Shaftesbury's voice was wheedling, honeyed, full of sweetness. 'We do not wish to upset you, Samuel. We simply want the truth. Would you like some wine, a cup of sack?'

'I would like to go home. I would like to know the true reason for being brought here.'

'I know what you are thinking.' Buckingham's podgy hand came flailing out. 'I can see how your brain works. Come, for your own sake, declare what you know.' Buckingham was oily-sweet, mouth gaping in a smile, eyes crinkled with amusement. 'We do not wish to hurt you, boy.'

'I am no boy.'

'What do you want?' Buckingham continued, ignoring the interruption. 'Honours, preferment? Just tell us the truth.' He sighed. 'However, my Lord Shaftesbury, let us break and wet our throats.'

Atkins sat and watched as the wine was served: these great lords wetting their throats, smacking their lips. Buckingham's jowls all a-quiver, Pembroke drinking as if it was his first for days. Compton the Bishop sipping at a cup, a disdainful look on his sour face. Atkins had now recovered from his first shock. Shaftesbury had nailed his colours to the mast. This was about the Plot and they would do everything in their power to trap his master. Atkins closed his eyes and quietly thanked God. When Godfrey had gone missing, Pepys had accompanied the King to Newmarket. But what about Maria Eleanora? Did Shaftesbury know about her?

'Mr Atkins, have you gone to sleep?'

'No, sir.' Atkins opened his eyes. 'I am just thinking what a nonsense this is.'

'A nonsense? A nonsense!' Compton stared fiercely at him. 'You regard plots and treasons as nonsense! Are you a loyal Englishman, Mr Atkins?'

'You couldn't find better, my lord.'

'Did you know Sir Edmund Godfrey?'

'Only by sight.'

'Do you take the sacrament?'

'Every month.'

'And how long have you been with Mr Pepys?' Buckingham demanded.

'Four years.'

'And how old are you?'

'Twenty-one.'

'Do you often visit the Duke of York at St James's?' Shaftesbury rejoined the hunt. He steepled his fingers together, peering at Atkins as if seeing him for the first time.

'You know the answer to that, my lord. The Duke of York is Lord High Admiral of England.'

'Do you ever visit Somerset Place?'

'The home of the Queen?' Atkins stuttered.

Shaftesbury's eyes grew hard. 'We know it's the home of Her Majesty the Queen, God bless her. Why are you so nervous, Mr Atkins?'

'I am tired. I cannot see why I am here.'

'Whom do you meet in the dead of night?'

Atkins's heart skipped a beat. 'I have told you, ladies of the night.'

'Furnish us with a name.'

'I can't remember any. They are just faces.'

'Just *faces*?' Shaftesbury taunted. He leaned back in his chair laughing. 'So, when you arrange to meet these ladies, you just send messages to faces?' He leaned forward, narrow eyes all a-blaze. 'Mr Atkins, you are a liar, you are a traitor! Tell us whom you meet in the dead of night.'

'I can't remember.'

'Where were you on the weekend Justice Godfrey disappeared?'

The clerk closed his eyes. He tried to recall days and dates but was unable to. He was frightened; these hounds were close to Maria Eleanora.

'I can't say,' he muttered eventually.

A collective sigh rose from the men behind the table.

'I cannot remember,' Samuel repeated.

'Mr Atkins.' Shaftesbury's voice became hard and brittle. 'Look at me, Mr Atkins.'

Samuel raised his head.

'Captain Childs has sworn a great oath that your master entertained ill-feeling towards Sir Edmund Godfrey, whose tortured corpse now lies in its cold grave, whilst his soul cries for vengeance to God.' The words came tripping off his tongue. The look on Shaftesbury's face was one of smug hypocrisy. 'You *must* know more than you have told us.'

'Are you protecting someone?' the Bishop of London asked. 'You see, my lords?' He lifted a hand, not waiting for Atkins's answer. 'He *is* protecting someone.'

The rest of the company joined in, banging hands on

the table, demanding that Atkins speak and tell the truth. The clerk, wild-eyed, glanced at their faces. They have me trapped, he thought, and I am in a cold terror.

'You will go to Newgate,' Shaftesbury decided. 'Yes, Mr Atkins, you will go to Newgate where you can sit and reflect. Only when you have decided to tell the truth, may you come back. We would like to know the truth about Master Pepys and, above all, we would like to know your whereabouts on the night of the murder. Whilst,' his voice dropped to a whisper, 'we are deeply interested in whom you meet at the dead of night.'

'Perhaps he should have a little more time!' Compton snapped.

Samuel felt the tip of Eastwell's sword prick his neck, forcing him to his feet.

'Very well, a few more minutes,' Shaftesbury agreed, staring at him. 'Captain Eastwell, take our young friend away.' He pointed across to a door halfway down the chamber. 'Put him in there and let him reflect.'

Atkins was bundled off the dais, Eastwell pushing him ahead. The door was opened, he was thrust into cold darkness. The door slammed shut. Atkins heard a laugh. He felt around: nothing but cold plaster. It wasn't really a closet, more of a cupboard in the wall, musty and dirty. The only light was a small chink beneath the door. He leaned back against the wall, pressing his hot, sweaty hands against the coolness and shivering, not so much with cold, but fear. All he could think of was Maria Eleanora, her beautiful face gazing beseechingly at him. He tried to marshal his wits.

'They have no evidence,' he muttered. Samuel slid down the wall. 'They have no evidence,' he repeated loudly. Little did he know such evidence was imminent, for the 'Devil on Horseback' had just arrived in London!

Chapter Four

William Bedloe was the Devil Incarnate. Warrants for his arrest were out throughout Europe, from Cadiz in the south to Antwerp in the north. A man of devilish tricks, a counterfeit, an artisan of infinite cunning, Bedloe rejoiced in the title of 'Captain' or 'Colonel', though he found it difficult to recall which regiments he had led or what battles he had fought in. A man who took to lying as a bird did to flight, William Bedloe, lately of Salamanca, quite recently of Brussels, and well known in the underworlds of London and Bristol, had come into his own. His was a villainous countenance, harsh and forbidding. A face full of malice and revenge, with beetling brows and savage eyes.

As he arrived in London at the beginning of November 1678, and dismounted from his black horse in the cobbled yards of the King's Head tavern in Fleet Street near Temple Bar, Bedloc was dressed in gaudy finery beneath his campaign cloak of royal gold braid; a battered hilted rapier slapping against his knee-high boots. William Bedloe took off his hat, adorned with a green plume, and tossed the reins of his horse to a gaping ostler.

'You ridden far, sir?' the ostler asked curiously, taking the measure of this striking-looking man.

'Where I come from and how long it has taken,' Bedloe wryly remarked, 'is not a matter for you or anyone else.'

The ostler searched Bedloe's cloak, looking for the tell-tale green ribbon. To be sure, a plume of the same colour adorned the hat but the servant had to be careful.

'Who shall I say has arrived?' The ostler's hand went towards the club which hung from his broad leather belt.

'Keep your hand well away from that!' Bedloe barked. 'And tell the tavernmaster that the Devil Almighty on horseback has returned to his own. Go on!'

The ostler scurried away. Bedloe swaggered across the yard, the hard heels of his boots clipping the dirt-strewn cobbles. Two guards sitting either side of the entrance got up, grasping their scabbards. When Bedloe threw back his cloak to display the hilt of his rapier, the men sat down again. The ostler came back through the door but Bedloe was already pushing him aside, stepping into the sweet warm fug of the taproom. Its floor was covered in freshly laid straw, lantern horns lit, tallow candles spluttering. Still it was a place of shadows, a broad room filled with tables, stools and broken chairs. A fire roared in the chimney-breast. Tap-boys, scullions and slatterns scurried about with trays of brimming jugs of ale. Pipes had been lit, the acrid tobacco curling up to the black-beamed ceiling. A little dog, trapped in a cage, aimlessly walked, keeping the spit above the fire turning slowly. A kitchen boy, his face brick-red, basted the pieces of roasting meat. Portions of beef, young ducklings, geese, a pullet: their savoury smell made Bedloe's mouth water.

A movement at the kitchen door caught his attention. He saw a maid, her blonde curly hair kept in place by a white mobcap. He glimpsed her low-cut bodice, merry eyes and a pert mouth. The young woman smiled, a little too quickly. Bedloe narrowed his eyes as he pushed his way into the room. Why had she been watching him so intently? Bedloe knew he was no Cavalier. He lacked the soft, foppish looks which were fashionable. He glanced again but the girl was gone. At that moment, the taverner came across. Jack Seagrave was one of Lord Shaftesbury's loyal lieutenants; he managed the King's Head on behalf of his patron and other powerful Green Ribboners. Seagrave was a taverner who brushed shoulders with ministers of the King's Council as well as highwaymen, footpads and paid assassins – men such as William Bedloe who came and went like thieves in the night.

'Master Bedloe!'

'Captain Bedloe to you, Seagrave.'

The taverner's broad, florid face broke into a smile. He stretched out a hand. Bedloe clasped it.

'Honest Jack Seagrave,' the taverner whispered.

'You've got a face as honest as a vicar and a heart as black as sea coal!'

'All in a day's work, Captain Bedloe.'

Seagrave brushed a lock of hair from his broad forehead, exposing the deep scar, a sabre-cut he had received whilst fighting in Cromwell's wars in Ireland. He bowed mockingly and gestured to the cushioned settle in front of the fire.

'A pot of ale, a pipe of tobacco?'

Bedloe unclasped his cloak and draped it over one arm.

'You have a wench – blonde hair, a proper doxy but innocent like?'

'Ah, that's our Cecily. Comes from the West Country.'

'And will she bounce in bed?'

Seagrave smirked. 'She bounces like a poppet. I have ridden her myself though she's choosy with her favours.'

'Noisy?' Bedloe asked.

'Like a bird on a branch. But she's not for you, Captain Bedloe.'

'Does she lodge here?'

Bedloe grasped Seagrave by the arm and led him across

to the settle. Seagrave broke free. Bedloe sat down and stared up, dark hollow eyes full of suspicion.

'Yes, she lodges here, in a small garret at the top.'

Bedloe stared through the fug. This was one of the few taverns where he could relax and not immediately spy out some window or narrow door through which he could escape. He glimpsed Cecily again bustling across with a tray of tankards for the gamblers in the far corner. She put these down, fought off a grasping hand and came hurrying back. Bedloe, tongue between his lips, watched intently. She was of medium height, broad-hipped and full-bosomed. A good piece of silk decorated her long, soft throat, and the front of her bodice was unbuttoned to whet the appetite of the customers, though she was certainly not free with her favours. Bedloe gnawed at a finger knuckle. He was sure he had seen her before.

Cecily lifted her head and glowered at Seagrave as she passed.

'Are you sure you've bedded her?' Bedloe taunted.

Seagrave glanced down at the hearth where the small dog, still trotting aimlessly, turned the wheels which moved the spit.

'I think it's your imagination.' Bedloe imitated a West Country accent.

'Let's just say I live in hopes.' Seagrave grinned. 'But now, Captain, how about that tankard and pipe, eh?'

'Is His Majesty here?' Bedloe whispered, raising his eyes to the ceiling. 'He is expecting me?'

'Like the breeze,' Seagrave replied, 'he comes and goes. We don't know whence or when but, if he arrives, I shall tell you.'

Bedloe made himself comfortable on the corner of the settle. He ordered the spit boy to cut him a piece of duckling; when the boy did so, Bedloe grasped it between his fingers, snorting noisily at how hot it was. He moved it quickly from finger to finger and bit into its white sweetness. The tankard and full clay pipe arrived. Bedloe snatched them from Cecily's hands. Despite the dirt and grease on her face, the maid was very comely, yet her smile was false, her wide blue eyes as hard as steel. Bedloe felt slightly uncomfortable. He took the tankard and placed it on the ground beside him.

'I need a taper!' he growled.

Cecily came back and thrust one into his hand. The Captain handed it to the boy who lit it and gave it back. Bedloe sucked at the pipe, watching the flame of the taper burn the brown tobacco black. Cecily still stood, hands on hips, staring down at him.

'I am sure I have met you before, Mistress. Your name is Cecily?'

The young woman nodded.

'And your surname?'

'Bannister.' Her voice was slightly harsh.

Bedloe, a cunning man, believed she was trying to disguise her accent.

'You are from the West Country, I hear. So am I.' He smiled.

'It's a large area.' Cecily's smile widened. 'My father was a farmer in Devon.'

Aye, and I'm a Cardinal of the Papal Court, Bedloe thought staring back. Perhaps he was just getting nervous?

'But now I am busy.' Cecily leaned down. 'If there is anything else, sir?'

Bedloe took the pipe out of his mouth; he stared at those sweet breasts peeping out from above their white linen bands.

'No, there's nothing else, Mistress, but if there is, I'll bear you in mind.'

Cecily flounced away. Bedloe enjoyed his tankard, puffed at the pipe and stared into the fire. The heat and glow were pleasant after his cold ride. It also woke memories, childhood nightmares about the visions of Hell and the fate of sinners. Bedloe coughed on the smoke. If any man was bound for Hell, Bedloe believed it was he. He comforted himself that he was in good company. He allowed his eyelids to grow heavy. He drained the tankard and dozed for a while. Memories came and went: the dark shapes and shades of different men he had killed, the women he had taken and the bag of mischief he'd recently let loose upon an unsuspecting world. Then Bedloe woke with a start. He took off his swordbelt and placed it on the settle beside him. He was safe here from the Sealed Knot, the likes of Dolius, who hunted men such as Bedloe, kept to their heels like snapping hounds.

'Captain Bedloe! Wake up, Captain Bedloe!' A pot boy shook his arm.

Bedloe opened one eye.

'What is it, lad?'

The youngster gestured with a finger to the ceiling. Bedloe grunted and got to his feet. He picked up his hat, cloak and swordbelt and went across to the door, then along a draughty passageway and up a winding narrow staircase. They reached the first gallery, the boy trotting in front. He stopped outside the second chamber guarded by two ruffians: these took Bedloe's swordbelt and searched him for weapons. The door was opened and he stepped inside. This was a far cry from the taproom below filled with bully-boys and brassy-eyed doxies. Its walls were completely covered in thick green leather quilts which deadened all sound, the ceiling likewise. The windows were shuttered, and small green curtains pulled across; soft carpets of the same colour covered the floor. A log fire crackled in the hearth. The table beneath the window was covered with parchments, an open ink-horn, quills.

'Captain Bedloe, you are most welcome.'

Shaftesbury's impish face peered round the corner of the armchair facing the fire. Bedloe went across. Falling to one knee, he kissed the green emerald ring on Shaftesbury's left hand. His Lordship put the small goblet of barley water down on the table in front of him, patted Bedloe's head as he would a dog, then gestured at the armchair opposite.

'You have had a hard ride?'

William Bedloe placed his cloak and hat on the floor and made himself comfortable in the armchair. Shaftesbury sat watching him intently from beneath heavy-lidded eyes.

'A warm cup of posset?'

Bedloe knew the ritual.

'My Lord, I have ridden well and hard but I've drunk enough for the time being.'

'And smoked a pipe?'

'Aye, my Lord.'

'And studied that little moppet Cecily?'

'I have seen her before, my Lord.'

'Have you now? Have you now? You are all suspicious, aren't you, Captain William?'

'My Lord, we have to be. The Sealed Knot are all about us and Dolius, whoever he is, could be prying from the darkness.'

'Yes, yes, he could be.'

Shaftesbury leaned back to look at the ceiling. Bedloe, who could never really guess what his master was thinking, this time prided himself that he had a very good idea.

'The Sealed Knot,' Shaftesbury murmured. He closed his eyes. 'You can talk here, Bedloe,' he continued, eyes still closed. 'This chamber is safe. No gaps and vents, no peep-holes, no listening cracks.'

'The Sealed Knot?' Bedloe demanded harshly.

'I don't know who they are.' Shaftesbury opened his eyes suddenly like a cat and glared at his guest. 'The King's own agents, eh? And Dolius is the worst. If only we could catch them.'

'If only you knew who they were,' Bedloe replied more rudely than he should have done.

Shaftesbury lashed out with one foot and caught Bedloe a painful crack on the ankle. The captain winced.

'Remember your manners, William,' Shaftesbury purred, 'and know where you are. This is the King's Head, the place of the Green Ribbon and I, William,' he turned his head and stared at Bedloe out of the corner of his eye, 'am your master!'

'My Lord, I apologise but—'

'But nothing! He lies buried, you know,' he continued, staring into the fire. 'Poor old Godfrey's corpse lay in state like a king's at Bridewell. Taken through the streets as if he was the glory of the people. What a funeral, William! Tears came to my eyes. People whispered how stricken to the heart the Lord Shaftesbury was! Thank God for mouchoirs.' He grinned. 'Otherwise the poltroons would have seen I was on the verge of fainting from laughter. Anyway,' he sighed. 'Godfrey's gone, the prying old fool, and we have the proof for our Plot! So, Billy boy, it's up Jack, up Jill, stir and agitate! In every tavern in London the tongues wag about the Great Plot, but we know the truth, don't we, my friend?'

Bedloe gazed blankly back.

'That's why I summoned you away from whatever shit-hole in Bristol you were hiding in. You've got another part to play.'

'Is that wise, my Lord?'

Bedloe immediately regretted his words. Shaftesbury's foot lashed out.

'I am sorry, my Lord,' he winced. 'I am on edge. I thought I would hide for a while.'

'Hide for a while, eh? Not from me! Tell me, do you know a man called Atkins, Samuel Atkins?'

'Of course I do, my Lord, you put me on his trail.'

'Yes, yes, so I did. You failed me badly there, silly boy.'

'In the last few months,' Bedloe hurriedly replied, 'Samuel has left his lodgings in Seething Lane.'

'I know where that runt lives!' Shaftesbury interrupted.

'And he goes to meet someone.'

'A woman?'

'No, my Lord, a man. Some young courtier who wears a hat with a scarlet plume.'

'A bum boy, eh?' Shaftesbury sniggered. 'So, Mr Atkins is of the way of Sodom?' He chewed on his tongue and, picking up his barley water, sipped from the cup. He grinned over its brim. 'But we can't have him accused of that, can we, eh? I mean, Master Bedloe, you too have certain habits which – how can I say this? – are not to my taste. We may sit in the same church but you perch on a different pew.'

Bedloe swallowed hard.

'Oh, I know about your little foibles,' Shaftesbury chattered on. 'And your love for a pair of round, sweet buttocks.'

'I've had my wenches as well.'

'Oh yes, you are Janus-like. You look both ways but you do have a problem, like our good friend Titus Oates, yes?'

Bedloe nodded.

'I believe you met him in Salamanca when Oates was pretending to train to be a Catholic priest? You know what happened there? He was expelled from the college because

75

of his unclean practices just like he was expelled from his Living on the south coast, not to mention being whipped out of the Navy. Master Oates sows his oats,' Shaftesbury chuckled gently at the pun, 'in a way proscribed by the Bible.' He pulled himself up in the chair. 'It wouldn't look good, would it, Captain Bedloe, if the two great heroes of the Plot, the Saviours of the Nation, were exposed as sodomites?'

'My Lord,' Bedloe croaked. 'If I could have a drink . . . my throat is dry.'

'I wager it is,' Shaftesbury nodded. 'But I couldn't care if it was cut!'

He abruptly leaned forward, eyes now wide open, the skin of his face tighter. Bedloe shivered. Shaftesbury in a temper was a fearsome man.

'I want you sober, Captain Bedloe.' Shaftesbury peered across the room to where a small clock stood on the table. 'You're soon to have an audience with His Majesty the King, God bless his poxy soul!'

'The King . . . !' Bedloe stuttered.

'Yes, the King, and you are my choirboy William. I have Oates chanting from one stall and I'll have you chanting from the other, a two-voiced harmony. So, back to Atkins. Forget about Scarlet Plume, though.' Shaftesbury lifted a finger. 'We could take that thread and twist it another way. Perhaps Master Atkins was meeting a priest? Or an agent from the Monsieurs?' Shaftesbury made a reference to the French Embassy. 'Or even a spy from the House of Spain. Well, whatever! Now listen, William, and listen well. I'll tell you a tale; Atkins is a player and this is the plot.'

For an hour Shaftesbury talked coolly, precisely. Every so often he would pause and make Bedloe repeat what he had said. The cunning man had a sharp memory and even keener wits. He quietly marvelled at Shaftesbury's churning, devious mind. Once he was finished, Shaftesbury questioned Bedloe, making him repeat the story, pressing him on this point or that. Bedloe was an apt pupil. The more he spoke the more confident he became. At the end Shaftesbury beat his hands in glee on the side of the armchair and stamped his feet as if preparing for a dance.

'Very good! Very good, Billy boy! What a fine fellow you are, Captain William Bedloe.' He dug into the recesses of the chair and tossed across a clinking bag of coins. 'Now come, come, William.'

Shaftesbury sprang to his feet and went to the door. The two burly ruffians came in, hats pulled low, faces almost covered by vizards. They hardly spared Bedloe a glance as they helped their master dress in his dark cloak and hat. Shaftesbury looked quickly in a small mirror. He pronounced himself satisfied and, ringed by his bodyguard, went down the back stairs, Bedloe walking beside him. They left the King's Head tavern walking quickly up towards St Paul's. Bedloe tried to contain his excitement. Shaftesbury informed him how the King was waiting in the Red Chamber at Whitehall. Once again Bedloe recounted to himself the tale he would tell. He would concentrate on that, nothing else! Link boys ran ahead of them, their lanterns glowing like beacon lights in the foggy dark. A biting wind carried the stench of fish from the river to mingle with the stink of the streets. Night had fallen but the city was as busy as ever. Stalls were being put away, the cries of tinkers and chapmen, anxious to earn a few more coppers before the bailiffs came, shrilled through the dark. Bedloe hugged himself. If it was not for the likes of Shaftesbury, that's how he would earn his keep. So he concentrated on his tale which would send Samuel Atkins to Tyburn and the cruel knife and axe of the quartering block.

*   *   *

'Did Abner die as a fool dies? And was not Abner buried in Hebron?' So the whisper ran through London like the wind through a cornfield, stirring and shaking. Hadn't Dr Lloyd proved, at least to the satisfaction of most citizens, that Sir Edmund Godfrey was Abner come again, whilst his assassins lurked in secret places and plotted more murderous mischief? Certainly arrests had been made. Papists had been taken up in the dead of night: their pale-faced wives watched whilst Master Oates and his bailiffs searched their papers. Oh, and the Lord be thanked and let Heaven ring with joy! Hadn't secret stashes been found in chimney-stacks or under floorboards? And were not suspects now laden with chains, imprisoned in the 'Little Susie' or 'Little Ease', the deepest condemned holds in Newgate?

People whispered above their tankards about what they had seen and heard. The crowds flocked to Somerset Place in the Strand where Charles's Catholic Portuguese wife held court. A Place of Treason, or so the hand-bills screamed, with its colonnaded front, deep courtyards, shallow steps, enclosed gardens and warren of passageways and chambers. The curious and the vulgar, not to mention the watch dogs of the Green Ribboners, kept Somerset Place under close surveillance. The King, seriously alarmed, had doubled its guard: his own soldiers, dressed in dark-red and black, breastplates shining, heads encased in steel morions, patrolled the perimeter armed with pikes and halberds, muskets and swords.

Inside Somerset Place, however, all lay quiet. The lights burnt low. The galleries were empty. Catherine of Braganza kept to her own apartments whilst her principal lady-in-waiting, Maria Eleanora, was sleeping in her own well-draped chamber. She had not retired for the night, was just dozing in the early hours of the evening before the low-burning fire, a book of love poetry resting on her lap. Maria Eleanora savoured the warmth and, once again, dreamed of Portugal, that same nightmare which always returned to haunt her in times of danger. Once again she was standing by her family villa, only a few miles from Lisbon. The gateway was open, the white, dusty trackway stretched under a blazing sun through a thick clump of olive trees to the far horizon. Birds sang as they wheeled in the steel-blue sky. Maria Eleanora's father sat on horseback, a dark-green jacket over his long silk-woven waistcoat with its golden buttons; a jewelled clasp kept his snow-white cravat in place. He had taken his hat off; his black hair was caught up and tied in a queue behind him. His long, dark face was wreathed in smiles as he leaned down and caressed his daughter gently on the brow.

'I will not be long, Maria Eleanora.'

She could remember every syllable, the way he looked – even the pattern on that beautiful waistcoat. His fingertips felt cool for she had been hot after running, going back to fetch the writing satchel he had forgotten. She was so proud as she handed it up.

'You must look after your mother and sisters,' he reminded her. 'I will be in Lisbon by nightfall and, God willing, home within three days.'

'Father, I love you,' she had cried out as he gathered his reins, moving his horse skilfully back. 'I shall miss you!'

'And I shall miss you, Maria Eleanora!' he called back, putting his hat on then taking it off in salute, his beautiful, black Arab horse caracolling upon its hind legs.

'I salute you, Maria Eleanora, jewel of my heart!'

And then he was gone, his servant behind, galloping along the trackway, thundering hooves raising white wisps of dust. Maria Eleanora had stood and watched until the dust cloud settled and her father disappeared into the distance. All sound had gone, leaving her under God's blue sky and the birds singing their hearts out. At this point, the dream always changed. The same gateway but this time at night, dark and cold. A bitter wind whipping up the flames of the torches. Men in cloaks trudging silently, mournfully up, her father's horse in the centre, his corpse laid across the saddle. When they brought him into the fountain courtyard, Maria Eleanora had screamed as if her very soul was leaving her body. They laid her father's body on a cloak strewn out on the cobbles. He looked as if he was asleep, eyes closed. In the torchlight his face had a deathly pallor, that hideous Burgundy stain on the gold waistcoat where the bullet had entered his left breast and pierced his heart.

'An assassin,' one of the riders had declared.

Someone hired by her father's enemies: they'd killed both him and his servant only a few hours after he had left his villa. After her one despairing cry, Maria Eleanora had laid down beside her father and stretched an arm across his chest as if they were in the vineyard, on that grassy bank which ran down to a small stream with the sun blazing above them. Her father would stroke her hair and tell her stories of the great heroes of Portugal's past. On that dreadful night Maria Eleanora had talked to him, as if her very words and love could withdraw the bullet, close the wound, breathe life back into his cold dead flesh. She was aware of her mother and sisters rending the night air with hideous screams. Still she had lain there, stroking her father's face, whispering words. At last they had dragged her from him. Someone had given her a drink, heavy wine laced with an opiate.

For the next few weeks and months Maria Eleanora had lived in a dream. She had watched her sisters recover but her mother's soul died, just shrivelled up and withered away. In a few months Maria Eleanora had become the head of the household, driving away her father's kinsmen, taking over the accounts, the running of the estate. She had hunted her father's assassin – an embittered nobleman – down, and settled accounts with him. One windswept night, on the quayside of Lisbon, as the man thought he would flee, Maria Eleanora caught up with him: she and her faithful retainers. The assassin had curled his lip, mocked her with his eyes, told her to go back to her embroidery. She killed him all the same, sword against sword. A swift lunge, a killing thrust to the heart, and his body was slipped over the quayside into the black waters below. No one mourned him, no one missed him. Maria Eleanora had returned to her estates and the dreams had begun. The same one: standing by the gate, the white dusty trackway, her father calling her, his hat coming off in salute . . .

'Maria Eleanora, I love you!'

The book slipped from her lap; she awoke with a start. Gripping the arms of her chair, she stared round at the heavy drapes pulled over against the windows. The dancing shadows as the wind outside seeped through cracks and vents, billowing the drapes as if someone lurked there, the spluttering candle-flame. She looked at the great cloak, a present from His Majesty, standing on a corner table, illuminated by two fat candles.

'Not yet eight o'clock,' she sighed.

Maria Eleanora picked up a pinewood log and placed it carefully on the fire, brushing her fingers on the napkin draped over the settle. Another hour and the Queen would send for her. Maria Eleanora pulled the thick embroidered shawl closer about her shoulders and tugged at the mittens she kept on her fingers. She recalled that dream, her life before coming to England. Something had died inside her when her father did, but meeting Samuel had healed the wound, fired her soul. She was ruthlessly determined; whatever he said, she would not stand by a gate, wherever that was, and watch someone she loved leave and never return. Maria Eleanora eased herself out of the chair and returned to the small writing desk just beneath the window. She lit more candles, drew across the ink-horn and took a piece of parchment from the small shelf just above her desk.

My dearest . . . The quill was not sharp enough. Maria Eleanora cursed, took up the small paring knife and sharpened it. The ink was thick and turgid. She moved the quill round and round to thin it. She must remember not to use Samuel's name, allow no hint. She had written once and he had not objected. Maria Eleanora closed her eyes at the pain she felt, the loneliness, the haunting, deep soul-biting sense of desolation. Oh, she missed Samuel so much! Her body, heart and soul ached. Even so, she appreciated the wisdom of Samuel's warning, was horribly aware of the mounting tension in London, the growing nervousness of the Queen, now a prisoner in her own palace. Sometimes this unease slipped into hysteria. The Queen demanded that her husband's most trusted officers be on call: she was reluctant, not only to leave her own apartments, but even to allow her ladies-in-waiting to stroll in the gardens.

'I must write.'

Maria Eleanora played with the small bronze bracelet Samuel had given her as a keepsake last May Day. She dipped her quill in the ink and began to form the following words:

> *My dearest, your face is beautiful to my eyes.*
> *Your smile bathes my life in light.*
> *Your touch keeps my heart beating.*
> *The very memory of you haunts my innermost soul.*
> *I miss you and wish our parting was not so terrible.*

Maria Eleanora paused and glanced up. She would never forget the sharp, bloody struggle at the mouth of that stinking alleyway. If that had not occurred, she would never have believed Samuel. Maria Eleanora smiled thinly. In a strange way, the struggle gave her comfort. It proved Samuel was telling the truth, that he *was* in danger. Perhaps that's why she had lunged first? Was it because of Samuel, or her dream, which had given birth to a determination never to be threatened, never be the victim, never stand and allow the malice to seep towards her? Maria Eleanora looked down at the parchment. The day Father died had forged her soul into fiery steel. He had been innocent, kept himself above the factions of Don Pedro's court. Now he was a voiceless ghost. Maria Eleanora gripped the quill so hard it broke and she had to look for a new one. She returned to her writing.

When I am with you, time ceases to exist.
No seasons, no winter nor summer.
No hour, second, minute of the day – only you.
How I wish to be one with you in all things.
I cannot really say why, except that is the Natural
    order of things.
I was conceived for you and can only conceive of you.

Maria Eleanora allowed a smile at what the poets called 'the subtle conceit' of her words. Her father had taught her well, her knowledge of English had been perfected by a Catholic priest living in exile. Maria Eleanora, like all the Queen's ladies-in-waiting, was trained in the courtesies and the subtle flatteries of court language. She tapped the parchment. Yet this was different, it sprang from her heart. She stared at the embroidered hangings, depicting a young woman gently soothing a lion with the feather of truth. Maria Eleanora could not recall the story but it was appropriate. Her father could never tolerate the false airs and graces of the court ladies and that, coupled with his desire to have a son, had made him lavish all his attention on Maria Eleanora, teaching her how to ride, duel, handle a pistol, hunt and fish.

'Be true to yourself,' he had urged.

'If I was that,' Maria Eleanora had retorted, 'I'd be surrounded by petticoats.'

Her father had laughed and hugged her.

'Be yourself,' he repeated. 'Be free.'

Maria Eleanora had followed his advice. Once she was away from the stifling court atmosphere of Lisbon, the strict protocol governing dress and manners, Maria Eleanora had felt as if she was liberated from a prison. She reflected wryly how everything had its own purpose. If she had been confined, strait-laced, she would never have dressed in disguise and slipped out of the Water Gate to meet her beloved Samuel. Balancing the quill on one hand, Maria Eleanora wondered if Samuel was writing to her. So far she was aware of what was happening and the dangers which threatened, but surely, these would pass? The hysteria would die. Despite the fog and the cold, Maria Eleanora loved England, London and the King's court. She loved the bustle and openness of the city, the freedom of the women here and, once suspicions were lulled, their warm welcome to strangers.

'The English are like a clear pool,' the Queen had once remarked. 'A good people: loyal, brave and stubborn. Nevertheless, they can be turned, especially the London mob.'

Charles had taken his Queen and their entourage out into the shires where the political and religious passions did not run so deep and the local lords were more concerned about the health of their dogs and the speed of their horses. Would he do that now?

Maria Eleanora returned to her writing.

One day this will surely pass? One week shall slip into another. The seasons will turn and spring will come. We shall be free again. But what then? We cannot live a life of dalliance and meetings.

Maria Eleanora paused and pursed her lips. Yes, that was the nub, the heart of the matter. What would the future hold? She was a Portuguese noblewoman, her own mistress. Would the Queen object? Maria Eleanora clicked her tongue. Perhaps she would ask the help of the King? She glanced towards the clock. Time was slipping away. She would have to finish this letter and ask one of her confidants Henry Berry or Robert Green to take it to Samuel's house. Which was safer? Mr Pepys's mansion in Seething Lane or Samuel's office at Derby House? She was about to continue her writing when there was a knock on the door. Three sharp raps, the pre-arranged signal. She got up and turned the parchment over. She smoothed down her dress, went across and pulled the door open a crack. Berry and Green stood outside in the passageway. Berry's normally good-natured face was dour. Robert Green's looked positively frightened.

'You'd best come in.'

They slipped through the door. Maria Eleanora returned to her chair before the fire. The other two sat on a foot settle. Both men were servants of the Palace. They were dressed in their own clothes – long brown coats, boots, dark waistcoats, rough serge shirts opened at the neck. Berry was tall and plump, bright eyes in a rubicund face, black hair thinning. He was porter and keeper of the Great Water Gate. Green was small and wizened, his face wrinkled and creased with lines. He insisted on wearing a red garish wig which looked rather grotesque but he was a kindly old man, a very devout Catholic. A crucifix was visible around his neck, another hung from his belt. Unlike Berry, who also kept a small ale-house further down the Strand, Green worked all the time in Somerset Place as carpenter and cushion-layer in the Queen's Chapel. Maria Eleanora had known the men for years and trusted both completely. Thanks to them, she was able to slip in and out whenever she wished. The two were now staring soulfully at her, trying to hide their agitation. Berry's boots were mud-stained, his face damp with sweat as if he had hurried far and fast. Green kept plucking at the crucifix round his neck.

'Gentlemen, what is the matter?'

'Mistress, we have served you well, have we not?'

She leaned over and grasped Berry's calloused hand.

'Henry, you have been a good friend. I trust you as I would a brother, a member of my own blood.'

'We know why you leave, don't we?' Green broke in.

'Well, of course you do,' Maria Eleanora retorted. 'You know how I love Samuel Atkins. I must see him. Henry brought me the clothes, the rapier . . .' Her voice trailed off; it was just the way they sat, slightly cowed. 'What is the matter?' She leaned forward. Despite the warmth, Maria Eleanora went cold. Heart in her mouth, she stared at these two men.

'We thought you'd best know, Mistress.' Berry's eyes filled with tears. 'You remember the beggar who lurks round the gates of Somerset Place? Josiah-Praise-the-Lord Stanker? Well, I pay him some of the money you give me, to find out what is happening in the city.' Berry coughed. 'Oh Mistress, Mr Atkins has been taken up!'

'Taken up? What do you mean?'

'He's been apprehended by the guards – taken to Warrington House to be interrogated by the Lords' Committee!'

'Oh no!' Maria Eleanora's hands flew to her face. She rocked backwards and forwards in her chair.

'Worse still, Mistress,' Berry came and knelt beside her, so close she could smell the ale fumes on his breath, 'he's been taken to Newgate and placed in the care of Captain Richardson the gaoler.'

'What does this mean?' Maria Eleanora gasped.

She crossed her hands over her stomach. She had never suffered from the vapours but now she felt giddy, light-headed, slightly nauseous. Once again she was at a gateway watching her beloved going away . . .

'It means, Mistress . . .' Berry wiped the sweat from his forehead with the back of his hand.

'Tell her, Robert!'

The little Irishman stared devotedly at this beautiful young woman who, as Green had secretly confided to Berry, always reminded him of a picture he had once glimpsed of the Virgin.

'It means, Madam, that Master Atkins has not given them the answers they want. He'll be placed in a cell and made to reflect.'

'Will he be tortured?' Maria Eleanora demanded.

'Ah no, Mistress, that's against common law,' Berry replied. 'But as you know, there's torture and there's torture. They'll not let him out, not Shaftesbury and his gang, until they've got what they want.'

'Tell me! Tell me!' Maria Eleanora grasped his hand.

'Shaftesbury and his gang,' Berry continued, 'have their guns trained on the Duke of York's palace and on this place. They'll make Master Samuel speak.'

'And if he does?'

'Then he will become their darling.' Berry's face was now pale. 'But he'll deliver others up. Master Pepys for one and the Queen for another.'

'But that is nonsense,' Maria Eleanora replied.

87

'Mistress, you don't know Shaftesbury and his gang. They can take night and call it day, Friday and call it Sunday. Godfrey lies buried, murdered by someone and they are now looking for culprits. They want to strike at the King but they'll do it through the Queen and the Duke of York.'

'So, we are in danger?'

'Mistress, we are all in danger. If Samuel breaks, if he confesses to meeting you they'll claim that *you* are the messenger between the Queen and Master Pepys, who is the Duke of York's man. They'll have the link to connect two lives together and so wrap the noose round all our throats. They'll discover that you leave at the dead of night. They may even pluck you up and ask you for your accomplices.'

'Have you told anyone?'

'Mistress, we took an oath. One other I *do* suspect. Someone here in the palace.'

'Not Lawrence Hill?'

Maria Eleanora referred to Berry's great friend: Hill was a tall, dark, bearded man who worked for the Queen's Treasury and often visited his friends in Somerset Place.

'Oh no, not him. Lawrence is as true as an oak. Do you remember the silversmith, Miles Prance? He often comes here late at night and has seen me down at the Water Gate.'

'But he's a friend, a servant of the Queen, a Catholic.'

'Prance has watched us.' Berry's gaze held hers. 'And, Mistress, I wager a tun of malmsey that someone else has watched Prance.'

But Maria Eleanora wasn't listening.

'I must go to Samuel,' she fretted.

Berry touched her hand.

'Mistress,' he pleaded. 'If you do, we might as well all go with you and take our own lodgings in the hideous dungeons of Newgate!'

Chapter Five

Charles, King of England, Scotland and Ireland, always prided himself on the mask he wore, that no man could see his true countenance. He sat in the Red Room at Whitehall at the top of the Council table and tapped his bejewelled fingers against the polished wood. He had dressed for the occasion, in a suit of dark-blue silk, his long jacket almost down to his knees, grey silk stockings tied with blue garters, whilst his shoes were gleaming black with silver-white buckles. He pulled at the lace of his cuffs; now and again his hand would touch the amethyst pinned into the dark-cream cravat. He kept smiling to himself as if savouring a secret joke: deep down he was furious. A violent rage seethed within him. For nineteen years he had bowed and smiled, turned and twisted to keep these hungry men, clustered at the other end of the table, away from his family, his throne, his crown. Now they were closing in and Charles felt powerless. He smiled down at them, his heavy-lidded eyes remembering where each sat, the look on their faces, the posture of their bodies. Shaftesbury lounging in a chair as if he was the King and Charles the subject. Around him, Pembroke, Buckingham, Coventry, Essex, Sir Robert Peyton and others of the gang. If I could catch you out in the open, Charles thought, I'd take all your heads and place them above Westminster Hall.

'Is Your Majesty ready?'

Charles languidly lifted a hand and stifled a yawn.

'God's truth!' he murmured. 'The hour is late and my Louise is waiting . . .'

'And after her?'

Again the lazy smile. 'I promised young Nell I'd call in. She'll come tripping down the stairs, tits bouncing, eyes all anxious. Louise . . .' Charles referred to his principal mistress, the Duchess of Portsmouth, 'has her yellow hair all frizzed and wishes to show me a gown fresh from Paris. Come now, Shaftesbury, you won't keep me from the ladies, will you? Now, who *is* this fellow Pedlow?'

'Bedloe, Your Majesty!'

'Ah yes, Bedloe, Captain William Bedloe.'

'Your Majesty.' Shaftesbury's voice was vibrant. 'I apologise for keeping you from the ladies but rogues plot the destruction of your crown and country.'

'Oh, I am sure they do,' Charles riposted swiftly. 'The problem, my Lord Shaftesbury, is deciding who these rogues really are.'

'I refer, Your Majesty, to the slayers of Sir Edmund Godfrey.'

'Aye, Shaftesbury – and so do I.'

The atmosphere in the room grew even more tense. Pembroke lunged forward as if to shout something but Charles waved a hand as a sign for silence. Buckingham sat scowling. Charles, still wearing his hat, brought the tip down closer over his eyes and glanced sideways at Henry Chiffinch. His squire of the back stairs raised a hand and scratched his cheek, a sign that all was ready: the King's agent, Dolius, was in place.

'Ah well, ah well!' Charles tilted his head back. 'We have heard the strains of music, the dance floor is ready. So, my Lord Shaftesbury, let us all dance to the tune struck up and dance we shall!'

Shaftesbury turned and muttered to Buckingham. The fat lord lurched from his chair, opened the door and brought in the dark-garbed Bedloe. The latter marched into the chamber as if he was the Angel Gabriel, made a low, stooping bow to the King. Shaftesbury vacated his chair and gestured for Bedloe to sit.

'He will sit when I tell him to!' Charles hissed.

Bedloe abruptly shot up again like a soldier standing to attention. The King ordered the candelabra to be moved further down so he could get a good glimpse of this man. As Charles looked at him full and hard, Bedloe's gaze never wavered. A true villain born and bred, Charles reflected. Never have I seen a face more fitting for Tyburn.

'Captain Bedloe.' The King leaned back in his chair and clapped his hands softly. 'Of which regiment are you? The Lifeguards? Or perhaps some other regiment I don't know about? I cannot recall your face or your rank. Your name means nothing to me. Yet I pride myself that I know my captains.'

'Your Majesty, I took my commission with the Prince of Orange.'

'Did you now? Did you now?' Charles drawled. 'And why aren't you fighting in Holland?'

'Your Majesty, I was homesick. I believed I could advance my affairs better in my native country.'

'Of course you did! Of course you did! So now you are one of Shaftesbury's men, eh? Well, sit down.'

Discomfited, Bedloe took his seat. Charles noticed how Shaftesbury tapped him gently on the shoulder in reassurance.

'Well, Captain Bedloe!'

Charles snapped his fingers. One of his clerks, standing in the shadows, came and sat down arming himself with quill, snapping open an ink-horn.

'We can give you a true account,' Shaftesbury interrupted smoothly, 'once Mr Bedloe has spoken.'

'I prefer to keep my own accounts,' Charles retorted. 'Now, Captain Bedloe, you have evidence about the murder of Sir Edmund Godfrey?'

'About October time, Your Majesty,' Bedloe began, 'I was in London on business.'

'What kind of business?'

'I was looking for fresh employment. I was approached by two Jesuits, Le Faire and Walsh.'

'Where are these?' Charles again interrupted. 'Secretary Coventry, do we have a list of Jesuits in this country?'

'We have, Your Majesty.' Coventry at the far end of the table raised his periwigged head.

Charles could never decide whether the Secretary of State was in his camp or Shaftesbury's, probably both, the King mused: a foot at either side of the fire. He quietly prayed the likes of Coventry would get their balls well and truly burnt.

'Does the name Le Faire and Walsh appear on that list?'

'No, Your Majesty.'

'They were probably false names,' Bedloe said hastily.

'You, sir,' the King raised his hand, 'will speak when you are told to. I do not doubt their names were false. They may be false, you may be false, your tale may be false, Captain Bedloe.'

But the good captain wouldn't be shaken. Ensconced amongst the Green Ribboners, he stared coolly back.

'I am all ears, Captain Bedloe. Let me remind you, the hour is drawing on.'

'Le Faire and Walsh, Your Majesty, offered me four thousand pounds if I would be one of a gang of four or six who had gathered to kill a man who was a great obstacle to their design. I agreed in order to discover the true extent of their wickedness. On Friday the eleventh of October, before Sir Edmund disappeared, I met Le Faire again, at about four o'clock in the afternoon in Grays Inn Walk. Le Faire told me to meet him the following day to carry out my design. I, not liking it, did not turn up.'

'Why not?' Charles enquired. 'Didn't you say you wished to discover their true wickedness?'

'Your Majesty.' Bedloe, all primed and ready, breathed in deeply like an actor about to deliver his finest line. 'Discovery of a plot is one thing, murder is another.'

'Continue,' Charles insisted.

'On Sunday the thirteenth of October, after Sir Edmund had disappeared, I met Le Faire by accident just near the entrance to Red Lion Court off Fleet Street. He accused me of cowardice but enlisted me in some other special business, saying that I should meet him the following Monday at the Palgrave's Head tavern. Le Faire accused me again of being faint-hearted, and warned me that I was not to forget our meeting.'

'You do seem to meet, to bump into, the Jesuit, accidentally, quite regularly?' Charles murmured.

'Yes, Your Majesty, but while *I* met him accidentally,' Bedloe smiled, 'he, undoubtedly, was following me.'

Charles waved a hand for him to continue.

'Between eight and nine on Monday night I met Le Faire in the inner courtyard at Somerset Place.' Bedloe paused for effect.

Charles raised his hand to stifle a yawn, really to hide both his fear and his fury. Keeping his head down, he glanced along the table. Shaftesbury had a triumphant smirk on his narrow face, Buckingham was beaming broadly whilst that idiot Pembroke, his mad eyes were all a-dancing with malicious glee. Charles pulled at his upper lip.

'I thought you were to meet him at a tavern?'

'Your Majesty, I received a second message changing our rendezvous.'

'How long did you stay there?'

'About half an hour, Your Majesty. He took me into the middle of a courtyard so he could speak without being overheard. "The person we have to kill is already dead!" Le Faire whispered. "His corpse lies in Somerset Place." He then promised me half of the original reward if I helped carry the body to a place where they had chosen for it to lie.'

Charles heard Chiffinch muttering furiously behind him. So we have it, Charles thought! They will lay the murder of Godfrey at the door of my little wife. They are going to impeach the Queen! Charles felt his fury boil over. Poor little Catherine with her anxious eyes and pouting mouth; her look of adoration for him, her complete dependence and her innate belief that he could protect her from anything except his own infidelity.

'Captain Bedloe.' Charles kept his voice languid. 'Do you know who lodges at Somerset Place House?'

'Why, yes, Your Majesty, the Queen and a gaggle of papists.'

'What happened then?' Charles demanded.

'Le Faire gave me the names of his other accomplices.'

'And who are these?'

'Four, Your Majesty. I think three of them work in Somerset Place.'

'And the fourth?' Charles asked pleasantly.

'Mr Samuel Atkins, clerk to Mr Pepys.'

'And you met these four?'

'Oh yes, Your Majesty. Le Faire took me into Somerset Place and led me into a chamber cloaked in darkness. When he pulled a lantern from beneath his cloak, I saw the four assassins clearly. I recognised Mr Atkins but not the others. My eyes were drawn to a shadowy object lying beneath a cloak on a table. They pulled this back, and underneath sprawled the corpse of Sir Edmund Godfrey.'

'Did you recognise it as him?' Charles asked, aware of how oppressively silent the Red Chamber had fallen.

'No, Your Majesty, not at first. I was told later, when they explained why they had killed him.'

'And how is this?' Charles's voice remained just above a whisper.

'Apparently Le Faire and Walsh, together with the four killers, persuaded Justice Godfrey to walk along the Strand where they would make a great discovery for him.' Bedloe coughed. 'So, Justice Godfrey called a constable.'

'Who?'

'I don't know, Your Majesty, but the fellow was supposed to meet him at Strand Bridge with power to take into custody anyone Justice Godfrey pointed out to him.'

'And?' Charles asked impatiently.

'In the meantime, Your Majesty, the killers persuaded Godfrey to walk into Somerset Place. They took him to a chamber used by one of the Queen's ladies-in-waiting.'

'Was she party to this?' the King asked languidly, leaning forward.

'I do not think so, Your Majesty. The chamber was empty. They stopped his mouth, bungled him in and stifled him with a pillow. The old Justice struggled so they grasped his cravat, tied it tightly about his neck and strangled him.'

'And the corpse?' Charles asked.

'The conspirators decided to carry it out of Somerset Place in a sedan chair at eleven o'clock that night.'

'Were you there when this happened?' Charles demanded.

'No, Your Majesty, I was not. I made my excuses and

escaped. The next day I met Le Faire again in Lincoln's Inn Fields. We adjourned to the Greyhound tavern in Fleet Street. Le Faire put his cane to my nose and reproached me for not helping them. "Who was the dead man?" I asked. "Why, Justice Godfrey," Le Faire replied. "He had Oates's depositions and had to be silenced." I asked him where the body had been put. He replied that they had taken it by sedan chair and horse and placed the corpse in a field, making a wound to the body and laying his sword nearby so it would seem he had committed suicide.'

Charles rested his elbows on the arms of his chair, head down, his face hidden by the brim of his hat, hand before his mouth. On any other occasion he would have burst out laughing. Bedloe's tale was a farrago of lies. But how could he prove it? In one fell swoop the lying villain had included Mr Pepys's man, therefore his own brother James of York as well as his Queen, Catherine of Braganza. What a mess, Charles reflected. Faces came and went. Little Catherine with her dumpy body and short legs. Master Pepys busy about his affairs; tall, strapping Atkins. If Bedloe's lies were believed, all of these would go into the dark.

'And what did you do?' Charles raised his head sharply. 'Why didn't you come forward and give this evidence immediately?'

'Your Majesty, I was terribly a-feared. I admit it.' Bedloe struck his breast gently. 'I played the coward and fled to Bristol, but the Lord works in wondrous ways . . .'

'Aye, He certainly does,' Charles interrupted.

'My courage returned.'

'And, like the Prodigal Son,' Charles smiled, 'you hastened into London to tell us the truth. Mr Bedloe, do you have anything else to add?'

'Your Majesty, I will go on oath.'

Charles looked across at the clock on the mantel hearth.

'Good Lord, is that the time?' He got abruptly to his feet and smiled to himself as everyone else did likewise.

'Your Majesty.' Shaftesbury couldn't hide his surprise. 'This meeting is over?'

'Yes, my Lord, this meeting is over. I have other business.'

'Your Majesty, Bedloe will go before the Lords tomorrow and make a full confession.'

'Of course he will. Of course he will.' Charles stifled another yawn. He waved his fingers. 'But, for the moment, leave me, leave me!'

Charles, one hand leaning on the table, had the satisfaction of seeing the gaggle of rogues troop out. As the last one filed out, Charles swaggered down the room and closed the door with a vicious kick. Then he took off his hat and stood leaning with his back to the door breathing deeply.

'Master Chiffinch,' he murmured, 'we are stuck in a morass. How, in God's name, do we get out?'

He marched back to his chair, threw his hat on the table and slumped down.

'The Duchess will be waiting.' Chiffinch hovered like a guardian angel beside him.

'The Duchess can go hang!' Charles muttered through clenched teeth. 'Master Chiffinch, you heard?'

'It was all naught but damned lies.'

'Bring in Dolius!' the King declared.

Chiffinch walked across to the wall and fumbled a while looking for the hidden lever. He found it and swung it open. The King's spy, the man known as Dolius, dressed in black from head to toe, apart from the white collar of his shirt, crept out from the secret chamber. A tall, thickset man, he wore no wig; his long hair, parted down the middle, fell just beneath his ears. An impudent face, Charles called it, with rather bulbous eyes, a snub nose, the full mouth not quite hidden by the rather thick moustache and beard. Dolius was one of the few men whom the King allowed to carry a sword in his presence. Without bidding, the spy walked across and sat down in a chair next to the King.

'Well, well, my friend,' Charles smiled. 'What do we have here, eh?'

'Why, Your Majesty, a murderer.'

'What?'

'Bedloe is a mercenary.' Dolius's voice was soft and musical, his Irish accent most evident. 'He doesn't know me but I know him.'

'So, keep yourself well hidden.'

'Oh, Your Majesty, I will, though sooner or later we have to show our hand.'

'We will, we will. Now tell me more about this Bedloe – he's a murderer, you say?'

'Your Majesty, look at the facts. Bedloe must have been in London when Godfrey was killed, yes?'

Charles nodded.

'If he wasn't,' Dolius continued, 'if it can be proved that he was in Dover or Bristol, his story would fall apart. What I suspect is that he killed Godfrey, or was a party to his murder, and then fled to Bristol for a while.'

'And now,' the King sighed, 'he returns with his revelations.'

'Your Majesty,' Dolius took up his story, 'Godfrey was definitely seen near the Strand and Somerset Place. I believe Bedloe and others abducted him, questioned him, killed him and used his corpse for this present mischief. Now this scoundrel Bedloe and his associates are going to see others hang for it. They'll strike at you through your Queen and your brother.'

'How vulnerable are we?' Charles demanded.

'If Atkins breaks, everything comes tumbling down,' Dolius said grimly.

'Atkins.' Charles scratched his chin and stared up at the ceiling. 'So that young man is our defence, is he? And how do we control him?'

'You know, Your Majesty – the girl.'

'Ah yes, our sweet, olive-skinned lady-in-waiting. Our woman of many parts, Maria Eleanora . . .'

'If she can stiffen him,' Dolius declared, 'if Atkins holds out, then . . .' He shrugged. 'All may be well. This gang, however, thirst for blood. I fear they'll taste it before the month is out.'

'We could kill the good captain,' Chiffinch broke in from where he stood just behind the King's chair.

'No, no.' Dolius shook his head. 'We can't provide them with another martyr. I will take care of Bedloe in my own time and a manner of my choosing.'

'Is the girl in place?' the King asked sharply. 'No, no, not the Portuguese, the other?'

'Like a cat in the shadows, Your Majesty, she watches the mouse-hole.'

Charles got to his feet and, picking up his hat, dusted the brim with his fingers.

'Tomorrow morning, Dolius, I shall go for a walk in the park. I'll have words with Mistress Maria Eleanora. You, too, shall have words with her.' Charles smiled. 'In your own time and a manner of your choosing.'

'And the others?' Dolius asked. 'The three servants at Somerset Place?'

Charles shook his head. He patted his spymaster on the shoulder.

'I am only God's King, not God Himself,' he murmured.

'I can save some but I can't save all. God help them! Aye,'
he added, 'and God help us all!'

Samuel Atkins squatted on the edge of the truckle bed in the
dark cell beneath Captain Richardson's lodgings. Richardson,
keeper of Newgate, had welcomed Samuel to what he called
'his infernal palace'. Samuel, despite his terrors, was more
than aware of how low he had fallen. Newgate was foul
and heinous, a kingdom of oozing muck and slimy rats. A
cavernous warren of weakly lit passageways and gloomy cells
– 'an abode of Stygian darkness' was how one writer had
described it. 'The very heart of Hell', another had proclaimed.
Even from where he sat Samuel could hear the harrowing cries
and shrieks of the Bedlamites, the insane, accompanied by the
racket from the common side – a mixture of drunken songs
and hideous curses, broken now and again by the slam of
iron-edged doors and the clink of fetters.

Captain Richardson, tall and gloomy-faced, had given him
a pomander to hold against his nose, but that did little to
offset the stench of the foul gases and fetid air. Atkins had
only been here hours but it felt like months. He had been
bundled from Warrington House and taken up to Newgate
by night, through the sludge of the butchers' stalls, the guts,
offal and blood, up Snow Hill and under the great arched
gateway flanked by its forbidding, six-sided towers. The
statues on their niches in the walls outside Newgate were
blackened by the sooty air. A huge, clattering windmill, fixed
above the main gate, tried to bring in air to this devilish
hive of grimy passageways. It did little to dispel the odour
from the filthy cells or the executioner's closet where the
dismembered limbs of felons were soaked in bay, salt, tar
and cumin seed before being exposed above the rooftops of
London.

Samuel gritted his teeth as the Bellman of Newgate, standing outside the main gate clanging his ominous bell, bawled his dire proclamation.

> *'You prisoners that are within!*
> *Who, for wickedness and sin . . .'*

Samuel tried to stop his ears as the bell was clanged twelve times, a warning to those who were to be hanged the next day.

'After many mercies shown you,' the crier continued, 'you are appointed to die tomorrow in the forenoon. Listen and understand! Wait for the bell of St Sepulchre which will tell the good people of this city that you are going to your deaths! So, fall on your knees and beseech God's grace . . . !'

The Herald of Death continued his lugubrious sermon, totally ignored by those for whom it was intended. They sprawled in their own dirt, drunk as sots, and still would be when they were brought down to the execution carts early the next morning.

Atkins recalled being aboard a man-of-war going into action and tried to muster the same resolve he had felt then: he must not panic, he must not give way to fear. He must ignore the squeak and scrabbling of rats, the overpowering din of this nightmarish place. Earlier, he had eaten some stew; it sat heavy in his stomach and he could still taste the brackish, water-soaked ale he had drunk. Putting his face in his hands, he conjured up the warmth and light of Mr Pepys's office and, especially, the beautiful face of Maria Eleanora. In that moment of anguish, Samuel recognised how deeply and truly he loved her. He would face anything rather than bring her into danger. He'd leap into the execution cart itself rather than betray her! Samuel felt all his inborn stubbornness surface. He took his hands away from his face.

'What am I frightened of?' he whispered to the slime-covered wall. 'Of death? But we all must die. Of disgrace? I have had my day in the sun.'

He paused, gnawing at his lip. He *was* frightened of two things – of breaking down and betraying Mr Pepys who had been so kind to him, and, most importantly, of placing his beloved in any danger. Samuel closed his eyes.

'Maria Eleanora,' he prayed. 'I have loved you, I love you. I shall always love you. We have drunk the loving cup. We have exchanged the kiss. If death comes, then death comes.'

When Samuel opened his eyes, he felt more confident, but his second fear remained. Ah, that was different! He feared for Maria Eleanora, her bravery, her impetuosity and, above all, her love for him. She was not the type to sit before the hearth with a piece of embroidery, weep copiously or give way to the vapours. She would fight back – and those who had trapped him, would certainly trap her. Atkins felt rage well within him.

'But I am innocent!' he cried. He nearly added, 'So is Maria Eleanora!' Yet he'd vowed, on his way to Newgate, that whilst he was circled by his tormentors, her name would never slip from his lips. He sprang to his feet and paced up and down.

'Oh please God!'

The young clerk felt guilty. He went to church but he was so often distracted. Now he had to beg for God's help. If only Maria Eleanora kept her wits. How could he help? He sat back down on the bed. Edmund Godfrey had disappeared on Saturday, 12 October. Where had Samuel been then? What alibi could he give? Everything was lost in a drunken haze. After leaving Maria Eleanora that fateful night, Samuel had sought out the company of carousers; from then on, one day merged with another, one dark night into one grey morning. So what story could he produce? What witnesses could he call on? He found one small crumb of comfort. If he hadn't made that declaration to Maria Eleanora, he would have been with her and they both would have been implicated. Who would believe a Portuguese lady-in-waiting to a Catholic Queen? They would have snatched that up and played with it like a hunting cat does a baby mouse. Atkins recalled Shaftesbury, the lord's clever, witty face. He had that same heavy-lidded glance as the King: a man who hid his soul and kept his cards very close to his chest. Shaftesbury was the dangerous one.

Atkins beat his fists against his temples. If only he could recall where he was, that fateful weekend! If he couldn't call up witnesses, Shaftesbury would produce liars like Captain Childs.

Atkins lay down on the bed and stared up at the grimy, cobwebbed ceiling. He had been let out of that closet in Warrington House, put back again, made to think as Shaftesbury and his gang tried to confuse him, muddle his wits, offering him the only gateway out of his misery: a damnable lie which would bring his master down. They had not sent him immediately to Newgate but returned to the attack. Captain Childs, his pipe glowing with tobacco, had been brought back in again as a veritable prophet come to judgement. Hadn't he talked to Captain Childs about the Great Plot?

'I saw him last in the middle of August, a little before Bartholomew's Fair but I am innocent of any treasonable conversation,' Atkins had protested.

'Are you?' Shaftesbury had purred. 'Then you are most unfortunate. Pray, Samuel, look Captain Childs in the face.'

Atkins had done so. The professional liar had dropped his glance and paled. At this, Samuel struck home.

'Look at him!' he cried. 'See? He won't hold my gaze. His face is as white as a ghost's!'

Then the horrible realisation had dawned. The lords didn't look at Captain Childs but lounged in their chairs, humming under their breath, glancing at the ceiling or examining their fingernails.

'This is not an examination,' Samuel had exclaimed. 'You just want me to confess. Whether it's the truth or not, is irrelevant. Any lie will do . . .'

At this, Shaftesbury had laughed in his face and Samuel had been bundled out of the chamber by his bully-boy Captain Eastwell.

A sound at the door roused Atkins from his reverie. A man, grey hair falling down to his shoulders, head bent, shuffled in with a tray. He kicked the door closed behind him.

'Some more food,' he croaked.

Atkins didn't stir. The man slammed the tray down on the table, then went and crouched in the corner where he couldn't be seen through the grating in the door. When he brought his head up, he was no longer the shuffling turnkey! The face beneath the dirt and grime was strong and resolute, lips parted in a smile, eyes bright with mischief. He gestured at Samuel and pointed to the stool.

Atkins, wary, swung his legs off the bed and came across.

'You've been sent to trap me, haven't you? You are one of Shaftesbury's men.'

The fellow turned, hawked and spat into the rushes.

'I don't come from Shaftesbury,' he whispered.

Atkins tensed at the Irish lilt in the voice. That alone half-convinced him that this man was, perhaps, a friend.

'My name is Dolius,' the fellow told him quietly.

'Dolius?' Samuel queried.

'An ancient king.' The smile widened. 'I come here to do you a mercy.'

'How can I trust you?'

'Don't,' the man replied simply. 'At least, not for a while.'

'How did you get in?'

'Captain Richardson may take bribes from Shaftesbury but the keeper of Newgate holds his office direct from the King.'

'Has Mr Pepys sent you?'

The man twisted his head back and laughed.

'Oh, I know busy little Mr Pepys – a great treasurehunter, isn't he?'

Samuel studied this man intently.

'I know what you are thinking,' Dolius continued. 'Very few people know about Mr Pepys searching the Tower for hidden treasure, but I do. I know a lot about Mr Pepys and even more about the Tower. But, as I have said,' he declared briskly, 'don't trust me, at least not for a while.' He glanced towards the door. 'We'll be having another visitor soon.'

'Who?'

'Why, your old friend Captain Childs! Now . . .'

Dolius stretched out a hand, most of which was covered by a ragged mitten but Atkins glimpsed the well-pared nails, the strong wrists and supple fingers; a duellist, he thought, a man of war.

'Now, when Childs comes in,' Dolius advised, 'be frightened, act concerned.' He shuffled closer, his face only a few inches from Atkins's. 'You are safe, boy.'

'I am not a boy!'

The light-blue eyes smiled. 'Samuel, I am sorry. You are *not* a boy. You are a man, and a good one – I can see that. Let me advise you. The easiest way is the worst way.'

'What do you mean?'

'It will be easy to confess. You will walk free but others

will come here to be despatched to a cruel death.' Dolius lunged forward and gripped Samuel's hand. 'You must keep faith, hold fast. Will you do that, Samuel?'

'Aye, but I am frightened for others.'

'Oh, I know you are.' Dolius's voice dropped to a whisper. 'That beautiful Portuguese, for one.'

Samuel withdrew his hand. 'How did you . . . ?'

Dolius chuckled deep in his throat.

'Samuel, Samuel, your secret's safe. Not a rat farts in London but Dolius doesn't know about it.'

'And will she be kept safe?'

'As long as you are honest, Samuel.'

Atkins recognised the threat.

'This is a game of Hazard,' Dolius insisted. 'The dice have been shaken, crowns and kingdoms lie on the table, not just pretty heads or soft necks.'

'If you know everything,' Samuel countered, 'tell me who killed Godfrey.'

'Ah.' The spy tapped the side of his nose. 'Knowing and proving are two different things. Let me put it this way, Atkins. The true assassin of Sir Edmund Godfrey will never be brought to trial, but that doesn't mean he won't face justice, both in this world and the next. What concerns me, Samuel, is where you were on Saturday, the twelfth of October when Edmund Godfrey disappeared?'

'I was drunk,' Samuel said shame-facedly.

'Balthazar's tits!' Dolius breathed. 'Is that the best you can come up with, lad?'

'What will Captain Childs say?'

'I'm not going to tell you. I want you to act surprised. Where were you, Samuel Atkins, on Saturday, the twelfth of October? Surely you should have been working in your master's house or office?'

106

'He was at Newmarket.'

'Yes, yes, so he was.' Dolius again gripped his hand. 'But where were *you*?'

Samuel closed his eyes. He recalled that week, his emotional turmoil over parting from Maria Eleanora: the late-night drinking bouts, the sense of freedom when Master Pepys slept. He recalled a tavern, lights winking, someone with his arms around his shoulder. There was a woman. Samuel swallowed hard. How could he explain that to Maria Eleanora? How could he confess that he was so distraught, in his cups, he didn't realise what he was doing?

'You've got to think, lad,' Dolius said grimly.

'I remember drinking. I remember a tavern. Oh yes, and water, black slimy mud . . .'

'Oh, for all the shit of Hell!' Dolius exclaimed. 'My Lord of Shaftesbury would love that! Can't you see, Samuel? If you confess that you were drunk he'll cry, drunk or sober, you were still involved in the murder.'

'But he has no witnesses.'

Dolius threw his head back and laughed.

'I could walk only a few yards from here and hire a shipload of witnesses who, for the price of a blackjack, would swear they had seen you carry Godfrey's corpse over your shoulder all round London!'

He heard a sound in the passageway and sprang to his feet.

'Will you help me, sir?' Samuel pleaded. 'And, if not, will you help Maria Eleanora?'

'I'll do all that, my boy, but you must remember you've got to help yourself.'

He kicked at the door, it swung open and Atkins's mysterious visitor disappeared into the icy darkness outside.

Samuel sat for a while, trying to follow Dolius's advice to help himself. He recalled an invitation during that week just before Godfrey disappeared. Who was it from? Ah yes, his old schoolmaster – but he hadn't kept that appointment. Samuel groaned. That would count against him! He lay back on the bed and pulled up the thin, moth-eaten blanket, but it stank so much he thrust it away.

'I'm damned if I do and damned if I don't,' he whispered. Mr Pepys would be livid at his carousing and would Maria Eleanora forgive him for being in his cups? Suddenly, Samuel burst out laughing. Here he was, facing certain trial for treason and murder, with the prospect of being hanged, dismembered and disembowelled – yet he was more concerned at Maria Eleanora's anger than anything else.

'I *must*,' he told himself. 'I *must remember* where I was.'

Eyelids heavy, he drifted into an uneasy sleep, dreaming that he was lost in some long, dark passageway, the ground and walls wet with slime. A light at the far end shone bright, beckoning him onwards. He opened his eyes. Captain Richardson stood over him with the lantern horn, a figure beside him. Atkins recognised the red breeches, the heavy sea boots, the dark brocaded coat. Dazedly, he sat up on the bed and pulled himself together.

'I have some visitors for you, Mr Atkins.' Richardson's harsh face broke into a smile. 'Come all the way from Warrington House, they have.'

Atkins heard a sound at the door and looked round. Eastwell lounged there against the lintel, hat in one hand, the other on the hilt of his rapier.

'Get them out!' Atkins yelled. 'They've come here to put words in my mouth, Captain Richardson. Please tarry a while and be my witness.'

'Come now, Samuel.' Captain Childs undid his broad belt, picked up the stool and came and sat beside the bed. 'Good morrow, young man. I am here on my own account.'

'I have orders from the Lords' Committee,' Richardson broke in, 'to leave you alone.'

Richardson and Eastwell left. Captain Childs stamped his feet and blew on his fingers. Even from where he sat Atkins could smell the brandy. Captain Childs swung his head backwards and forwards.

'Samuel Atkins, you are all undone.'

'How?'

'By the Lord, a man's come,' Captain Childs groaned. 'He's taken an oath against you, that you were at the scene of the murder. He can identify you. He claims Godfrey's murder was committed in Somerset Place. By the light of a lantern horn he glimpsed you standing over Godfrey's body.'

'He's lying,' Samuel protested. 'You know he's lying – as you lie. I have done you no ill. I have even lent you money.'

The captain spread his hands. 'We are all liars: that's not the point. It's how we come out of this.' He leaned forward, his face earnest. 'Samuel, we could emerge from this affair as wealthy men laden with heavy purses and honours. You *were* there, weren't you? You can identify the others?'

'Of course I wasn't there! I tell you, I was not there!'

'But you were,' the other man insisted. 'Don't you remember the mist?' He laughed gently. 'You drank a few bottles.'

Samuel went cold. This man was following him into his nightmare, stretching into the deepest part of his soul to stir up the fires of fear.

'Perhaps you've forgotten,' Captain Childs soothed. 'Perhaps your mind's so tormented it's playing tricks. If you weren't there, Samuel, just where were you? At a tavern in the Strand, playing a game of Hazard, or perhaps watching a cock-fight? No?' His eyes rounded in amazement. 'Or perhaps you were with some doxy – some fine, bouncing girl with juicy tits. You'd remember, surely? And if you can't remember Friday or Saturday, do you remember waking up on Sunday morning?'

'I won't tell you.' The clerk felt trapped.

'Why not?' Childs pulled the stool closer. 'What have you got to hide, Samuel? You are a wealthy young man. You work in the Admiralty, you have to remember this and you have to remember that – yet you can't remember where you were that weekend?'

'I know where I was.' Samuel put a brave face on it. 'But I shall not tell you lest you trap me.'

Childs's smirk proved that the captain didn't believe him.

'You are going to be questioned, my fine young fellow. Shaftesbury will send his hounds to the right and left. They'll circle you and hem you in. Have you ever been to Somerset Place?'

Atkins swallowed hard.

'You have, haven't you? You'll have to answer that. And there's worse to come. They'll ask you where you go at night. They'll call Mr Pepys and put him under oath. Then everyone will hear how worried your own master gets about where you go and what you do after hours. He has been for months.'

Captain Childs got to his feet and banged at the door.

'Just remember what I have said, Samuel. Lie there on your rotting bed and think it over. The easiest way is the best way.'

The door opened and the Judas man left. Atkins crossed his arms to control his shivering. Captain Childs's words had struck home. What happened if he was right? Where *had* he been? And what exactly had he done on that fateful weekend?

'*You prisoners that are within . . . !*' The crier had returned with his hand-bell.

Samuel Atkins closed his eyes and fought against the terrors which threatened to engulf him.

Chapter Six

Charles of England was in fine fettle. Dressed in a light-blue morning suit, he ambled through the courtyard of Whitehall Palace and into the gardens. It was one of those bright, clear autumn days when, Charles thought, if you closed your eyes and ignored the cold, you'd think summer had returned. The sun was high in a cloud-free sky, birds busy in the trees, thickets and bushes. Charles cocked the hat further back on his thick, rich black wig and tried to hide his smile. Despite Bedloe's revelations, the King was convinced that the game was not yet over. He stopped at the entrance to the park, brushed the crumbs from the front of his coat and leaned on the ebony-headed walking stick. All around yapped his spaniels, Charles's 'lovely lads', eager to be free. They raced across the grass at their usual quarry, the plump pigeons who, as customary, regarded them with the utmost disdain before soaring off into the sky.

'You'll never learn, will you.'

Charles watched as the spaniels, ears flapping, careered around barking and yelping. Charles swirled his stick and stared up at the gaunt branches of a great oak tree. The sight always provoked memories of that dreadful flight from Worcester, Cromwell's soldiers searching the foliage and brambles beneath him.

'Well, they never caught me then,' he murmured. 'And begad, they'll not catch me now!'

The doting spaniels thought Charles was speaking to them: they all raced around, leaping up, begging for his attention.

'No, no, you are naughty boys.' Charles smiled at them. He patted the bulging pocket of his coat. 'And these are not for you, they are for the ducks. You eat well enough.' He patted his own stomach. 'And, like your master, need regular exercise.'

Charles whistled a ditty under his breath. He'd certainly had enough exercise last night with pretty Louise, an experienced and enthusiastic lover. Charles had not fallen asleep until the early hours but he had risen early, checked on one of his experiments, signed some papers, and now he was going for his walk.

Secretary of State Coventry and the other gaggle of ministers, courtiers and gentlemen of the chamber, were all gathered at the far side of the courtyard. All carried scrolls and petitions, eager to do the business of the day.

'I have to exercise my spaniels,' Charles told them, taking off his hat and planting it on the back of his head. 'I must also feed my ducks; of all my subjects, they are the most loyal.' Charles sniffed the back of his hand, savouring the cologne he had rubbed there. 'Right, gentlemen.' He stared down at the spaniels. 'I wager a bone to a bottle of wine I can walk faster than you.'

Charles headed off across the grass, the spaniels swooping on either side of him. The grass was still wet underfoot, the slight hoarfrost not yet burnt off. Charles stopped by the stone sundial and studied the thin, triangular shadow. Was it accurate? he thought. He leaned against this as his dogs coursed out across the chessboard of grass plot and flowerbeds, haring round the rather battered marble and bronze statues. From where he stood Charles could hear the noise of the city drifting through the line of poplars which hid the iron railings. He looked up, as if admiring the different weather cocks, brilliant against the sky, which topped every cupola, spire and jutting tower roof of the palace buildings. According to rumours, if Charles was to be assassinated, then it was here in his private garden. If Mr Bedloe was to be believed, dozens of assassins lurked in the long grass or took careful aim from behind a hawthorn bush. Charles laughed to himself.

'My spaniels could do a better job,' he murmured.

As he walked on, the King repeated to himself the sacred rules of his behaviour: 'Never drop the mask, never show your true feelings. Never say the game is lost before it is over.' Then, invigorated, he walked on until he reached the edge of the lake where the ducks were waiting like stately barges on its smooth, silvery surface.

'Ladies and gentlemen of the court,' Charles declared. 'My lord drakes and my lady ducks, I have brought you sustenance.'

He took the bag out of his pocket and began to throw the crumbs. Just like my courtiers, Charles reflected as the ducks fought over these juicy morsels. One spaniel, not so bright as the rest, whom Charles secretly called 'Canterbury' after his revered Archbishop, splashed into the lake frightening off the ducks. Charles, forgetting he was wearing his best shoes, went to the edge and, grasping the miscreant by the neck, pulled him out. He glanced sideways. Good, she was waiting. The young lady, cloaked and hooded, was sitting on a marble bench overlooking the ornamental lake. Charles threw more crumbs to the ducks, told the spaniels to behave and sauntered over. The woman rose as he approached, pulling back her hood, and went to curtsey.

'Oh, for God's sake, don't do that,' Charles smiled, doffing his hat and giving her the most courteous salute. 'Maria Eleanora, pull back the cowl of your cloak and sit down.'

He approached closer and chucked her under the chin, admiring her lovely, oval-shaped, olive-skinned face, the brilliant eyes, those full red lips. Charles quietly thanked God that the Duchess of Portsmouth or Nell Gwynn couldn't see this. Louise would certainly indulge in one of her screaming fits of jealousy.

'You are well, my dear?' He sat down beside her.

'As well as can be expected, Your Majesty.'

Maria Eleanora felt nervous. She had dressed in a high-necked, dark-blue gown of sarcanet fringed at the neck and cuffs with white lace. Silver buckled boots on her stockinged feet, over her shoulders a thick blue cloak of best wool, one of her first purchases on arrival in England. Charles glanced sideways. Maria Eleanora's raven-black hair was gathered and held in place at the back with silver clips covered by a lace-fringed hairnet. Pearl drops hung from her delicate earlobes. He watched the sheen of light on her high cheekbones.

'You are not nervous of your King?' Charles spread his feet, tapping the ground with his cane.

'Should I be nervous of Your Majesty?'

The King grinned. He grasped Maria Eleanora's hand and kissed her fingers, allowing her to withdraw them gracefully.

'I have a reputation, Maria Eleanora. Old Rowley, the merry monarch, literally the "Father to his People".'

Maria Eleanora laughed.

'If anyone sees me with a beautiful woman,' Charles drawled, 'they think I am bent on seduction. Well, I'm not, though in your case I would make an exception.'

'A conundrum, Your Majesty, a puzzle?'

'No, Maria Eleanora, I am just teasing you.'

'But your courtiers will see me.'

'If any courtier approaches within ten yards of that lake,' Charles indicated with his cane, 'I'll make him take my spaniels for a thirty-mile walk. And, should he lose one, he'll spend thirty days in the Tower. No one will see you come, Maria Eleanora, and no one will see you go. I am not here for seduction, my dear, though the prospect is enticing. It would be enticing, wouldn't it, Maria Eleanora?' he couldn't resist adding.

'Your Majesty, flattery is the most delicate perfume,' Maria Eleanora replied. 'You dab it on your neck, not your tongue.'

The King grasped her arm and squeezed it affectionately.

'You remind me of my Minette, Maria Eleanora, my beautiful sister. Sharp as a razor, pretty as a flower.'

Charles stared at the faint bank of mist which still hung over the centre of the lake.

'Are you in love, Maria Eleanora? No.' He held up a finger. 'I *know* you are in love. Yet you come from Portugal, a Catholic court where protocol and etiquette weigh as heavy as manacles on a prisoner.'

'The Portuguese are as amorous as the English,' Maria Eleanora retorted sharply. 'They only hide it better.'

'Touché,' Charles retorted. 'You are quite a duellist, aren't you? A master, or should I say, mistress of the sword?'

'Ladies at your court, Your Majesty, are just as proficient.'

'I don't think so,' Charles replied. 'With the knife, perhaps, or the biting tongue, or the long, red-nailed finger.' He sighed. 'Do you think I'm a knave, Maria Eleanora, to forsake my own wedding bed, my own wife?'

'The Queen loves you deeply.'

'And I,' the King coughed, 'have the deepest affection for

115

her though, Maria Eleanora, I have never loved. I want to, I would love to, but I never have. I have had more mistresses than many a man would in a dozen lifetimes. My confidants tell me I am searching for something. Father Huddlestone, the Jesuit who hid me after Worcester, says I am a prince addicted to pleasure.'

'And the truth, Your Majesty?'

'I have already told you. I have always wanted to love, to fall deeply in love, not just a passing passion or an amusing flirtation . . .'

Maria Eleanora stared at this strange King with his long, dark, handsome face, heavy-lidded eyes, the drawling speech, the constant hint of self-mockery.

'Sometimes I lie awake and stare into the darkness and wonder why. My father – now he loved my mother, Henrietta Maria, with a passion beyond all understanding. She loved him just as deeply. They were locked in one world, that was part of Father's problem. He could never see beyond that love. The only real advice he took was from my blessed mother and he paid for that with his life.'

'Do you envy him, Your Majesty?'

Charles leaned over and pinched the back of Maria Eleanora's hand.

'I do envy my father and the love he enjoyed. I adored my mother and Minette my sister. Yet I cannot make the same mistakes as he did. I do not want to be sent on my travels. I do not want to plunge my kingdom into civil war. I want every one of my subjects to live peacably under their own vine and cultivate their own fig tree.'

'But you are King?'

'Power is a two-edged sword, Maria Eleanora.' Charles whistled across his spaniels who, now rather tired, came trotting over to rest at his feet. 'I know the game my Lord

Shaftesbury is playing: let's provoke the King until he's a despot and, when he's a despot, let's attack him for being one. If he doesn't respond, our attack will still be successful, not because he's a despot but because he's weak.' Charles swung the cane backwards and forwards, tapping the inside of his shoe. 'They are like swordsmen, Maria Eleanora. I move to the left, they move with me. To the right, they follow. Fall back, they pursue. Go forward and they defend. Stand still and they mock me.'

'So, what will Your Majesty do?'

'I shall play the cunning cat. I shall drop my sword, walk away and let them beat the air. To do that, my dear, I need you.'

'Your Majesty?'

'Maria Eleanora, you are a lady-in-waiting who has fallen deeply in love, God knows for what reason, with that long, burly streak of honesty known as Samuel Atkins, clerk to Master Pepys. No, don't get me wrong.' Charles lifted a hand. 'I have every respect for Mr Atkins, as I do for his master.'

'How did you know?' Maria Eleanora pulled her cloak closer.

'I know because I have to know. I have a man, Dolius. He heads my league of ruffians, my own spies and bully-boys who rejoice in the dramatic title of the Society of the Sealed Knot. I put more faith in them than I do those lords who claim to support me. Now Dolius and his crew watch Somerset Place. They have often glimpsed the dark-garbed, red-plumed young man who slips out through the Water Gate and hurries deep into the city.' Charles blew his lips out in a long sigh. 'And why should I object? What can I say? You are old enough to know, whilst I have no right to comment on anyone's morals. But now,' his voice became firmer, 'now is different. Atkins is in prison. My Lord Shaftesbury is going to try and break him.' He ignored Maria Eleanora's gasp. 'So, let me see what metal you are made of, young lady. Do you really love Samuel Atkins?'

'Yes, Your Majesty.'

Charles held her gaze. 'No, do you *really* love him? More than life itself?'

'You have my answer.'

Charles's eyes grew sad. 'Then you are more fortunate than I am,' he murmured.

'If Your Majesty knows about us, why not Lord Shaftesbury?'

Charles crossed his legs and drummed his fingers on his thigh. 'Shaftesbury regards the Queen as a pawn. It's me and my brother he's after. Atkins could break and, if he does, God help us all!' He paused. 'Tell me, Maria Eleanora, why do you love him? I apologise for the distraction, but what do you see in a naval clerk?'

'A person I have never met before. A man I have always loved and one I always shall love.'

'And if you come through this?'

'I hope to marry.'

'Let us see. Let us see,' Charles murmured. He rested the cane against his leg, took out his bag of crumbs and threw them on the ground for his spaniels. 'Whatever happens, Maria Eleanora, I want you to continue to visit Samuel Atkins. I know he is in prison.'

Charles dug into his inside pocket, brought out a small scroll and handed it to his companion. She undid the scarlet ribbon and read the contents:

To all officers and loyal servants of the Crown, greetings. Charles, King of England, etc. orders that the bearer of this warrant be allowed to do what the writer of this requires, without let or hindrance. Charles Rex.

'Is that all, Your Majesty?'

'You can show that and go wherever you wish. Some will accept it without hindrance, others may object. Only use it if you have to. You will also have the support and loyalty of Dolius and his crew. They will make their presence known and their assistance felt. You are to strengthen Atkins's will. He comes from the West Country, well known for its stubbornness and determination. Tell him to hold fast.'

'And the allegations?'

'I do not wish to hurt you, Maria Eleanora, but I gather you and Samuel had a difference, a quarrel?'

'He claimed our meetings were becoming too dangerous.'

'In that he was correct,' the King agreed. 'He must never confess to them: there must be no link between Mr Pepys and the Queen.'

'Is Samuel so vulnerable?'

'On the weekend Godfrey disappeared,' Charles continued, 'Master Atkins cannot recall where he was or who he was with. His conduct that week leaves a great deal to be desired. He drank deeply and was often seen in the company of ladies of the town.' Charles glanced quickly at Maria Eleanora. 'Does that upset you?'

'On the one hand, yes, Your Majesty, but I would be more stricken to the heart if Samuel had left me and went about his business, whistling under his breath without a care in the world.'

'Good! Good!' Charles murmured. 'Now is not the time for the vapours or silly jealousy. I will be blunt with you, Maria Eleanora, I cannot save Atkins by some decree. If I issued a pardon, Shaftesbury would pounce. "Look," he'd declare, "the King hides traitors, protects the enemies of the realm." I can only save three people through my prerogative: my brother, my wife and Father Huddleston who hid me when I fled from

Cromwell's men. Shaftesbury knows this. He may strike at all three but he knows that might be too dangerous. He will only attack them when he's ready, when he has the so-called evidence or proof. But the rest of his victims?' Charles shook his head. 'At the moment I am powerless.'

Maria Eleanora stared across the lake. She felt like screaming objections, like demanding protection – yet she was versed enough in court politics to understand the King.

'Atkins must save himself,' Charles said quietly. He whistled softly under his breath. 'Yes, he must save himself. If he holds fast, he's halfway there. Shaftesbury will do two things: he must get witnesses who will swear, without reservation, that Atkins was involved in Godfrey's murder. And . . .' He paused. 'He must make sure that Atkins does not produce a convincing alibi. If Samuel can do that, then he may yet walk away with both his life and his love. You must work on that.' He leaned over and grasped Maria Eleanora's hand. 'The news is bad. Shaftesbury already has one witness – a rogue called William Bedloe.'

'No, no, no!' Maria Eleanora exclaimed. 'It cannot be!'

'Bedloe is a liar born and bred. There's another danger, one Shaftesbury must now be plotting.' A bell began to clang. 'I have no doubts,' Charles declared, 'that Atkins was drunk on Saturday, the twelfth of October. What I fear is the company he kept. Did my Lord Shaftesbury's Green Ribboners follow him from tavern to tavern?'

Maria Eleanora's mouth was so dry she found it difficult to swallow.

'You follow my thread, Maria Eleanora? How do we know that Atkins was *not* present, even though he was unwitting and unwilling, when Godfrey was killed?'

'But Samuel is not a drunkard, a killer!'

'Of course not.'

Charles banged his stick on the ground so hard his sleeping spaniels sprang to their feet and looked owl-eyed at him, mouths open, little pink tongues lolling.

'No, no, my boys,' Charles whispered, patting one on the head. 'It's not home yet for milk and biscuits. What I dread, Maria Eleanora, is that Atkins was so drunk he can't remember what he did, where he was or who he was with. Can you imagine that, eh? Before the Lords' Committee or Chief Justice Scroggs? I can just imagine my Chief Justice roaring at him red-faced, blue eyes popping. "And where were you, Master Atkins, on the night of Monday, fourteenth October?"' The King let the question hang in the air.

'Samuel will say,' Maria Eleanora shrugged, 'that he can't remember.'

'"Ah no!" the Chief Justice will bawl back. "Can't – or won't!"'

Maria Eleanora hid her hands beneath her cloak. They felt icy cold. She couldn't stop trembling. She felt the King's arm around her shoulders, a slight hug.

'There's the rub,' Charles whispered. 'The hanging jury would promise not to be slow, they would hardly be out before they were back. I don't mean to frighten you, Mistress, but that's the danger we all face.' He leaned closer and pecked her on the cheek. 'But you and Samuel have a fire within you.' He grinned. 'And where I can help, Maria Eleanora, I will.'

The King rose to his feet, tapping the cane against his leg.

'Use your wits, my dear. Use your strength and your skill. Leave Samuel out of this.' He doffed his hat and gave the most courteous bow. 'And, believe you me, Lady Maria Eleanora, I shall be eternally in your debt.'

And then Charles was gone, walking along the narrow path, whistling up his spaniels as if he hadn't a care in the world.

Maria Eleanora watched him go, disappear behind the line of bushes. The spaniels yapped, the sound of voices echoed then was followed by silence.

The cemetery of St Mary-Le-Bow standing off Cheapside was truly a place of the dead; the receptacle of corpses for hundreds of years, its ground was full of bones. Here and there coffins had been disinterred and white gleaming bones peeped through a thin coating of soil. Tombstones lay overturned beside statues and crosses, battered and weathered by the passage of time. Nevertheless, in one place in the far corner shaded by yew trees, the dead slept with more honour and dignity. It was a place of secrecy, well away from the eyes of the intruder, the spy or the Government agent. A place where Cecily Bannister could pay her loving respects at the tomb of her husband, Jonathan, barbarously slain two years previously.

Cecily crouched before his gravestone, eyes hungry for that inscription: JONATHAN BANNISTER, BORN 1650, DIED SEPTEMBER 1676. WELL BELOVED PHYSICIAN, RESPECTED MEMBER OF THIS PARISH, LOVING HUSBAND OF CECILY. The widow rearranged the wild flowers on the small mound before the tombstone.

'I hope you like these,' she whispered. 'I took them from the common. They are fresh, perhaps the last flowers of the year.'

She didn't cry because Cecily Bannister had cried so much she had no tears left. Whenever she could, she came here to invoke memories, recall the past and mourn for this man she had so deeply loved. This morning was different. A cold, clinging mist hung over the cemetery and, although it muffled the sounds of the city, the cries of hawkers, the crash of carts and the yapping of dogs, Cecily felt she wasn't truly alone. On her head was a broad-brimmed hat to hide her face as well as provide warmth, and around her shoulders was the maroon woollen cloak Jonathan had bought her one winter. Cecily dug her long, white fingers into the rich, brown earth. If only she could stretch out and touch Jonathan's sweet, kindly face. She sighed, withdrew her hands and made herself comfortable, sitting with her back against a gravestone covered in dark green moss. Oblivious of the damp, cold ground, she rearranged her cloak. Nothing would interfere with this vigil.

Cecily's face was often described as sweet; some even called it beautiful, with its large cornflower-blue eyes and ivory skin with its slight sheen. At the King's Head tavern she was regarded as a beauty with her long graceful neck, full bosom, slim waist and long legs. Cecily thought of the customers there, greedy-eyed and hungry-mouthed, hands constantly touching her, hot whispers in her ear, the offer of this, the offer of that: assignations in her chamber or some other place where a loving tryst could be kept. In return Cecily acted the saucy, buxom wench, hinting much but giving away nothing. Eyes and ears open, collecting tidbits of information for her master Dolius. Cecily knew his true name but never used it in her role of tavern wench. Seagrave had employed her for at least twelve months and Cecily had acted the part to perfection.

'As I used to, Jonathan,' she whispered tenderly. 'Do you remember?'

Then Cecily lost herself in sweet reveries. She and Jonathan had owned a house in Farringdon, just near Grays Inn. Jonathan, a graduate of Oxford, had soon established himself as a notable physician, a man who read not only the recently published tracts and learned works but investigated the new theories of medicine coming from abroad. Such a comfortable life! Cecily, the daughter of a London merchant, had fallen in love with Jonathan at first sight. A true love match. They had been married here in the church, determined to build their lives together.

'How many children, Jonathan?' she crooned. 'Was it six or seven? I know you wanted three boys and three girls.' Now the tears did come. 'You wouldn't believe me now, my love, how I act the part and play the hussy.'

She recalled the small plays she, Jonathan and their neighbours used to put on at Midsummer, Christmas and May Day. She and Jonathan had visited every theatre in the city, eager to see this work or that, arguing heatedly over the respective merits of each. A comfortable life! Her husband had built up a practice which attracted patients not so much amongst the great ones but the wealthy merchants. Then it had all come tumbling down like heavy rain would spoil a children's game. One beautiful autumn evening, they had been over the water to Southwark to visit a theatre in Bankside. She and Jonathan had taken a barge back across the river and landed at East Watergate. They were walking up the street arm-in-arm. It had been so simple, so innocuous. A man hurrying down, slightly drunk. Jonathan's shoulder had hit his, he had turned to apologise but the man had already drawn his sword. Cecily had watched in horror as the shining blade snaked out, taking her husband deep in his beloved heart. The assassin had stepped back, head up, wondering whether to attack again but the hue and cry had been raised. He had fled like a shadow but Cecily could always remember that twisted smile, the arrogant, hollow eyes of Master William Bedloe, swordsman and member of the Green Ribbon gang. Jonathan had died in her arms, whispering, 'I love you. I love you,' interspersed with prayers. 'Jesus have mercy.' Then he had shuddered, given a deep sigh and was gone.

For months afterwards Cecily had lived as if in a nightmare: distraught, adrift like a ship without its anchor, being pushed this way and that. She had been aware of friends and neighbours gathering round, words of comfort, the funeral service in a cold, bleak church. Jonathan being buried here. Eventually reason had returned – slowly, surely, like the night giving way to dawn. Cecily Bannister was left with one purpose in life and one purpose only, the utter destruction of her husband's assassin. Although at that stage she did not know his name, she would always recall his hateful visage. Despite her grief, Bedloe's face remained as clear in her mind as if she had glimpsed him only an hour ago.

After the funeral, Cecily had sold her house in Farringdon and taken comfortable lodgings in Mugwell Street near St Giles Cripplegate. She also sold all her possessions, taking only a few keepsakes, together with Jonathan's pistols, his dagger, rapiers and his great chest of medicines. In her bereavement, she had become hard of heart and iron of will. She'd made careful search in this tavern and that, but had not found the man with the twisted smile. Instead, Dolius had found her. He had come like a thief in the night: she'd returned home to find him sitting merry-eyed and saucy-faced on a stool in her chamber.

'How did you get in?' Cecily demanded.

Unafraid, she'd put her basket down and moved across to the bed and the pistol, primed and ready, placed beneath the bolster.

'Oh, don't look for your pistol,' Dolius had teased. 'I have already removed it. I mean you no harm, lady.'

'How did you get in?' Cecily repeated.

Dolius pointed to the small casement window.

'Madam, there's not a wall I can't climb or window I can't break through.'

'Who are you?'

'My name is Dolius.'

Cecily sat down in the high-backed wooden chair. She recognised that this stranger was no threat, posed no danger; she was more intrigued by his cool arrogance, the sheer effrontery of him sitting there, now and again turning to pluck a sweetmeat from the dish.

'I bought these myself,' he declared, offering her one. 'I borrowed the dish from your scullery.'

Cecily had taken one, a piece of sugared marchpane.

'They are fresh.' Dolius chewed like some schoolboy.

Despite the rags and the dirt on his face, Dolius was an educated man, a gentleman pretending to be a beggar.

'You are very pretty, Mistress Bannister.' He placed his hands on his heart and gave a mock bow.

'You've come all this way to tell me that? You name isn't Dolius, is it?'

'Of course not. My name is Captain Thomas Blood. I was born in County Meath, Ireland.'

'Ah, I recognise your accent.'

'Oh, I can speak many accents and many tongues: French, Spanish, Italian. I am a master swordsman, a great drinker, a seducer and ravisher of beautiful women.'

For the first time in months Cecily laughed.

'Aye, and a great liar and a boaster. Wait!' She stood up in surprise. 'You are the same Captain . . . ?'

Dolius rose to his feet and made the most graceful of bows.

'The same man!' He stood like an actor on the stage, head thrown back. 'Captain Thomas Blood of County Meath, Ireland. A gentleman who has fallen on hard times!'

'And who, a few years ago, tried to steal the Crown Jewels from the Tower,' Cecily interjected. 'You should have lost your head.'

She could well recall the details of this famous exploit, one which linked Blood with her dead husband Jonathan, for he had been full of the news during their courting days. A daring, audacious feat! Blood had actually entered the Jewels Chamber before the alarm had been raised. Cecily forgot her own troubles.

'Are you insane or a liar?'

Yet she could sense the truth. This man *was* Thomas Blood, she could tell just from the way he stood with all the easy arrogance of a born scoundrel.

'You were taken before the King but were pardoned?'

'I had an interview with His Majesty,' Dolius conceded. 'We discussed a number of matters. I made him laugh.'

'And he pardoned you for that?'

'No, it's a long story.' Blood clicked his tongue. 'But let me try and explain, Mistress Cecily.' He leaned forward. His eyes were a tawny brown; Cecily had never seen so much mischief in a man's gaze before. 'Let me put it this way. Charles Stuart, King of England, God bless him, had a similar interest in the Crown Jewels as myself. He was desperate for money as your own loyal servant here.'

Cecily couldn't help laughing. The captain was playing with the ring on his finger. He took it off and threw it at her. She caught it deftly. A simple gold circle, it bore a small crest displaying the arms of England.

'I work for the person who gave me that,' he told her.

'What work?'

'Against His Majesty's enemies, both here and abroad.'

'And what has that to do with me?'

'Why, Mistress Cecily, pray don't be sharp. You have a cask of good Bordeaux in the scullery. If we can share a loving cup? I promise, I will never bore you.'

'I don't think you bore many people, stranger!'

'You can call me Captain Thomas but only in your heart. To you, and to everyone else, I am Dolius, a mythical Greek King who worked in the shadows.'

Cecily, much taken by his impudence, went to the scullery and filled two goblets to the brim. She handed one over. He grasped her hand, kissed it and looked steadily at her.

'You are not frightened, Mistress Cecily? No hysterics, no screams?'

'I have no fear.'

'I know.' Blood smiled thinly. 'And that's why I've come to visit you. A woman without fear is even more dangerous than a man like myself.'

'Why did you search me out?'

As Cecily sat in her chair cradling the goblet, she realised she had absentmindedly taken down the two goblets she and Jonathan used to share, deep-bowled and chased with silver.

'We have an acquaintance in common.'

'I have no acquaintances, Captain Blood.'

'Oh, but you do. I have come for two reasons: to help you and to tell you to be careful.'

'Why be careful?'

'Your husband lies buried in St Mary-Le-Bow, a beautiful tombstone beneath the yew trees, yes?'

'Have you followed me there?'

'From a distance. I have seen you weep.' Blood's face became sad. 'I'll be honest, Mistress, and I speak the truth from my heart. I have silently wept with you and for you.'

Cecily looked up and her heart skipped a beat. For the first time since Jonathan's death someone had touched her soul. Blood was no longer the arrogant swaggerer; he sat slightly crumpled, face sad, eyes watchful.

'I have also loved and lost, my dear, and I have not loved again. Oh, I am a roaring boy, a drinker of sack. I have heard the bells toll the curfew. I have fought and I have lusted and, God forgive me, as the psalmist says, "My sin is always before me". But you, you are different. You search for a man, our mutual acquaintance: he is lean-visaged, hollow-eyed and smirking-mouthed, with a spot here high on his cheek, a mole – the Devil's mark since his birth.'

Cecily leaned forward so quickly the wine slopped onto her gown.

'You know this man?'

'Yes. His name is William Bedloe, and he is a rat in human form! A killer! A baseborn whoreson! A man who would draw a sword and kill a gentleman like your husband but run like the wind if confronted by someone like myself.'

'Do you hunt Bedloe as well?' Cecily spoke low.

'Since I entered the King's service I hunt Bedloe and his ilk. He calls himself Captain but he's really a Judas man born and bred. He'd betray his own mother, and probably did, for a couple of coins dropped into his clack dish. He killed your husband like he has dealt with many of his victims. The sudden drawing of a sword, yes? The swift thrust to the heart before your husband even knew that his death was streaking towards him.'

Tight-lipped, Cecily nodded. This stranger's story brought all the memories flooding back.

'Dressed in all his tawdry finery is Captain William Bedloe! Foul of soul and foul of temper. A true Pistol – you remember the man from Shakespeare's play, full of angry oaths and hot air? Oh yes.' He sighed. 'A veritable windbag.'

'Now I have his name,' Cecily interrupted, 'and his description, I'll go before a magistrate.'

'If you do that, Mistress, you'll have your throat cut.'

'I can defend myself.'

Blood snorted with laughter.

'Fine, fine.' He waved a hand. 'So, you are protected by the King's own lifeguards and go into court. Master Bedloe will be summoned and he'll turn up with a hundred witnesses to say how, when your husband died, he was in Bristol.'

'But that's a lie!'

'Of course it is. Bedloe wouldn't know the truth if it jumped up and bit him on the arse. He's well protected. A Judas man, he's a Green Ribboner, one of my Lord Shaftesbury's darlings.'

Cecily closed her eyes. She and Jonathan had not been bothered about the politics of the city but everyone knew Shaftesbury and his Green Ribboners, well aided and financed by the great London merchant Sir Robert Peyton.

'Ah, I see you have sense as well as beauty, Mistress Cecily. If you want Bedloe, and I swear by all that is holy that one day you shall have him, then come and work for me and my gang of lovelies.'

Cecily opened her eyes. 'And who are those?'

'King's men.' He smiled widely. 'And women. Agents who work directly for the Crown at His Majesty's bidding, who scurry through the dark and keep an eye on Master Shaftesbury, Bedloe and others. Especially now, since they are presently plotting something very devious and dangerous.'

'And how can I help?'

'By being a spy.'

'For what reason?'

'To kill Bedloe.' Dolius winked. 'At the appointed time. Also, to help me find out what plots are forming in Lord Shaftesbury's teeming brain.'

'And why else?'

'For the love of the King, sweet Mistress. For protection. For monies paid to you directly via a goldsmith in Cheapside from a secret fund.'

'Captain, the pie smells beautiful but why should I eat?'

'Well, I'll come to my final reason: because you need me. Oh, you are very good, Mistress Cecily. You move from tavern to tavern pretending to be this or that and always asking the same question. It's only a matter of time before a Green Ribboner realises for whom you are searching. You won't be the first corpse fished out of the Thames.'

Blood got up and, carrying his stool, came and sat closer. He grasped the young widow's cold hand and kissed it in a friendly gesture, rubbing it between his own warm hands.

'I have watched you, Cecily. You may be only a physician's widow but you are strong of heart, fearless.' He cocked an eyebrow. 'Beautiful, too.'

Cecily snatched away her hand.

'And you can act. Lord save us, Mistress Cecily, you can act!' He held out his hand again. 'Cecily, are you with me?'

She clasped it immediately. Blood leaned over and kissed her gently on the brow.

Afterwards he sat and told her all about the wickedness of Lord Shaftesbury and the evil deeds of William Bedloe. Cecily realised she was entering a world of dim lights and shifting shadows, of battles being fought in the alleyways and taverns, the brothels and dank places of the capital, of sword fights by torchlight, of treachery and treason, of a ruthless world where no pardon was offered and none taken. As Blood spun his web, that lilting voice, full of self-mockery, changed to hardness. After listening to him, a man resolute on serving the King, whom he described as 'great and as merry a rogue' as he himself was, Cecily had agreed to an alliance. Before long, she had moved to the King's Head tavern and become a scullion, a serving maid. Blood had told her to keep her own name, playing the part of a gentlewoman fallen on ill fortune.

'Bedloe won't remember you,' he reassured her. 'But, Cecily, I must have your oath that you will only strike when I tell you.'

She had given her word. Now she had met Bedloe. She had glimpsed him on a few occasions from afar, but now she had his full measure . . .

A twig snapped and Cecily broke from her reverie. The graveyard still lay silent but the feeling that she wasn't alone had suddenly intensified. The mist too, had grown deeper. Scrambling to her feet, she picked up the basket, her hand going beneath the cloth for the small musket concealed there.

'Don't be afraid, Cecily my sweet. It is only I.'

Dolius, wrapped in a cloak, stepped out of the mist, hat in one hand, the other holding a staff.

'I have decided to become a preacher.' He smiled. 'I have a sermon to preach, Cecily, the King's work to do. The good Lord knows the time is upon us!'

He stretched out his hand, and Cecily grasped it.

'Are we close?' she whispered.

He leaned forward and brushed her lips with his.

'Closer than you think!'

Chapter Seven

Samuel Atkins sat miserably under the canopy of the great Westminster Barge; its oarsmen, backs bent, strained at the oars, fighting the current as they cut through the morning mist down to Westminster. Now and again the mist broke and the prisoner felt a pang of homesickness at some of his favourite sights: the high brick wall of the Temple, the red tiles of the merchants' houses, their white plaster now grimed with sooty dirt borne by the autumn winds. Occasionally another barge passed them. Samuel stretched to ease the cramp. On either side sat armed, burly guards and, facing him, Captain Eastwell humming some ditty.

The barge-master called out an order. The oarsmen rested as the boat was caught by another wave and juddered sickeningly from side to side. Samuel clutched his stomach. He felt nauseous, a combination of agitation and the miserable victuals served at Newgate. At least he was out of there! He could breathe God's air and, perhaps, this was the last time the Lords' Committee would interview him? Perhaps they would even free him, he thought hopefully. Then Eastwell caught his eye and smiled cynically.

No, no, they won't do that, Atkins reflected. He had tried to rack his brain, recall where he had been on that fateful weekend – and now, suddenly, the river jolted his memory. Had he been on a barge like this? But where was he going, up- or downriver? And who were his companions? He could remember torchlight, lantern horns. People garbed in black coats, hats pulled over their eyes. Samuel shivered and crossed his arms as his nightmare threatened to return. Had he, in a drunken stupor, been involved in something nefarious? Did he have something to hide?

He peered longingly towards the bank on his far right. Somewhere in the huddle and maze of buildings was Somerset Place. He wondered what Maria Eleanora was doing, and once again prayed that she would not be too rash or audacious. As he had left Newgate, Samuel had glimpsed figures standing in doorways, their gaze intent on him. They were hardly waiting for him to escape, not from a place like Newgate. Was it his imagination, or were they waiting to see who might try and visit him?

Eastwell pulled down his cloak which covered his mouth and leaned forward.

'I hope you have your wits about you this morning, Mr Atkins. My Lord Shaftesbury is in fine fettle. He'll demand questions and you must give answers.'

'I'll speak the truth,' Atkins declared hotly.

He lifted his hand to his face and felt his unshaven cheek; then he stirred on the bench and sniffed: his clothing stank of that foul prison.

'You have been treated gently so far,' Eastwell commented. He winked at the soldier sitting on the young clerk's right. 'Come, come, Master Atkins,' he whispered, his narrow eyes bright with malice, 'where were you that weekend? If you can't tell us, Captain Childs and his men will swear your life away. You'll be doing the Newgate dance before you know it.'

Samuel stared back.

'And come, come, Master Atkins.' Again the taunt. 'We

have met before, you know we have. Do you recall that alleyway outside the theatre? An invitation offered and curtly refused.'

'So it *was* you!'

Samuel would have lurched forward but the soldiers grasped his arms and pulled him back.

'I didn't say it was,' Eastwell declared. 'Though it was an invitation you refused. Perhaps if you and your companion had accepted, a great deal of these present troubles might have been avoided. So, tell me. Share this secret. Who *was* that young man in the broad-brimmed hat and scarlet plume?'

'I don't know what you are talking about.'

'Do you like fancy boys, Atkins? Do you ever visit a molly house to hire a set of nice, rounded buttocks?'

'You seem to know more about it than I do. Just because—' Samuel bit his tongue.

'Just because what?'

'Just because I have my own friends, that does not mean I will betray them to every footman and lackey hired by my Lord Shaftesbury.'

Eastwell stretched out and jabbed Atkins viciously beneath the chin.

'Watch your tongue, clerk. Otherwise we will meet again!'

'Wherever you wish,' Atkins retorted. 'Just the two of us, eh, Captain Eastwell? Sword against sword, dagger against dagger. None of your bully-boys or molly friends, eh?'

Eastwell lifted his hand again.

'I wouldn't do that, sir.' The corporal sitting on Atkins's left spoke up. 'Remember how Lord Shaftesbury said the prisoner was not to be harmed? If he appears in court bruised,' he sniggered, 'old Justice Scroggs will believe the poor little lamb has been tortured.'

Eastwell, back in control, swallowed his anger and pulled his cloak high to cover his mouth.

'True, true,' he murmured. 'Old Scroggs will take care of you, Atkins. A quick trial and a speedy cart to Tyburn, eh?'

Ignoring him, Samuel stared across the river. The barge-master issued an order. The oarsmen turned, those on the right lifting their oars whilst the others pulled lustily, steering the barge so it could nose its way over towards King's Steps. The barge reached the quayside, shuddering up against the muddy steps. Ropes were thrown, the oarsmen, nimble as monkeys, slipped up the steps and secured the craft. Atkins was bundled out and pushed up onto the quayside which stank of salt and mouldering fish. The Palace was fairly deserted apart from beggars, hands extended, whining for alms.

Westminster was quiet that day, for neither Commons nor Lords were sitting. A few pedlars and chapmen came hurrying up, offering pies and strips of pork warmed over their makeshift ovens. When they glimpsed the red uniforms of Eastwell and his group, they slunk away.

The captain led his party across the cobbles into the main courtyard of Westminster Palace. They passed the Great Clock, went up a flight of stairs and along a warren of stone-paved, hollow-sounding passageways. Clerks and scriveners hurried by, servants and scullions from the kitchens. Here and there soldiers stood on guard. Dark-garbed lawyers, papers in their hands, stood huddled together, heads nodding. They reminded Atkins of a group of crows come to feast on carrion.

The group marched past the Great Hall where the courts were held and up chipped steps to an oak-panelled chamber. Within, a fire roared in its hearth, and further up the Lords' Committee sat like judges around a polished walnut table. More of them had gathered this time. Shaftesbury sat at the top, combing his fair wig with one hand, the other holding a small gilt hand-mirror. He was dressed in his usual light-green suit with a large emerald fastened into his snow-white stock: on his left sprawled Pembroke, on his right Buckingham. Atkins quickly studied the other faces. Next to Sir Robert Peyton sat a dark-wigged, cunning-faced, hollow-eyed man dressed in a braided military cloak, who raised his hand in greeting as if he recognised Atkins. Eastwell shoved him into a chair at the end of the table.

'Give our Master Atkins some wine,' he ordered.

The others now took notice of his arrival. The conversation died. All faces turned towards Atkins. He saw no hint of compassion there, nothing but hard glances in sour faces.

'We have been very busy on this affair,' Shaftesbury called out.

He paused as Eastwell slammed a half-filled goblet in front of Atkins. The clerk drank it greedily.

'Full red Burgundy,' Shaftesbury smiled, leaning forward, placing his hand elegantly on the table beside him. 'Just think, Samuel, there's more of that, aye and a fresh partridge pie, if you come to the point and tell the truth. You do like partridge pie, Mr Atkins?'

'I am partial to it, my lord.' Samuel's voice echoed so clearly, he stared round.

This was part of the old medieval Palace. The plaster above the oak wainscoting was flaking but the windows, long and broad, were filled with glass, their shutters pulled away, allowing the light to stream through. The ceiling was black-beamed, from which two huge wooden candelbra hung on stout cords.

'You find it strange, Master Atkins, after your lodgings at Newgate? But look, sir, would you not like a partridge pie? A cup of warm posset? A bag full of coins and the approval of your colleagues?' Shaftesbury paused. 'And your betters?'

'I have spoken the truth.' Atkins's eyes roamed the table. He didn't like the way the black-wigged man kept staring at him, fingers tapping his cheek. 'I have told the truth,' he repeated.

'Nonsense!' Pembroke bawled, banging the table with his fists. 'You are a liar, Atkins. Captain Childs has already sworn that you were involved in the plot to murder Godfrey.'

'I was not,' Atkins replied steadily.

'Tell me.' Shaftesbury picked up the hand-mirror and wiped some of the white powder from his face.

Atkins was sure the old rogue had also reddened his lips. Now he could view him clearly, Shaftesbury looked a frightening figure, so precise, so neat, the false bonhomie, his painted face, those cunning, flickering eyes. Atkins felt as if he was on the verge of walking into a trap yet there was nothing he could do to save himself.

'Tell me.' Shaftesbury moved the mirror as if concerned with the beauty spot placed high on his cheek. 'Tell me where you were on Friday the eleventh of October, Saturday the twelfth and Sunday the thirteenth?'

'I can't remember, my Lord.'

A growl of disapproval greeted his answer.

'Do you have a ladyfriend?' Peyton drawled, turning to look fully down the table at Atkins. 'You've served in His Majesty's ships of war, I believe. You are a man of action as well as a clerk, Master Atkins. The juices must run full and hot within you. Surely you have a doxy? Some strumpet or whore?'

'Perhaps some merchant's wife?' Pembroke interrupted.

Peyton turned and glared, but Pembroke wouldn't be checked.

'Perhaps that's why Master Atkins won't tell us. He's been sowing his oats in someone else's fields. Is that true, Atkins? By the cock, man, you look a mess!'

Atkins stared at Pembroke's wild eyes, bristling beard and moustache, the shock of greasy hair.

'My Lord, in which case I must return the compliment.'

Pembroke would have leapt to his feet but Shaftesbury restrained him.

'You'll have your time for jests, Mr Atkins. And your time for jigs. If you are not careful, at the end of a rope! Let's come to the point. You leave your master's lodgings in Seething Lane. Whom do you meet at night?'

Atkins blinked as if that very gesture could clear the beautiful face of Maria Eleanora from his memory. He compressed his lips. Shaftesbury was watching him closely.

'There is somebody, isn't there?'

Atkins shrugged. 'A lady of the night.'

'Dressed like a man?' Peyton bawled. 'With olive skin?'

Atkins's mouth went dry. He was sure these men could hear his heart thudding. He was about to object but Pembroke, eager for another thrust, banged the table with his goblet.

'He's a sodomite!' he belched and made an obscene gesture. 'He buggers young men!'

'Do you have any business at Somerset Place?' Shaftesbury asked tersely.

'No, my Lord.'

'So, why have you been seen there? Look, look, you lie!' Shaftesbury caught Samuel's discomfiture. 'You've been seen prowling round the streets there. Whom have you been waiting for? What have you been doing? You were there when they murdered Godfrey, weren't you?'

'I was not!'

'Yes, you were.' The black-wigged man was now on his

feet, finger pointed accusingly. 'It *is* you! I saw you in the light of a dark lantern horn.'

'Are you sure, Captain Bedloe?' Shaftesbury asked smoothly. 'Do you truly believe this to be the man?'

'Yes, my Lord.'

'And he told you his name was Atkins, a clerk belonging to Derby House?'

'This is a lie!' Atkins roared. 'I don't even know you, sir!'

'It is *not* a lie,' Bedloe retorted, re-taking his seat. 'I knew you as soon as you entered this room.'

'Well, well.' Shaftesbury leaned back in his chair. 'Here's evidence that will hang. Were you at work in your office on Monday, the fourteenth of October, a date we're very interested in?'

Atkins closed his eyes. The trap had sprung shut.

'We have already checked the records.' Shaftesbury smiled thinly down the table. 'Your master was away at Newmarket.' His voice took on a sing-song tone. 'When the cat's away the mice do play, do they not, Mr Atkins? You were missing from your desk. You didn't reappear until the following Tuesday morning. Where were you that weekend and, above all, that Monday?'

'I . . . I can't remember.' Atkins closed his eyes.

'What can you remember?'

'I remember leaving my work on Friday afternoon.'

'You speak here of the eleventh of October?'

'Yes, my Lord.'

'Captain Bedloe?'

'I saw him!' Bedloe's voice rolled like a peal of thunder round the chamber. 'I saw this man standing over the body of Sir Edmund Godfrey on the night of Monday, the fourteenth of October!'

'Perhaps he expects a pardon?' The Duke of Buckingham spoke up. 'Perhaps he thinks Mr Pepys will do him a favour?'

'Three hundred to one he won't,' Shaftesbury snarled. 'Captain Eastwell, take the prisoner back to Newgate. Have him loaded with irons.'

'This is nonsense!' Atkins sprang to his feet. 'I am the King's most loyal subject. This man is lying!'

'Now, sir, come quietly.'

Perhaps it was the malice on Eastwell's face but suddenly Atkins could take no more. The blood roared in his ears. He was aware of these men grinning at him, prepared to send him to a hideous death for no other reason except that he wouldn't perjure himself or others. Leaping up and knocking his chair over, he picked up the goblet and flung it hard down the table. The wine flew out, spilling all over the papers, as the goblet bounced crazily along the surface.

Eastwell grabbed an arm, that smirk still on his narrow face, and Samuel, using his free hand, brought his fist back and punched the captain straight in the mouth, sending him staggering back across the chamber. As the other guards closed in, Atkins lashed out with boot and fist. He was aware of Pembroke hurrying down the chamber, then a soldier jumped on his back. Atkins twisted to punch him but took a blow on the side of his head, a sickening thud. The roaring in his ears grew worse. He staggered and then fainted into a black unconsciousness.

When he awoke, Samuel ached from head to toe. His skull and the back of his neck were wracked with pain, mouth dry, stomach heaving. He stared round. At first he thought he was in a dungeon cell. He could see no door or windows, nothing but a flickering lantern horn fixed on a hook against wet mildewed walls. He tried to lift his hands but the manacles which secured him allowed little movement. Similar chains held his ankles fast.

Samuel watched in horror as a black, furry body slipped across his leg. The rat turned, snout twitching, little greedy eyes studying Atkins as if he couldn't decide whether this prisoner was alive or dead. Atkins screamed. The rat scurried away. Samuel turned to vomit. He leaned his head back against the wall. His legs and arms hurt because of the way he had been punched and kicked. The tip of his tongue licked the blood-encrusted corner of his mouth. His right eye was half-closed, he could feel the bruise forming there. The shooting pain at the back of his head made him nauseous; was he going to faint again? He gazed around again at the ill-lit, fetid chamber, the black slush which covered the floor, the dripping walls.

'Oh God!'

Atkins closed his eyes. He must be in the Little Susie, the dank, underground holding pit of Newgate Prison. Was he alone? He peered through the murky gloom. He could see chains fastened to the walls but no one else was there.

'I am an innocent man!' he screamed.

He made out a trapdoor in the roof.

'I am innocent!'

Much to his relief, the trapdoor was pulled open. A bright lantern dazzled his eyes. When he peered again, Samuel made out Captain Richardson's craggy, severe face.

'Everybody sings that song, Mr Atkins. Now, if you behave yourself, I can bring you out. Find you more comfortable quarters, a nice dry cell. You have a visitor who is prepared to pay your chummage.' Richardson referred to the fee that well-to-do prisoners paid to secure a more salubrious pit or cell.

Relieved, the young man swore he would behave himself.

A cage was lowered on a creaking, rusting chain, a turnkey inside. The fellow came out and threatened Atkins with a huge bunch of keys.

'If you try anything,' he warned, 'I'll hit you with these and you can stay here for a month.'

'Just get me out,' the clerk begged weakly.

He wanted to be away from here; he was also curious as to who his visitor could be. Surely someone like Maria Eleanora would be turned away, whilst Shaftesbury, or any of his cronies, wouldn't need to come here to question him. The gyves were released. He was dragged to his feet and thrust into the cage which was then raised. At the top, two other turnkeys guided the cage in, unlocked the gate and took Atkins out before sending the contraption back down for the turnkey. Captain Richardson tapped him gently on the shoulder.

'They say you became violent, Mr Atkins. You won't become violent with me, will you? You'll be a proper gentleman and behave yourself.'

Richardson mockingly gestured him to walk forward. As they left the condemned hold and made their way along narrow, link-lit passageways, the light was poor, the stench offensive. They passed gratings where mad eyes in dirty faces peered out at them. Sometimes Richardson's presence brought forth piteous cries, more often maddened curses or obscene jibes. The keeper, in his light-blond periwig and red buff coat, strode on as if he was totally unaware of his surroundings. They climbed some steps. Here the gallery was cleaner, better lit. Richardson stopped at a door, unlocked it and pushed Atkins inside.

'The best lodgings Newgate can provide.' He opened his hand to show the silver and gold coins and smiled. 'Go on, laddie, show your gratitude. At least say thank you.'

Atkins went across to the narrow cot bed and sat down. He still felt dizzy and light-headed, but was aware of clean plaster walls, fresh straw on the floor: a table, stools, chair and a two-branched, rusting iron candelabra. Pots and cracked cups stood on the shelf. The bed had blankets, even a soiled bolster.

'It's better than Little Susie.' Richardson crouched down before him. 'Now look, Mr Atkins, you'll have three square meals a day. Ale in the morning, wine at night.'

'Who's my visitor?' Atkins demanded.

'Oh, very well.'

Richardson left the cell. He returned within a short time accompanied by a male figure. Atkins knew immediately it was Maria Eleanora. She was dressed like a court Cavalier in a dark suit and military cloak, her hat pulled low. Richardson, however, acted as if he could see, hear and smell no one. He didn't even look at Samuel's visitor but waved to a stool.

Atkins was so curious he forgot both his surprise and his own situation.

'Captain Richardson, do you have permission for this?'

Maria Eleanora made no welcoming sign as she pulled across the stool.

'Don't be long!' was all the gaoler said as he closed and locked the door behind him.

'Don't touch me!' Maria Eleanora warned.

She pulled down the front of her cloak. Atkins saw her lips, her eyes bright. Was it with fear or desire?

'Don't touch me,' she repeated hoarsely. 'Samuel, we must talk in a whisper.' Her own gloved hand went out then fell away. 'Good Lord, my love, you look terrible. You have been tortured?'

'Just beaten.' Samuel grinned, then gave way to despair.

'Maria Eleanora, you've signed your own death warrant by coming here.'

'No, listen.'

Maria Eleanora swiftly described her interview with the King and what was happening outside the prison. Samuel heard her out.

'That's no protection,' he hissed, 'against a dagger, sword or musket ball!'

The young woman breathed in. She was shocked and frightened by Samuel's appearance. Eyes sunken, he had lost weight in the very short time he had been in prison. His face was grimy and unshaven, there were large angry bruises round his mouth and under his eyes, and his lovely hair was clotted with filth. Maria Eleanora could smell the rankness of his clothes. She hated this place. She had heard tales about how heinous and horrid it was. In Lisbon she had helped the good Sisters in the military prison outside the city, an old disused barracks, but even that had not been as foulsome as this antechamber of Hell.

'Why are you here?' Samuel demanded.

'Because I love you.'

'If you love me,' his voice caught in his throat, 'you would not be here.'

'If I loved you and did not come,' she said painfully, 'Then, Samuel, that means I would be dead.'

Atkins blinked away his tears. He leaned across as if she was a priest listening to his confession.

'I am not as evil-used as you think,' he whispered. 'I met the man who attacked us, Eastwell, an officer in the pay of Shaftesbury and his gang. They want me to confess.'

He explained exactly what had happened at the different meetings: the taunts of Shaftesbury, the veiled bribery, the lies of Captain Childs and William Bedloe.

'Sometimes,' he concluded hoarsely, 'when I sit here, I think I should lie, confess, tell a tale as tall as the ship's mast and walk free.' He glimpsed the doubt and uncertainty in Maria Eleanora's eyes.

'Could you, would you do that?' she asked softly.

For some strange reason Atkins abruptly recalled Mr Pepys sitting at the head of the table at his house in Seething Lane last Christmas. A huge goose rested on a silver platter at one end, crisp and succulent, and a roasted haunch of beef at the other, cooked in wine and smelling sweetly; Pepys telling jokes, his small kindnesses. Samuel glanced up and held Maria Eleanora's gaze.

'If I did that,' he replied, strongly now, 'I would not be Samuel Atkins and, if I am not Samuel Atkins, then how can Maria Eleanora love me?'

Her hand crept out and brushed his. Samuel couldn't resist the cry which came from his very soul. He went to grasp her but she stood up, kicking the stool aside, then walked to the door to peer through the grille.

'Richardson will leave us alone,' she said agitatedly, 'but Samuel, they must not know who I am. I must sustain this disguise.'

'Your voice has changed,' Atkins broke in.

'What are you talking about?'

Atkins grinned. Maria Eleanora's voice had become deep, accurately echoing the London twang.

'If you vant,' she continued, imitating a city-dweller, 'if you vant, I vill . . .'

Samuel laughed, biting his lip so the sound wouldn't carry.

'When you are at court, Samuel,' she lectured him, 'wearing a mask is the only way to survive. You only show enmity when you are hidden in your own closet and can ridicule and imitate your enemies to your heart's content. It's the same here in Newgate.' Maria Eleanora shook her head. 'God knows what peep-holes the walls have, so be careful! Richardson can be trusted. He knows where his true loyalties lie. His politics are very simple. What he doesn't see, hear and understand he can't tell. Now you, Samuel,' her fingers brushed his, 'you must wear your mask and remain firm, whatever happens, whatever these evil men throw at you. You must be like one of your oaks, bracing itself against the tempest.'

She pulled her cloak further down. Samuel noticed the bead of sweat running down her cheek. He touched this lightly and licked his fingers.

'Or like a ship at sea,' he replied hoarsely. 'Run before the wind though God knows what rocks await us!'

'Samuel, I must ask you a question: where were you on that missing weekend?'

'I can't remember – and it's Monday the fourteenth which might hang me.'

'For God's sake, Samuel!'

Panic surged within him at the fear in his beloved's eyes.

'I was distraught,' he confessed. 'I was in my cups. God knows, Maria Eleanora, who I was with! Before I met you, I was friendly with a number of ladies of the town.'

The smile returned to her eyes.

'I missed you,' he said sheepishly. 'I tried to drown my sorrows. You've heard the English expression?'

'As long as you didn't try to drown yourself!' she quipped. 'Whatever you did, my love, I don't really care. You love me, don't you?'

'Of course.'

'If I was with you you'd want no one else?'

'You know that.'

'Then you must remember! At all costs *you must remember*!'

'If I don't come through this,' Samuel began.

'You will,' she said hastily.

'No, no, listen. If I don't,' Samuel grasped her fingers and held fast, 'promise me you will leave England. Get out and never come back.'

'Samuel!' Maria Eleanora's voice became choked with emotion.

'I am not going to lie,' he said steadily. 'Maria Eleanora, I may have signed my own death warrant. If the King can't have his way and I am for the dark, promise me you will not come and see me die. Feign some excuse, any lie. I have friends, captains of ships.' Samuel paused. Something pricked his memory but he was too distraught. 'Go and talk to Mr Pepys. He will see you safely out to Lisbon.'

Maria Eleanora's shoulders were shaking with sobs. 'I love you, Samuel Atkins. I always have and I always will. For the sake of us both, for the sake of our lives, for the life we will have, and the love which we share, you must come through this. You must remember.'

Her voice was so impassioned, her face so resolute, that Samuel's courage failed. He dare not tell her about his nightmare. How, as he lay in this narrow, close place, he sometimes wondered if he *had* done something wrong. Had he been used, trapped deep in his cups? Did Shaftesbury and the others have evidence which they kept hidden for the time being?

'Samuel, listen, tell me.'

Atkins wetted his lips.

'Do you want some wine?' Maria Eleanora was all concerned, her face only a few inches from his.

'No, no, it's my stomach.' He plucked at his jacket. 'I do not feel well.'

Now, recovering from the onslaught of the attack at Westminster and the shock of seeing Maria Eleanora again, Atkins felt distinctly uncomfortable. At one time he felt cold, other times hot. His hand went to his throat. He dabbed at the sweat forming there.

'My love,' she said urgently, 'in the days before you met me, you went carousing, like all young men. Who did you go with? What did you do?'

'I can't remember.' Samuel smiled queasily. 'My life began when I first met you.'

'Samuel, please concentrate!'

'I used to go to Greenwich,' he confessed. 'I have many friends, acquaintances, officers in the Navy. We'd hire a room in a tavern and dine on pheasant pie, jugs of ale and cups of sack. We'd toast each other on our good fortune . . .'

There was a banging on the door.

'Master Soames! Master Soames, your time is up!'

'That's me,' Maria Eleanora whispered. 'I had an English nurse, Mathilda Soames.' She smiled. 'Remember this, Samuel Atkins, whatever Hell spits at you, I am here. I shall return. I shall always be with you!'

Samuel leaned forward. Maria Eleanora held one gloved finger against his lips and pushed his head gently back.

'Keep faith,' she murmured. 'For the love of me, Samuel, keep faith.'

She got to her feet and pulled up the cloak to cover her face, lowering the brim of her hat, eyes gazing hungrily at him. He made a sign with his hand, placing his fingers on his lips. The cell door swung open and she was gone.

Samuel watched the lantern glow fade in the passageway, heard the soft shuffle of feet receding. A bell began to toll. He became aware of the noises from the prison: the banging of doors, the rattling of keys, distant singing and the shouts of the turnkeys. He smelt his fingers: for a moment he caught her fragrance, a soft musky perfume. Samuel couldn't stop shivering. He gazed round the bleak cell recently transformed by Maria Eleanora's presence. He recalled the way she had stood there, breeched and booted, heavy cloak swathed around her, and prayed that she would be safe. To him she was his great love, but to others, she was just a handsome young cavalier, soft-faced and bright-eyed. Yet she had taken a terrible risk. Samuel recalled the watchers outside the prison gates. Unable to control his fear, he took the heavy serge blanket from the bed and wrapped it round his shoulders; then, lying down, he prayed as he had never done before that the love of his life would be safe.

As soon as she stepped out of the prison Maria Eleanora was aware of the danger. Dusk was falling. The cobbled courtyard in front of Newgate was lit by cresset torches fixed into the ground or lashed to poles jutting out from the towers. It was a cold, empty space. A few of the curious thronged to stare up at the windows. The chilly evening breeze carried the bloody stench of the butchers' stalls. People hurried about, cloaked and hooded. Maria Eleanora looked to her left at the scaffolding around a newly built church. As the shouts of the workmen echoed down, she glimpsed the two watchers standing in the doorway of an ale-house.

'People don't stand in ale-house doors,' she muttered. 'Not on a cold November evening.'

Making her way across the stinking, slippery cobbles, she turned abruptly right down Dyers Lane, hand on the hilt of her rapier which Richardson had returned to her before she had left his lodgings. Ignoring the curses and shouts, Maria Eleanora hurried on, pushing her way through the throng. A beggar stepped out of the shadows, a clack dish was thrust in front of her face. She knocked this aside. A chapman selling ribbons and geegaws tried to block her path. She pushed by. A whore lurched out of the ale-house and grabbed her arm. Maria Eleanora gazed down at the bloated, leering face, the yellow straggly hair.

'Won't you keep us company, a nice boy like you?'

Maria Eleanora stepped aside. A man with a hand-bill hurried up.

'Do you want to see it?' he screamed in her face. 'The Great Curiosity! A negro with white hair and beard! A dog with two heads? Come and see Mr Arkwright's curiosities!'

Maria Eleanora ignored him and strode on. She hoped to go towards the river, turn into Thames Street and so elude any pursuers. As she crossed Bowyers Row, the dark mass of the new St Paul's loomed up on her left. She turned down Carters Lane, a dingy, narrow place. Shadows lurked in the doorways and at the mouth of the numerous alleyways.

'Master Atkins!'

Maria Eleanora froze. She paused and glanced over her shoulder.

'Master Atkins!'

The beggar boy came running down the street.

'What is it?' Maria Eleanora put out her hand to stop him.

The boy was spindle-shanked, with thin arms, large eyes in a white pale face, hair cropped too close to his head. He was dressed in threadbare rags, old sandals on his feet, a size too big for him. When he opened his mouth, Maria Eleanora glimpsed the sore on his upper lip. The poor half-starved creature looked like a dream-walker.

'Master Atkins,' he repeated as if he was learning something from rote.

'What is it, boy?' Maria Eleanora crouched down.

'I don't know.'

The child looked frightened. A ripple of cold fear caressed the back of Maria Eleanora's neck. She dug into her purse and brought out a silver piece and pressed it into the urchin's hand. He stared speechlessly at her.

'Master Atkins,' he babbled. 'Master Atkins.'

'Why do you use that name?'

'I don't know,' he whispered. 'They told me.'

The young woman got to her feet and stepped back. Four men had followed the boy down the alleyway. They moved softly and silently as padding cats.

'What shall I do?' the lad whimpered. 'I am sorry, Master. They gave me a coin.'

'Go away! Run along now!'

Maria Eleanora pushed him gently aside and he scuttled away and was gone. She looked quickly over her shoulder. The alleyway was long and narrow as a needle; it was bounded by dingy tenements, their upper storeys jutting out. Battered signs creaked and clattered, the occasional dull light glowed at fly-blown windows. Maria Eleanora gazed at the four men. She recognised fighting bucks, roaring boys just by the way they swaggered, cloaks pushed back, hands caressing the hilts of their swords. Even in the fading light she could make out their tawdry finery, the glint of an earring, the silver chain around their throats.

She backed slowly down the street wondering what to do. If she ran she might slip. Did they carry muskets? Were there others waiting further down? Then she heard the scrape of steel. A decision had been made: all four had drawn their rapiers. Very well. She drew her own, along with the lethal duelling dagger from the back of her belt.

The four men shuffled forward, their leader slightly in front.

'Who are you?' he taunted. 'Let's see your face, pretty

boy. Don't be angry, now. Just lower your sword and come closer.'

He darted in, blade flickering. As she blocked it, Maria Eleanora felt his strength, the power of the cut, and gripped her own sword more tightly. Curbing her panic, she stepped back, careful of the sewer which ran down the middle of the street. The four men followed warily, as Maria Eleanora kept stepping away. She recalled a thin runnel which should lie just to her left, but she needed something to protect her back. Again the leader came forward, this time joined by one of his companions. The alleyway echoed with the rasping clash of steel, the grunts of the attackers. Maria Eleanora felt the wall behind her. Thank God!

One man came in, hoping to take her from the side. A fatal error. Maria Eleanora skilfully knocked his sword aside, lunged in with her dagger. The point of her blade caught him just beneath the neck, and he screamed in agony as he fell to his knees. Enraged, the others moved in, but cautiously. Again the feints and parries. Two of her attackers were clumsy, nothing more than slash and cut. It was the leader in the middle she must counter, Maria Eleanora knew. Head down, determined to conceal her face she fought on; it was thrust and parry, blow and counter-blow. As the sweat broke out on her brow, she realised that these men were in no hurry. They hoped to wear her down, were obviously determined to take her alive and learn her identity. Whoever had hired them had paid well for this. The men ignored their former companion, who was nothing more than a bundle of clothes lying next to the sewer, clutching at the bubbling wound high in his chest. Again the leader came in, this time faster, the point of his sword snaking out towards Maria Eleanora's face. She blocked him swiftly. The alleyway had fallen silent. She looked across the street and, just for a second, glimpsed a girl's face pressed against the dusty window of a house opposite.

'Well, well, well!' The voice came from behind the attackers.

The three men whirled round. A man stood there. He was dressed only in shirt, breeches and heavy boots, like those of a sailor, his hat pushed to the back of his head. In one hand he carried a sword, in the other a dagger. Maria Eleanora couldn't make out his features but she was aware of the man's strength just by the way he stood, legs slightly apart, shirt unbuttoned at the top.

'Go away, stranger!'

The leader stood sideways, gazing quickly at Maria Eleanora, then back at this stranger.

'This is not your quarrel,' he snarled.

'Oh, but it is. When has four against one been a fair fight, good sir? Now I would ask you to let this gentleman by. Why don't you collect your groaning companion and go back to the sewer you slunk from?'

The leader sucked on his lips, his eyes flickering briefly at Maria Eleanora. His scarred, unshaven face was soaked in sweat, his features a mask of malice. Maria Eleanora had not seen him before. She quietly prayed she never would again. He looked what he was, a killer, a man without a soul.

'I am going to count,' the stranger said pleasantly. 'I shall count to ten and then I shall kill you. One! Two! Three! Four!'

The leader of the attackers suddenly sheathed his sword and flung his hands up in the air. He had no choice. Maria Eleanora was on one side, this stranger on the other.

'This to he who fights and runs away,' he snarled, then spat contemptuously.

'Five!' the stranger continued unmoved.

The leader chattered in a patois to his two companions who, panting, sheathed their weapons and went across to pick up their fallen companion. Cursing and muttering, they dragged him up the alleyway. Maria Eleanora brought her hand up and wiped the sweat from her face on the back of her hand.

'Thank you,' she whispered hoarsely.

The man bowed gallantly, putting on his jacket.

'Madam, your humble servant.'

Chapter Eight

'Who are you?'

'My name is Dolius.'

Maria Eleanora brought her sword up.

'I expected you, but how do I know who you really are? This could be a trap.'

'I am a friend of Samuel Atkins.'

'That's what the others said.'

'You looked beautiful, Maria Eleanora, when you were in Whitehall Gardens by the lake, talking to the King. "There," I said to myself,' the stranger smiled with his eyes, '"there goes a beautiful woman and Samuel Atkins is a very lucky man." Mind you,' he sheathed his sword, '*I* am also a very lucky man.'

'Why is that, sir?'

'Because I know two courageous, beautiful women. In this vale of wickedness two of anything is a great profit, but *two* beautiful, courageous women? Madam,' he bowed again, 'I am your most fortunate and humble servant.'

When Maria Eleanora still refused to lower the sword, Dolius sighed.

'You carry a warrant from His Majesty. I'm here to help you. Now you can stand there, the brave Cavalier, till darkness falls and Weasel Eyes, who has just struggled away, returns with more of his friends.' He approached closer.

Maria Eleanora studied the handsome face, the impudent tawny eyes.

'I mean you no harm,' he whispered, his voice thick with an Irish brogue. 'By St Patrick and all the saints in Heaven, I've never hit a woman in my life.' His smile widened. 'Unless she really wanted it. Come, Maria Eleanora, we have to talk.'

She sheathed her sword and dagger. Dolius grasped her hand and, without asking, linked her arm through his. He smelt of leather and horse and some fragrant soap. She noticed his face was freshly shaved, his hair slightly oiled. He walked with a swagger, planting his hat back on his head.

'You don't wear a wig?' she asked.

'Madam, if it makes you happy I'll buy one, though every part of my anatomy is what God gave me and I am proud of that.'

'Where are we going?' Maria Eleanora demanded.

'Why, Mistress, into the very pit of Hell.'

He led her back up the alleyway chattering as if he had known her for years, pointing out different ale-houses and taverns. They went through the old city wall, along Fleet Street and right into Shoe Lane; a dingy, foulsome part of the city. The houses were much decayed, almost toppling over to meet each other, blocking out the light. The lane was littered with mounds of refuse and dead carrion: thin-ribbed dogs came rushing out, lips curled in a ferocious display of yellow, sharp teeth. Dolius lashed out with his boot and swaggered on. Whores and prostitutes thronged the doorways. Men hidden in the shadows watched them go by, gleaming eyes measuring their wealth.

'Aren't you frightened?' Maria Eleanora whispered.

'Of course I am,' Dolius replied. 'But the trick is, my dear, never to show it. That's what I want to teach you. To swagger, to curse.' He turned, hawked and spat. 'To spit and stand aside for no man.' He grinned down at her. 'Unless he's bigger and stronger than you are, of course!'

Now and again one of these figures would slip out of the house, pluck at Dolius's sleeve and chatter away in a slang Maria Eleanora couldn't understand. She grasped the fustian of her protector's sleeve, noting that while the jacket was of good quality, it was nothing special. Nor did he wear any jewellery – so why did these creatures of the night seem so eager to catch his attention?

'I call them my squirrels,' Dolius answered her unspoken question. 'My little squirrels who perch in doorways and windows, watch the world go by and tell their master.'

'Why do you call yourself Dolius?'

'When I was a lad, not much bigger than a grasshopper, I had a love for schooling. They've great scholars in Ireland, the very best in Drogheda, or used to, until Cromwell's bastards killed them. Anyway, I had a teacher, a Mr Thomas Fogarty. He believed in teaching you the Classics the percussion way.'

'The what?' Maria Eleanora asked.

'The percussion way. He'd beat it into you. However, he was a great story-teller. He'd studied the *Iliad* and the *Odyssey*. You remember Ulysses, don't you? He was King of Ithaca and left his pretty wife Penelope to go and fight the terrible Trojans. Well, whilst he was gone,' Dolius patted her arm, 'Penelope was besieged by suitors – but one man helped her to keep them at bay. His name was Dolius and he was loyal to his King who, after many years' absence, came back to hearth and home.'

'And you are loyal to your King?'

'Oh yes, to Charlie boy. He's my darling. We've had the occasional difference of opinion. Some say I even tried to murder him, but that's a lie. I like playing jokes on him, though.'

'What's your real name?'

Dolius didn't answer until they had reached the end of Shoe Lane. He paused, staring into the mist seeping up from the river, dulling the sound of carriages and carts, turning the passers-by into shapeless wraiths.

'My name? My real name?'

He leaned down and kissed her on the brow. Maria Eleanora did not object. All she could think of was Atkins shivering in that hideous cell; this man was going to help her free him.

'Captain Thomas Blood,' he whispered, 'late of County Meath in Ireland: adventurer, soldier, freebooter, pirate, lover of beautiful women, drinker of the best claret. His Majesty's most loyal servant at your service.'

Maria Eleanora laughed; her companion patted her gloved hand.

'But you must always call me Dolius.' He freed his grip on her. 'Now, where we are going, we don't want to be taken as two molly boys.'

'Which is where?'

'As Virgil said to Dante, follow me!'

They crossed Holborn and entered a maze of alleyways. Dolius moved quickly, pushing people aside, hurrying down one runnel than back up another. Maria Eleanora found it hard to keep up. Darkness was falling and these alleyways were dangerous underfoot, strewn with filth and rubbish. She realised, as she glanced down one side street, that they must be somewhere near Smithfield, the great open expanse where the busy horse-fairs were held which the Queen occasionally attended. Down another alleyway and they stopped beneath a faded sign depicting an angel blowing a trumpet. Underneath was the title *The Golden Angel*. The windows were all shuttered, the heavy oaken door closed. Dolius pointed to the sign.

'Now I understand the meaning of the phrase "Satan can appear as an Angel of Light",' he joked. 'Stay close by me!'

He kicked at the door. A grille high up was pulled back.

'Who's there?' a voice grated.

Maria Eleanora could hear the faint noise of fiddle music; the stench of cooking and tallow grease seeped out.

'Who's there?' the voice repeated irritably.

'Satan and all his Angels!' Dolius swore. 'Will you come on down and open up or I'll kick the door in!'

'Oh sorry, my apologies.'

To the sound of locks being turned and bolts pulled back, the door was finally opened. The passageway within was stone-flagged and ill-lit, its walls covered in posters. The man who'd opened the door now hid behind it. Dolius ignored him and led Maria Eleanora by the elbow down a long passageway. She was surprised because the floor was clean, the plaster on the walls snow-white. Bills and posters were pinned there, including one advertising a monstrous cannibal giant brought from overseas: *To be seen at Mr Cooper's Store House in the Vintry for the price of a shilling.* Someone had written underneath: CANCELLED. THE POOR BUGGER'S DROWNED HIMSELF. Dolius paused before this notice and abruptly walked on. He stopped again and Maria Eleanora looked at him curiously.

'What's the matter?' she asked.

'Just read the poster,' he replied, 'so the watchman can check you.'

Maria Eleanora did so. It proclaimed another monstrosity: *To be seen next door to the Black Raven in West Smithfield during the time of the Fair! Being a living skeleton taken by Venetian galleys from a Turkish vessel! This is a fairy child!*

Maria Eleanora felt her arm being pulled and they walked

on until they reached the door at the far end, which swung open. There she was ushered into a large oaken taproom. Fresh straw lay on the floor, tables and stools stood about; hams hung from the rafters. More pictures and posters hung on the walls, above the huge counter in front of a row of barrels and wine tuns. Maria Eleanora gazed round in astonishment. The room was one of the largest she had ever seen in such a tavern. Everyone had left their tables to crowd round the cockpit at the far end; even the lackeys and scullions had put down their trays. Dolius walked across, muttering to Maria Eleanora to keep her face hidden. The occasional drunk, heads on hands, lay on the floor fast asleep. The crowd around the cockpit were silent. Dolius pushed his way through. The fight was just about to begin.

The two men in the pit opened their sacks and released the red and black fighting cocks. These strutted out like duellists, heads high, little legs taut, bodies quivering with aggression. A great roar greeted their arrival. Men and women were shouting bets, some offering wagers, others taking. The two cocks circled each other then attacked in a flurry of feathers, pecking and clawing, hacking at each other with their spurs. Maria Eleanora stood and watched. The combs of the fighting cocks began to bleed as crop and abdomen were shredded by razor-sharp spurs. At last one cock collapsed of his wounds. A great roar greeted the victor, who was scooped up and placed back in his sack. People now went hunting for their bets. One young man, unable to pay, was bundled into a basket which was winched up to the ceiling. Maria Eleanora stared round in astonishment. The customers could not be categorised or classed. They consisted of ladies of quality, dandies, fops, well-to-do merchants, lords in their silks, ladies in their satins, prostitutes, pedlars and chapmen.

'What is this place?' she whispered.

'A place where you can drink, dine, whore and gamble,' Dolius replied. 'Without the constables fingering your neck. It's the best place to be, my dear.' He led her across the taproom. 'You may think its dangerous, but in a place like this, no one meets your eye. No one is interested, whilst the Golden Angel has more entrances and exits than there are paths to Hell.'

They reached the other end of the room and climbed a wooden staircase built into the side of the tavern. One storey up, they moved off along a dusty wooden passageway. Dolius stopped at a door and rapped twice: this swung open and they entered a small chamber, its windows shuttered. Maria Eleanora was aware of capped candles on tables and ledges; clothing was strewn across a bed. A woman stood there, her face and figure hidden by the shadows. Dolius closed the door and pulled the bolts across.

'Sit down, Maria Eleanora, and let's see your true beauty.'

Maria Eleanora took off her hat and cloak, and let her raven-black hair fall down. At this point, the other woman came out of the shadows. She was fair, with her golden hair gathered up at the back; she had a beautifully formed face with large, expressive blue eyes and full, red lips. She wore no jewellery and her gown was like that of a Puritan's, deep black with a white, lace collar, bands of the same colour round the cuffs.

'Maria Eleanora, may I introduce Cecily Bannister.'

The woman studied Maria Eleanora carefully as if trying to memorise every detail. She would have looked vulnerable except for the hardness in her eyes and the set to her lips. When she thrust out her hand, Maria Eleanora grasped it self-consciously.

'So, you are the Portuguese.' Cecily looked Maria Eleanora up and down, from head to toe. 'Do you often dress like a man?'

Maria Eleanora bit back her reply. The other woman's solemn face suddenly broke into a fetching smile.

'I've done it myself,' she confided, 'but I can never imitate a man's swagger, not like Captain Thomas here.'

'Ladies, ladies.' Dolius fussed round them. Shabby chairs were pushed up to the table. 'They are the best we have,' he said apologetically.

He gestured for them to sit close together whilst he sat on the bed and gazed at them.

'Yes, a pretty pair.'

Cecily began to laugh.

'Some wine?' he asked.

Dolius didn't wait for an answer but got up, went across and brought back a jug and three cups. Maria Eleanora noticed how the candles were placed to provide light but, at the same time, keep certain parts of the room in the shadows.

'I like this place,' she told him.

He filled each cup to the brim, then brought up a stool, sat opposite them and lifted his goblet in a toast.

'Ladies, to the hunt!'

Maria Eleanora tasted the wine.

'It's good, isn't it?' Dolius smacked his lips. 'The best claret brought in by smugglers. It tastes even better when it's stolen. Now, don't worry, this room is secure. The door is of stout wood, the bolts are good and there's a staircase outside the window: that's the way you'll leave, Maria Eleanora.'

Dolius sipped at his wine, staring at them both from over the cup.

'What's the matter?' Cecily nudged Maria Eleanora with her elbow. 'Thomas, you are staring at us as if we are two turtle doves!'

'You do look a pretty pair,' Dolius repeated. 'But now, ladies, we have business and it's urgent.'

Dropping all the bonhomie, with a brittle tone to his voice, he introduced each of them to the role they were to play. He quickly described Atkins's capture, Shaftesbury's politics and gave a pithy summary of Cecily's role and the dangers posed by 'that professional liar and killer, the so-called Captain William Bedloe'. Maria Eleanora drank her wine. After the sword fight in the street and Dolius's frenetic hurrying her through the streets to this mysterious place, she felt rather sleepy, but the more she listened, the more reassured she became. She was convinced of two things: Dolius's loyalty to the King, and the hatred of the woman beside her for a man who was prepared to destroy her beloved Samuel.

'What are we to do?' she broke in. 'Attack Newgate? Free Samuel?'

'No.' Dolius ran his finger round the rim of the goblet. 'We are going to become as cunning as Shaftesbury and his gang. So, let's start with Godfrey. According to the King,' he paused, 'or rather according to his agents, Godfrey was first approached by Titus Oates, another perjurer, with revelations of an intended plot. After that, Godfrey disappeared.' Dolius shook his head. 'Now, no doubt Godfrey was killed on Shaftesbury's orders. I wager Bedloe had a hand in it. The magistrate's corpse was dumped on Primrose Hill and Bedloe fled to Bristol. Once the hue and cry had been raised, Bedloe came swaggering back and we know why. He wants Atkins to break, to implicate our good friend Mr Pepys and so attack the King's brother James, Duke of York.' Dolius smiled from under his eyebrows at Maria Eleanora. 'I have learnt a lot about your beloved. He likes his claret and a pretty face, and he's a better man for that. He is also loyal and stubborn. He won't lie. So, Mistress Cecily, what do you think our Shaftesbury will do now?'

'He'll cast about,' she replied sharply.

'Good lass.' Dolius smiled. 'He'll cast about and look for someone else.'

'What do you mean?' Maria Eleanora demanded.

Dolius tapped his fingers against the cup.

'Well, the Duke of York and Mr Pepys are relatively safe for the moment. They were at Newmarket when Godfrey disappeared and was murdered. Shaftesbury, like the fox he is, will try another entrance to the hen coop. It won't be the Duke of York's Palace he'll attack, it will be Somerset Place.'

Maria Eleanora caught her breath.

'Oh yes,' Dolius agreed. 'If they can't get at the King's brother they'll try and implicate the King's wife, his Catholic Queen. Atkins is the clasp which will link Somerset Place to the Duke of York. Your Samuel is much smitten with you, Maria Eleanora. Did you know that he was often seen outside the Queen's lodgings, gazing soulfully at the entrance or up at the windows?'

Maria Eleanora felt a lump in her throat; tears stung her eyes.

'There, there, lass!' Dolius stretched across and stroked the back of her hand. 'He really does love you. Now, Shaftesbury and his Green Ribboners know about Samuel's interest in Somerset Place, but they don't know why. They also know that your Samuel met someone muffled and disguised in different places around the city. This intelligence came to them rather late which is why they attacked you some time ago and why "Weasel Eyes" wanted to take you alive.'

'But they failed,' Cecily added softly.

'Yes, they failed. Well, well, well!' Dolius got up and filled his goblet. 'Shaftesbury is in a quandary now,' he continued. 'He recognises that Atkins is as stubborn as a mule, so he's concerned. You see, if I understand His Majesty correctly, and His Majesty,' he grinned at Cecily, 'does have spies amongst the Green Ribboners, Samuel Atkins may not know where he was that weekend – but neither does Shaftesbury. Our ignoble Earl is frightened that Bedloe may go into court, swear an oath that he saw your beloved in Somerset Place and that Samuel was involved in Godfrey's murder, only to have built his house on sand. What if young Master Atkins can suddenly produce convincing evidence, corroborating witnesses that he was elsewhere?' He held his hand up, emphasising the points with his fingers. 'Your Samuel will walk free and Bedloe will be seen for what he is, a liar and a perjurer.'

'But Samuel can't remember where he was, especially on that Monday!'

'God help the poor ninny,' Blood declared. 'He'd better remember, for all our sakes.'

'But Shaftesbury and Bedloe won't wait, will they?' Cecily demanded.

'Correct, my pretty one. They have now kicked the door open at Somerset Place. They said Godfrey was taken there and murdered. It would be marvellous if they could tie Atkins to the murder, but if that's not good enough, others must be involved.'

Maria Eleanora felt the warmth drain away. Dolius was watching her curiously.

'These men have a hunger for blood,' he said softly. 'What you don't know, Mistress . . .'

'I know what Samuel told me in Newgate,' she interrupted. 'But I didn't know it had gone this far.'

'Oh, it's gone further than that. Earlier this evening warrants were issued for the arrest of other suspects.'

'For what reason?' She felt a stab of fear.

'Oh, Shaftesbury's divided the plot between the doers and the plotters; the latter are now being swept up into the net.'

'And?' Maria Eleanora demanded.

'They'll go searching for the other so-called murderers.'

'Who?' Maria Eleanora's throat felt dry.

'Anyone associated with Somerset Place.'

Maria Eleanora's hands went to her face, and Cecily put an arm round her shoulder to comfort her. Maria Eleanora sensed the unnamed fears and terrors growing around her. She had friends like Green and Berry at Somerset Place.

'Shaftesbury is too cunning,' Dolius whispered, 'to strike directly at the Queen, just like he's too wily to lunge straight for James, Duke of York, or even Pepys. Instead he turns his attack on Atkins.'

'Could he attack me?' Maria Eleanora asked.

'I doubt it very much. You are Portuguese; the worst he could demand is your removal from the kingdom.' He smiled at the look on Maria Eleanora's face. 'Though that would be hell enough for you, it seems. Secondly, although you disguised yourself as a man, Shaftesbury must be careful not to lose public opinion. It doesn't do to bully a woman, at least in public. Oh no, it will be someone else.'

'I have friends, Green and Berry, they are minor officials.'

'Yes, people like that. I've heard other whispers. You know Miles Prance?'

'The silversmith? He does some work in the Queen's Chapel.'

'Now Prance is a dyed-in-the-wool papist. He's married, has a wife and family in Covent Garden. Prance is a mysterious character, a convert to Catholicism. He likes intrigue and so makes himself vulnerable. He also has access to Somerset Place; being a silversmith, he has every right to go in there.'

'How do you know all this?' Maria Eleanora broke in.

She studied Dolius's clever face. Was this man totally trustworthy? Or did he play on both sides of the fence? What was that English phrase – 'run with the hare and hunt with the hounds'?

'Don't doubt me, dear lass,' Dolius smiled slyly out of the corner of his eyes. 'Young Cecily has also suspected the same. Oh yes, I can be a turncoat but not with the King. No, to answer your question bluntly: when Shaftesbury's men go hunting, I go hunting *them* – that's how I found you this afternoon. They are also keeping Prance's shop under close scrutiny. They're rather mystified,' he grinned to himself, 'about where Miles goes at night.'

'Where *does* he go?'

Dolius tapped the side of his nose. Cecily withdrew her arm from around Maria Eleanora's shoulder.

'It's a little surprise we have arranged,' she whispered in the other young woman's ear. 'Miles Prance is not what he claims to be.'

'Now!' Dolius rapped the table-top with the edge of his hands. 'We must find out where Samuel Atkins was, that fateful weekend. We must also take care of Miles Prance or, indeed, anyone else who is taken up and clapped into Newgate. If I can follow Shaftesbury's cruel mind, he won't have Atkins committed for trial until he's resolved this problem of our young clerk's whereabouts. He's also got to try and find someone who will bear testimony against him.'

'You mean Miles Prance?'

'Prance is a coward,' Dolius mused. 'Oh, he'll be stubborn for a while but, once he's spent a night in Little Susie, his tongue will clack like a beggar's bell.'

Dolius paused suddenly, then got to his feet, went into the darkness and returned with two horse muskets primed and ready. Cecily, too, was tense.

'What's the matter?' Maria Eleanora breathed.

Blood lifted a hand and listened.

'A tavern is like a piece of music, Maria Eleanora; it has a certain tempo, a flow of sound. But, never mind, we must get to Prance and threaten him.' He shrugged. 'To do that we all need to work in unison. Now,' he gestured with his hand. 'Get closer, both of you.'

Cecily giggled. Maria Eleanora felt slightly embarrassed as she moved the chair closer.

'Put your arm round her,' Dolius ordered.

Maria Eleanora blushed slightly but obeyed. She was rather surprised when Cecily laid her head gently on her shoulder. She was aware of the young woman's golden hair and the fragrance from her clothes. In times less dangerous Maria Eleanora would have envied Cecily's colouring, the ivory paleness of her skin.

'Clasp her close!' Dolius said impatiently.

Maria Eleanora did so.

'Now, *that's* what you are going to be,' Dolius declared. 'A young Cavalier and his paramour.'

Cecily burst out laughing and drew away. Dolius sat, head to one side.

'What a very pretty picture. It fair sharpens the appetite.' Then the smile faded from his face. 'That's what you are going to have to do,' he told them, deadly serious now. 'It will confuse the enemy, who will be looking for one person, not two. It will also heighten your disguise, Maria Eleanora.'

'Is it necessary?' she demanded.

'At times, yes, it will be. Not tonight but . . .' he squinted up at the ceiling '. . . perhaps tomorrow. We'll meet here at about six o'clock and I'll prove to you, Maria Eleanora, that you are not the only person in London who travels in disguise.'

'And Samuel's whereabouts when Godfrey was mur-dered?'

'That is for your young man to tell us. If he doesn't . . .' Dolius shrugged. 'Then we'll have to discover it for ourselves.'

'Do you love him?'

Maria Eleanora turned. She was surprised at the passion in Cecily's voice. She noticed how the faint bloom had returned to her cheeks, her eyes were no longer so hard but searching, as if she was trying to discover the truth.

'Do you really love him?'

'If I cannot live with him,' Maria Eleanora replied slowly, 'then my life will never be full. There will always be something missing. A part of my soul which will wither, a dulling of the wit, a frost in the heart.'

'Are you a poet?' Cecily teased, leaning closer. 'Will you write poetry for me, your newfound paramour?' she added coquettishly.

'And what do you live for, Cecily Bannister?' Maria Eleanora asked.

Cecily drew away. She glanced across at Dolius who was watching them intently.

'You live and love,' Cecily whispered. 'That is the best many of us do. Perhaps one day I can do that again. Once in my life I didn't just live and love but lived *for* love. Bedloe took my love from me. I will not rest until he has paid the forfeit, until justice has been carried out.' She glanced down at the table, running her finger through a spot of wine. 'Once I have done that,' she continued as if talking to herself, 'once it is finished, perhaps I can live again.'

'And you, Master Dolius?' Maria Eleanora prompted, eager to find out as much as she could about her new companions.

'I am not so fortunate.' Dolius's voice had lost its harshness, the Irish brogue now strong. 'I did have a love but now she has gone.'

171

'Dead?' Maria Eleanora asked.

'No, she betrayed me. No, that's not right.' He lifted a hand. 'I must fight against self-pity. If her heart had been as fair as her face, then she would have been fairer still and I would have called her the fairest of them all.' He clapped his hands softly. 'There we have it, poets all! So . . .' He scraped back the stool then lunged forward and grasped the pistols.

'What?' Maria Eleanora exclaimed.

'Hush!'

Dolius held up one of the pistols and sat listening. Cecily had crept to the door.

'We have visitors, haven't we?' Dolius murmured. 'Listen, Maria Eleanora. Notice how quiet the alleyway's become?'

Maria Eleanora hadn't noticed, but now she realised that all the clatter from the gallery outside had died. It lay silent, then she heard it: the creak of a floorboard, the scuff of a boot.

'Arm yourselves.'

Dolius handed one of the pistols to Cecily and sprang to his feet, strapping on swordbelt, picking up cloak and hat. He grabbed two saddle bags and began to fill them with different possessions. Now and again he would stop and listen intently.

'Some are on the stairs,' he said quietly. 'There must be others outside.'

He went over and doused the candles; his voice sounded hollow in the darkness.

'I have gathered all my possessions, the little I have.'

Maria Eleanora got to her feet. She felt Dolius touch her arm as he handed over her swordbelt.

'Put it on,' he whispered. 'They must have followed us here. Ah well,' he mocked. 'It's time we moved house.'

'What shall we do?' Cecily demanded.

'If I know these bully-boys, they'll come through the

172

window and force us back into the gallery where the others are waiting. So, which way do we go?'

Maria Eleanora stood, stomach tingling with excitement. She breathed in deeply, trying to control her own fear and panic. Dolius was correct. She could feel the danger. They were trapped, both outside the house and in the alleyway beyond.

'Right, Cecily my darling, what I am going to do is this,' Dolius announced. 'First, give me the pistol.'

Cecily handed it over.

'If we go out into the gallery, they might trap us. So, keep that door bolted and locked. We are going to go through the window.'

Maria Eleanora peered nervously at the chink of light between the shutters.

'It's quite large,' Dolius told her. 'More like a small door. The stairs are just below it. Let's go that way.'

Cecily made sure the bolts on the top and bottom of the door were pulled across, then Dolius noiselessly lifted the bar of the shutter; at which the cold night air gushed in. Wearing his hat and heavy military cloak, and balancing both pistols, Dolius then climbed carefully through the window. Maria Eleanora heard the stairs outside creak. She gestured Cecily forward.

'You'd best go next.'

'No,' the woman replied. 'Draw your sword. You go first. Dolius will need all the help he can get.'

Maria Eleanora obeyed. Climbing over the windowsill, she could just make out the narrow wooden staircase built into the back of the tavern. Lantern horns, hung on hooks further down the alleyway, provided a little light but to her left it was pitch dark. Maria Eleanora controlled her fear. She could see or hear nothing, but she sensed the lurking danger.

'Come on!' Dolius hissed. 'If we separate, go to the

Morning Star in Catte Street near the old Guildhall. It's owned by friends, members of our community.'

'Garrulous as ever,' Cecily whispered behind Maria Eleanora, who now lowered herself onto the steps. She turned and helped Cecily climb over. They reached the bottom. Dolius was already peering into the darkness.

'Move backwards!' he urged.

Even as they obeyed, figures seemed to step out of the night, hats pulled low, vizards covering their faces, swords and daggers out. They padded softly forward like hunting cats.

'What now, my boys?' Dolius called out cheerfully. 'You have mistaken us, surely?'

As their assailants approached, Maria Eleanora heard shouting and banging from above as more attackers tried to break through the chamber door. Dolius didn't wait any longer. He lifted both pistols, and fired. A deafening flash echoed through the alleyway. One musket misfired but the ball from the other took the leading assailant full in the face. He fell back screaming. Dolius threw his pistol at the others and drew both sword and dagger.

'Take Cecily,' he growled out to Maria Eleanora. 'Get her away! You know where to?'

He then lunged forward, sword and dagger flickering out. The night was shattered by the clash of steel. Maria Eleanora paused but Dolius was a fighting man. In this first attack he disabled one assailant.

'Go!' he shouted over his shoulder.

Maria Eleanora didn't wait a second time. Grasping her sword in one hand and Cecily's arm in the other, she hurried down the alleyway. They passed the first lantern horn and had almost reached the second when three figures came out of an entrance. Maria Eleanora caught the glint of rapier and dagger. She thrust Cecily behind her.

'Well, well!' a voice drawled.

Maria Eleanora drew away. Despite the darkness she realised that 'Weasel Eyes' had returned.

'Won't you and your pretty friend come quietly?'

All of a sudden, Maria Eleanora's patience broke. Resentment, anger, fear – the sheer tragedy of Atkins's condition – it all boiled over. All she wanted to do was help the man she loved and this ruffian, who cared for nothing, was foolishly trying to stop her. Maria Eleanora forgot her tiredness. She was aware of Cecily behind her and the three assailants before her. The alleyway rang with the clash of steel from Dolius's struggles at the far end. This time there would be no help. Determined to fight both for her life and that of her beloved, Maria Eleanora lunged forward. The fury of the attack surprised her assailants; they had expected a spirited defence but were unprepared for this fierce cavalier. Maria Eleanora recalled the words of her Lisbon duelling master: 'A good swordsman fights to kill,' he had always told her. 'He no longer cares for himself but for one thing and one thing only – the total defeat of his opponent.'

Remembering this, Maria Eleanora used every parry, feint, lunging attack and sharp defence she had been taught. All the tricks of the duelling school came into play. She wasn't even aware of her success except that one opponent withdrew from the fight, clawing at a savage wound in his chest. She pressed her attack further. 'Weasel Eyes' she kept isolated, defending his parries with her dagger whilst she lunged at the man on her right. He now panicked, lost control and exposed his belly to a death-bearing lunge which sent him crashing to the cobbles. 'Weasel Eyes' drew off once again. He was now nothing more than a black shape, but Maria Eleanora danced forward. If the man had considered flight, then it was too late.

'I am going to kill you,' Maria Eleanora gloated through the dark. 'Because you deserve to die!'

'Weasel Eyes' fought back, but as an average swordsman he had never met anything like this and, all on his own, didn't stand a chance. Maria Eleanora drove him further up the alleyway. She pretended to slip and he came running forward straight into the trap, sword pulled back for a killing thrust, a hideous mistake. He had exposed his guard. Maria Eleanora drove his sword back with her own and, jabbing forward, aimed the stiletto deep and hard under his ribs. She let go. He staggered back, dropping his sword, clutching at the wound, the blood gurgling in his throat. Then he collapsed to his knees, gave a sigh and fell to one side.

Maria Eleanora leaned over him, pulled out her dagger and wiped it on his cloak. Her body was laced in sweat and the night air was chilling; her legs felt weak, and were trembling.

Cecily came up beside her, grasping her by the arm.

'The other two are dead,' she murmured. 'Maria Eleanora, are you well?'

'Never call me that! Not in public. And Dolius?'

'He's gone.'

'Where?'

'He finished off his assailant,' Cecily explained, hurriedly, 'and went back up the staircase. These three must have been waiting for us in the gallery outside. They realised we'd escaped and came down to help their comrades. Should we go back?'

Maria Eleanora shook her head.

'Dolius may have forgotten something. He can take care of himself. What is important is that we must not be seen, not like this.'

She pushed Cecily ahead of her to the mouth of the alleyway. Here they paused. Cecily fastened her cloak more tightly, drawing the hood up like a cowl round her face. Maria Eleanora sheathed her weapons, rearranged her cloak and pulled down the hat which, she quietly thanked God, the fight had not displaced. Cecily reached up and touched the sweat on her friend's face with the back of her gloved hand.

'You must be careful,' she soothed. 'A chill on a night like this could bring more than the rheums. You don't want the coughing sickness.'

'I will not be sick,' Maria Eleanora replied through gritted teeth. 'I cannot afford to be ill as long as Samuel Atkins remains in Newgate. It will be warm enough at the Morning Star.'

They left Smithfield, going down through Aldersgate into St Martin's Lane, past Goldsmith's Hall. It was a dark, cold night. The stalls had now been cleared, the shops all shuttered. Only beggars and the occasional chapman wandered the streets. They passed a party of constables but one glance at Maria Eleanora's attire and they left such quality alone. Every so often Cecily would grasp Maria Eleanora's arm, and they would pause and look back.

'We are not being followed,' Cecily reassured her. 'And it's time we acted the part.'

They made their way down the alleyway which led across Wood Lane and into Catte Street. The Morning Star was halfway down: a well-lit tavern, with savoury smells wafting out onto the street from its kitchen. The ale-wife stood just within the doorway, cheery-faced, breasts bulging out of her bodice.

'Come on in, sir.' She gestured at Maria Eleanora. 'And bring your ladyfriend with you.'

'Has anyone been here?' Cecily asked.

'What do you mean, dearie?'

Cecily dug into the pocket of her cloak, took out a piece of string and tied a knot in it.

'Which number?' she asked.

'Just the one,' Cecily replied.

'He has not returned.'

'Then we'll wait a while.'

Cecily plucked at Maria Eleanora's sleeve, led her past the tavern door and further down the street.

'Dolius has not yet arrived,' she whispered. 'I don't think we should go in. At least, not for a while.'

'I must go,' Maria Eleanora said anxiously. 'I have been from my duties for some time. Her Majesty insists that I join her late in the evening.'

Cecily grasped her hands and held them fast. She peered into Maria Eleanora's face.

'I never knew,' she whispered. 'I thought only I could love as passionately as that.' She abruptly kissed Maria Eleanora on each cheek and let go of her hand. 'Farewell.' And she walked back towards the tavern even as a link boy raced down Catte Street, lantern in one hand, broadsheet in the other.

'More traitors have been taken!' he yelled. 'The instigators of the Plot have been arrested!'

His yells brought customers out of the tavern. Cecily turned, lifted her hand slightly and joined the throng. Maria Eleanora watched her go then disappeared into the night.

Chapter Nine

Miles Prance, silversmith, slipped out of the doorway of his shop in Princes Street, Covent Garden. He wore his shabbiest cloak, and scuffed riding boots. He carried a sword thrust into the belt round his slim waist, whilst a battered hat kept his fair wig in place. Miles had a pale, rather austere face, with close-set eyes and a sharp, pointed nose; his front teeth protruded slightly. He stroked his face thoughtfully; it was smooth as a piece of satin. For a while he simply leaned against the doorpost of his shop, watching the world go by. Inside, his wife and maid were seeing to the children. From where he stood, Miles could hear his offspring's screams and shouts. He felt slightly guilty yet, tonight, he had to get out of the house. He had been so busy and every man needed to relax, indulge himself for a while.

Miles stared up and down the street; there was the occasional passerby but nothing untoward. He was pleased that a mist was curling in for, on a night like this, Prance became a creature of the dark. He had told his wife he was attending a Guild meeting, matters of pressing urgency, so he had the evening to himself. He glanced about once more, seeing nothing but idling lovers. Satisfied that he was alone, Miles hurried down the side of the street, ducking the overhanging signs. Using well-established lanes and runnels, he made his way south. Near Bride Lane, just off Fleet Street, he paused outside a ramshackle tenement, took a key out of his purse, unlocked the door and went in. Prance was there a while, at least half an hour, and when he came out he still wore the same cloak and hat but his shoes were now polished and buckled. Even from where they stood, hiding in the shadows, Maria Eleanora and Cecily could smell his heady fragrance.

'What is he up to?' Maria Eleanora whispered.

'Wait awhile and see!'

They followed him down Bride Lane, as they had through Covent Garden. Maria Eleanora allowed Cecily to guide her, one arm round her waist, broad-brimmed hat pulled down; to all intents and purposes they looked like a young buck and his paramour out for a night's pleasure.

In truth Maria Eleanora felt tired, heavy-eyed. She had returned to Somerset Place the previous evening to discover the Queen's household in uproar over the arrests and the Queen herself in a near state of panic. So engrossed was she in calming Catherine's nerves, and discussing the tidbits of gossip, that Maria Eleanora had little time to reflect on what had happened to her in the company of Dolius and this beautiful young woman who walked, head resting against her shoulder, guiding her expertly whilst keeping Prance in full view.

'Are you tired?' Cecily asked.

'If my legs were chalk they'd crumble,' Maria Eleanora yawned. 'I slept late but, every time I walk through Somerset Place, I remember Dolius's warning.'

'They are going to cast their net wide.'

They have already, Maria Eleanora reflected. In the late afternoon she had been given time to herself just before Dolius's message arrived – delivered, she suspected, by Josiah-Praise-the-Lord Stanker. Green the porter had brought it up: all it gave was the time and place. Maria Eleanora had spent the waiting hours fretting. She felt sorry for anyone who worked in Somerset Place but her beloved Samuel was taken up, confined in that hideous gaol, already marked down for death. On one occasion, for a few minutes, Maria Eleanora had begun to panic: a soul-chilling, heart-rending wave of anger and terror about what might happen. She found that the only way she could compose herself was to take down a sheet of vellum, and write to Samuel, as if they were both in a different place, deeply in love with no real divide between them. She found that when she gave expression to her heart the panic ceased, the words soothed her soul.

Maria Eleanora quietly thanked God that the Queen retired early whilst the rest of her household went into the large drawing rooms or kitchens to discuss the news. Taking advantage of the lull, Maria Eleanora had disguised herself again, crept out of her chamber down the secret passageway Green had shown her and out through the Water Gate. Cecily had been waiting on the corner of the alleyway near the Morning Star tavern and now they were in pursuit of Prance.

Maria Eleanora concentrated her mind. She believed Dolius knew more than he had revealed. He and his royal master seemed to be involved in some macabre game of chess, in which they tried to anticipate Shaftesbury's next move. Maria Eleanora truly believed the man they were now following through these foul winding streets was a real threat to her beloved Samuel. She wondered what Prance intended. He had now hired two link boys and, as they entered the warren of alleyways around Whitefriars, walked more confidently, letting his cloak slip, swinging the elegant walking-cane like a true gentleman of the city.

'Does he have a lover?' she murmured in Cecily's ear.

The other young woman squeezed her waist. 'Always

remember,' she murmured, 'that everyone has secrets. You have secrets, I have secrets and so does Prance.'

They passed the watch, led by lantern-horned jacks, the bailiffs who carried the lights to search out miscreants and footpads. They didn't trouble Prance nor Maria Eleanora and Cecily as they crossed the dirty wasteland, past the crumbling remains of the old Carmelite monastery. When Prance turned down an alleyway and disappeared into the light-filled doorway of the Sigh of Mourning tavern, Cecily and Maria Eleanora followed suit.

'Is Dolius here?' Maria Eleanora breathed.

'He may be but he won't show his hand.'

Inside, the taproom was packed, well-lit, thick with the fug of tobacco. Cecily forced Maria Eleanora to stop.

'Act the part,' she murmured. 'Keep Prance in view.'

'What do I have to do?'

Cecily gazed up, eyes bright with mischief.

'Flirt with him. Do whatever you have to do. Play along.' She patted her own bodice. 'You are well formed, Maria Eleanora, but fortunately, small-breasted. Keep the folds of your cloak hanging down,' she added cheekily, and repressed a laugh, tugging Maria Eleanora into a shadow-filled corner. 'Don't let him touch you. Speak as little as possible.'

'What happens if Prance doesn't take a fancy to me?'

'Oh, I think he will.'

'Why here?'

Cecily was now biting her lip. 'For the love of life, Maria Eleanora, open your eyes! By the way, Prance is now wearing a black wig. He's over in the far corner. Go on – just act the fop!'

And then she was gone back out of the doorway.

Maria Eleanora sighed and gazed around. Maids bustled about with tankards, trays, cups of canary and sack. She abruptly realised how the Sigh of Mourning differed from other inns. Most of the customers were young men dressed very foppishly, bunches of lace at throat and wrist, faces heavily painted. Some talked in a mock falsetto as they ogled and smiled at each other. Maria Eleanora realised why Cecily had left her. She had picked up enough London cant to recognise a molly house, the meeting place for homosexuals. Similar establishments could be found in Lisbon, talked about in hushed whispers but tolerated by both Church and State, probably because both Church and State were well represented here. Such men were allowed their private licence on two conditions: they kept it private and were never caught.

'Samuel Atkins,' Maria Eleanora whispered, 'if we ever come through this to love and laugh, don't ever say I never cared!'

Summoning up her courage, one hand on her sword hilt, the other hanging elegantly by her side, Maria Eleanora pushed her way through the throng, walking with that arrogance, that certainty so characteristic of the court bully-boy, a man who didn't give a damn about anything under Heaven.

Most of the customers sat round tables talking, gambling, playing cards or Hazard. Others moved from table to table. They would stand, leaning hand on shoulder, head bowed, whispering to this person or that. Maria Eleanora noticed how the taproom had at least three entrances whilst a staircase at either end was thronged with people busy going up and down: both were guarded by burly sentries armed with sword and club. Different couples would go up, slipping a coin into the outstretched hands of these Guardians of the stairs. Occasionally some man would catch her eye and wink. One old roué, dressed flamboyantly in the French style, blew her a kiss.

When Maria Eleanora reached the far corner, Prance was sitting by himself, leaning back against the wall, staring out across the taproom. She took a table nearby and ordered a cup of wine. Thankfully, most of the men kept their hats on and so did she. To all appearances she was a young man out on a night's carousing, ready for whatever else might happen. She did not look directly at Prance but glanced casually around, cradling her wine cup. The swordbelt became uncomfortable so Maria Eleanora stood up and carefully removed it; as she did so, she looked directly across at Prance. The silversmith had transformed himself. He was now dressed in a white shirt and fashionable coat. A heavy, ornate black wig cascaded down to his shoulders, his face wore make-up, his lips were heavily rouged; a beauty spot was placed strategically under his left eye. .

Maria Eleanora wondered if Dolius would make an appearance. Was he the old man over there pretending to be asleep, hat pulled over his eyes? Or the gentleman in the middle of the room wearing the bright red periwig? Or was he even one of the Guardians on the stairs? She sipped at her wine, feeling apprehensive not so much at the company she was keeping but more about what might happen next.

And yet Maria Eleanora had been in more turbulent taverns, where knives and swords were drawn at the wrong cast of a die, an insult hurled, the allegation of cheating or flirting with some doxy. The customers of the Sigh of Mourning were more civilised, as if eager to keep well away from the eye of the law. Maria Eleanora closely studied its different customs and mannerisms: there was no shouting or shoving, pushing or raucous behaviour. Now and again a man would come up and gesture at the empty stool beside her. Maria Eleanora, imitating what she had seen, simply shook her head and the man would walk away.

'Are you here by yourself?'

Maria Eleanora looked up. Prance was staring across at her.

'I've been watching you for some time. Would you like to join me?'

Maria Eleanora picked up her cup and took the proffered chair. She turned slightly as if she wished to speak to Prance over her shoulder. The silversmith had drunk his wine rather fast, and now his face was very flushed under its white paint.

'Who are you?' Prance lisped. 'I've never seen you before.'

'I've just come into the city,' Maria Eleanora answered shyly, keeping her voice just above a whisper. 'I'm here on business for my father.'

'Who is?'

Maria Eleanora smiled. One thing she had learnt, listening to the hushed conversations around her, was that the customers of the Sigh of Mourning gave as few details about themselves as possible.

'My name's Charles,' she answered quickly. 'I am my father's son and I look for a quiet night, some wine.'

Prance's hand stole across the table and brushed hers.

'And some company?'

'If the company is suitable.'

She let Prance's hand rest on hers. In any other circumstances Maria Eleanora would have thrown her head back and laughed. She loved the theatre and here was a scene the most outrageous playwright could not begin to imagine: a young woman pretending to be a young man, in turn pretending to be a homosexual. She smiled quietly at the irony: even in the greatest lies some truth could be found. Encouraged by her smile, Prance's grip tightened. She swiftly withdrew her hand.

'I am sorry,' he flustered. 'I don't mean to give offence – Charles.'

'None taken,' Maria Eleanora answered languidly.

'Are you frightened?' Prance leaned across the table. 'If I were you I would not be frightened. You are very handsome, my dear boy, very elegant. I noticed the others watching you.'

Maria Eleanora smiled demurely. She desperately wondered how long this would continue. How long could she sustain this act – and what would happen if something went wrong? What if her disguise was seen through? She looked nervously across the taproom, then decided there would be no trouble here, certainly not from the customers. They seemed to tolerate and show no animosity to the maids and slatterns who served them. However, what if Shaftesbury's Green Ribbon boys were present, desperately searching for Dolius and his mysterious companions who had slain so many members of their company?

'Are you waiting for someone?' Prance asked. 'Do you often come to such a place?'

Maria Eleanora caught the alarm in Prance's voice.

'I have been to similar establishments in Oxford,' she whispered over her shoulder, 'but this is my first time here.' She turned up the brim of her hat. 'I'm glad you invited me over.'

Prance relaxed and dabbed at a bead of sweat coursing down his cheek.

'Would you like some wine?' he asked hoarsely.

'I would love to share some with you,' Maria Eleanora replied flirtatiously.

Prance got to his feet, gesturing at a slattern.

'The best Bordeaux!' he ordered shrilly.

The wine was served. Prance and Maria Eleanora toasted each other.

'What's your name?' Maria Eleanora asked.

Prance opened his mouth then giggled.

'My name? Why, you can call me Johnathan – yes, Johnathan will do nicely. Perhaps . . .' he leaned over and plucked at a piece of dirt on Maria Eleanora's cloak, 'perhaps as the evening draws on we can be more honest with each other?'

'You mean reveal our innermost hearts?'

Prance swallowed hard and dabbed at his lips with a lace kerchief.

'Are you a swordsman?' he asked, pointing to the belt Maria Eleanora had placed on the ground beside her.

'I can defend myself,' she replied tersely.

'But not now, surely? You are in the company of a friend.'

'I am,' Maria Eleanora agreed, smiling with her eyes. 'In the company of someone who, I hope, may be more than a friend.'

Prance had risen to the bait. He was trapped but what next? Maria Eleanora was determined not to remove her hat or gloves.

'What business are you in?' she asked sweetly.

'Precious metals,' Prance told her, his eyes all hungry. 'You are olive-skinned,' he continued in a rush. 'You seem shy – have you a slight accent to your voice?'

'My mother was Portuguese,' Maria Eleanora revealed. 'My father a wine merchant from Bristol.'

'So, you are a papist?' Prance asked in a hushed whisper.

'Master Johnathan, in here, I am nothing but your companion.'

For a while they feinted and parried; Prance asking questions, Maria Eleanora answering as evasively as she could. She noticed the silversmith drank quickly; as he did so, he became less guarded, making slips and errors. Maria Eleanora managed him as she would a pompous courtier. Prance began to boast about his wealth, his connections. Other customers began to stare across at them.

'Why not take off your cloak?' Prance offered suddenly. 'Your hat? Or shall we go somewhere else where it's not so warm and crowded?'

Maria Eleanora raised her eyebrows and Prance nodded towards the stairs. Maria Eleanora decided she had had enough. She rose to her feet and grasped her swordbelt. Prance stared up in alarm.

'Are you leaving?'

'No, no. Perhaps above stairs may be more comfortable!'

Maria Eleanora didn't wait for him but walked towards the stairs. Prance eagerly brushed by her and dropped a coin into the Guardian's hand; the fellow nodded and let them through.

'Go up,' he grated. 'The boy will show you which room.'

When they reached the top of the first flight of stairs, a boy dressed in gaudy colours led them along the ill-lit passageway, where plaster peeled off the walls between the shabby doorways. They stopped at a chamber at the far end. The boy pulled a key out and handed it over with a cheeky smile.

'You have no more than an hour,' he said with a nod and a wink.

Prance unlocked the door and Maria Eleanora stepped inside. The window was shuttered, a large lantern horn glowed on the table. The room contained a few sticks of furniture and a shabby four-poster bed with curtains pulled back to reveal crumpled linen sheets. The blankets lay upon the floor. A huge chamber pot stood in the far corner. The place smelt stale. She walked away as Prance, hands trembling, closed the door and turned the key. Prance leaned against it and stared across the room.

'You are agreeable to this, Charles?'

Maria Eleanora stood examining the bed. If Prance laid a hand on her, she'd draw her rapier and leave. Just then, he came forward rubbing his hands, swaying slightly on his feet.

'We should have brought some wine,' he said nervously.

'You won't be needing that!'

Prance stopped as if struck by a musket ball. Maria Eleanora looked in shock at the bed. Dolius pulled himself up on the far side and dusted himself down. Clamping his plumed hat on his head, he came round and studied Prance from top to toe.

'Well, well, well!' he whistled. 'How are you, Master Miles Prance, silversmith of Prince Street, Covent Garden? Husband to Amelia, father of Robert, David and Mary?'

'I am not! I am not!'

Blood pulled the wig from Prance's head. The silversmith stood unresisting, hands down by his side, as if he was already in the dock being sentenced by a judge for sodomite practices.

'Does Amelia know about your little visits here? Or the garret in Bride Lane?'

'I don't know. Oh, God help me.'

Maria Eleanora felt sorry at the stricken look in the silversmith's eyes. Dolius, dressed like a street brawler in his short cloak, tattered hat and high-heeled boots, picked up a stool and forced the man to sit down, throwing the black wig into his lap. With his shaven head and painted face, Prance looked grotesque and pathetic. Dolius walked around, fingers strumming the hilt of his rapier.

'Oh Lord save us!' Prance whispered. 'What is this, blackmail? Do you want money? I have some silver, a little gold.' He glared across at Maria Eleanora. 'And who are you? Why have you done this? I cannot help myself.'

'Oh, but you can.' Dolius crouched down before him.

'Look at me, Miles. Look at me, don't be frightened. Nothing is going to happen to you. Others may hurt you but we will not. I want to ask you one question and one question only. Do you know a man called Samuel Atkins?'

'I've never heard of him.'

'Very well. I ask you again. Do you know Samuel Atkins?'

'No!' The answer came in a screech.

'As long as you say that, Miles, we mean you no harm, whatever anyone else may ask you to say. Whatever else they may ask you to do, your answer must always be: "I DON'T KNOW SAMUEL ATKINS! I HAVE NEVER MET SAMUEL ATKINS!" Do you know who this person is?' Dolius pointed at Maria Eleanora.

Now he was without his wig, Maria Eleanora vaguely recalled Prance's face; she'd glimpsed him along the galleries at Somerset Place.

'No, I don't know.'

'Good,' Dolius soothed. 'But if you ever say you know Samuel Atkins, we will tell your wife, your family, your friends and the local justice all about this.'

And, patting Prance on the shoulder, Dolius walked over to the door, beckoning at Maria Eleanora to follow.

Dolius now took Maria Eleanora by the hand. They slipped through the door and were making their way back towards the stairs, when they heard Cecily call out from behind them. She was dressed as if she was a serving wench in the tavern; she'd even obtained an apron and napkin with a white mobcap for her hair.

Dolius pointed to a staircase leading to the gallery above. Maria Eleanora noticed he had blackened his teeth and daubed soot on his face and neck.

'Are you so sure that Prance is the right person?' she asked. 'What if . . . ?'

'My guess is good.' Dolius grinned.

'I have noticed something else,' he told both women, and went to the bottom of the second set of stairs. 'Maria Eleanora, come with me. To all intents and purposes,' he grasped her arm, 'I am a rough-looking customer with a pretty boy. Cecily, you are a serving wench who will perhaps join us in our merriment. I want to show you both something.'

Arms linked, with Cecily trailing behind, they slipped up the darkened stairs. Another guard at the top stopped them. Dolius showed him a ring and slipped him a coin.

'The end chamber,' the fellow muttered. 'Take off the picture.'

'Which one?' Dolius asked.

'The Spanish galleon riding at anchor.'

As they went along the poorly lit gallery, Maria Eleanora heard sounds from the rooms they passed: laughter, cries, the clink of glasses.

'The Devil's own playground,' Dolius commented. 'Every practice under the sun takes place here.' He sighed. 'My friend the landlord now and again allows special clients to watch the frolics and pastimes of his customers. I can't believe what I have just seen.'

'What?' Maria Eleanora whispered, trying to keep up with him.

The door of the last chamber was of polished wood with a shiny knob. The narrow passageway at the end led to a further, third staircase. On the walls hung a series of dingy paintings. Dolius carefully took the painting of *A Galleon at Anchor* from its hook and placed it gently on the floor, revealing the peep-holes in the wall. Dolius crouched down and peered through.

'Well, I never!' he chuckled softly to himself. 'Well, I never!'

'What is it?' Maria Eleanora asked.

'Don't exclaim,' Dolius warned quietly. 'Look and see.'

Maria Eleanora crouched down and peered through. At first her eyes were unaccustomed to the bright candlelight which bathed the room in a golden glow. She glimpsed a heavy, oaken four-poster bed on which a young man and woman, naked as the day they were born, lay locked, arms and legs together. Both were very comely. The girl had long red hair whilst the young man was olive-skinned, vigorous in his love-making, his blue silk suit and white lace hat scattered on the floor beside the bed. Maria Eleanora felt guilty watching them.

'To the right, can you see him?' Dolius murmured.

Maria Eleanora looked again and stifled a gasp. A large, overweight man sat in a great oaken chair before the fire, goblet in one hand, the other covering his crotch. He sipped and watched the couple on the bed with growing excitement. He had taken his wig off; it lay on the floor beside him. Maria Eleanora noticed the heavy paunch, the portly thighs, the face with harsh red spots high in the cheeks. A beak-like nose jutted over a cruel mouth, the lower lip was wet with wine. His greedy eyes were like two black holes fixed intently on the bed.

'Who is it?'

'Oh, don't you know?' Dolius teased. 'No less a person than Baron William Scroggs.'

Maria Eleanora withdrew her gaze. Where had she heard that name?

'Sir William Scroggs,' Dolius enlarged. 'Baron, Privy Councillor, former soldier and now Chief Justice of England.'

'What use is he to us?' Maria Eleanora asked.

'When the blood-letting begins,' Dolius replied, pulling her away, 'Scroggs will be in at the killing. He likes nothing better than to prove his loyalty. Oh yes, when the hounds begin to bay, Scroggs will lead the pack. He's already sent a number to their deaths. One day your Samuel Atkins will appear before him.'

'But how can this help us?' she demanded. 'Scroggs's peculiar tastes must be common knowledge?'

'Oh, they are,' Dolius agreed, moving the painting further along the wall. 'Yet even in times like these, the Commons, that bunch of hypocrites, have objected to the scandalous rumours surrounding their Chief Justice's private life.'

'Would you blackmail Scroggs?'

Dolius returned to the eye-let: he put a finger to his lips, covered the hole with one hand and turned.

'Maria Eleanora, go back down to the landing below,' he instructed. 'Stay in the shadows and watch for anything suspicious.'

Cecily touched her arm as she passed.

'You look a handsome young buck,' she teased. 'Be careful no more customers approach you, be they man or wench.'

Maria Eleanora, pulling her hat brim further over her eyes and clutching the hilt of her sword, went down the stairs and across to a dimly lit corner on the first floor. The revelry in the taproom below had increased. She could hear the faint strains of a violin and the lilting call of the lute. People came and went: customers, vizards up over their faces, pot boys, serving wenches. A man lurched out of a chamber much the worse for drink and found it difficult to manage the stairs. He slipped and crashed to the bottom amidst loud curses and shouts. Maria Eleanora felt the sweat break out on her neck: she wondered why Dolius was delaying and what he intended to do about the Chief Justice.

This Sigh of Mourning was a house of peculiar delights, she reflected. Maria Eleanora was about to come out of her hiding-place and go back up the stairs to her friends when a man came striding along the gallery. He wore no hat or vizard. Maria Eleanora was instantly repelled. Never had she seen such an ugly, vicious face. A blood-red wig framed lean, cadaverous features, disfigured by a hideous birthmark. The others behind him were undoubtedly his bully-boys.

'You are sure?' The red-wigged stranger turned, his close-set eyes glittering.

'I am positive,' a voice piped back.

The man stretched out his hand and dragged the small pot boy closer.

'So, he must be around here somewhere. You two go back to the yard and keep those dogs quiet.'

The man walked away, the pot boy and his companion going in the other direction. Maria Eleanora sneaked off up the stairs; as she did so she caught the distant baying of a hound. Dolius and Cecily were coming towards her.

'I heard that baying,' Dolius remarked. 'What is it, Maria Eleanora?'

'A man, his body covered by a cloak but—'

'Never mind that,' Dolius interrupted. 'Did he have a red wig? An ugly, stained face?'

She nodded.

'Hell's teeth!' Dolius muttered. 'Blue-skin the thief-taker! We are not going that way.'

They hastened back, past the room where Scroggs was still enjoying himself and up the stairs leading to the loft. Dolius pushed open the door at the top. He grasped the lantern horn and tinder placed just inside: after some scraping, he lit the thick tallow candle within.

'You seem to know this place,' Maria Eleanora said.

'Like the palm of my hand,' Dolius agreed. 'My good friend the landlord always leaves this here, just in case.'

The loft was mean and draughty, and as black as night. Maria Eleanora heard the scamper of rats and mice. The floorboards were covered in dust. Dolius stepped forward, holding the lantern horn up, and Maria Eleanora glimpsed timbered rafters and a small door in the far wall. Dolius pulled back the bolts, and the door swung open, a gust of cold night air chilled her face. Dolius beckoned the women forward and guided them down the wooden stairs into a narrow, evil-smelling runnel.

'Be careful,' he warned. 'At the bottom, wait for me.'

Teeth chattering with the cold, for she had come without her cloak, Cecily crept down behind Maria Eleanora. At the bottom they paused. They heard the door closing at the top of the stairs. Maria Eleanora peered down the alleyway and glimpsed the glow of light at either end. Dolius came clattering down.

'Right, my beauties,' he declared. 'It's into the dark for us!'

They had hardly gone a few paces when they heard a shout. Maria Eleanora whirled round. There were figures clustered at the end of the alleyway and again that ominous baying of a hound.

'Run!' Dolius ordered.

He pushed the women ahead of him. When they reached the end of the alleyway Maria Eleanora's heart skipped a beat. They were in the very heart of Whitefriars, crumbling houses, narrow passageways lit here and there by a candle or oil-lamp. Shadowy figures crept about. The smell was rank and offensive. It was the stench of poverty. Dolius urged them on. Maria Eleanora was aware of stumbling along pitch-black alleyways, slipping, missing her footing on the rubbish and ordure. Battered signs, their paint peeling, hung dangerously low just above her head. People slithered in and out of doorways to the snarls of a dog or the hiss of an angry cat. An occasional scream or curse echoed from some noisome courtyard. Dolius had now drawn both sword and dagger and these kept people away. Maria Eleanora hastened on, no longer aware of where they were or what was intended. At the end of one alleyway she stopped, clutching at the pain in her side. Here the night mist was thicker, the shifting vapours like long-lost ghosts.

'Can't we stop and fight?' she gasped.

'Not here,' Dolius warned.

Maria Eleanora couldn't make out Cecily's face but she could hear her laboured breathing. Abruptly through the night air like a gallows bell, came the baying of the hounds once more.

'Who is this Blue-skin?' Maria Eleanora panted.

'Thief-taker of London and the biggest thief of them all,' Dolius replied, also catching his breath. 'I don't fear him but I do his dogs. He calls them the Angels of Hell. They are mastiffs, ill-bred curs with a good nose for a scent and teeth which have torn a living man apart.'

'Where to?' Maria Eleanora demanded, trying not to panic.

'Follow me!'

Down another alleyway they hurried, into the shadowy ruins of the old Carmelite monastery. Beggars and night-walkers skulked, ready to pounce, but the sight of naked steel, gleaming in the poor light, drove them away. Dolius led the women down some ruined steps. Fumbling about, he produced a half-burnt sconce torch, and muttering and swearing under his breath, he managed to fire this. The pitch spluttered and burst into flames. As he led them into the darkness, the stench worsened, catching the nose and throat. Cecily gagged and retched as Dolius strode ahead, torch held up, a moving pool of light.

'Welcome to the Great Stink of London!' he called out over his shoulder. 'One of the ancient sewers of the city runs here.'

'And I suppose you know it like the palm of your hand,' Maria Eleanora retorted queasily. She pulled up the hem of her cloak and wiped the sweat from her face.

'Why here? Can we get out?' Cecily asked. 'I am tired of running.'

But Dolius walked on. 'I have unfinished business with Master Blue-skin,' he said grimly, 'and now is as a good time as any to do it. You are safe here, ladies.'

The baying of the hounds seemed to mock his confidence.

'They've found our scent!'

Maria Eleanora slipped. Cecily caught her arm to steady her. They rounded a corner, Dolius warning them to be careful. He lowered the torch and the underground river was revealed, a dark sludge of filthy water, oozing and bubbling, moving slowly into a great dark cesspit. On either side of this ran a ledge about two widths across.

'Keep to the wall,' Dolius said tersely.

Maria Eleanora stared up. The brickwork looked ancient; grey mildewy stone. Now she could hear faint voices, the barking of dogs. They rounded another corner away from the foul-smelling river; the ground, covered in wet filth, stretched into the darkness.

'We are nearly there.'

Maria Eleanora was going to protest when Dolius abruptly stopped and lowered the torch. She caught a glimpse of two broad trestle-tables laid across the passageway like a barricade. Dolius moved quickly. He lit the sconce torches fixed into crevices so that part of the underground passageway flared into light. Then he became busy. Maria Eleanora could see nothing except the tables, taken from some tavern.

'What is this?' she demanded, her endurance at its limit.

When Dolius disappeared into the shadows, she stomped after him. He was crouching down, removing bricks from the wall, humming softly to himself. He pulled free a heavy canvas bag tied at the neck; undid this and brought out a thick horse blanket. Ignoring Maria Eleanora's increasingly angry questions, he unrolled this and smiled up at her gasp of surprise.

'Six good horse pistols,' he said with great satisfaction. 'Well kept, polished and oiled. Can you fire a pistol, Maria Eleanora?'

'My father said I had a steady hand and a sharp eye,' she told him, mollified.

'Good!'

Dolius was already priming them, pouring in the powder from a small pouch, pushing balls down the heavy muzzles.

'Every so often,' he explained, 'I have to flee for my life, and believe me – there's no better feeling than when the hunted becomes the hunter. Blue-skin is a knave and has been since the first day he drew breath. He has the blood of two of my friends on his hands. He poses as a thief-taker but only fingers the collars of those he is tired of. He's amassed wealth by organising gangs, taking a portion of their plunder and then returning the rest to claim the reward. Sometimes, if he feels so inclined, he'll lay information against those whom he organised to perpetrate the robbery in the first place. He's a base-born mercenary who sells his services to the Green Ribboners.'

He paused as the baying drew nearer.

'There's my beauties! Nice and leisurely,' he hissed through the darkness. 'They think they've got us trapped, at the very most, one small pistol between us. Now is the day we meet the Angels of Hell!'

Cecily, who had been crouching down near one of the tables, came across. Her face was laced with sweat, she had lost her mobcap and her blonde hair hung all a-tangle round her face. She looked even more beautiful, like an angel from a painting. Dolius stared up at her.

'Our haste has put a bloom on your cheeks, Mistress. Now, if you can fire one of these?'

'You know I can,' she retorted.

Dolius handed the pistols over.

'Two each,' he said, getting to his feet. 'Six in all. Now, this is what will happen.' He pointed back down the passageway. 'Blue-skin will bring his Angels round here and glimpse us in the darkness. Keep the pistols down, concealed behind the tables. The three dogs will come like lurchers hunting a hare. They'll divide, running fast, bellies low, close to the ground. Only fire on my say. Not both pistols together! Shoot, wait, and if the first ball has not stopped the brute, fire again. Cecily, you will take the one on my right, Maria Eleanora the one on my left. For all our sakes,' he smiled at both of them, '*don't panic*. And don't run. Once you turn your back on these brutes they will have you.'

He led them across to the man-made barricade.

'I have similar traps,' Dolius declared, 'all over the city. So far my luck has not run out. Mistress Fortune favours me. Pray that she doesn't forsake me tonight.'

As they took up positions, Maria Eleanora began to feel calm after their hasty flight. Her sweat was cooling. She was aware of the night chill, the pool of light, the darkness stretching before her: Dolius on her right, Cecily in the shadows beyond. She looked down at the table and noticed the purple candle grease and idly wondered if these came from a church. The sounds of the pursuers drew closer. She heard a man's voice and appreciated how cunning Dolius was.

Blue-skin thought that, like foxes, they had gone to earth: it was simply a matter of digging them out and allowing his hideous hounds to finish the task.

Maria Eleanora calmed herself. She thought of the orchard at her father's house, the cool shade, fruit heavy on the branch, the sweet smell of the summer air. Night was falling, a beautiful dusk, the stars gleaming above her, the refreshing sound of the fountains. One day, she vowed, she would take her Samuel to a place like that. Away from these horrors – the sword and the dagger, the bloody pursuit in the dead of night. She smiled. If her mother or the Queen could see her now . . . She suppressed a giggle. She could only imagine their vapours, the quick screech for the smelling salts, the flutter of handkerchiefs and the rustle of petticoats.

'What are you smiling at?' Dolius asked, his head slightly turned, straining for the sounds of their pursuers. 'Do you enjoy this, Maria Eleanora? I think you do. Take this as a compliment, my lady. You are a better man than many men I have met.'

Cecily heard this and laughed softly.

'Hush now,' Dolius ordered. 'Remember, hide your pistols!'

The sound of boots, muttered curses and the occasional howl of a dog drew closer. Maria Eleanora curbed her panic. Clutching the pistols out of sight, she watched the torch-lit corner. The first shadow emerged: it was as if the very mouth of Hell had gaped. A group of men appeared, lantern horns in their hands. Maria Eleanora glimpsed hats and cloaks, the glint of rapier, sword and dagger, and three great brutes, dark formless shapes straining on leashes. Their muffled gasps and whines echoed through the cavern. The men stopped. One of the dogs howled.

'Good evening, sirs,' Dolius called out. 'What business do you have here in my kingdom?'

'You are under arrest!' a strident voice shouted out.

'On what charge?' Dolius replied.

'House-breaking.'

Dolius bellowed with laughter.

'You refuse to accept our warrant?' the voice enquired. 'Then I have no choice. Release the hounds!'

Chapter Ten

As Maria Eleanora watched the dark, hideous shape loping towards her, for a brief second she recalled her father's hunting dogs. They were friendly, docile animals, but these were different; these were killers. She was aware of the light at the end of the tunnel, of Dolius tense beside her. There was a glitter of eyes, the whiteness of sharp fangs, curled-back lips, a massive head, ears back. An age seemed to pass.

'Aim!' Dolius shouted.

Maria Eleanora brought up one of the pistols. It weighed heavily in her hands. She looked along the sights.

'Now!' Dolius roared.

The cavern exploded as if a man-of-war's cannons had been fired. The centre dog was down. Dolius's ball must have taken it clean in the head. Cecily's was writhing on the ground. Maria Eleanora watched, horrified. She had missed. The musket ball had gone clear. Her hound was close, mad eyes glaring, fangs exposed, its great body arching for the leap. She couldn't move. The smoke from the pistol caught her nose and mouth. She tried to lift the second one but it knocked against the wooden barricade. As the hound gathered itself to spring, she was pushed aside. Dolius snatched her second pistol, aimed and fired. Again the roar, the flash, the burning smoke. The animal didn't leap but crashed into the wooden barricade, knocking it over in its death agonies.

'Maria Eleanora, for the love of God!' Dolius snapped.

He raised his own second pistol. Blue-skin's gang, screaming curses, were running towards them. Dolius aimed the pistol, Cecily likewise. Once more the roar of musket fire thundered through the cavern. Two of the pursuers fell, the rest hastily drew back. The underground passageway had become a scene of carnage; one of the dogs still lay writhing, two of Blue-skin's men were down. Another tried to crawl away, holding his side and yelping for help. His companions lay still in widening pools of blood gushing from their wounds.

'You'll hang for this, you bastard! You whoreson knave!' Blue-skin's voice echoed. 'I'll see you dance at Tyburn!'

'Aye,' Dolius screamed. 'And I'll see you dance with me! You'll wet your breeches before I do mine.' He was hastily priming the musket again. 'Come on, my roaring boys,' he bellowed. 'We have enough powder and ball for all of you. I know you, Blue-skin, though you may not know me. You have no legal warrant. I am sorry for your animals, but self-defence is self-defence.'

He was deliberately talking, gaining time so the musket could be primed. Cecily crouched on the ground beside him, feverishly working with priming rod and powder horn. Suddenly, Maria Eleanora lifted her musket and, without bidding, fired towards the end of the cavern. This proved too much for Blue-skin and his gang. The ball went wide but they withdrew, shaking their fists.

'Are we safe?' Cecily gasped. 'Or are they coming after us?'

'No, they've had enough and more. They'll let us retreat. Blue-skin will want to mourn his poor creatures. He brought them to their deaths. The thieves and cut-purses of Alsace will rejoice at hearing the news: those mastiffs have even brought down a child.'

'I am sorry,' Maria Eleanora intervened. 'My aim was not as good as I thought.'

Dolius smiled and chucked her under the chin.

'You did well enough.'

He gazed down the cavern. The wounded man had been dragged away but the corpses of the attackers and their animals lay still.

'We must be gone,' he said. 'And the sooner the better.'

He took the pistols, placed them in the leather sack and stowed them away.

'How did you come by all this?'

Maria Eleanora sat down, her back to one of the tables, and stretched out her legs. The cold seeped through her clothing but she didn't care, she felt so tired and drained.

'Do you always live like this?' she asked. 'Scurrying down secret passageways? Risking your life with musket and sword?'

Dolius hid his weapons in the far wall, replacing the bricks carefully.

'Don't worry yourself, child,' he replied, his voice burred by a broad Irish brogue. 'I like the stalk and the chase. Believe you me, Maria Eleanora, when you have been hunted by Cromwell's men up mountains and across rivers, you get a taste for it all. But, come, let's be gone before friend Blue-skin returns.'

The three left the cavern, padding wearily down stinking, empty passageways and up another set of steps into the Temple.

'Fleet Street's over there,' Dolius remarked, pointing to the glimmer of lights, hazy now in the swirling mist. 'I think we're safe.'

He led the exhausted women across the wasteland and

into a maze of streets, pausing under the sign of the Merry Mouth tavern.

'We'll eat and drink here.'

The taproom was fairly empty but remarkably clean for such a dingy-looking place. A fire roared in the great mantled hearth, fresh-cut herbs and sawdust were strewn on the floor. Mine Host, a small, genial-looking man, who shook Dolius's hand and chattered away in Gaelic, led them across to a private booth. Maria Eleanora was concerned about the time but Dolius told her not to be so anxious. They sat quietly for a while, not speaking. A slattern and pot boys brought brimming tankards and platters of hot tasty meat and soft white bread. They ate quickly. Dolius reassured them that the taverner was an old acquaintance and would keep a sharp eye out for any would-be pursuer or Green Ribbon spy.

'Why did we strike tonight?' Maria Eleanora asked, finally putting down the horn spoon.

'I have studied Shaftesbury and his gang,' Dolius replied. 'They strike first for the little people and then move higher. They are not really hunting Samuel Atkins, they simply hope he'll lead them to the Duke of York. They also want to attack the King's Catholic Queen but they'll do that in a more cunning way. So, what I ask myself is, right my bucko boy, who would you sweep up at Somerset Place?' He held his hand up, fingers splayed. 'You have four Papists: Green, Hill, Berry and Prance.'

'But Prance is not a member of the Queen's household.'

'No, but he does work in her Chapel. One, or all four of these, will be attacked.'

'But the other three,' Cecily demanded. 'Green, Berry and Hill. Do they lead secret lives?'

Dolius shook his head.

'So, why tonight?' Maria Eleanora repeated.

'Because time is running out for all of Shaftesbury's intended victims.'

Dolius leaned across and grasped her hand. Maria Eleanora had now taken off her hat, her black hair was still tied up. The Irishman's sharp bright eyes scrutinised her face.

'You really do love him, don't you? You know, Maria Eleanora, in Ireland they say that such love only comes once in a thousand lifetimes.'

Maria Eleanora swallowed hard. 'Will he escape?' she asked huskily.

Dolius pressed her fingers. 'The King loves Master Pepys. He has a special affection for him. He will do everything he can to protect Pepys so he will do everything he can to safeguard your Samuel.'

'But Green, Berry and Hill?' Maria Eleanora insisted.

'This is going to be a cruel business,' Dolius whispered. 'Isn't it, my pet?' He turned to Cecily sitting beside him on the bench, arms folded.

'A bloody business,' she echoed, hard and determined in her stare.

'The King will promise pardons. He's already done so for Sir Edward Coleman, the Duke of York's former secretary.'

Maria Eleanora shivered at the steel in Dolius's voice.

'But he won't keep his word, will he?' she faltered.

Dolius shook his head. 'A hard and cruel business, Maria Eleanora. I suspect the same offer will be made to Green, Berry and Hill: if they keep their mouths closed, before they are turned off the execution cart, a messenger will arrive with a pardon. In fact, there'll be no pardon.'

'This is murder!' Maria Eleanora exclaimed. 'Hasn't the King the power to do what he wants in his own kingdom?'

'Of course he has!' Dolius snapped. 'But he's a general, dear lady. He's determined to win the war, not just the battle.

Like any general, certain of his troops have to be sacrificed. The King doesn't *want* their deaths. Shaftesbury hopes that Charles can be depicted as a tyrant like his father was. He wants Charles to intervene, issue pardons to convicted felons. "Ah!" Shaftesbury will cry, throwing up his hands. "Here we have another Stuart King ignoring Parliament, putting aside the verdict of judge and jury. How can such a man govern this great kingdom?".'

'Civil war?' Maria Eleanora whispered.

'Civil war, indeed. Towns and villages burning under the sky. Widows in their droves. Orphans screaming for their fathers. I fought Cromwell. Have you ever heard about a town called Drogheda in Ireland levelled with fire and sword? No mercy shown, no pardon given. The innocent and guilty despatched to God. To avoid all that, our King must bide his time. He will lie and he will cheat. He will smile and smile again and be as villainous as Shaftesbury. If he survives, the kingdom survives. By Sweet Mab's tits!' Dolius squeezed her hand. 'Maria Eleanora, we are no different. We could have died in that cavern, been torn to pieces, and Blue-skin wouldn't have turned a hair. He would have swaggered back to his tavern to eat his steak pie, drink his tankard and pick at his stinking teeth. He'd collect his reward and never give you a thought.'

'And you?' Maria Eleanora asked, slightly ashamed that both Dolius and Cecily had risked their lives for her tonight.

'You know why we are here,' Cecily replied.

'It's because she loves me,' Dolius teased.

He tried to embrace Cecily but she broke free.

'I have no life left,' Cecily declared bitterly. 'I will kill William Bedloe and do as much damage to those who protect him as I can.'

'And you?' Maria Eleanora repeated to Dolius.

'Once upon a time I was Captain Thomas Blood of County Meath in Ireland. I fought for the King's late father. During Cromwell's reign, whilst our noble King lived in exile abroad, his party convened a secret coven of spies, assassins, thieves and scurriers. We called ourselves "The Secret Knot". We worked hard to break Cromwell's rule and bring about the Restoration to this kingdom of its legitimate prince.' He shrugged. 'We achieved that. The King returned in glory. London's bells rang for days, there was feasting in the streets, wine along the conduits! But, Maria Eleanora, certain men, the great nobles and the powerful merchants, had their appetite for power whetted. They didn't want a king but a figurehead who would take all the responsibility whilst they wielded the power. Our Merry Monarch, with his lazy smile and sardonic wit, would never agree to that. So, we have this deadly dance.'

'And the jewels in the Tower?' Maria Eleanora asked abruptly. 'All of London heard about your escapade. How was it the King met you privately and offered you a pardon?'

Dolius picked at his teeth with a fingernail.

'He had no choice, my love. True, I tried to rob the Crown Jewels from the Tower, but *I did so at the King's behest*.'

Cecily began to laugh.

'What?' Maria Eleanora gasped, dumbfounded.

'Money, my young friend. Charles Stuart is penniless. He's bankrupt. I was to take the jewels, replace them with plaster imitations and use them as a pledge to raise urgent funds.'

Still she stared in disbelief.

'You don't believe me?' Dolius smiled. 'Shall I also tell you what Shaftesbury's game is? I can tell you the truth because no one would believe it and you, Maria Eleanora, are in this right up to your pretty neck. Shaftesbury suspects that our noble King is in secret negotiations with the French, his

Cousin Louis XIV, who has more wealth than he has sense. In return for certain concessions, Louis has offered to pay a huge bribe to our King: a yearly pension to keep English troops well away from France's northern borders.'

Maria Eleanora listened, astonished.

'Shaftesbury would love to find out the terms of these secret negotiations. If he could, he would use that in rousing the mob, and public hysteria would spread. He'd claim Charles is bringing French troops across to Dover, hiding them away in Windsor Castle or under the cellars of Whitehall.'

'But what has my poor Samuel to do with such important matters?'

'I have told you. If Samuel breaks and indicts his own master, Shaftesbury will have Pepys – and Pepys knows all about these negotiations.' Dolius smiled at Maria Eleanora's long sigh. 'Oh there's more to this dance, child, than meets the eye. But the end,' he pulled a face, 'is very clear. There are three possibilities. One: Charles successfully beats Shaftesbury, takes the French pension and has no further need of Parliament or its taxes. Two: Shaftesbury wins and Charles remains as a figurehead, a puppet. Three: if Shaftesbury so wishes, Charles Stuart goes back into exile and England has a new Lord Protector, no less a person than Anthony Ashley Cooper, Earl of Shaftesbury, self-proclaimed Saviour of the Nation.'

Maria Eleanora drank from her tankard.

'He's truly the King's man, is our protector!' Cecily said. She edged closer to Dolius and linked her arm through his. Maria Eleanora wondered if they were sweethearts.

'Does Shaftesbury know who you really are?' she asked.

Dolius pulled a face.

'Perhaps. He might suspect that Captain Thomas Blood and Dolius are one and the same person but he really doesn't care.

210

He knows I am the King's man, so what's the use of picking me up and thrusting me into Newgate? He has no evidence whilst I have very-powerful friends amongst the city folks. No, as regards me, Lord Shaftesbury is much more simple and stark. He would like me dead, cold as Sir Edmund Berry Godfrey. However, before I die, I am sure he would like to ask me a number of questions.'

'Is that what happened to Godfrey?'

'Oh, there's very little mystery about *his* death.'

Dolius paused as the door to the booth was opened and the taverner came in to refill their tankards.

'Godfrey was only a catspaw,' he continued once the man had left. 'A God-fearing London Justice of the Peace. He was probably abducted by Bedloe and his gang, tortured and murdered, his corpse then taken out to Primrose Hill.'

'Bedloe?' Maria Eleanora queried.

'Oh yes, our sweet William, that's why he fled to Bristol. When I attended the coroner's inquest, I was intrigued by the bruising on Godfrey's chest and stomach and knew immediately that it was Pembroke's work. Our Earl of Pembroke is a madcap, ladies. He attacks without warning. On a number of occasions he has thrust his victim to the floor and violently jumped on their chest and stomach. Once he actually killed a man – but escaped his just deserts because of his high position and powerful friends. So, thinks I, if my Lord of Pembroke was present at Godfrey's murder, so too was Sir Anthony Ashley Cooper.'

'And Chief Justice William Scroggs?' Maria Eleanora asked.

'Oh, he'll play his part though Scroggs is not a murderer.' Dolius sipped from his tankard. 'Nor is he corrupt in matters of the law. He's a bully-boy, that's all. He likes to play to the gallery.'

'And what we saw tonight?'

'It's futile to openly bribe or threaten Scroggs.' Dolius put the tankard down. 'But what we saw might be useful in pushing him in a certain direction. He wouldn't be corrupted, but he might be influenced. Now, my pretty, before you ask me how, remember this, and the same goes for you, Cecily! We are like swordsmen: if Scroggs gives us an opening, we will use it. Somehow or other he must be reminded of the young man in blue.' And when Maria Eleanora looked baffled: 'Scroggs is well-known for his love of venery – his bawdy licentiousness is a byword. Why, he'd squeeze our Cecily's tits and have a hand up her skirts swifter than a fish through water. Yes, he's a notorious lecher, but what we saw tonight . . .' Dolius narrowed his eyes, 'Master Scroggs would *not* like that to become public knowledge. So remember, my pretties, the young man, so active on the bed, who left his clothes draped over a stool: a blue ensemble with a white lace hat. Our Chief Justice will remember that – and so shall we.'

Dolius lifted his horn spoon, ran it round the bowl again and licked it slowly.

'We have a card to use against Scroggs and that is most fortunate. If Green, Berry and Hill are taken up, the King will deal with them differently. Shaftesbury might pounce on Prance; that little silversmith will break, he'll want to walk free. Prance will agree to whatever Shaftesbury says, except knowing anything about Samuel Atkins.'

He put the horn spoon down, dug into the pocket of the great military coat he wore and drew out a leather pouch. He handed this across to Maria Eleanora; it weighed heavy in her hands.

'Place it carefully away,' Dolius warned. 'It's a small, silver-chased pistol fit for a lady like yourself, designed by

212

the best gunsmith in Woolwich. It carries a priming rod and a carton of musket balls.'

'Why will I need this?' she asked.

'Because this is our last night running the wild streets of London. We have done what we can to silence any would-be detractor of Samuel Atkins, and now we must search out the truth of where Samuel was during those days when Sir Edmund Godfrey disappeared. You must stay at Somerset Place, Maria Eleanora. No, no.' He lifted a warning finger. 'Enough is enough. No more journeys to Newgate, not unless it is necessary. Samuel Atkins will be closely watched.'

'But what am I to do?' She wanted to know.

'Watch and wait. Cecily and I will be in correspondence. There's a beggar who often prowls the streets around the Queen's palace. You may have seen or heard of him – a base-born rogue called Josiah-Praise-the-Lord Stanker? He will be our Mercury, the bringer of messages.'

'Can he be trusted?'

'He's mortally a-feared of me,' Dolius grinned. 'He'll come to the Water Gate and say,' he squinted up at the ceiling, 'that he brings scriptural texts to turn the Queen from her papist ways or some other password.'

'But he'll be ignored, sent packing!' Maria Eleanora exclaimed.

'Not if you tell the gatekeepers and porters that you wish to have words with this impudent fellow, to give him good advice not to bother the Queen.' Dolius spread his hands. 'A clumsy device but Josiah will not be a common visitor.'

'And the pistol?'

'Carry that with you always, close upon your person. You never know, in this vale of tears, when a musket ball may help lift some of the darkness.' Dolius got wearily to his feet. 'And now is the time for all of us God-fearing people to be in our beds.'

Dolius and Cecily returned Maria Eleanora safely to Somerset Place by secret, circuitous routes. She slipped through the Water Gate, glimpsed the lantern still burning in the porter's lodge and felt guilty about Green, Berry and the others who, unsuspecting, were being hunted by a malevolent pack of men. Yet what could she do? Dolius's warnings might be nothing but hot air. Yet any revelations by her would provoke fear, even flight, which would only increase the accusations against any of the Queen's household when they were tracked down by Shaftesbury and his Green Ribboners.

Maria Eleanora entered the palace by a side door and changed in the small closet near the stairs. She stowed the secret clothes, now crumpled and filthy, in a large leather sack, lit a candle and made her way along the deserted gallery. The palace lay silent except for the whine of a cat and the scurry of mice in the corners. Occasionally a sleepy-eyed servant would pass, hand half-raised in salutation. As she went deeper into the palace, Maria Eleanora realised that the King had sent in some of his own chosen officers: these lounged in chairs at doorways and entrances to antechambers. They looked up as she passed. Some doffed their hats, others nodded. No one challenged her but Maria Eleanora felt nervous. What excuse could she give for wandering the corridors and galleries so late at night? She reached her own chamber, unlocked the door and slipped inside. She placed the candle on the table and gasped: Catherine of Braganza, Queen of England, sat in the high-backed chair before the dying fire. She was dressed for bed in a gorgeous gold and pink nightrobe which fell down to her silver slippered feet, her thick black hair, parted in the middle, cascaded down to her shoulders.

She wore no paint or cosmetics but sat like a graven image, large dark eyes staring intently at Maria Eleanora.

'Your Majesty.' Maria Eleanora remembered protocol and sank to one knee, hand on her chest. 'Your Majesty startled me.'

'Maria Eleanora, where have you been?'

'Madam, I . . . !'

'Look at your face.' Catherine leaned down and gently touched Maria Eleanora's cheek. 'Not a touch of paint, or beauty patch.' She brushed the young woman's lips. 'No carmine. Your neck is sweaty. I cannot smell any fragrance. I know you, Maria Eleanora. You love no one in this palace. You are not some wench to be tumbled in one of the garrets or stables here. I let you go tonight and have looked for you ever since.'

Maria Eleanora tightened her lips in alarm and annoyance.

'No, no, don't worry.' The Queen patted Maria Eleanora on the head and gestured to the chair opposite. 'I have not raised the alarm. No one will become suspicious about my principal lady-in-waiting. You have not been here, have you, Maria Eleanora?' The Queen clutched her stomach. 'We live in dangerous times. Spies are on the prowl . . .'

'I am no spy, Madam!' Maria Eleanora broke in hotly.

'Of course not! Of course not!'

Catherine smiled and, getting to her feet, went to a side table. Maria Eleanora protested and made to rise.

'No, no, don't,' the Queen called out over her shoulder. 'If the truth be known, Maria Eleanora, I would prefer to serve than to reign. I have brought some white wine, not Spanish or Portuguese, but specially imported from the Loire Valley. My father acquired a taste for it and passed it on.'

She filled the goblets, brought them back and thrust one gently into the young woman's hand.

'You are not a spy, Maria Eleanora, but you are headstrong. I saw your father once: a kestrel amongst the peacocks at court. Do you know why I chose you as my lady-in-waiting?' She didn't wait for an answer. 'Because you are honest. Oh, you have your faults, you are hot-tempered and your tongue speaks before your mind reflects, but you *are* truthful. You live in the truth. You swear by it.'

Maria Eleanora leaned her elbows on the arms of the chair. Catherine's voice was strong but her eyes were pleading. The Queen was clearly frightened. You don't know where to turn, Maria Eleanora thought. You are married to a King who has more mistresses than many a man has hot dinners in a year. She gazed at the little Queen and recalled her piety, her good works, her compassion for others. She felt a spurt of anger at the likes of Shaftesbury, Blue-skin, Bedloe and others who wished to bring her down.

'Where have you been, Maria Eleanora?' the Queen asked, sharply now. 'And whom do you love?'

When only silence followed her questions, Catherine laughed and toasted Maria Eleanora with the goblet.

'I am Portuguese, my dear. I am small. The children I conceive die in my womb.' She blinked away the tears. 'I am not, as the English say, a fertile field. My body is dumpy – no, no.' She held a hand up. 'I know I have been called comely, even pretty, but my body is not elegant. My legs are short and fat. The ladies of the court call me plump – others, who are more cruel, call me "The Portuguese Donkey". The King comes and sits with me for a glass of claret, or a dish of chocolate. He kisses me on the lips and, like Judas, slips through the door to other pleasures. I have nothing except a few friends, my prayers, my good works. At night I sleep in a cold large bed. I curl up like one of the King's little spaniels and dream that I am far away from this cold island, that I can

216

feel the sun on my back and the smell of the fruit orchards on the morning breeze . . .'

'Your Majesty,' Maria Eleanora broke in.

'Your Majesty nothing!' Catherine snapped. 'The English have a phrase, do they not, about judging a book by its cover? I am not what I appear. What they don't know, but I do, is that I am deeply in love.'

'Madam, the King?'

'The King.' Catherine's face was now wreathed in a brilliant smile. 'My darling Charles.'

'He loves you, too, Madam.'

'Oh yes, I know that. It's another of my little secrets.'

'But the Duchess of Portsmouth? Nell Gwynn?'

Catherine made a rude sound with her lips and clicked her fingers.

'They don't know Charles like I do. He's frightened of love. He told me that once. He believes everybody he loves becomes tainted, is marked down for death or tragedy. His father was executed, his mother sent into exile; his younger brother died, so did his friends who fought for him. Charles is a great lover but is frightened of what he feels so he hides behind a mask. The Merry Prince, the Cynical Politician. I have seen behind that mask, Maria Eleanora, and I love him for what he is, for what he will be. Whatever he does, I shall never ever stop loving him.' Catherine smoothed out the creases in her night robe. 'I am Catherine of Braganza whom people laugh at behind their fingers and tell funny stories about; they mimic the way I talk, the way I walk. Yet they don't know me, they don't know Charles and, above all, they don't know the love which exists between us.'

'And this present danger, Madam?'

'This present danger will whirl round me like a storm,' the Queen retorted. 'It will not hurt me: the King has sworn that, but it will hurt those close to me. That's why I am worried about you, Maria Eleanora.' The Queen sipped from her goblet. 'What I am trying to say,' she paused, searching for words, 'is that while I may not be in danger, *you* certainly are. But I think you already know that. More importantly,' again the smile, 'I know about love. I can, therefore, recognise passion in others.'

Maria Eleanora blushed and lowered her eyes. She felt embarrassed, not so much at being found out, but at her own arrogance: the way she patronised this plump, innocent-looking woman whose bland face and funny ways hid a sharp mind and a keen wit.

'You have been in love for months,' the Queen continued. 'I know about your secret comings and goings and, God forbid, perhaps others do, too. You are in love?'

Maria Eleanora nodded.

'With an Englishman?'

'Yes, Madam.'

'A Catholic? Maria Eleanora, you are your own mistress: the indenture you signed when you entered my household said that you were a companion, not a servant, but this is England, not Portugal. Is the man you love a Catholic?'

'No, Madam.'

'Deo gratias!' the Queen whispered. 'Thanks be to God! Who is he?'

'A clerk in the Admiralty office: Samuel Atkins, Secretary to Mr Pepys.'

The Queen's hand shot to her mouth to stifle a gasp.

'Oh Jesus Miserere!' she whispered. 'Maria Eleanora, is this so? I think I met him once. Tall, broad-shouldered? He looked like a sailor, fresh-faced, keen-eyed, Master Pepys's man? The one taken up and imprisoned in Newgate on this ridiculous plot?'

'The same, Madam.'

Maria Eleanora sat and told the Queen exactly what had happened. How she had met Samuel and fallen deeply in love with him. She made no reference to Dolius or Cecily.

'And so you went out at night to meet him?'

Maria Eleanora agreed.

'And now he is taken up?'

'I go in disguise to visit him in Newgate, Madam, but that's growing nigh impossible.'

The Queen put her goblet down on the table beside her and sat deep in her chair, head pressed back against the rest.

'I am sorry, Madam,' Maria Eleanora continued. 'I did not know that my love for an honest clerk could put us all in great danger.' She gestured at the dying embers of the fire. 'Are you cold, Your Majesty? Shall I build it up?'

The Queen shook her head.

'There is nothing I can do for him. You know that?'

'I know, Madam.'

'I insist you be careful. You *must* be careful, Maria Eleanora.'

Maria Eleanora recognised the threat. She might be the Queen's principal lady-in-waiting, her companion, but Catherine did have the authority to order her to leave the palace and take lodgings with the Portuguese Ambassador or, even worse, request she return to Portugal forthwith.

'Do you love him, Maria Eleanora?'

'More than life itself.'

'Are you sure of that?'

Maria Eleanora stared round the comfortable chamber with its wall hangings and dark, oaken furniture; the soft carpets, the padded chairs and foot-stools, the glittering bric-à-brac on ledges, the clock ticking in the far corner.

'Madam, if necessary, I would leave all this and go out onto the Strand in my night shirt for him.'

Catherine sighed; she stared long and hard at the fire.

'Then this is what we shall do, Maria Eleanora.' She paused.

'Yes, Madam?'

'Let them come,' she whispered. 'Let them do their worst. You must follow your heart, for why should I deny to you what I claim for myself? But remember this.' The Queen's head came up. 'True love knows no fear, no compromise, no limitation, no end. Love is greater than any threat which challenges us, any menace which may try to curb it. In the end it could cost you your life. Are you prepared for that?'

'Of course.'

'I thought so.' The Queen spoke low. 'I would have hoped so. Very good, Maria Eleanora.' She got to her feet. 'Say your prayers, love with all your heart. And forget this conversation ever took place!'

Samuel Atkins was dreaming. He had left the horrors of Newgate and was resting under the shade of an oak tree in St James's Park: the sun was hot, the heady smell of flowers curled everywhere. Maria Eleanora was kneeling beside him, a napkin spread out on the grass, a flask of wine, two goblets, bread, cheese and cherries freshly picked. A wood pigeon was cooing somewhere. Maria Eleanora was leaning close, beautiful eyes in that exquisite face. She was laughing at him, teasing him, as she often did, speaking Portuguese or Spanish and finding his consternation amusing. Samuel extended his hand. He wanted to grasp her. Yet he found it difficult to move his arm and, when he did, an invisible wall of stone separated them. He beat at this and awoke to find himself lying twisted on his bed, hitting his fist against the slimy wall of Newgate prison.

For the first time since his arrest Samuel Atkins felt like bursting into tears, not from self-pity but sheer rage: a murderous fury at those who had taken him up and trapped him. He eased himself up on the stinking bed and gazed round the narrow cell. At least he wasn't in chains! A faint chink of light came through the grille at the top of the sturdy oaken door. He breathed in. The stench was still offensive, despite assurances that the gullies outside were washed with vinegar and water. Samuel began to shiver and pulled the cloak firmly round his shoulders. He was perspiring and felt nauseous but, looking round the cell, he forced a smile and began to whistle under his breath. He had been in worse places. The King's men-of-war beneath decks were no pretty pleasance. It was the same here: the slops, the dirt, the foul smells, the poor light. The sounds of the prison were like those of a warship preparing for action though there was no camaraderie, no one to come through the dark and pat him on the shoulder or tell him all was well. There was no way out, no steps leading up to the fresh air, no prospect of a pleasant port. Above all, no Maria Eleanora.

Samuel clutched his stomach. He had a number of fears. What would happen to him? And what would happen to Maria Eleanora? Samuel was frightened of nothing. He'd often boasted the same. He'd stood on the quarter-deck and heard the roar of cannon, the whistle of grape-shot. Now, by himself, he secretly confessed he was a little frightened of Maria Eleanora. She was so impetuous, so daring. She reminded him of a young officer he had once known who had revelled in danger and paid for it with his life. Would Maria Eleanora, ever headstrong, plunge into this affair and trap herself? Surely someone could help. Samuel recalled the advice of an old captain.

'Cowardice and bravery, Mr Atkins,' the old sea dog had

trumpeted, 'are two states of mind. A coward imagines every-thing and terrifies himself. A brave man forgets everything and concentrates on the task in hand.'

'What is the task in hand now?' Samuel whispered to the darkness.

He was accused of murder but that was arrant nonsense.

'Yes, it is nonsense!' he exclaimed. 'I like my claret and my friends, but I am no assassin!'

So how could they convict him? How could that evil-faced Shaftesbury, and the pack he led, bring him down? Samuel shivered and pulled the blanket closer. They could produce evidence but nothing in writing, that was too dangerous: a forgery was easy to disprove. Witnesses? Ah yes, the likes of Bedloe. But if a witness lied and was proved to lie? Samuel went back to the problem which had vexed him time and time again.

'Where *was* I?' he nagged himself. 'Where the devil was I on October the fourteenth?' He had been sad and upset after his last meeting with Maria Eleanora, frightened lest they would never meet again. And then, because Master Pepys was absent, he had gone drinking. Samuel remembered his old teacher, Mr Edward Littlejohn, who had sent him an invitation to join him for dinner on the eleventh, but Samuel had been remiss and not turned up. Now that was dangerous! If Shaftesbury found out about Littlejohn he could make great play of it to taunt, tease and bait him. Samuel's mouth went dry. In fact, it was worse than that. Littlejohn had written to him and Samuel had accepted the invitation many weeks before but had rudely failed to put in an appearance. He could just imagine Shaftesbury proclaiming this around court. What was so pressing that Master Atkins, who had accepted an invitation from his old teacher, a man he was deeply fond of, had failed to turn up at the appointed time and place? Not only that, Atkins hadn't even sought him out or written him a letter of apology!

'You are a fool,' Samuel agonised. 'You failed to act prudently.'

And the following days? He closed his eyes. The memories were drifting back but they were patchy, like drops of ink on parchment. He remembered a boat. He was crossing the Thames to a ship riding at anchor. A hearty, cheery man greeted him. A dark chamber, lamps glowing. Wine being served and drunk like water, his back being slapped. Samuel went cold. Had a sword been drawn? He beat his hands against his head. Another boat. A lantern horn in the stern, stumbling back to his lodgings and waking up, his head thick, ringing like a bell. He had lain in his bed for hours.

Samuel rose and paced up and down the cell, half listening to the sounds of the prison, the tolling of a bell. He heard another sound, too, a slither of footsteps which stopped outside his door.

'Master Atkins! Master Samuel Atkins? Can I hear your confession?'

The clerk went back and sat on the edge of the bed.

'Master Atkins!'

The voice came in a hiss: just the way his name was pronounced, and from the malice behind the whisper, Atkins was sure it was Captain William Bedloe.

'What do you want?' he demanded. 'What do you want of me?'

'Come to the door, Master Atkins. Perhaps I can help you?'

Atkins got up and walked closer.

'You are Bedloe, aren't you? Captain William Bedloe?'

Atkins was sure that Richardson wouldn't allow this man into his cell, but the passageway outside had been cleared so that Bedloe could talk uninterrupted.

'You are in great trouble, young man,' the voice hissed on. 'Why don't you just confess? I am sure I saw you standing over Godfrey's body.'

'That's a lie!'

'So, where were you on Monday the fourteenth of October?'

'It's none of your business.'

'Oh, but it is. As it will be the court's. Tell me, Master Atkins, do you have friends? Is there anyone who will come forward and take the oath and say you were at such and such a place?'

Samuel swallowed hard. What was Bedloe hinting at? Did they suspect Maria Eleanora? Or was it something else? Behind the grille Bedlow sniggered.

'Are you a loyal subject, Master Atkins?'

'You know I am. You are a liar and a perjurer!'

'And you are the gentle clerk! What are you thinking about as you sit on your bed?' Bedloe taunted. 'Do you remember your schooldays?'

Samuel's heart skipped a beat.

'Do you remember Mr Littlejohn? We are looking for him, Master Atkins. We think he might be able to help.' Bedloe's voice took on a sing-song tone. 'And the night of the theatre, the young man you met . . . You've been seen together before. They say he's of Italianate extraction, smooth-faced and slim. Are you a bum-boy, Master Atkins? Are your pleasures of the bed chamber different from ours? We'll ask such questions in court.'

Samuel felt himself shaking with fear.

'But all we want are a few words,' Bedloe continued. 'Just the truth. Perhaps I didn't see you at Somerset Place? Perhaps I was mistaken? However, nothing in life is free except, of course, the execution cart to Tyburn. So, where do you go at night, my young buck? Whom do you see, especially in October?'

Bedloe stepped away.

'Go back and think, Samuel. Go back and pray.'

Chapter Eleven

*Winter is now here. The mist hangs heavy till midday
and the grass in the palace grounds remains frozen
from morning to night. Daylight seems to have shrunk
to a few hours. The wind is biting cold. The gardens
reflect the state of my heart and the ravages of my soul.
I am in my own winterland, bereft of your warmth, the
soft tenderness of your touch. At night I dream that I
lie, arms around you, protecting you against all the
hideous horrors. I never go out now. My friends do not
approach me. I learn about what is going on from Her
Majesty and the tittle-tattle of courtiers and servants.
Bells toll the passing hours. I attend Mass in the morning and Mass in the evening. The Queen's Chapel is
dark. A sombre place where the daylight never seems
to reach. Candles glow all the time. The place reminds
me of a tomb my father visited many years ago. The
Queen is a good comfort. She is kind and understanding. She has never referred to that conversation . . .'*

Maria Eleanora heard a sound in the gallery outside. Putting
down the quill, she rose stiffly from the chair and walked
across in a rustle of taffeta, hoping that her soft red slippers
would hide any sound. Was that an eavesdropper? She opened
the door. The gallery outside was cold and empty.

'Nothing but ghosts,' Maria Eleanora murmured.

She closed the door and went and sat on a small tasselled foot-stool near the fire, stretching out her cold, numbed fingers to the warmth. The windows were all closed and shuttered, hangings pulled across yet somehow the freezing cold seeped through the cracks and crevices. Maria Eleanora glanced across at the journal she kept, the diary of her love for Samuel. She wrote in a Portuguese cipher learnt at the Lisbon court. If the book was seized no one would make any sense of it.

Maria Eleanora turned her fingers. One of the pine logs spluttered and broke, grey-white ash amidst red sparks. She wondered what was happening in the seething politics of the city. Public hysteria was now as common as the air they breathed. What was the date now? Ah yes, it was 24 November, the year of Our Lord 1678. The arrests were continuing, the whispering campaign spread like Deadly Nightshade. French soldiers had been seen in barges along the Thames: Spanish men-of-war were supposedly slipping into coves and inlets, landing troops, traitors, spies and munitions. The murderers of Edmund Berry Godfrey were mustering all the powers of darkness. Londoners were to be murdered in their beds! The Guildhall seized, Westminster occupied! No one really knew who was organising all this, the mysterious evil genius plotting to wreck Crown and Church, to bring about the total destruction of Lords and Commons!

Maria Eleanora shook her head in silent disbelief. She couldn't believe how the Londoners, usually so friendly and level-headed, good-natured and kind to many foreigners, were all ablaze with hate at this unseen enemy. The prisons were packed, Newgate, the Fleet and Marshalsea. More troops had been brought into the city. The Commons demanded that the King summon the city bands, the powerful city militia, but

Charles would do nothing. He strolled through his parks, became more interested in his chemical experiments, visited the Queen, entertained his mistresses, played languidly at chess or tried to cheat at cards.

A week had passed since Blue-skin's attack. Neither Dolius nor Cecily had made an appearance. No message, no secret cipher or letter had been delivered. On one occasion Maria Eleanora had glimpsed Prance the silversmith. She had been in the small sacristy and spotted him at the far end of the Queen's Chapel, examining a silver candelabra. Taking her courage into her hands, she had walked down and stood beside him; he scarcely gave her a second glance. He certainly looked worried, engrossed in his work. Maria Eleanora suspected Prance would prefer to have nothing to do with any member of the Queen's household. She'd also seen Green, Berry and Hill. Green and Berry were a more common sight, going about their duties. Hill, tall and broad with his luxuriant black beard, was a servant of the Queen's Treasury. They were all papists and had become increasingly nervous, as had many of the Queen's household. The common topic on everyone's lips was when would the finger of accusation be pointed at them? Already desertions were taking place. People feigning sickness or declaring they had to visit this cousin or that relative somewhere in the shires.

Now and again Maria Eleanora would go down and look through the great gate leading onto the Strand. Carriages and carts clattered by. Figures muffled in cloaks, hats pulled down, went hurrying about their business. Maria Eleanora wondered how many of them were spies keeping the Queen's residence and household under close scrutiny? She dare not return to Newgate, that was too dangerous even though her heart ached for Samuel. She had learnt, much to her cost, about the appalling conditions in the prison but drew comfort from the fact that Samuel was a hale and hearty young man, of strong physique and sturdy constitution. Often she was racked by fears. Had he been tortured? Fallen ill? Beaten up? What happened if a so-called accident was arranged?

She would pace the galleries or, when the looks became too curious, stay in her chamber walking up and down, wondering what Dolius and Cecily were doing. If she could only find out where Samuel had been, the weekend Edmund Godfrey had been murdered! The more she reflected, the more Maria Eleanora was inclined to visit Master Pepys and ask for his help. A clock struck deep in the palace. A man's voice shouted. A door opened and closed. Maria Eleanora stifled a yawn. The hour was late. She should retire, though when she went to bed, she couldn't sleep. She heard a rap at the door.

'Who is it?' she called.

'Robert Green, ma'am.'

Maria Eleanora sprang to her feet and hastened across. Green stood outside, the cowl of his cloak laced with raindrops. He looked anxious, haggard-eyed.

'Robert, what is the matter?'

'You must come! You have a visitor,' he whispered, staring up and down the gallery.

Maria Eleanora grabbed her greatcoat and quickly put on a pair of soft boots. She followed Green out, locking the door behind her. They went down the galleries and passageways, out across rain-drenched courtyards where mist tendrils hovered. As they crossed the bitterly cold gardens, the mist seemed to envelop them. They walked quickly, silently, along the twisting, narrow track to the Great Water Gate at the far side of the palace. Now and again either Maria Eleanora or Green missed their footing, stumbled and slipped.

'I dared not bring a lantern horn, Mistress,' Green said hoarsely. 'No light.'

Maria Eleanora felt in the pocket of her greatcoat. The pistol Dolius had given her was primed and ready. Every morning she checked to ensure nothing was wrong.

'Do you know who it is?'

Green, stumbling behind her, muttered, 'I think he's a beggar, Mistress.'

'No one else?'

'As far as I could see.'

When they reached the open enclosure before the gate, Green stayed in the shadows whilst Maria Eleanora hastened across. She pressed her face against the wet bars, one hand on the pocket of her cloak.

'Where are you from?' she asked.

'I am from Ithaca.'

Maria Eleanora breathed a sigh of relief as the unexpected visitor gave a password. She opened the small wicker gate and stepped through. In the faint light she could make out the shapes of trees and bushes. One of these rustled and a figure emerged. Maria Eleanora could smell him before he came much closer: the sour reek of sweat-ridden clothes on an unwashed body. She slipped her hand into her pocket and felt the serrated pistol handle. The figure shuffled closer.

'Stop where you are!' she ordered. 'Who are you?'

'I come from Ithaca, Mistress. I beg along these shores.'

As Maria Eleanora's eyesight grew accustomed to the dark, she saw the tousled hair and craggy features of the beggar who constantly prowled round the palace gates.

'Master Stanker. You may approach.'

Josiah-Praise-the-Lord Stanker drew closer. Maria Eleanora smelt cheap ale, the stench of fish.

'What message do you bring?'

'Dolius said be ready, here before dawn.'

'And why is that?' Maria Eleanora asked curiously.

'A certain prisoner has been committed for trial in Westminster Hall.'

The young woman exclaimed in horror.

'Tomorrow morning! Are you sure?'

'Tomorrow morning it is,' Stanker said heavily. 'Dolius of Ithaca says you are to be here at six of the clock. Farewell, Mistress.' And he withdrew.

Maria Eleanora was so shocked she couldn't move. This was one thing she hadn't thought of: Samuel being dragged from his prison and committed for trial before any real defence could be organised. Had Shaftesbury and his gang found enough evidence? What could Samuel do? Maria Eleanora felt the panic seethe within her. Tomorrow was 25 November. The trial might last a day, two days. If he was found guilty . . . She couldn't stop the trembling in her legs.

'Oh no!' she prayed. 'Oh, sweet Lord, not now.'

'Mistress, Mistress!' Green's voice hissed through the darkness. 'Mistress, are you well? We must return!'

'Aye, we must.' And, turning round, Maria Eleanora moved like a sleep walker back into the palace.

Maria Eleanora slept very little that night. She tossed and turned, breaking in and out of dreams which always turned into nightmares full of chilling unnamed fears and unseen terrors. She listened to the clock, the minutes and hours ticking away. She was up, washed and dressed in her disguise long before she was due to meet Dolius. She wrote a swift note to the Queen, sealed it with a blob of wax and left it on the table. The palace was still sleeping as she made her way along the passageways, down the stairs and back to the Water Gate. The mist hung thick and heavy. She waited impatiently and started as a hand came round and covered her mouth.

'Hush now!' Dolius whispered. 'No chattering, no talking!'

He took his hand away. Maria Eleanora spun round. Dolius and Cecily stood swathed in great cloaks. Dolius took off his hat. Maria Eleanora hardly recognised the King's man in his fresh blond wig, rouged cheeks and painted lips. He even had a beauty spot beneath his left eye.

'I am a man of the city,' he lisped. 'Doing business before the King's courts.'

'I hardly recognised you,' Maria Eleanora smiled.

Dolius put his finger to his lips. 'Let me talk,' he whispered. 'You say nothing. Now, may I introduce my sweet wife?'

Dolius pointed at Cecily who pulled back her cowl. She, too, had changed; her face pasty-white under a black heavy wig.

'The poor girl's not well.' Then Dolius's voice changed, charged with an Irish brogue. 'But she is as anxious as I to see justice done. Now, come.'

They led her along the trackway which wound across some wasteland down into the streets of the city, and then hired a wherry to take them over the freezing river to the King's Steps at Westminster. The journey was silent. Maria Eleanora felt as if they were the only people alive in London. The mist was so thick and heavy it dulled all sight and sound to about an arm's length from them. However, when they reached Westminster the mist was beginning to lift. People were already arriving for the business of the day. Tinkers and chapmen stood before the gates and in the courtyards, offering trinkets and mementoes. Cookshops had been opened, selling pies and spiced sausage cooked over a grill, a warm cup of posset and freshly baked bread from the local bakeries. The lawyers were busy, the men of the Temple Bar, Lincoln's Inn or Gray's Inn dressed in their black cloaks lined with ermine. Clerks and scribes scurried behind them, arms laden with learned tomes. The air smelt of scent and tobacco, as well as the fine claret many

233

of these men downed in drinking bouts which lasted all night in the underground boozing-kens of Westminster nicknamed 'Hell', 'Purgatory', 'Paradise' and 'Heaven'.

Dolius knew his way around. Now and again he made some pithy comment, ridiculing the lawyers under his breath, quietly confiding that more roguery flourished here than in any prison in the kingdom. They went up some steps and into the Great Hall, a sombre, awesome place which, Dolius explained, was nicknamed the 'Great Stone Jug'; its soaring roof was almost hidden by the mist which curled in and the constant fug of tobacco. The windows were high, the daylight weakly filtering in. Candles, torches and lantern horns had been lit.

Despite the early hour the hall was already busy. Along the left-hand wall were the makeshift shops of the haberdashers, booksellers and instrument-makers. Maria Eleanora, her face almost hidden by the black hat and vizard, stared around. This did not look like a place of justice. Rogues and ruffians thronged all around. Dolius explained how many of these were professional witnesses who would swear away a man's life for a shilling. They pushed through the throng, past a young seamstress who sat behind a stall shouting that she would mend any of the fine beaver hats of the lawyers, if they so needed. Next to her a powerfully built woman stood shaking her fist at a young clerk.

'God's tittle!' she screeched. 'Where is your master? He's supposed to be here. The court will open soon!'

Dolius swore at her as he passed, but the woman took no notice, more intent on her present victim. They went deeper down the stone hall to where the three great courts of the realm met: King's Bench, Chancery and the Court of Common Pleas. They went up a set of shaky steps which separated two soaring wooden partitions.

'Chancery stands on the right,' Dolius indicated. 'King's Bench on the left.'

They were stopped by a tipstaff at the entrance. Dolius showed him a scrap of parchment, the tipstaff looked blearily down but smiled at the silver coin which Cecily pushed between his grimy fingers: he stood aside and let them through. A straight and narrow place, Maria Eleanora found King's Bench forbidding and dark. At the far end against the wall stood a raised dais with a huge oaken table. To the right of this, a high wooden box with raised seats for the jury and, on the left, a similar platform for the accused. Below the dais was a green baize-covered table for the clerks and scribes. The court was already filling. Constables walked officiously about; clerks and scribes scurried in, faces anxious under their dirty white wigs. The paraphernalia of the court was then brought in. A broad, red cloth was unrolled along the great table and three high chairs set behind it. Quills, ink-pots, documents were distributed, and a shield bearing the royal escutcheon was hung from the wall above the central chair. Slowly but surely the ritual of justice gathered pace. Ushers began to call for silence. Tipstaffs, armed with white wands, came to the foot of the spectators' bench and glowered up as if challenging anyone to make further noise.

Dolius had secured good seats at the top. Maria Eleanora on the end of the bench near the hard cold wall, Dolius to her right, Cecily just beyond him. The journey had been chilly but now Maria Eleanora began to perspire under her cloak. Although she was fascinated by the people milling below, her gaze was always drawn back to where the accused would stand.

'Now we can talk,' Dolius murmured, 'but keep your hat on, Maria Eleanora. Try not to draw attention to yourself.'

Dolius studied the bench in front of him and the one below

it. He pronounced himself satisfied: he could see or detect no Green Ribboned spy close by, though he was sure there would be some in the court.

'Why so quickly?' Maria Eleanora asked. She found it difficult to speak. There was a lump in her throat, and her mouth was bone dry.

'I don't know,' her protector replied softly. 'But that's the way of justice, blind and uncaring.'

'And what can we do to help?'

'Very little,' Dolius said compassionately. 'Hush now.'

He gripped Maria Eleanora's knee as the clerk of the court, dressed in red and black, a white wig on his head, came up the narrow stairs which led to the Judge's table. He walked in front of this and unrolled a parchment.

'Oyez! Oyez!' he proclaimed. 'All those who have business before His Majesty's court of King's Bench must now approach and be heard!'

The clerk paused for a while.

'Therefore, all ye who are present, stand to greet His Majesty's Chief Justice, Sir William Scroggs!'

Everyone in the court sprang to their feet. Up the narrow stairs came a fat, red-faced, popping-eyed gentleman garbed in red scarlet and ermine, a thick white wig framing his sweaty face. He huffed and puffed his way into the great chair, fleshy hands shimmering with rings. He gave the smallest nod to those present and plumped himself down. Once he was seated, glowering at the court, another line of lawyers entered, led by the Attorney-General, Sir William Jones, sour-tempered and peevish under his silk black coif. This cruel-faced man was, Dolius murmured to them both, nicknamed 'Bull-Face Jonas'.

'Lord help us!' he then whispered. 'We have all the three bottle lads here.'

He pointed out 'Bull-Face's' assistants – Serjeant Maynard with his old, wizened face and clever eyes, and Sir Francis Winnington the Solicitor General, who had the features of a bulldog and looked as if he relished a fight. All three came, bowed before Scroggs and took their places at the table just before the rail which separated the Judge's table from the rest of the court.

'Oyez! Oyez!' the clerk began again. 'If any man can give evidence on behalf of our Sovereign Lord The King against William Staveley, let him come forth and he shall be heard!'

Dolius started in surprise. 'It's not Samuel! They have changed the prisoners. We've wasted our time.'

'Can we leave?' Cecily murmured, leaning across.

'No!' Maria Eleanora had forgotten her discomfort. 'I want to see what happens. If my Samuel is to be tried,' she ignored Dolius's look of warning, 'I want to see how it is done.'

Her words were hushed by the cries and exclamations of the court as the prisoner was led up and placed in the dock. Dark-haired, thin, narrow-faced with starting eyes and quivering lower lip, William Staveley stared out over the court.

'Who is he?' Maria Eleanora whispered.

'One of the little ones caught up in The Plot,' Dolius replied. 'Maria Eleanora, I am sorry, but last night our man's name was posted. For God knows what reason, they've changed it!'

Dolius fell silent as Maynard sprang to his feet, hand extended, and accused Staveley in a bawling voice of being party to 'The Great Plot' to destroy the King and overturn the will of the Commons and Lords.

'A man deeply steeped in treason!' Maynard trumpeted.

The charges rolled on.

'How do you plead?' Scroggs demanded.

'Not guilty, my lord.'

'Call the witnesses to prove the offence!' Scroggs replied.

Maria Eleanora watched as the macabre dance of law and evidence began. Time seemed to fly. She was no longer aware of Dolius sitting beside her, or of other people in the court, just the sharp interchange as 'Bull-Face Jonas' brought forward evidence to convict William Staveley. The prisoner reminded Maria Eleanora of a doe brought to bay by ravenous hounds. He did his best and fought back, but 'Bull-Face' had him by the throat. Witnesses were called who clearly perjured themselves. Two paid informants, evil-looking rogues, Carstairs and Sutherland, related how, on 14 November last, in a cookshop at Kingston, they had overheard Staveley in a conversation with a Frenchman. Staveley had uttered treason. A constable had been called and he had been arrested.

'Where is this Frenchman?' Staveley cried.

'He's in prison, my lord,' the Attorney General blithely replied, putting an end to the prisoner's plea. 'And in prison he will stay.'

Maria Eleanora stared open-mouthed. 'This is a nonsense!'

'Hush,' Dolius counselled. 'If you want, we can leave.'

'No, no, no,' Maria Eleanora said hastily. 'I want to see this.'

Staveley was following the same route her beloved Samuel would have to take. The trial did not last long. At the end, summing up, 'Bull-Face Jonas' made the point that Staveley's trial was a warning to so many others. A claim Scroggs took up.

'Aye,' he boomed with a sinister look at the jury. 'You shall do well to begin with this man, so that he may be a deterrent to the rest.'

The jury retired, promising they would not be long. They kept their word and soon trooped back.

'Look upon the prisoner!' the clerk bellowed.

Staveley was now standing, right hand raised.

'How do you find him?'

'Guilty!' the foreman cried.

The verdict was greeted by a smug, nodding smile from Scroggs. The Attorney-General and his fellow officers began to congratulate themselves. The spectators cheered. Staveley, still protesting his innocence, was grasped by the constables and hustled from the dock.

By the time they left Westminster Hall it was past midday. Maria Eleanora felt unsteady on her feet, a little faint as she had sat tense for so long. Dolius grasped her by one arm, Cecily the other. They avoided the cookshops and the taverns and made their way down to a small overgrown park next to the Thames. It was proving to be a bitterly cold day. The sky was a leaden grey. The mist had not fully lifted; even the hoar frost on the grass had not melted. Dolius kept looking round, ensuring no pursuers skulked in hiding. He led them across to a derelict pavilion shrouded by trees.

'No one's about,' he muttered, 'except a small boy with his dog. Well, what do you think, Mistress Cecily?'

'God help anyone who comes before Lord Chief Justice Scroggs. The trial was mummery from beginning to end. They may as well have taken Staveley out to Tyburn and hanged him and saved themselves both cost and time.'

Maria Eleanora pulled down her vizard and hid her face in her hands. Cecily put an arm round her shoulders and hugged her close.

'Will that happen to Samuel?'

'Not if we can help it,' Dolius intervened cheerfully. He leaned closer. 'You must have faith. You must not lose hope.'

'But why?' Maria Eleanora sat back. 'Why wasn't Samuel brought today?'

'That,' Dolius replied, getting to his feet, 'is what I intend to find out.'

They returned to King's Steps and took a wherry back upriver to East Water Gate. Maria Eleanora felt more composed now. Dolius claimed he was ravenously hungry so they stopped at a tavern close to the ruins of Castle Baynard where they broke their fast. Once they had finished, Dolius hired a small garret above the taproom and told Maria Eleanora to stay there.

'Where are you going?' she demanded.

'Why, Mistress, to Newgate. We must see what happened to poor Samuel.'

He and Cecily left, still in their disguises. Maria Eleanora bolted the door and lay down on the shabby bed, half-listening to the sounds of the taproom as she fell into a fitful sleep. She dreamed how the love of her life was standing in that hideous court with 'Bull-Face Jonas' bellowing whilst Lord Chief Justice Scroggs had a gibbet set up beside him. She was woken by a knocking on the door. At first Maria Eleanora didn't know where she was and stared wildly around.

'Mistress, are you well?'

She looked at the window. The daylight was already fading. She hurried across to the door and pulled back the bolts. Dolius and Cecily slipped in. One look at their faces and Maria Eleanora felt a fearsome chill in her stomach.

'Oh no!' she moaned.

Cecily led her back to sit on the edge of the bed. Dolius drew up a stool opposite, sweeping off his wig and hat and throwing them on the floor.

'Samuel?' Maria Eleanora asked shakily. 'He's still alive?'

'Oh, very much so, Mistress, but they were playing games with him. It's a common enough trick, to tell a prisoner he's due for trial and then keep him waiting. However, there's more.' Dolius's eyes were sombre. 'Brace yourself, sweetheart, and be strong.'

'What is it?' Maria Eleanora demanded.

'He's ill with gaol fever,' Cecily said gently. 'We bribed Richardson to let me in and I found your beloved on the felons' side, a narrow, evil-smelling place. He has a terrible fever, his body is soaked with sweat and he's gibbering nonsense.'

'I suspect,' Dolius spoke up, 'that when they baited Samuel with the prospect of a trial, that was the final straw. He succumbed to some pestilence.'

'Will he recover?'

'That's why we were so long,' Cecily explained. 'Our good friend knows a physician, a wise man who lives in a shop above the Shambles near Newgate.'

'I bought some powders from him,' Dolius said, 'and gave them to Richardson. He has promised he will take care of Samuel. Our good keeper of Newgate suspects who I am. I will get a message to the King: Samuel must recover.'

'Did he speak to you at all?' Maria Eleanora asked.

Cecily shook her head. 'Nothing but nonsense. He talked of a boat or a ship. A man called Mr Littlejohn.'

'Ah, that's his old teacher. What else?'

'He was talking about food,' Cecily continued. 'About a bottle of sack and victuals.'

'Victuals?' Maria Eleanora was puzzled.

'Yes, he kept repeating the word time and time again. How he needed victuals.' Cecily shrugged. 'I put that down to the fever.'

'We have done all we can.' Dolius got to his feet, kicking back the stool. 'I want to leave here before dark. Come, Maria Eleanora, we will see you back to Somerset Place.'

'And poor Staveley?' she asked.

'He'll be dead within forty-eight hours. They are all a-hungry for blood. The real Terror is about to begin. But take some comfort, my dear. Samuel's illness may be a godsend. If he's sick he'll be too weak to stand trial. We must use that time to save him from Staveley's fate.'

They left the tavern, hurrying back through the misty gloom via narrow alleyways and mean streets. Maria Eleanora, who had once prided herself on her knowledge of the city, realised how little she knew. At times she declared herself lost but Dolius, true to his word, brought her safely back to the Water Gate and into the grounds of Somerset Place. She made a hasty farewell and returned to her chamber: the letter she had left for the Queen had been taken. Maria Eleanora changed quickly and made herself comfortable. Her duties were light and the Queen often stayed within her own apartments. Robert Green knocked on the door and assured her that the Queen herself had come into the room and taken the note.

'How is Her Majesty?' Maria Eleanora asked.

Green shrugged. 'Nervous, withdrawn. You've heard the news from Westminster? Staveley will hang and others will be committed for trial soon. Madam, you must be careful.'

Maria Eleanora looked sharply at him.

'The messenger last night,' Green said. 'Can he be trusted?'

'I think so,' Maria Eleanora assured him.

Green, shaking his head, walked back down the gallery. Maria Eleanora closed and locked the door. She sat for a while until a chambermaid came to build up the fire.

What can I do? Maria Eleanora reflected. I cannot stay hiding in a hole! Samuel was ill. She prayed that he would recover, and deep in her soul she knew he would – but what then? Hadn't she heard how the English courts sat according to the seasons? Today was 25 November. Soon it would be Advent Sunday and the preparations for Christmas would begin. The courts would rise; they would not sit again until January. What was it called? The Hilary Term? Maria Eleanora quietly hoped that Samuel's illness would keep him out of danger for a while. She recalled Dolius's warnings but all the same she resolved to do *something*. A knock came on the door and Maria Eleanora absentmindedly looked up. She remembered the maid leaving. She rose and answered it: Catherine of Braganza slipped into the room. Maria Eleanora curtseyed, the Queen snapped her fingers.

'None of that! None of that!' she said, turning the key and locking the door herself. 'You were gone today – did you go to the court?' She clasped her lady-in-waiting's hands. 'You look pale as a ghost, and your hands are freezing!'

'I thought it was Samuel who was to be on trial.'

'You could have asked.' Catherine's eyes flashed angrily. 'I do have some influence!'

'I had to go.' Maria Eleanora held the Queen's gaze. 'It was disgusting. That poor man Staveley, it was like pitting mastiffs against a fawn. They dragged him down.'

'I know. I know.' The Queen let go of her hands and went to sit in the chair in front of the fire. 'What other news?'

'Samuel is ill with gaol fever.'

'I can do something about that. But what else?'

Maria Eleanora explained how she and Samuel had separated shortly before Justice Godfrey's disappearance; how she believed that her lover, upset and distraught, had whiled away in drinking the very days the Justice had disappeared. Now he was unable to recall specific events or produce witnesses who would discredit the allegations laid against him.

'There is only one thing we can do,' the Queen replied. 'We must seek the advice of Master Pepys.'

'But Samuel hasn't told him about me. He claims Master Pepys will be in a terrible rage.'

'Master Pepys will be in a terrible rage,' the Queen answered drily, 'if his clerk is hanged at Tyburn.'

Maria Eleanora was about to reply when voices echoed along the gallery, and there was the sound of a booming laugh. The Queen rose swiftly to her feet, face wreathed in smiles.

'The King!' she said happily. 'His Majesty has decided to visit us.'

She ran to the door like a young woman, unlocked it and flung it open. Maria Eleanora followed her out. She always thought the gallery was dark and sombre with its candle-holders and dusty paintings, but now it was transformed. The King was strolling down it, dressed in an exquisite suit of rich, dark Burgundy, a white froth of lace at his throat, silver stockings and black, gold-buckled shoes; his broad-brimmed hat boasted a white plume. The King paused, resting on his silver-topped walking-cane. He swept off his hat and gave the most elegant bow, ignoring the gentlemen who thronged about him.

'Madam.' Even in the poor light Maria Eleanora could see Charles's eyes dancing with mischief. 'Your humble servant.'

'Charles.' Catherine's words came as a whisper.

The King straightened his hat, tapping it firmly on his head and playing with the oiled locks of his luxurious wig.

'Strewth!' he declared. 'What a pretty sight. Two Portuguese ladies by candle-light. Any artist would pay good gold to paint such a scene!'

'Your Majesty is well?' Catherine didn't move from the doorway.

'His Majesty is *very* well,' Charles replied, head back. 'And all the better for seeing you, Madam. I wish a few words. I will not tarry long.'

'You may tarry and tarry and tarry yet again,' Catherine dimpled. 'And still the time will be too short.'

For a few seconds Charles's face grew sad. He blinked and glanced away as if distracted by a painting on the wall.

'Oddsblood, Madam,' he drawled. 'You have a way with words. Your command of our language grows better by the day.'

'Heart speaks to heart,' Catherine replied in Portuguese. 'And love never lies. Love always finds the will, the way and the words. Love is a fire which rages and seeks its own opening. You may disguise the flame but never the heat!'

Maria Eleanora recognised the lines from a Portuguese love song. She was sure Charles understood, even though his gentlemen murmured amongst themselves. The King made an elegant movement with his hands, fluttering his fingers as if unable to comprehend or reply to the Queen's sweet words. He then replied in French, so swiftly Maria Eleanora couldn't understand but the Queen did. She answered with another quotation:

'*De siècle à siècle*: for ever and ever.'

Charles spoke over his shoulder to the assembled gentlemen, a veritable gaggle of peacocks in their plumed hats and gorgeous apparel, and they withdrew further down the gallery. Charles sauntered up. Once again he bowed to the Queen and touched Maria Eleanora gently under the chin.

'Inside,' he whispered. 'And quickly!'

He followed them into the room, closed the door and leaned against it. Dragging his hat from his head, all the poise and elegant charm disappeared. Charles looked tired, haggard.

'You've heard the news?' he said quietly, staring up at the ceiling. 'Poor Staveley! I knew his father, a goldsmith. The man is going to die, yet he's innocent. The poor fellow has done no wrong. They are waiting for me to act, to issue a pardon. God forgive me!' The tears in the King's voice were obvious. 'I can do nothing. I can do nothing to save him from a barbaric death. And there are others . . .'

'Your Majesty, should I withdraw?' Maria Eleanora curtseyed.

'No, no.' Charles raised his hand. 'I would like, Madam,' he stared sorrowfully at his wife, 'to say I have come to see you, but that would be a lie. I always lie, don't I?' he added harshly. 'I am a liar and a rogue, a wencher and a roisterer.'

'You are Charles the King.' The Queen stepped forward, pressing herself against him, staring up into his heavy-lidded eyes. 'You are my Charles,' she said fiercely. 'My Prince, my King. You are what you have to be. What men like these have made you.'

'I wish to God I was what I should be!' Charles retorted.

Leaning down, he kissed Catherine sweetly on the lips. He murmured something to her again in French. Catherine did not reply but pressed her head against his chest. They stood together for a while, so poignant, so sad. Maria Eleanora glanced away. When she looked again, the tears were streaming down Charles's face. He leaned his walking-cane against the doorlatch and put his arms around his wife, hugging her gently to him. Catherine murmured something. Charles, grasping her by the arms, kissed her on the brow, picked up his walking-cane and stepped around her. He walked across the room as if fascinated by the clock in the corner and Maria Eleanora realised he was composing himself.

'Strewth!' he drawled finally and turned round. He dabbed at his moustache and ran a finger along the cleft of his chin. 'How I do love clocks, watches and anything mechanical. How are you, Maria Eleanora?' He stopped before her, resting on his cane held slightly to one side. 'I bring you news.' He glanced towards his wife who was standing near the door. 'Samuel Atkins is ill with the gaol fever but I think you know that. I have sent instructions,' he gestured with his finger, 'that if Atkins dies in prison, I will hold Master Richardson personally responsible. He will recover, but there's another pestilence I cannot control. You must have the wit and the courage to combat it. Captain William Bedloe, God knows how, has discovered that, on the day before Sir Edmund Godfrey disappeared, your Samuel was supposed to dine with his old teacher Master Littlejohn. He did not turn up. Nor did he send any letter of apology or explanation.'

Maria Eleanora felt the blood drain from her face.

'What is worse, Bedloe has found a witness – someone we can't control. A young man of dissolute character.'

'His name?' Maria Eleanora demanded harshly, ignoring all etiquette and protocol.

'I do not know his name,' the King replied quietly, 'but he is well schooled. So far, Bedloe is the accuser. He has summoned up the service of Captain Childs but he is a poor witness. A sea captain who strikes his colours will not be popular in an English court.' The King moved closer. 'They may do great damage here,' he continued hoarsely. 'Yet, even if they have the entire Queen's choir,' he smiled grimly, 'arrested and placed in Newgate, their testimony would be,' he made a *moue*, 'scarcely as strong as . . .'

'As what we could counter with?' Maria Eleanora interjected.

'Correct,' the King agreed. 'Witnesses who ostensibly have nothing to gain, who are not trying to save their own necks. I have sent a message to my good servant, our mutual acquaintance.' He glimpsed the despair in Maria Eleanora's eyes. 'Hope,' he whispered. 'Always hope. We have time on our hands. In a few weeks the courts rise for Christmas. I may not be able to save others but, pray God, I can save your young man and my good servant Master Pepys. Now, Catherine.' He turned briskly. 'Madam, a few words with you in private?'

Maria Eleanora curtseyed. The door opened and, when she glanced up, the King and Queen had gone, leaving her alone in this shadow-filled chamber.

Maria Eleanora heard the gentlemen chattering outside. She sat down at her writing desk and, picking up the quill, began to write again as if Samuel Atkins was free, as if their love could run true and untroubled, as if the sun shone, the wine was rich and strong and all these terrors were a mere passing fancy.

Chapter Twelve

Cecily grasped the tankards and moved away from the ale butts. Despite the very late hour, the King's Head in Fleet Street was bustling and noisy. She glanced out of the corner of her eye at the slightly raised platform at the end of the sprawling taproom. Two oafs, wearing ribbons on their jerkins, and armed with sword and cudgel, guarded the stairs up to the dais. The Green Ribbon leaders, wreathed in pipe tobacco, sat round a table discussing the events of the day. Shaftesbury was absent but Pembroke had made an appearance: the nobleman had drunk himself into a stupor and lay sprawled across the table. The rest of the crows had gathered: Captain Eastwell, Bedloe and Blue-skin. The great liar, Titus Oates, very rarely graced the tavern with his presence; jealous of Bedloe's growing fame, Oates held court in his own chambers across the city. Cecily felt no fear. Blue-skin had not glimpsed her face and she had changed, pulling back her straw-blonde hair and fastening the mobcap more securely. She wore a low-cut dress, the bodice revealing more than it concealed. Holding the tankards carefully, she tripped across the room, knocking aside with her elbows any lecherous touch or responding to bawdy remarks with a withering look.

Cecily worked quietly and without causing comment. Seagrave the taverner welcomed this, allowing her to sleep in a garret above. Cecily had fabricated her own story about an ancient sick mother and a fictitious family. She never acted suspiciously, showed no interest in what was going on and so she was accepted for what she pretended to be: a not too intelligent tavern wench, who kept herself to herself and wouldn't tolerate any naughtiness. The men whose tankards she carried were different from the rest of the customers. Cecily found it difficult to look at Bedloe, afraid he would see the hate glowing in her eyes. On one occasion, when leaning over to serve him, she had glimpsed a carving knife on a platter and had had to fight the urge to pick it up and thrust it deep into his dirty, villainous neck. She approached the steps and smiled. The green-ribboned oafs stood aside, and up she traipsed, holding the tankards in one hand, lifting the hem of her skirt with the other. She placed the tankards on the table. Bedloe raised his head and stared full at her. Cecily smiled with her eyes.

'Hey, you! Clear these pots!' Blue-skin shouted.

Cecily was glad of the opportunity to linger. She picked up a tray from a nearby stool, placed it on the end of the table and slowly began to clear away the empty tankards. The men were talking about Staveley.

'He'll certainly hang,' Bedloe remarked. 'And within the week. Good riddance, I say, to a traitor!'

He lifted his brimming tankard. No one responded. Eastwell was staring down at the table much the worse for drink, whilst Blue-skin was seething.

'Three dogs in all!' he roared. 'Three good hounds, each with a musket ball. I'll see that bastard hang!'

'Who?' Eastwell asked bleavily.

'The man who calls himself Dolius or whatever. I'd like to take him by the heels and find out who he really is.'

'He enjoys high favour,' Eastwell replied pompously, and

belched. 'You know he does.' He laughed abruptly to himself. 'And you know the rules of the game. Our masters may bow and scrape and smile at each other but, unfortunately, there is only so much we can do. We must keep within the law.'

'Will Atkins be next?'

Cecily froze as if fascinated by the tankards.

'I am not too sure,' Eastwell slurred. 'My Lord Shaftesbury has received information that he now lies sick in Newgate, not fit to plead. Aye, Bedloe, how are you doing with our new witness?'

Cecily picked up the tray but, ostensibly seeing another tankard she had deliberately left, she put it down and moved along the table. She slapped aside a questioning hand, one of Pembroke's henchmen, sitting tipsily on a stool rocking backwards and forwards.

'I am going to see him in a moment,' Bedloe declared.

'The hour is late.'

'It's the best time!' Bedloe snapped. 'What the eye doesn't see, the heart can't grieve over.'

'And he'll testify against Atkins?'

'Oh, he'll testify, but now . . .'

Bedloe was watching Cecily curiously. Picking up the tray she smiled back, realised she had tarried long enough and went down the steps. She elbowed her way through the throng and went into the large, steam-filled scullery where she tipped the tray of dirty tankards into a great vat of boiling water. Seagrave the taverner was sitting in his high-backed chair, clay pipe between his fingers. A sly-eyed rogue, Seagrave had attempted intimacies with Cecily when she'd first arrived but now knew his place. She would catch him gazing lecherously at her, smiling beatifically to attract her attention. He was now staring at a point behind her. Cecily felt the sweat on her back prickle cold: even before she turned, she knew William

Bedloe was standing in the doorway. He came slowly into the scullery, high-heeled boots tapping on the flag-stoned floor. He winked at Cecily, went up to the tavern-master, whispered in his ear and dropped a silver coin into his lap.

'You can ask but whether or not she'll agree . . .'

Bedloe came sauntering back, his narrow, close-set eyes all hot with cheap ale and wine, his sallow features flushed. Cecily braced herself. On a night like this, she thought, with your hat and cloak on, you slew the love of my life and killed the life within me. Cecily prayed, to the spirit of her dead husband, that the mask she wore would not slip, that her eyes or lips wouldn't betray her heart.

'So, you are Mistress Cecily?'

Bedloe performed what he thought was an elegant bow. He straightened up, one finger resting against his cheek, head slightly sideways.

'Do you know, Mistress, I have seen you somewhere before, but, for the life of me, I cannot place you.'

'You are mistaken, sir.'

'No, no.' Bedloe shook his head. 'I never forget a face though sometimes the details slip my mind. I would never forget someone as pretty or as comely as you.'

'Why, thank you, sir.'

'I enjoy the favour of Lord Shaftesbury.' Bedloe leaned closer. 'I am a man of considerable importance. I have the ear of those who matter.'

'Then, sir, you are most fortunate.'

'I wish your company, Mistress.'

'Sir, I serve ale. I am not any man's strumpet.'

'No, no, no.' Bedloe imitated the foppish manners of an elegant courtier. 'I have asked Master Taverner for your company. The rain has stopped, the night is not too cold . . .'

'I have duties here.'

'You can be relieved of them.'

Cecily bit her lip as if considering his offer.

'I have a man to meet: an inmate of Bedlam.'

'Why, sir, in which case you do not need my company.'

'No, no, I would just like to walk with you, enjoy a little company, get to know you better.'

Cecily made the decision. She glanced at the tavern-master who nodded imperceptibly. Cecily slowly undid the apron, took it off, smoothing down the folds of her shabby gown.

'Just a walk and then I must return, nothing else.'

'Why, Mistress, you will be safe with one of the Saviours of our Nation.'

Cecily smiled, excused herself. She hurried out up the back stairs to the garret at the top of the tavern which she shared with three other wenches. A cramped, dingy closet, it held four cot beds and a few sticks of battered furniture. Cecily took off her slippers, put on the sturdy walking boots bought in the Cheapside market and took down her cloak. She moved to the corner, raised a floorboard and drew out a wicked-looking Italian stiletto in its red brocaded sheath. Cecily slipped this into her inside pocket and sat on one of the stools.

'Am I doing right?' She could control her hatred if the journey might prove to be profitable. 'Oh Maria Eleanora,' she whispered. 'If you only knew the debt you owe me.'

Cecily stared down at the scuffed toes of the boots. She liked the Portuguese girl with her fiery eyes and passionate love; she reminded Cecily of herself in the days of her courtship. Now all that was gone, only Dolius remained. Cecily lifted her head. She felt confused about the Irishman. Sometimes she feared him, other times she didn't know whether she loved him as a brother or a man; albeit with a different, weaker form of love than she had felt for her husband. Undoubtedly, a bond had existed between them;

their very souls had touched. Cecily grasped her cloak and patted the pocket. What would happen tonight if she withdrew that dagger and thrust it between Bedloe's ribs? She could do that. How would she feel? What purpose would remain in her life? Did she live just for revenge? No, that wasn't true. She wasn't full of hate, not like those men below. All she wanted was justice. She wanted Bedloe to suffer, and suffer he would.

Cecily rose to her feet and went downstairs. Bedloe was waiting near the door, booted and cloaked, a broad-brimmed hat in one hand, the other resting on the hilt of his sword. The brave warrior home from the wars, Cecily mockingly thought. Bedloe imitated the posture of a professional soldier. He beckoned Cecily closer, opened the door and ushered her through. She half-heard some ribald remark thrown from Bedloe's companions but she didn't care. Outside, the street was still busy. Carriages and carts rattled by. Bedloe, without asking, linked his arm through hers and drew her closer. Cecily didn't struggle.

'I am sure I have met you before,' Bedloe repeated, his face only a few inches from hers. 'You are comely enough, Cecily. I am proud to have you on my arm.'

You are a fool, Cecily thought, smiling back, a base-born coxcomb but I'll act the part. She fluttered her eyelids.

'Sir,' she cooed. 'What do you wish with me? I am only a poor tavern wench and you sit at table with the high and mighty.'

'I sit because I am needed,' Bedloe retorted.

A chapman, hurrying by, knocked him slightly on the shoulder and Bedloe glared round. Cecily repressed a shiver. A simple knock like that, a petty accident had taken her lover's life yet she had the measure of Bedloe: a cunning coward who was not as intelligent as he appeared.

'You could have someone else,' she purred sweetly, nestling up closely.

Bedloe preened himself like a cock.

'I have had my eye on you for some time, Mistress Cecily. Your face bathed in candle-light, your bosom, your slim waist and long legs. You have a haughtiness about you, like some great lady of the court.'

Aye, Cecily thought. You'd like me on some truckle bed with my legs kicking high above you so you could boast to all your cronies about the pleasures you had taken.

'Will you walk out with me again, Mistress Cecily?'

'Why, Master Bedloe, it depends on this evening. You do have great influence with my master.'

Bedloe steered her down Fleet Street and up into Shoe Lane. The houses here hung close together, their upper stories jutting out so close, the night sky was reduced to a mere strip.

'A pleasant enough evening,' Bedloe commented.

He walked with a swagger, his left arm through Cecily's, the other throwing back his cloak so his fingers could beat a tattoo on the hilt of his rapier: a warning to all those who lurked in alleyways and doorways that here was a bully-boy. Cecily suspected the broad green ribbon pinned to Bedloe's cloak was more than enough protection for this narrow-eyed assassin.

'How goes this business?' Cecily asked.

'What business?' Bedloe asked sharply.

'Oh, the doings of the court. All the tavern wenches are talking about a man, Stourley?'

'Staveley!' Bedloe corrected her. 'William Staveley, an attainted traitor.'

'And did you have a hand in his capture? It must have been very dangerous.'

'More's the pity, no,' Bedloe replied pompously. 'I would have loved to have been involved in his apprehension. Oh no, no, no, I hunt bigger game than the mice and hares of the field. Staveley,' he leaned closer like a conspirator, 'Staveley was mere froth on the water.'

Cecily smiled and gave what she hoped was an adoring glance to this makeshift hero.

'What game?' she whispered back.

Bedloe paused and pulled her in under a shop sign. Cecily's hand fell to the dagger as his arms circled her waist and pulled her close.

'Oh, sir, not now! Please!' She struggled.

Bedloe must have taken comfort from the phrase 'Not now!' for he kissed her full on the lips. Cecily, wide-eyed, simply froze. Bedloe stepped back, still preening himself.

'There's many a lady in London, Cecily, who would pay dearly for such a kiss.'

'Sir, I am only a simple tavern wench,' Cecily simpered.

Bedloe stepped into the trap.

'Not if you are my friend, Cecily. I have secrets, as well as influence.'

'What secrets?' Cecily gasped round-eyed. 'Sir, you are teasing me. You are lying. You are simply trying to impress a poor country girl!'

She didn't object as Bedloe stretched out his hand and pressed her breast.

'Many men tell lies,' she pouted, looking at him coyly. 'And wish to take the garter from my legs.'

'Is it a lacy garter?' Bedloe asked throatily.

'Of course, sir, one bought specially.'

'Have you ever lain with a man?'

Cecily smiled and decided to gamble all on one throw.

'I, too, have a secret, Captain Bedloe! A city merchant, I cannot give his name.'

'Who is he?' Bedloe asked.

Cecily chewed her lip, more to control the laughter bubbling within her than to appear frightened and coy.

'Who is this man?' Bedloe thrust his head forward.

Such a fool, Cecily thought, deserves to be trapped.

'I cannot give you his name, Captain, but it does not matter now because he's dead.'

'Dead?' Bedloe's head came back.

'He died during our pleasures.' Cecily breathed out as if upset. 'He used to buy me silks and liked to disport himself with me. He said I gave him so much pleasure, and then one night he died.'

She watched Bedloe's Adam's apple bobbing up and down like a bird on its perch.

'So much pleasure,' he said hoarsely.

Cecily found it difficult to contain her laughter. She only hoped this varlet would take her trembling as excitement. Cecily recalled the plays she and her husband used to stage: the bawdy romps, the salacious stories of innocent country maids being seduced by city gallants. She could hardly believe Bedloe could be so easily deceived. Arrogant, Cecily thought, arrogant and greedy. She felt more confident in her disguise. Bedloe grasped her hands and stared longingly at her.

'I am what you think I am.' She smiled. 'A country wench, who gives great pleasure in bed.'

'Oh Cecily!' Bedloe's eyes glittered.

'Anyway, sir.' She glanced away. 'Ever since then, I have been most prudent in my personal matters. You will not tell anyone my secret?'

'Oh, no, no!' Bedloe flustered.

Of course you won't. Cecily glanced out of the corner of her eye. You think you've found a honey pot for Captain William Bedloe's use only.

'Must we tarry here?' she whispered. 'I am slightly cold and . . .'

Bedloe, grasping her by the hand, led her along Shoe Lane lost in his own lecherous thoughts.

'Do you have secrets?' she asked, clenching his hand even tighter.

'I am Lord Shaftesbury's lieutenant in this matter.' Bedloe spoke like any rogue on a stage. 'We have a villain lodged in Newgate called Samuel Atkins. We search for evidence against him.' He paused and pressed his lips against her ear, brushing it with his tongue.

'He was involved in Godfrey's murder.'

Cecily was only too pleased to step away, all horror-struck.

'No, sir, that cannot be true!'

'A murderous villain,' Bedloe declared.

'But if that's the case, why do you need evidence?'

'It's what the law says,' Bedloe told her grandly. 'Evidence is demanded, so evidence will be obtained.'

They hurried along Shoe Lane, going towards Holborn when Bedloe dragged her down an alleyway leading into Farringdon Ward – a foulsome, evil runnel. He stopped and knocked at a brass-studded door. This swung open and an old crone, mobcap on her wiry hair, wrinkled face all sleepy-eyed in the light of a lantern horn, ushered them in. Servile to Bedloe, she gave Cecily a lecherous look.

'Is he still up there?' Bedloe demanded.

The crone nodded.

They went up the battered, wooden steps. Cecily sniffed and pinched her nostrils.

'The air stinks,' she whispered, 'of rotting vegetables.'

'It's not the King's Head,' Bedloe retorted. 'But it will do for the purpose.'

He went along a poorly lit gallery, stopped at the first door and knocked. The young man who opened it had a lean, grey face, lank brown hair and deep-set eyes.

'You haven't been drinking, have you?' Bedloe accused, pushing him back into the evil-smelling chamber.

'I must have something to drink,' the man slurred. 'And who's this? A doxy for my pleasure?'

Bedloe pushed the man so hard, he went crashing back against the table.

'Don't you know a lady when you see one?'

The man licked slobbery lips.

'Mistress Cecily, may I introduce Jeremy Prinkheart, formerly scholar of Eton College, former student of Christ Church Oxford, formerly a clerk in the Duke of Newcastle's household, but now a scholar from Bedlam.'

Cecily studied the man's empty eyes, the pitted cheeks, the chamber that smelt like a midden-heap.

'When you come into court,' Bedloe barked, 'you'll have to look better than this. Cecily my dear, would you stand outside and guard the door?'

Cecily did so. She heard the bolts being drawn and, pressing her ear against the wood, listened to the murmured conversation.

At first Cecily found it difficult to hear. Prinkheart was slurred but Bedloe's voice was decisive, sharp as he enjoyed the power he exercised. The gallery was deserted. Cecily had a good view of the stairs and, knowing Bedloe, he had chosen a place where few would dare to enter. Prinkheart was moaning.

'I have little to eat and not enough to drink.'

'You look hale and hearty enough,' Bedloe snorted. 'Too many cups of sack and your tongue runs away with you. Now, what is your name?'

Prinkheart gave his personal details. Cecily could now hear very clearly. She marvelled at how the Green Ribboners had groomed this vicious young man in perjury. His dissolute life was ignored, and Prinkheart was portrayed as a capable young man of good family who had fallen on evil times. Cecily grew impatient but, at last, the two conspirators reached the heart of the matter. She froze as Bedloe moved onto the events of Monday, 14 October.

'Where were you then, Master Prinkheart?'

'I was hired by certain men.'

'Who were they?'

Prinkheart gave the names of several Catholic priests.

'And did you know who they were?'

'Oh no.'

Bedloe moved him smoothly on. Cecily grew frightened. Despite his dissolute life, Prinkheart was a consummate actor and played the role of the frightened, wide-eyed innocent to perfection. In a strong but quavering voice he described how he had been hired and taken by secret routes into Somerset Place; he spoke of men in black cloaks, vizards and hats, of gloomy passageways, pattering footsteps and moving shadows; of a ghastly corpse being viewed by candle-light, of Prinkheart's own fear and disgust. When he realised a gruesome murder had been committed, his terror had turned to seething panic when he recognised the slain man as none other than the Justice of the Peace, Sir Edmund Godfrey.

Bedloe, like a tutor at an Oxford college, interrupted occasionally to correct the heightened impression. The role he and his fellow conspirators had written for Prinkheart would move the heart of any jury and have the London mob howling for vengeance and justice.

'And who did you see round the corpse?' Bedloe asked in the tone of a proper Job's comforter. 'Think clearly now, Master Prinkheart.'

'I am not too sure,' Prinkheart stuttered. 'The light was poor. My heart was beating fast and tears stung my eyes. I was praying to the Lord Almighty to rescue me from the snare of the hunter, from the pit which had been dug, the evil which pressed . . .'

'Enough of that,' Bedloe taunted. 'The jury want to hear the story, not your prayers.'

'I glimpsed Prance.'

Cecily caught her breath.

'Prance! Who's this Prance?' Bedloe asked, all innocent. 'And how do you know it was he?'

'One of the conspirators let slip his name.'

'Oh, come, come.' Bedloe acted the lawyer. 'Would conspirators make such a mistake?'

'They were all in a hurry and a fluster.'

'Very good! Very good!'

Cecily heard the clink of cups.

'And what else did you see?'

She pressed her ear firmly against the wood. She had an instinct, a premonition, that Prance was not Bedloe's real quarry.

'I am not too sure. I don't want to swear a man's life away.'

'But you won't, you won't.' Bedloe reassured him. 'You are on oath, Mr Prinkheart. Your allegiance is to the Crown, Parliament and this court.'

'I saw Samuel Atkins.'

'Who is he?'

Prinkheart's voice quavered.

'Oh come, Master Prinkheart.'

'I don't wish to be the downfall of any man.'

Again the quaver. Cecily could imagine Prinkheart, hands clasped, eyes staring heavenwards.

'But you have heard the rumours?' Bedloe urged.

'He's Mr Pepys's man and works at Derby House.' The words came out in a rush. 'I've heard he's been taken up and lodged at Newgate.'

'Are you sure it was he?' Bedloe pressed his point.

'I saw him in the dim light of a lantern horn.'

'Very good! Very good!' Bedloe soothed. 'Now, Master Prinkheart, you may have more wine.'

Again the clink of cups. Cecily strained for further sound. She heard a creak on the boards so she stepped away and sat in a narrow window-seat, tapping her foot. The door swung open, and Bedloe, face smiling evilly in the light of a tallow candle, slunk out like a demon.

'You are well, Mistress Cecily?'

'I am impatient, sir. But I will wait for you.' She rearranged her cloak and leaned forward.

Bedloe's eyes fell to her bodice.

'We have to tarry a little longer, Mistress Cecily, but I won't be long, I promise you.'

The door closed again. Some instinct warned Cecily to remain seated. It opened again, and Bedloe came out with a goblet of wine. He thrust this into her hands, his fingers brushed her bodice and he swaggered off. Cecily sniffed at the wine and, seeing a gap between the floorboards, poured it away. She waited a while and returned to her listening post. Bedloe was congratulating Prinkheart.

'Is Atkins the guilty one?' Prinkheart demanded. 'Will he dance at Tyburn?'

'Atkins is a strange one,' Bedloe commented. 'He lies sick in Newgate but we hope and pray that he will come to Judgement.'

'Why a strange one?' Prinkheart demanded.

'A man who likes the pleasures of the flesh.'

'Don't we all,' Prinkheart joked.

Cecily heard a cry of pain; Bedloe must have struck his protégé. She listened carefully. Prinkheart was crying. Bedloe, like a school bully, was offering him false comfort.

'Master Atkins *is* strange,' Bedloe declared. 'Because, for the last few months, he has slipped out of his lodgings to meet someone, a young man of Italianate extraction. We wonder if he's from a foreign embassy, Portugal, France or Spain? Or, better still, one of the Queen's servants at Somerset Place. However, we cannot find a man who fits his description. The Queen has no young fellows in her retinue. Anyway, my masters are on it . . .'

Cecily's mouth went dry.

'You met Mr Blue-skin,' Bedloe chattered on. 'He brought you here. He's had his eye on a beggar called Stanker – you may have heard of him. He's a snapper-up of trifles, a wheedling, cunning man. We think he takes messages to Somerset Place. This very evening Master Blue-skin is going to pick him up and take him there.'

Cecily bit her lip or she would have cried out. She listened carefully but Bedloe had returned to tutoring Prinkheart in his prepared script. Cecily walked back to the window-seat and stared fearfully into the darkness. Had she made a mistake? Had Bedloe brought her here deliberately? Did he know that she was eavesdropping? And what could she do? The hour was late. If she disappeared and tried to warn Dolius or Maria Eleanora, would Bedloe pursue her? Or worse still, was there someone lurking downstairs or out in that night-black alley waiting for her to flee? If she did so, what good could she do? She returned to the door and listened carefully. Bedloe was now showing Prinkheart how to stand, how to talk. Cecily went back to the window-seat. She had no choice. She thought of Atkins racked with fever in Newgate, of the impetuous Maria Eleanora, and prayed to the love she once had that the villainy planned would come to nothing.

> *If I loved you and did not say,*
> *Then my tongue would lie and*
> *My heart be perjured.*
> *If my heart did not speak of the love*
> *It holds, then my soul would dry*
> *And my tongue would remain dumb.*

Maria Eleanora paused and stared down at what she had written.

'Dumb or mute?' she mused. 'I love you, Samuel Atkins.'

She looked fondly at the little keepsake, a bronze paper-weight, resting at the far end of the writing table, that Samuel had bought her at St Bartholomew's Fair. She gazed round the chamber. Everything was in order. To compose herself, she had whiled away the long hours tidying her room, going through her papers. She had written letters to her friends and family in Portugal, attended to the Queen, immersed herself in the chatter of the royal household. Nevertheless, despite all this, Maria Eleanora felt as if shadows stood at her elbow, threatening, menacing. She had resisted the urge to don her disguise and slip out through the Water Gate, for that would be foolish. The wolves were at the door and, if she moved hastily or unpreparedly, she might bring great danger to those who were helping her. Maria Eleanora felt as if she was imprisoned: her only consolation was that Samuel in

Newgate would be well tended and the fever would pass. She returned to her writing.

> *All my soul is yours. It always has been,*
> *And always shall be.*
> *When God created us, He made us one*
> *Before we became two,*
> *So we could become one again.*

Maria Eleanora threw down the quill.

'But when?'

She hurled the question across the lighted chamber. Surely every nightmare ends, and darkness finally gives way to the light of day? Maria Eleanora reflected on her life. In her soul she was convinced that Samuel was for her and she for Samuel. They had been made for each other, but how would it end? A noise echoed in the passageway. She hid the piece of parchment and got to her feet. A knock at the door. She hurried across. Robert Green stood there, a lantern horn in one hand, a thick serge cloak over his arm.

'Madam, you have a visitor.'

Maria Eleanora's heart leapt.

'At the Water Gate!'

Maria Eleanora took a cloak, doused the candles and followed Green down the passageway and out across the windswept courtyard. The same path, the same ritual. As she reached the Water Gate, Stanker shuffled out of the shadows.

'Mistress.' His voice quavered. 'I have a message for you.'

Maria Eleanora looked over her shoulder. Green had retreated deeper into the shadows. She stared up at the sky; it was cloud-filled, but the wind was not so biting, the cold not so cutting. She recalled a line Samuel had once whispered to her: 'A night for lovers and conspirators'. Maria Eleanora, hand on the gatelatch, stared out at the dark shadowy form. She felt uneasy, a premonition of danger.

'Is everything all right, Master Stanker?'

'Mistress.' The man moved from foot to foot. 'I have an urgent message. You must take it!'

Maria Eleanora went through the gate. Stanker moved backwards. She followed and exclaimed in horror as a shadowy figure slid out from behind a bush. Then the cold muzzle of a pistol pressed against her cheek.

'Well, well, well.'

Maria Eleanora smelt a rank odour of sweat, mixed with tobacco and wine. She dared not move but stared beseechingly at Stanker.

'Bring the lantern horn!' the voice ordered.

Stanker hurried away and returned with the lantern. The man holding the pistol took it, and when Maria Eleanora turned her head slightly, she was staring into the mottled, wicked face of Blue-skin. His hat was pushed back on his head and he'd pulled down the edge of his cloak, covering his nose and mouth. He moved the muzzle, pressing it against Maria Eleanora's neck.

'What is your name, my pretty one?'

'That is my business!' Maria Eleanora replied hotly.

'I had no choice,' Stanker wailed from the darkness. 'Mistress, he was waiting for me. I had no choice.'

'Shut up!' Blue-skin snarled. He wetted his lips, eyes on Maria Eleanora. 'Pull back that hood!'

She did so.

'I wonder . . .'

Leaning forward, Blue-skin grasped one of her breasts. Maria Eleanora stood rigid, her hand falling to the pocket but, in her haste, she had brought the wrong cloak! The pistol wasn't there! As if he could read her thoughts, Blue-skin put the lantern horn down on the ground and searched her roughly, his hands moving freely. Maria Eleanora blushed but Blue-skin's pistol was primed: this man would have no compunction in murdering her and Stanker.

'I wonder if we have Master Atkins's strange friend?' he hissed. 'It would make sense.' His hand caressed Maria Eleanora's face roughly. 'A pretty young Portuguese girl dressed like a man. A plump pigeon pretending to be a hawk. What's your name?' His tone became more menacing.

'Maria Eleanora.'

'What a nice name! What a pleasant name! Look at you now in your dark dress with your petticoats peeping out.' Blue-skin's voice turned thick and ugly. 'What a treasure! What a prize! How can Master Atkins answer this? Taking messages to and from Somerset Place?'

'I love him!' The words came out before Maria Eleanora could think. 'To be in love is not treason.'

'Oh, you love him!' Blue-skin taunted. 'Well, well, Master Stanker, you'd best go.'

The beggarman fled into the night, stumbling and cursing. Maria Eleanora looked back, but there was no sign of Green. In a way she was glad; she had brought this trouble on herself. Blue-skin was studying her.

'I have never taken a Portuguese.' He pressed the pistol into the pit of her stomach, pushing her back. 'One of the Queen's great ladies, eh?'

Back and back he pushed her, up against the cold metal grating, the damp seeping through her clothes. Blue-skin had the pistol muzzle pressed firmly. She moved her hand but he grasped it. She felt his wiry strength.

'Are you a woman or a man?' he said thickly. 'Shall I search and discover? Shall I claim lands not yet entered?'

His hand snaked out and undid the clasp of her cloak. Maria Eleanora felt the cold air. She tensed, horror-struck by this evil man.

'I'll have a little pleasure for my pain,' Blue-skin muttered.

He undid the buttons of her gown, hands slipping down to her breasts, calloused fingers scoring her nipple. She dare not move. She wanted to scream and fight back, but perhaps that was what Blue-skin wanted?

'I'll take you down to Newgate,' he whispered hoarsely. 'They'll have the pleasure of you but I'll take mine first. If you let me – well, I might even put a kind word in for you.' His hand went down to her skirts and he lifted the hem of her dress. 'Petticoats,' he muttered. 'White and thick, eh, like cream on a tankard.'

His hand brushed her thigh and stopped at the lacy garter. Maria Eleanora felt as if she was going to be sick.

'Well, well, well!'

She winced as the iron butt of the pistol pressed deeper. She thought of Samuel, Dolius and Cecily.

'If you scream,' Blue-skin warned, 'I'll put a ball in your midriff. I have the proof.' His hands scrabbled underneath her clothing, his stinking breath making Maria Eleanora flinch. 'I'm becoming lost,' he whispered frustratedly.

'Why, good evening, Master Blue-skin.'

The thief-taker froze. The voice came soft and mocking out of the darkness.

'I'd step away if I were you.'

'I'll kill her!' Blue-skin spoke over his shoulder.

Maria Eleanora, eyes filled with tears, peered into the darkness but her vision was blurred: a shape seemed to emerge from the ground behind Blue-skin. She heard a click as a pistol was pressed against her violator's head.

'Isn't this a pretty pass?' Dolius's voice murmured. 'Your

pistol against her stomach, my pistol against your head. Do you know, Blue-skin, I've prayed for such an opportunity, to catch you out in the open, alone in the dark.'

'I have others.' Blue-skin's head was still turned. 'In the alleyway leading from the Strand.'

'Oh, don't worry about them,' Dolius mocked. 'They are dead.'

Maria felt Blue-skin stiffen.

'I know what,' the Irishman continued, 'I will withdraw my pistol, and you take yours away. We'll settle this matter man to man, sword to sword. It's the only way out.'

Blue-skin swallowed hard.

'You don't want to die, do you?' Dolius's voice was soft and cunning. 'You don't want to die here, out in the dark?'

'I'll kill her,' Blue-skin warned but there was a tremor in his voice.

'Then kill her,' Dolius purred. 'Do it. I'll kill you and that will be the end of the matter. She's nothing to me. I'm stepping away.'

Maria Eleanora heard the scuff of boots.

'Step away too!' Dolius urged. 'We'll settle this matter man to man and, if you win . . .'

Blue-skin, teeth slightly jutting out, glanced at Maria Eleanora, a calculating look in his eyes. She noticed how his hand had fallen away; he was searching for a second pistol.

'Musket to musket, sword to sword!' Dolius's voice echoed.

Blue-skin kept the muzzle pressed against her stomach.

'Do I have your word?'

Blue-skin's eyes were now slits of malice.

'You have the word of Dolius.'

'I don't think I have,' Blue-skin replied. 'I have to think of this. What if—?'

Suddenly he turned, bringing his musket round. The night air exploded into flashes and billowing acrid smoke. Maria Eleanora watched in horror: Blue-skin was still standing. He was walking but then his legs buckled. She heard a rasping, choking sound as he fell to his knees and crumpled sideways to the ground. Maria Eleanora let her body relax and slid down against the iron gate. She crossed her arms. Dolius seized the lantern horn and brought it over. He placed it next to the corpse and turned the body over.

'He always was a lying bastard! Now he's dead!'

Blue-skin's livid face looked ghastly: mouth open, eyes rolled back as if he was trying to see the great black hole in the centre of his forehead.

'You could have missed,' Maria Eleanora whispered.

Dolius crouched before her. He wore no disguise; in the lantern-light he looked younger, fresher, eyes sparkling.

'I have the luck of the Irish, Mistress. As regards Blue-skin,' he shook his head. 'I would never have missed.' He helped her to her feet. 'Where is the musket I gave you?' His voice was harsh.

'I forgot it.' She shook her head.

'Ah well. I saw Cecily leave the King's Head with Bedloe. If I am not sleeping or plotting, I keep that nest of vipers under close observation.' He sighed. 'Anyway, Master Stanker said he thought he had been followed. When I saw Blue-skin and two of his bully-boys leave the tavern, I thought, Ah, there goes mischief. So I followed.'

'The corpse?' Maria Eleanora asked. She found she could not stop shivering.

'Go back, Maria Eleanora,' Dolius urged, rearranging her cloak about her shoulders. 'Go back and stay safe. I'll take care of the corpse. And you, my bonny, take care of yourself, for the storm is about to break!'

Chapter Thirteen

Tribulation upon tribulation, like waves upon the sand!

Maria Eleanora wrote the words in her journal. Despite the Portuguese cipher, they seemed like the searing lines from one of the many hand-bills being distributed across London. After Blue-skin's attack, Maria Eleanora had been ill for days. The speed, the savagery of his assault, his callous touch, his foul body pressed up against hers! Ugh! She could smell the stench of his breath for the rest of the week and recalled his cruel gimlet eyes and thrusting hands. Once she had returned to her chamber, she had stripped herself naked and given the Queen's almoner every item of clothing she had been wearing. She did not wish to see or touch them again. She had bathed herself carefully and, making the cold weather an excuse, confined herself to her chamber. She was so relieved Dolius had arrived. Blue-skin's attack had made her realise how her protector's warnings were not ill-judged. Shaftesbury and the Green Ribboners were locked in a fight to the death. So, what did it matter if a Portuguese lady-in-waiting suffered an unfortunate accident? She had later asked Robert Green why he hadn't stayed, but the poor man's fear was answer enough.

'I could not tarry, Mistress. Why, what happened?' he asked plaintively. 'I am a member of the Queen's household, and I am a papist. I must be careful.' He'd added something inaudible.

'What is it, Robert?' Maria Eleanora had demanded.

'We are being watched,' he whispered. 'Berry, Hill and myself. Nothing significant, just the same faces in taverns which we saw the previous evening. As we go about our business, meet in Paternoster Row or out near Cripplegate, we glimpse these men watching us. Mistress, I am a-feared. I do not wish to be drawn into anything dangerous. I urge you to follow my advice!'

After that she hadn't seen the porter of the Great Water Gate again. Over the succeeding days Maria Eleanora realised Green's fears were truly founded. Shaftesbury and his coven were howling for blood. Titus Oates and Bedloe were like a braying chorus chanting the same lines. William Staveley had died a horrible death at Tyburn, half-hanged, cut down, his entrails and vital organs plucked out, his body quartered. A grim warning of the terrors yet to come. Edward Coleman was next. This feckless former secretary to the York household was brought to trial on 27 November: face wasted, eyes hollow, so the hand-bills described him. Coleman had licked dry, bloodless lips as he stood in the dock at Westminster Hall and Titus Oates and Bedloe damned him as a traitor. The news of the trial seeped like black, fetid smoke into Somerset Place. Maria Eleanora did not need Dolius or Cecily to tell her which way the wind was blowing. Coleman was accused of plotting to kill the King, of proposing to give the Queen's physician, Sir George Wakeman, ten thousand pounds for a powerful poison. All a tissue of lies but Coleman had been imprudent. He had written letters which damned him out of his own mouth.

Chief Justice Scroggs had bellowed at the jury.

'Gentlemen, if your consultation shall be long, then you must stay at it all night and I'll take your verdict in the morning. If it will not be long, I am content to wait.'

'My lord,' the foreman replied. 'Trust us, we shall be brief.'

They were very brief. When Coleman was told to stand, raise his hand and face the jury, he was marked down to follow the same grisly path as William Staveley. The verdict came at the end of November. Maria Eleanora had to forget her own problems in comforting the Queen and trying to put a brave face on it. The only ray of light to pierce the murk was news smuggled in by Dolius: her beloved Samuel Atkins was still feverish but the worst was past. Maria Eleanora asserted herself. The Queen needed her. The days passed one into the other. Despite the King's reassurances, Shaftesbury aimed for the heart. Oates and Bedloe were brought before the bar of a packed Commons, the doors closed and guarded. Oates, supported by Bedloe, portrayed himself as a martyr. He spoke all a-blather, his great chin wagging, his protuberant eyes glaring round the chamber. He insisted that Catherine of Braganza and all her household should be removed from the kingdom. A courier brought the news hotfoot to Westminster. Maria Eleanora was with the Queen as she crumpled into a heap on the floor and sobbed bitterly. The young woman crouched next to her, stroking her face, whispering endearments in Portuguese.

'What shall we do?' a sad-eyed chamberlain moaned.

'There are guards outside!' Maria Eleanora yelled. 'Have all doors closed and locked. Tell the royal officers to protect every approach to the Queen's apartments!'

She helped the sobbing, tear-soaked Queen to her feet, pushing her out along the gloomy passageways to her own private bedchamber. Yet, in the end, Oates had struck too far, too fast. Outside Westminster the mob refused to accept the lie. Maria Eleanora was with the Queen, sitting on the bed beside her, when the King, hat in one hand, sword in the other, surrounded by his gentlemen and officers of his guard, swept into Somerset Place. Maria Eleanora had grown used to the languid Prince with the cynical eyes and heavy-lidded glance but this Charles was different, his face a mask of fury. He leaned over the Queen and kissed her, cuddling her close. On one occasion he turned away; Maria Eleanora could tell by his shaking shoulders that he was sobbing as bitterly as Catherine. He composed himself and looked over his shoulder at Maria Eleanora.

'What you have seen today you must not reveal,' he whispered, 'but I tell you this.' The words came out in a hiss. 'They think I will divorce and get a new wife but, God forgive me, I love my Catherine. I will not see an innocent woman abused!'

He extinguished the dim lamp on the bedside table and lay down beside the Queen who had cried herself into an almost trance-like state.

'I swear, Catherine,' the King said passionately, 'at my time and in my place, at a moment of my own choosing, I shall meet these gentlemen who have managed this. If there be a God in Heaven, the reckoning will be terrible.' He kissed the Queen, flung himself off the bed, came round and glanced down at Maria Eleanora. 'Samuel Atkins is getting better,' he told her, 'but we must pray God for a miracle. I could not save Staveley and I cannot save Coleman. The dogs are loose, Maria Eleanora. God knows whom they'll bring down next but I must protect my Queen!'

Charles was true to his word. Maria Eleanora appreciated that his loving words for Catherine were not merely hot breath on cold air. The following day, when the Commons 'Address for the Removal of the Queen' came to the Lords to be debated, Charles himself led the attack. He dropped the heavy-lidded, sardonic approach and spoke bluntly and passionately. The Lords refused to accept the Address by eight votes. Shaftesbury was discomfited whilst Oates was confined to a chamber. The King had shown his hand. More soldiers were placed in Somerset Place. On 30 November Parliament demanded the city militia be placed under their control.

'My father lost his head because of such measures,' the King replied tartly. 'I will not lose mine by letting the militia out of my hands.'

The Terror grew. At least two thousand troops circled London. Wealthy merchants started to send their families abroad. On 3 December Edward Coleman was dragged on a sledge through the mud and slush to be butchered at Tyburn. He stood shivering on the scaffold staring out across the mob who had gathered to watch him die. One of the Queen's maids told Maria Eleanora how Coleman had expected a pardon but, when it did not arrive, the condemned man whispered, 'Put not your trust in princes,' followed by another quotation from the Psalm: 'There is no faith in man.' He died bravely. Two days later, five Catholic lords were sent to the Tower and, as the city prepared for Christmas, more priests were committed for trial.

Maria Eleanora was exhausted. Now confined to her chambers, she could only pray and express her love for Samuel in writing letters which were never sent; composing poems she could only whisper. Sometimes she felt as if her heart was going to break. At others she recalled Dolius's cunning and the courage and tenacity of Cecily.

'He is not dead! He is not dead!' she whispered. 'My Samuel is still alive and I must not give up hope.'

On one occasion she persuaded another lady-in-waiting to go out and visit the shops and stalls along the Strand. She hoped that Josiah-Praise-the-Lord Stanker might be waiting, or some other emissary from Dolius but the captain of the guard insisted that he and four of his men accompany her. After a short walk in the cold December air, Maria Eleanora returned to her quarters in Somerset Place.

That same day she attempted her disguise but got no further than the first court. She peered through the thick mullioned glass of the stairwell and glimpsed the soldiers milling outside warming their hands over a brazier. She had no choice but to retreat back to her chamber. 'Tribulation upon tribulation! Wave after wave!' The words seemed to haunt Maria Eleanora but then the real storm broke. A pedlar came and whispered the words to one of the soldiers who guarded the main entrance to Somerset Place: Shaftesbury had returned to the attack. The news alarmed the Queen's court. Miles Prance the silversmith, a constant visitor to the Queen's Chapel, had been taken up in the dead of night and lodged in Newgate for questioning. Catherine, eyes red-rimmed in her ghost-like face, decided to brave the storm. At Maria Eleanora's insistence she opened her coffers and bribed those servants who'd remained to bring news and information. Maria Eleanora quietly thanked God that Dolius had struck before Shaftesbury had.

At first Prance held out. He knew nothing about Justice Godfrey's death.

'May I be damned to the pit of Hell,' he cried, 'if I know anything of his murder or the Plot.'

'No, no,' Bedloe replied. 'I saw you there in a light flaxen periwig.'

Maria Eleanora read these words in a hand-bill, so freshly printed the ink stained her fingers. She closed her eyes and recalled Prance at the Sigh of Mourning tavern. She only hoped that Bedloe did not know the full truth. Prance, however, refused to give satisfaction. He explained that he'd once worn a light flaxen periwig made from his wife's hair

276

but he had not worn it for many a day. Bedloe laughed at him. Prance was carted off to Newgate, loaded with irons and lowered into the underground cell. According to witnesses, he'd screamed and screamed to be released. After a short while in that perishing-cold, foulsome hold, he'd agreed to speak. He was dragged up, teeth rattling, and carried out of Newgate to Shaftesbury's residence at Thanet House in Aldersgate. Shaftesbury's gang played him like the cruel men they were. Maria Eleanora could only wait. Christmas was forgotten. They had reached the eye of the storm! Would Prance name Samuel Atkins? Or would he try to save both his life and reputation?

Dolius's prophecy proved correct. On Christmas Eve, Prance signed a confession to say that he had been present at Somerset Place. He had glimpsed the murderers and he gave names. Henry Berry, porter of the Great Water Gate at Somerset Place. Robert Green, cushion-layer and minor carpenter at the Queen's Chapel, and Lawrence Hill, also attached to the Queen's retinue. Green was depicted as the principal murderer. According to Prance, Green had flung the hapless Godfrey to the ground, beaten him on the breast, throttled him and twisted his neck until he broke it. Maria Eleanora heard the news, gabbled out by a breathless messenger, someone who had bribed one of Shaftesbury's servants. He delivered the news in the Queen's own chamber. Catherine lifted a finger, a sign for Maria Eleanora to remain silent.

'These are lies,' she whispered. 'Was any other name given?'

'Your Majesty, I do not think so. Green, Berry and Hill, that was all.'

Maria Eleanora had to grasp the arm of the chair to steady herself; her body went hot and cold. The Queen was about to continue her questioning when they heard a tumult, raised voices, footsteps hurrying along the gallery. The door was flung open and the captain of the guard, hatless, his wig askew, leaned against the lintel and fought for breath. The Queen half-rose.

'Sir, what is this?'

'Your Majesty, I apologise. My Lord of Shaftesbury and others are now within Somerset Place. They have brought the silversmith Miles Prance to show them where Justice Godfrey was supposedly murdered.'

The messenger fled. The Queen slumped back in her chair. Maria Eleanora made her comfortable and followed the officer out.

'Can't you stop them?'

'They have the writ of the Commons,' the hard-faced officer replied.

'They must not approach the Queen,' Maria Eleanora insisted.

'They will not!' the officer swore, taking up position outside the Queen's bedchamber.

Maria Eleanora heard the noise below and hurried down the stairs. She glimpsed red-coated guards. Berry and Green, already under arrest, hands tied behind them were being bundled out into the darkness. Maria Eleanora kept to the shadows. The sound of voices grew. The glow of lantern horns and torches lit up the dank, cold courts and doorways. Prance, dirty and dishevelled, led the committee and their hangers-on around Somerset Place. He was almost hysterical. Maria Eleanora followed him and the rest as they went up stairways, through the vast maze of rooms and galleries. Prance pointed out how Godfrey had been brought within, imprisoned, attacked and killed. Voice high with anxiety, Prance gibbered and chattered, eager to save his own life, then they were gone like some rushing wind. Maria Eleanora found herself outside the chapel. She went in, crouched down on a prie-dieu and sobbed bitterly.

The arrest of Green, Berry and Hill brought new terrors to Somerset Place. Prance was returned to Newgate where he was given more comfortable quarters but acted hysterically, screaming, 'No murder, murder, guilty, not guilty, plot, no plot!' Nevertheless, despite all his ranting lies, he had not named Samuel Atkins. Green, Berry and Hill, however, were another matter. Maria Eleanora was terrified that they would follow the same path as Prance and name anybody Shaftesbury and their coven wanted. She found it difficult to eat or sleep. She began to neglect her appearance and seemed unaware of the half-hearted Christmas festivities, the greenery, the red-berried holly and ivy which decorated the principal chambers of Somerset Place. The carols and the whispered chapel services came and went like dreams in the night.

As the old year gave way to the new, Maria Eleanora was awakened one morning by a lusty singing outside her chamber. She recognised an old carol. Picking up her robe, she put it round her shoulders and opened the door in annoyance. An officer of the Life Guards stood, back to the door, in the splendour of his scarlet coat, black shiny boots, a blond wig under his gilt-edged, tricorne hat.

'I beg you, sir,' she said tartly, '*not* to sing here at such an hour.'

'Why, Madam.' The man turned and doffed his hat. 'Your servant, Ma'am. Jonathan Harding. Colonel in the King's own regiment.' His rubicund, fat face broke into a smile.

Maria Eleanora peered closer. 'Dolius!' she whispered.

'I beg your pardon, Ma'am.' The hat was planted with a flourish back on his head. He stood, one thumb looped through the pocket of his waistcoat, the other beating a tattoo on the basket hilt of his rapier.

'Do . . . Do . . . Do . . .' he mimicked. 'Ma'am, I suggest you go back to sleep.'

He almost pushed her into the chamber and, leaning down, kissed her smackingly on the lips. Then he took off both wig and hat.

'What a dance, eh? Green, Berry and Hill are in Newgate whilst Prance blathers like a babe.'

'Where have you been?'

'Hither and thither, the far side of the moon,' Dolius replied. 'Do you like my disguise?' He preened a blond moustache. 'A very clever dye from a barber's surgeon I know in Threadneedle . . .'

'Shut up!' Maria Eleanora intervened. 'How is my Samuel?'

'"My Samuel",' he teased, 'is feverish, still weak but getting stronger by the day.'

'Has he recalled any matters?'

'No. It is now common knowledge that he was supposed to have supper on Friday, October the eleventh with Mr Littlejohn his tutor. He never kept the appointment, nor did he apologise for his absence. I am sure our good Captain Bedloe has heard this. Your Samuel, and my Samuel, will be depicted as being with Godfrey's assassins from Friday to Monday.'

'But Prance hasn't named Samuel?'

'Thanks be to God,' Dolius replied briskly.

'And Green, Berry and Hill?'

'That's what I'm here for, Ma'am. I am to escort you to Newgate.' He winked knowingly. 'Because Catherine is a tender-hearted woman, you are being sent from the royal household to bring comfort to three former, hapless members of the Queen's entourage.'

'And Samuel?' Maria Eleanora asked.

'You will see his face for a brief while, but you must not let slip anything. Oh, and I've brought you some company.'

He opened the door and went out into the gallery.

'Where is that bloody wench?' he bawled. 'The one I hired to accompany me and give me comfort!'

Maria Eleanora heard the tip-tap of footsteps as Dolius led Cecily into the chamber. She, too, was disguised. A curly red wig was on her head, paint was rubbed into her cheeks, and a false beauty spot adorned her upper lip. She was dressed in tawdry finery under a thick, blood-red cloak; even her fingernails were garishly painted.

'Cecily, it's so good to—'

'Garn!' Cecily acted the loud-mouthed harridan from the Fleet.

'Very good, isn't she?' Dolius put a fond arm round Cecily's shoulder.

She put her basket down, freed herself from Dolius's embrace and, grasping Maria Eleanora's hand, kissed her on the cheeks.

'You look as if you've been harrowed from Hell,' she whispered. 'You must not give up hope, my love.'

'What's been happening?' Maria Eleanora asked. 'Blueskin?'

'At the bottom of the Thames,' Dolius shrugged. 'A good piece of iron shot tied round his neck. He's poisoning the fishes.'

'And the rest?'

The Irishman's smile faded. 'Maria Eleanora, I am going to take you to see Green, Berry and Hill. The King cannot save them.'

'Oh no!'

'Oh yes.' Dolius's eyes were sad. 'There is no way they

can be saved. They will be offered a pardon if they tell the truth, but nothing else.'

Maria Eleanora recalled red-haired little Berry crouched over his work bench, peering at her with his weak eyes.

'It has to be done,' Cecily declared. 'Green, Berry and Hill could bring everyone down.' She tightened her lips. 'It's hard, Maria Eleanora. For the last few weeks I've allowed myself to be fondled and caressed by the man who murdered my husband. The only comfort I can offer you is what I give myself.' Cecily paused. 'Revenge.'

Maria Eleanora's heart softened at the stricken look in her friend's eyes. She went forward and embraced her.

'Are you in danger?'

'No,' Cecily replied. She laughed self-consciously and pushed Maria Eleanora away. 'Men have one great vice, their arrogance. Bedloe thinks I am smitten with him. I'm only too willing to play the reluctant maid.'

'Will you kill him?' Maria Eleanora asked.

'Oh, I will kill him,' Cecily replied coldly. 'But only when I am well and truly ready. Bedloe deserves to die. He's an assassin, a reprobate who has sent far too many good men to their deaths.' She glanced away. 'I am, at least for Captain William Bedloe, God's reckoning.'

Dolius intervened, telling Maria Eleanora to act quickly. She gathered up the clothes she always wore and they slipped down the gallery. Maria Eleanora marvelled at the way Dolius could swagger and carry off the role of the haughty royal officer. No one gave him a second glance as they went downstairs. Maria Eleanora closeted herself in the small tiring room where she changed, hid her court clothes and emerged, once again, dressed in dark colours, broad-brimmed hat and heavy cloak.

'A handsome man,' Cecily winked. 'I could take a fancy to you myself.'

'It's the company you keep,' Dolius riposted. 'I am beginning to wonder about my two girls. But come. The day
draws on.'

They left Somerset Place and entered the Strand. It was
a cold, bleak, iron-grey day, the fog rolling like clouds of
cannon smoke, bringing with it the different smells of the
city. Sedan chairs were carried by, link boys running ahead
with lighted tapers and lantern horns. Candle-light gleamed
through thick mullioned glass. Voices shouted, people going
about their business. The Yuletide festivities were over and
the harsh reality of another new year beckoned. Dolius
swaggered ahead, Cecily, acting the little maid, pattering
behind them.

A light drizzle began to fall as they tramped on up across
the muddy cobbleways of Snow Hill to where the great
towers of Newgate loomed. They entered a postern door.
Captain Richardson, surly as ever and smoking a clay pipe,
beckoned them forward. Today he wore a tricorne hat and a
thick military cloak. Maria Eleanora noticed how Richardson
acted very busily but never ever really looked at them, as if
the keeper's personal motto was: What the eye doesn't see,
the heart cannot grieve over. The letters Dolius carried were
returned. They left the porter's lodge, went across the press
yard and entered the filthy warren of passageways and cells,
dungeons and pits. Maria Eleanora kept her head well down,
unwilling to hear the cries of the prisoners or be aware of the
dirt and the squalor.

Green, Berry and Hill shared a cell at the far side of the
prison. A narrow, dirty room with a small window high in
the wall, the place smelt worse than a sewer. Maria Eleanora
stood in the shadows with Cecily whilst Dolius swaggered
across and crouched before the three prisoners. Green and
Berry looked in a pitiful state, their hair, face and clothes

covered in dirt and mud. Berry couldn't stop trembling and had to walk away to relieve himself in a cracked pot in the far corner. Green was stricken, withdrawn, but Hill, who Maria Eleanora knew by sight, was of stronger stuff: he loudly declared his innocence. For a while Dolius listened to their different complaints.

'I'm here to ask you one question,' he declared in a voice deep and rich as port wine. 'I come directly from the King. Are you three men innocent of all charges?'

'As newborn babes,' Hill bellowed. 'And there's not a shred of evidence to convict us.'

'Very good! Very good!' Dolius replied in a most soothing voice. 'But, tell me now, gentlemen, how will you plead in court?'

'Not guilty!' Hill spoke for the rest.

'But what happens if my Lord Shaftesbury offers you a path out, like he did to Master Prance? If he asks for names?'

Hill turned away, hawked and spat.

'I can't speak for the rest,' he declared, 'but I'll not follow the liar's path. I'll bring no innocent men to suffer what I have.'

'Good! Good!' Dolius said. 'Then this is my offer. Speak the truth, plead your innocence and, whatever happens, the King will pardon you.'

The change in all three men was remarkable though Hill looked suspicious.

'Wasn't Master Coleman promised a pardon?'

'Never,' Dolius retorted. 'But the conditions are very simple. You *must* plead your innocence. You must *not* convict anyone else. Do that and a pardon could be yours. I assure you of that.'

'And who are these?'

Berry and Green had ignored Maria Eleanora and Cecily but Hill edged forward, eyes screwed up.

'A young man and a maid come to see a woman prisoner on another matter.' Dolius was already on his feet. He clasped each of the men's hands. 'Have no fear. The King will keep his word.'

Dolius turned on his heel and walked to the door. Even as he did so the expression on his face changed. Maria Eleanora, eyes hidden by her hat and the thick folds of the cloak, stared pityingly at the three prisoners. They were men whom no power on earth could help. They were lambs for the slaughter. Green and Berry were terrified, their wits so disordered, they hadn't realised who Maria Eleanora really was, though, she reflected sadly, Green had only ever seen her as a dark shadow slipping through the Water Gate at night.

Outside in the passageway a turnkey was waiting. Dolius imperiously beckoned him away.

'Richardson,' he whispered in Maria Eleanora's ear, 'has given us permission to pass Samuel's cell. You will have no more than a few heartbeats. Promise me now,' Dolius gripped her arm and squeezed so tightly that Maria Eleanora winced, 'promise me that you will not put all our lives at risk! They've put a prisoner in with Samuel – a man called Beecham. He's no more a prisoner here than I am; he's a professional witness brought in by Shaftesbury and Bedloe to observe what happens. Promise me now!'

Maria Eleanora nodded.

'Right, gentlemen.' Dolius called to the turnkey. 'Lead on, Macbeth!'

The man looked perplexed.

'It's Shakespeare!' Dolius bellowed. 'Oh, forget it.'

The turnkey, fat and shambling as some squat toad, shrugged and led them off.

'When I begin to whistle,' Dolius whispered, 'we are not far from Samuel's cell.'

They turned a corner; the walls were wet and slimy, cell doors either side. Mad eyes glared out at them. Curses and obscene suggestions were directed at Cecily. Maria Eleanora's heart lurched as Dolius began to whistle. She kept her eyes down. When Dolius tapped the wall, Maria Eleanora realised which side the door was. She knew it even before they reached it.

'Fine prisoner we've got here!' Dolius stopped before a cell.

Maria Eleanora, a lump in her throat, stared into the pale face of Samuel Atkins. She would have stretched out and touched those fingers; her heart nearly broke at how thin and pallid his face had become but his eyes had immediately brightened and crinkled in amusement.

'And who are you?' Samuel turned to Dolius. 'A captain in the King's Guard, eh?' His eyes moved hungrily back to Maria Eleanora as he spoke. 'Come to gloat over a poor prisoner, have you?'

Maria Eleanora pulled down the folds of her cloak and mouthed the words. 'My heart I love you. I will always love you.'

Samuel's passionate stare, the way his fingers splayed as if he could put them through the bars and caress her cheek was answer enough.

'I tell you this.' Atkins kept up the pretence. 'If you've come to stare at a man like me then take pity. Once I was a clerk to the grand Mr Pepys who works in the Admiralty at Derby House.' Samuel's eyes were now staring at Maria Eleanora, pleading with her to understand. 'Tell him all I need is victuals – food and drink. Victuals, victuals and victuals!'

'The fellow's mad,' Dolius drawled. 'Fool's gone witless.'

He pushed Maria Eleanora on. She shot one last lingering passionate stare.

'Go tell grand Mr Pepys!' Samuel bawled behind them. 'I'm a-hungered and thirsty, and all I need is victuals!'

In his cell Samuel stood by the door banging his forehead against the wood.

'Oh, Maria Eleanora,' he whispered beneath his breath. 'Oh, how I love you! How I miss you!'

For a moment Samuel just stood, his entire body pressed against the wooden, iron-studded door, head going backwards and forwards as if, by very force of will, he could break through and follow his beloved. He heard a sound behind him.

'Are you well, Master Samuel?'

Atkins closed his eyes and turned. He felt weak, still nauseous after his fever but he had been given good physic. He glared across at Beecham – a thin, cadaverous-faced man with lank, greasy hair, sunken cheeks pitted with smallpox and a mouth like a gaping hole. Samuel had soon grown to hate him.

'What's this about victuals?' Beecham clamped his arms together. 'Captain Richardson has given you a good stew, nourishing pottage, wholesome oatmeal.'

Samuel smiled back, baring his teeth.

'What day of the year is it?'

Beecham shrugged. 'January the year of Our Lord 1679 though God knows the date!'

'And how long have you been with me?' Atkins leaned against the door.

'Don't you remember? I joined you soon after Yuletide because of purse-picking.'

Samuel rubbed his face between his hands.

'Shall I tell you something, Master Beecham?'

287

A wary look appeared on the Judas man's face. Atkins walked over. Beecham recoiled.

'I am sick to my heart,' Samuel glared down at him, 'of your whines and your mock friendship. You are no more a cutpurse, Master Beecham, than I am. You have been placed in here to keep an eye on me and listen to what I say. I would like my freedom. I would like a slab of roast beef but, above all, I would like to meet you out on a piece of wasteland, armed with a musket or sword, where I could kill you!'

Swallowing hard, Beecham backed into the corner.

'You are witless!' he croaked. 'You are mad! You are insane!'

'No, I'm not.' Samuel followed him over. 'I'm an innocent man, falsely accused, deprived of my freedom, whom your masters wish to see swing at Tyburn.' He bent down, his face only a few inches from the cowering Beecham. 'So, do you know what I am going to do, Master Snooper? I am going to give you a beating which you will never forget. And when your cries bring Richardson here, you will be released. You can hasten back to your masters then and tell them this: Samuel Atkins is a loyal, Godfearing Englishman.'

Beecham slipped by him and ran towards the door, screaming and banging on the wood.

'Let me out! Let me out! This man's for Bedlam! This man's for Bedlam!'

Samuel slid down the wall. He joined his hands, bowed his head and prayed that Maria Eleanora, and those who were with her, would reflect on what he had said. For he had finally remembered where he was in those fateful October days – but would his beloved find the evidence? And if she did, could she save him from the hangman's noose?

Outside Newgate, Dolius, Maria Eleanora and Cecily had

walked up through the Shambles, along St Martin's Lane and into the noisy taproom of an ale-house.

Everyone made way for Dolius in his red coat and military manner. He commandeered a table and ordered tankards of ale, bellowing at the pot boys to hurry up. Maria Eleanora sat mutely, deeply upset by what she had seen, trying to hide her panic at the plight of her beloved.

'Well, well, well,' Dolius breathed. 'Our Samuel's hale and hearty.'

'He was sending a message.' Cecily spoke up, tankard shielding her face. 'That business about you telling grand Mr Pepys that he needs victuals?'

'But Pepys doesn't know anything about me,' Maria Eleanora objected.

'No, he doesn't.' Dolius drained the tankard. 'And I think it's high time he did.'

He gave the women no choice but to follow him all the way to Derby House. Even Maria Eleanora, unused to the city and the politics of the Green Ribboners, realised the building was being carefully watched. Beggars lounged on the steps, others lurked in nearby ale-houses. Dolius didn't give them a second glance but, acting the part of the brave, bold officer, he strode up the steps, grabbed a clerk by the scruff of his neck and forced the hapless man to escort them up the wide-sweeping internal staircase to Mr Pepys's office.

The Secretary of the Navy's chamber was spacious and grand, with a polished wooden floor, elegant drapes round the windows, and the silver-chased candelabra standing on shining oaken furniture. A great fire roared in the canopied hearth. The rather dimunitive Secretary was seated behind a desk piled high with papers. Pepys had taken his coat off. When Dolius strode in, still clutching the struggling clerk, Pepys sprang to his feet.

'What is this, sir? What is this? Upon my honour, what is this? Who are you?'

'Get out!' Dolius roared at the scribes and clerks clustered about. 'Everyone get out! I am from His Majesty the King!'

Dolius let go of the struggling clerk who joined the rest in their flight from the room. Pepys, however, remained calm. Maria Eleanora realised some secret sign must have been passed between himself and Dolius. Once the door was closed, Pepys sauntered over, pulled the bolts across and returned to stand with his back to the fire.

'Well, I never – Captain Thomas Blood!'

'I don't know who he is, sir,' Dolius replied, taking his hat off and giving the most mocking bow. 'Me, I'm from Ithaca.'

'Do you bring help?' Pepys's voice was low. 'For our cause seems ruined.' He fished in a waistcoat pocket and brought out a pair of spectacles which he placed carefully on his nose, then he stared at Maria Eleanora and Cecily. 'Who's the young man swathed in black and the red-haired maid? Can these be trusted?'

'Upon my life they can be, but are we to stand here like actors on a stage?'

Pepys shrugged and walked back to his desk, gesturing at them to sit in chairs arranged in front.

'My clerks have fled so I might as well hear you. Pray be brief.'

Dolius plucked the hat off Maria Eleanora's head and pulled back her cloak. Pepys nearly shot to his feet again.

'Upon my honour! Begad! What is this?'

'May I introduce Maria Eleanora Gonzales Esqueba de Valeroma, lady-in-waiting to Queen Catherine of Braganza and the ardent beloved of your own Samuel Atkins.'

'Upon my honour!'

Pepys sat back in his chair and, grasping a sheaf of papers, began to fan himself furiously, his short-sighted eyes rounded in wonderment. His face showed a range of moods: surprise, interest, even appreciation for Maria Eleanora, followed by a petulant anger.

'The young fool!' He threw the sheaf of papers back on the desk. 'To be courting a Queen's lady-in-waiting, a papist at a time like this!'

'What time?' Maria Eleanora asked coolly. 'I believe you were once married, Mr Pepys?'

The Secretary's face softened.

'Elizabeth, wasn't it?'

'Elizabeth.' Pepys half-smiled. 'I loved her then and I love her now. Not a day goes by that I don't think of her.' He gestured at a painting on the wall of a dark-haired, pale-faced woman garbed in a gauze-like, very revealing blue dress. 'She drove me to distraction when alive,' he said in a half-whisper. 'Even dead, she does the same.'

'I love Samuel Atkins,' Maria Eleanora declared. 'I couldn't care if he was papist, Protestant or, indeed, a blackamoor in the court of the Great Cham. If he was here, he would say the same about me.'

'And who are you?' Pepys abruptly turned to Cecily.

'One of my little helpers,' Dolius spoke up. 'Don't worry about her. Just concentrate on the Portuguese. For heaven's sake, man!' Dolius leaned forward and banged the table. 'She's making a confession about love; if that was a crime we'd all be swinging by our necks at Tyburn. I can vouch for her.' His voice became soft. 'If a woman like Maria Eleanora loved you, or me, like she does Samuel Atkins . . . well, I for one would die a happy man. Now, we know Atkins is innocent. Lord Shaftesbury is really pursuing *you*. We have come for your help, sir. Are you going to give it, or sit on your arse and lecture us?'

'How can I help?' Pepys sat back in his chair and stared at them. He gave a great sigh, fluttered his eyelids and started strumming his lower lip.

'If you don't help us,' Maria Eleanora told him, 'Samuel will die and so will I.'

Pepys sighed and leaned forward. 'I know what you are after. When Godfrey was killed, I was in Newmarket – I can vouch for my actions. However, Samuel, on the other hand, spent the weekend carousing – though nobody knows where or with whom. I've made my own enquiries. None of the scribes or clerks here can help. If I could, I would. I like Samuel.' He added testily, 'But my hands are tied. I can go nowhere near him, my every movement is watched. You've seen the men outside . . . ?'

Dolius nodded.

'We visited Samuel this morning,' Maria Eleanora declared. 'He told me how he worked for the grand Mr Pepys. He was acting witless but kept saying I must ask you for *victuals*.'

Pepys cocked his head sideways. 'Did he, now? Are you sure of that? Samuel was a good trencherman. He liked his food . . .'

'But why should he ask for victuals so insistently?' Maria Eleanora demanded. 'I am sure it was a secret message.'

'How strong is Shaftesbury's case?' Pepys asked.

'They have perjury witnesses.'

Pepys sighed again.

'Matters are not helped by Samuel's inability to remember anything.'

'So, why *is* he asking about victuals?' Pepys got to his feet, pushing back his chair. He walked over to a window and stared out. 'I wish I could give more assistance but I have duties here – ships preparing for sea.'

Then Pepys went rigid and, turning, did a small jig.

'Now who's witless?' Dolius murmured.

'Victuals!' Pepys roared, clapping his hands. 'Victuals indeed! Oh, Samuel, you are wise beyond your years! A man of keen wit. Why, of course, ships ready for sea!'

Watched by a surprised Maria Eleanora, Pepys hurried back to his desk and searched amongst the papers. Dragging out a calfskin ledger, its cover emblazoned with gold letters, he almost thrust it into Maria Eleanora's face.

'Do you know what this is?'

'For love's sake!' Dolius growled.

'This,' Pepys declared triumphantly, 'may well save our Samuel!'

Chapter Fourteen

The coach was the best Dolius could hire – a great ornate, four-wheeled affair painted completely black and pulled by powerful bays. It stood on the cobbles near the gateway to Westminster Hall. Outside, the February morning was freezing. Inside the coach, Dolius had arranged for a small chafing dish to be brought full of glowing coals; this lay on the floor between them. The blinds were pulled down, a large lantern horn rested in the corner. Now and again the horses moved and Maria Eleanora would steady herself. She glanced across at her two companions and once again marvelled at their clever disguises. Dolius was dressed as a lawyer in a gown as black as night edged with silver-white fur, a coif upon his head. Paste rubbed into his face turned his features longer and older, fine ash had been applied beneath his eyes to make them more hollow. When he sucked in his lips, he looked the epitome of a sharp-faced lawyer hungry for a brief. He even had the mannerisms, turning his head slightly as if hard of hearing, and his fingers were ink-stained. When he had shuffled into the coach, Maria Eleanora had truly believed he was a lawyer come to assist poor Samuel.

'Are you well, Maria Eleanora?'

She glanced across at Cecily. She, too, had been transformed – into a grey-haired housewife. Extra clothes thickened her figure and the paint on her face made her look heavy-cheeked. A grey wig planted under the dark-brown felt hat completed the transformation.

'Are you sure you won't be recognised?' Maria Eleanora asked.

'My dear child.' Dolius's voice took on a West Country twang. He leaned forward pretentiously, grasping the scrolls wrapped with red ribbon. 'My name is James Bartlett of Gore, lawyer.' He then mimicked an Irish accent. 'Or should I say "liar" come to do business in the Court of Common Pleas and distracted by the case of young Atkins. This is Mistress Barbara Touchwood of the Parish of St Clement's, come to push her claim in the Court of Chancery regarding certain tenements and messages bequeathed to her by her late husband . . .'

Dolius's teeth were now jutting out, flecks of spittle formed on the corners of his lips.

'Very good! Very good!' Maria Eleanora applauded. 'But can we help Samuel?'

'He's hale and hearty,' Dolius replied. 'He loves you more than he ever did. I know that because I learnt it straight from the horse's mouth. The coachman driving us is one of our men. He visited Newgate on pretence – slipped the keeper a few coins – and thus ensured that Samuel will appear in court unchained, in fresh apparel, and cleanly shaved though his hair will be cropped. He'll be rather weak-legged and pasty-faced despite a good breakfast of kidneys, eggs and a large cup of malmsey.'

'How will it go?'

Dolius stared back. Maria Eleanora closed her eyes. January had slipped away, one terror-filled day after another. Green, Hill and Berry had been brought to trial. She had received the Queen's permission to attend with one of the other ladies-in-waiting. Maria Eleanora had left the court in white-knuckled terror. Here were three men completely innocent of any charge, yet the Green Ribboners danced round them like children about a Maypole. Green and Berry had virtually collapsed under the sharp questioning of the Attorney-General 'Bull-Face Jonas' and the hostile attitude of Chief Justice William Scroggs. Only Hill had fought the good fight, challenging witnesses, demanding the evidence against him be more precise and not so circumstantial.

For a while Maria Eleanora and the other ladies had held their breath, thinking that the prosecution's case would either collapse or be withdrawn, but Bedloe's lies held. Scroggs terrified any opposition, so when all three were confronted by the jury, they were declared guilty. Their deaths had been preordained, as Dolius remarked; they were sacrificial lambs for the bloody slaughter. Green, Berry and Hill were presently lodged in Newgate awaiting sentence and there was no doubt about what that would be. Jack Ketch of Tyburn had been very busy with his rope and knife, his fleshing table and buckets of pitch and tar. The dismembered limbs of other unfortunates caught up in the Great Plot and executed, now decorated the approaches to London Bridge.

Maria Eleanora could not bear considering such a fate for Samuel. She opened her eyes and stared at Cecily.

'And Bedloe is full of himself?'

'Like a cock on a manure heap,' Cecily replied. 'They think they have Samuel bought and sold, what with Captain Childs's evidence, Bedloe's own and, of course, that degenerate Jeremy Prinkheart.'

'Do they know anything about our defence?'

'A little,' Dolius intervened. 'It was inevitable. I just pray to God that everyone turns up.' He leaned across and pulled back the blinds of the carriage. 'The mist is still thick and that will aid our cause. What hour of the morning do you think it is?'

'Not yet light,' Cecily replied.

'We do have one problem,' Dolius said, chewing on his lip. 'Sir William Scroggs is becoming rather tired. He may decide that the court should not sit but take its Lenten break.'

'Oh no!' Maria Eleanora moaned. 'Samuel has been in Newgate for three months!'

'If Shaftesbury has his way,' Dolius replied, 'he will spend another three months there. So, let's remember our tactics. We will go to court, because Samuel will now be accused of being an accessory to murder, rather than of the murder itself. He will be brought to the Bar before King's Bench. We must get very close to him. To do that I will have to use all my authority. Once I am there, let me stand next to Samuel, get as close as I can. The prosecution will present their case, produce evidence and summon up witnesses. Let them run like a ship before the wind. Let's see the trim of their sail and how their cannons fire. But remember.' He pulled back the blinds of the coach. 'If we are watching them, they will certainly be watching us.'

'What is the matter?' Maria Eleanora asked anxiously. She had broken her fast rather hastily and donned her disguise. Now she felt hot, stifling, her stomach nauseous; the strain of the last few months was beginning to tell. She slept badly at night and felt heavy-headed during the day.

'Maria Eleanora, you are a brave girl.' Dolius let the blind fall. 'What we do is a matter of faith, but for you . . .'

'For me, sir,' Maria Eleanora responded hotly, 'it's my life and my love. If I have no Samuel, I have no love. If I have no love, I will never have a life.'

'Oh, that will pass,' Dolius murmured sadly.

'No, it won't.' Cecily spoke up. She, too, was now perspiring. 'You know, Thomas.' It was the only time she had ever used his real name. 'You know it never passes.' She smiled gently at Maria Eleanora. 'You come to terms with it. You compromise but you never forget.'

'Is Bedloe still pawing you?' Maria Eleanora asked, not wanting to appear selfish.

'He grows more lustful and lecherous by the day. He's had my petticoats up and seen my garters.' Cecily did not flinch. 'And he's seen me kick my legs and strain and groan, but he hasn't had his full pleasure yet. Like a fish coming towards a hook, he is. I think he likes the hunt better than the kill.' She leaned forward. 'Are you well, Maria Eleanora?'

She was about to reply when the door of the carriage was suddenly thrown open. Dolius's hand went to the pistol hidden in the folds of his cloak but it was only a pie boy with a tray of freshly baked pastries.

'Are you hungry, sir? Are you hungry, Mistress? Brooks's pies are the best, you know. Pastry soft and tender. The meat and gravy hot and sweet.'

'Go away, lad!' Dolius flicked a penny onto the tray.

The boy was about to continue arguing, but something about the way he was looking round the coach made Maria Eleanora uneasy. He stepped back and Dolius slammed the door shut.

'By the King's balls!' The Irishman wiped his mouth on the back of his hand. 'That was no accident, was it?'

'Do you think he was sent?' Cecily asked.

Dolius undid the door and got out. The carriage moved slightly and, although they couldn't hear distinctly, they knew Dolius was questioning the coachman. A short while later he clambered back.

'He sends his apologies.' Dolius pointed at the roof. 'He claims the boy stole up before he even glimpsed him. The mist is still rather thick. People come and go like ghosts.'

'He was sent,' Cecily repeated. 'The oldest trick but a good one. Take an innocent, give him a coin and ask him to find out who's in the coach.'

Dolius lifted the blind again and peered out.

'I can see no one,' he murmured.

Maria Eleanora became agitated. 'What could they do?' she asked.

'Try and stop us.' Dolius glanced across. 'Do you feel rather hot, Maria Eleanora? Would you fancy a short walk? Take the morning air?'

'You mean, see who is following us?'

'You have your sword,' Dolius replied.

She was about to object but he grasped her hand and squeezed it.

'My love, they have someone here who will try and impede us, stop us getting close to Samuel. They know this coach. Cecily hired it, collected you and collected me. They are suspicious about Blue-skin's disappearance. They must now know who I am. I suspect they are looking for you – the olive-skinned stranger, the young man dressed in dark clothes who was seen with Samuel before his arrest.'

'They are still talking about it at the King's Head,' Cecily agreed. 'They know Blue-skin went to Somerset Place and did not return. They have a great interest in you.'

'Do you think they suspect?'

'They have a list of the Queen's household but no young man of olive-skinned appearance.'

'You must go,' Dolius declared.

Maria Eleanora agreed.

'But wait!' He lifted the small pistol out of his pocket but put it back. 'On second thoughts, just go for a walk down some lonely alleyway.'

'What happens if there's more than one?'

'I doubt if there will be,' Dolius said. 'They do not wish to be too conspicuous. I suspect it's someone in authority – the pie boys of Westminster are notorious for their impudence. It would only take a coin and a threat.'

Maria Eleanora agreed, pushed open the door and stepped gingerly out. The coachman, shrouded in his cloak, sat like a statue carved out of stone. He looked over his shoulder then glanced away. Maria Eleanora closed the carriage door. The air smelt of the river, fish and cordage, pungent with the savoury odours from the nearby cookshops. The mist still curled, like steam above a pot, deadening sound. Figures flitted by. Maria Eleanora pulled up the edge of her cloak to cover her nose and mouth and, grasping the hilt of her sword, walked across the cobbled expanse and down a narrow alleyway which led to a broader thoroughfare. This was a derelict, lonely area: the buildings of the Westminster Palace on one side, a black brick wall on another. Weeds and plants sprouted amongst the mud and dirt. At the far end she glimpsed lantern-horn lights and heard a woman shouting beyond the wall but, otherwise, it was deserted.

Her high-heeled boots crunched on pebbles, the only sound as she walked slowly on. Halfway down she turned swiftly and glimpsed a figure. Maria Eleanora decided to return and investigate. The figure had vanished, but now reappeared, stepping out of a small enclave to block her path. She recognised the red coat and gold buttons of an officer. The man had his head down. When he glanced up, tipping back the brim of his hat, she saw it was Eastwell!

'Let me pass, sir.' Maria Eleanora kept her voice low and clipped. 'I have business in the courts.'

'As do I,' Eastwell taunted. 'I also have business with you.'

He pushed back his cloak and stood, hands on his hips, showing off his dark-green waistcoat as well as letting Maria Eleanora glimpse the rapier hanging on his side.

'I just wondered who you are. And the coach you come from – who's inside?'

'Didn't the pie boy tell you?'

'Your voice is strange.' Eastwell stepped closer. 'Let me see your face.' His hand stretched out.

Maria Eleanora slapped it away.

'Sir, you have no warrant or commission.' She tried to keep her voice to a growl. 'You block my path and insult me.'

Eastwell stepped back, right hand going to draw his sword.

Maria Eleanora decided to strike first. Instead of going back as Eastwell expected, she lunged forward, at the same time drawing her sword – a trick her duelling-master had taught her.

'Always remember,' the old man had advised, 'that many a sword fight can end before it really begins. The rules of fairness do not apply.'

Her sword leapt from the scabbard. Surprised, Eastwell tugged at his own. Then he stumbled. Maria Eleanora paused for a second but this morning was vital: Samuel's life hung by a thread. Eastwell used the delay; his sword was out, coming up. Maria Eleanora danced sideways and, changing hands, drove her sword deep into Eastwell's chest. She pushed, forcing him back. He tried to lift his own weapon, his face a mask of surprise.

'You cannot . . .' he gasped.

'I can and I have!' Maria Eleanora pressed on the sword.

Eastwell coughed, blood bubbles frothing at his lips. She drove her sword in once more, withdrew it and stepped back. Still grasping his weapon, the dying man stumbled against the wall, then his sword fell from nerveless fingers, he gave a cry and crumpled to the ground. Maria Eleanora waited for a few seconds, staring up and down the alleyway. It still remained deserted. She took off her glove, leaned down and pressed her hand against Eastwell's neck but could detect no pulse; her thrust had been deadly and deep into his chest.

Maria Eleanora wiped her sword, sheathed it and walked

along the alleyway. The nausea had disappeared as had the weakness in her legs. She re-entered the cobbled enclosure. More people were there. She heard someone shouting Eastwell's name. A man with a green ribbon pinned to his cloak was running up and down. She ignored him, went across, opened the door of the coach and almost threw herself in. Only then did she begin to tremble, the sweat break out on her face. She took off her hat, pulled down the cloak, ignoring Cecily's questions and Dolius's protests at removing her disguise. Maria Eleanora sat for a while. She found the sword an encumbrance and realised the scabbard had moved on her belt. Her two companions fell silent. Dolius offered a flask, the stopper pulled off.

'The Water of Life,' he murmured. 'The best brandy smugglers can bring in.'

Maria Eleanora grasped the flask and took a mouthful of the fiery liquid which warmed her throat and stomach. She coughed a little, took another swig and handed it back.

'There was someone, wasn't there?' Dolius murmured.

'Eastwell,' Maria Eleanora replied. 'I went down an alleyway. He followed me. He wanted to know who I was . . .'

'And you fought him?' Cecily asked.

'I never gave him a chance. He was drawing his sword. I drew mine and struck first.'

Dolius whistled under his breath and toasted her with the flask.

'I've used that trick myself but not as effectively.'

'I didn't kill him in fair fight,' Maria Eleanora replied. 'But I don't care.'

'No, you shouldn't, my little flower,' Dolius soothed. 'Eastwell was mean, vicious and a good swordsman. He would have killed you and not turned a hair.'

'That's what it's come to.' Maria Eleanora glared at him. 'They kill us or we kill them.'

'That's the spirit.' Dolius laughed softly. 'When you enter the snake pit, you forget all the rules of honour. Kill or be killed. God forgive us, we are worse than any creatures of the night. So, at least we are warned.'

He offered the flask to Cecily but she refused. Dolius muttered to himself, staring across at Maria Eleanora.

'I never thought you could do it.'

'Neither did I.'

Cecily seized her hand. 'A few more hours,' she reassured her. 'Just a few more.'

They heard a cry from outside.

'They are bringing the prisoner up!'

Dolius opened the door and stepped out of the coach followed by Maria Eleanora and Cecily. They glimpsed a line of torches coming through the mist, the gleam of a red coat as an officer led Samuel Atkins, surrounded by turnkeys, up from the river and the prison barge which had brought them from the city. Dolius gripped Maria Eleanora's arm. She was aware of other people gathering round. She glimpsed lawyers, clerks, arms full of bundles of parchment but she was only interested in one thing: that ring of torches! The escort drew closer. Dolius's grip tightened. The ensign in front marched stolidly, the turnkeys behind. Samuel was in the middle, fastened by chains. She noticed how cropped his brown hair was; his face seemed longer, paler. He was staring round, looking for her.

'Now there goes a bully-boy! Fit carrion for Tyburn!' Dolius bellowed at the top of his voice, shaking his sheaf of parchment. 'God save the King says I, and God damn all traitors, be they Lord or commoner!'

Samuel glanced across. Maria Eleanora pulled down the edge of her cloak, their eyes met. Samuel went to smile but remembered himself. Yet his gaze told her everything. How much he loved her. How much he'd missed her and how determined he was that he would survive these cunning machinations which threatened to entrap and kill him.

Maria Eleanora would have walked forward but Dolius, still shouting, held her fast. Cecily moved slightly in front ready to block any approach her friend might be impetuous enough to make. Maria Eleanora felt herself go hot and cold, her legs so stiff, the muscles tense and cramped. She wanted to move. Cecily grasped her arm.

'For God's sake, no!'

Dolius was still shouting threats as the escort passed, making its way up through the gates of Westminster Hall.

'Good girl,' Dolius breathed. 'We've seen our quarry. Now, let's go in hot pursuit!'

Dolius urged them on, pushing his way through the gathering throng, knocking aside hucksters and chapmen, traders and pie men until they were virtually behind the escort. Dolius kept himself firmly in front, Maria Eleanora behind, her arm held fast by Cecily. They went up the steps. The escort swept through. Dolius showed the guards some papers and followed the other group closely.

The day's business had now begun. Lawyers and plaintiffs were busy, with scribes offering their help. A whole legion of traders were looking for custom. Maria Eleanora was aware of the soaring roof, the babble of voices, the different smells, but she concentrated on that figure in its dark-brown jacket, the close cropped hair, the strong neck and muscular shoulders. She kept whispering 'Samuel', until Cecily nudged her sharply in the ribs. They were down the hall, up the steps to King's Bench. Dolius shouldered his way by one of the ushers, coins in one hand, papers in the other, and they were through.

The full panoply of law was waiting inside the screened

enclosure. Maria Eleanora recalled her previous visit. Nothing had changed: the great oaken table, the scarlet cloths, the Royal Arms above the Judge's chair. Tipstaffs, ushers, scribes and officials were all a-bustle. Samuel had been taken along the central passageway. On the right were the raised seats for the jurors, on the left the empty dock. Maria Eleanora half-expected to see the ghost of Staveley standing there. Cecily, in a hushed whisper, explained how Samuel would be brought to the bar rather than the dock.

Dolius was determined to get as near to Samuel as possible, shoving and pushing his way through. Maria Eleanora felt a deep glow of happiness; tears pricked her eyes at the courage of this wild, eccentric Irishman who seemed to love the plot and counter-plot of this seditious, treacherous game. A master of disguise, he was supremely confident. Dolius shouldered his way through until only a turnkey, standing on Samuel's left, separated Maria Eleanora from his would-be protector. Cecily was whispering advice. Maria Eleanora found the heat uncomfortable but she kept her hat low whilst the folds of her cloak hid the lower part of her face. The stench of unwashed bodies and cheap perfume hit her like a gust of hot air from an oven. Spectators were taking their seats, eating, drinking and shouting greetings. Maria Eleanora reached the great wooden bar which separated the Judge's table from the rest of the court and turned round. Amongst the spectators were many wearing the green ribbon pinned to their cloaks.

'Don't worry,' Dolius whispered. 'We have kept our witnesses well away. They'll arrive by special coach. I have it in hand.'

The prosecutor's lawyers filed in, led by 'Bull-Face Jonas' arrayed like a ship-of-war in his black, red and ermine, the silvery white coif clasped on his head, his bulbous sweaty face all set for conflict. He was assisted by other principal law officers gathering like great feathered crows to what they considered to be an easy plucking. Maria Eleanora gazed past Dolius; Samuel was gripping the wooden bar, staring steadfastly before him. Dolius had slipped coins into the turnkey's hand and, for some unknown reason, the fellow disappeared leaving Dolius free to whisper advice whilst, at the same time, keeping Samuel and Maria Eleanora separate. Cecily was still urging her to keep calm and not to betray them. At one moment the excitement was so much Maria Eleanora felt herself sway and prayed she wouldn't faint. She tried to distract herself.

'Are you sure our witnesses will come?'

'Of course!' Cecily's face was also bathed in sweat. 'Dolius has everything in hand. Just pray that all goes well.'

The court was now preparing. The Judge's table was laid with tomes, documents, writing-trays, quills and ink-pots. The Clerk of the Court, his face almost shrouded by a heavy white wig, processed solemnly up the stairs, an usher carrying a white wand on either side.

'Oyez! Oyez!' he shouted. 'All ye who have business before His Majesty's Chief Justice, Sir William Scroggs, take ear and draw close!'

'Bull-Face Jonas' and the prosecution immediately sprang to their feet and handed the clerk a scroll. The fellow undid it and read the contents as if he was seeing them for the first time.

'Oyez! Oyez!' he proclaimed. 'All ye who have business against the accused Samuel Atkins draw close and lay your petition!'

He rolled up the scroll. The two ushers banged their white wands against the bar of the court. The noise subsided.

'Oyez! Oyez!' the clerk proclaimed again. 'All faithful subjects of His Majesty the King, make way for his Chief Justice Sir William Scroggs!'

This terror of the court, this scourge of traitors, solemnly processed up the staircase and onto the raised dais. The clerk hurriedly remembered and ran round the baize-topped table and pulled back the chair. Scroggs looked as toad-like as ever with his red, fleshy jowls, jutting lips and popping eyes. He surveyed the court as if he would hang every man, woman and child present, then his eyes fastened on Samuel. Maria Eleanora was sure she glimpsed a supercilious smile.

The Judge bowed to the court and sat down like a king on his throne. 'Bull-Face Jonas' jumped up and delivered a fiery speech, peppered with 'Your Honour', and 'my Lord'. Maria Eleanora's heart skipped a beat. The Attorney-General was not laying the indictment but pointing out that the court did not have time for the business in hand and that there should be an adjournment. This brought groans and protests from the spectators. They had turned up to taste blood and blood they would have.

Scroggs waved his hand. 'Bull-Face Jonas' paused.

'This court is too dark!' Scroggs barked.

The scribes and clerks, sitting at the small table just beneath the dais, leapt to their feet like imps to do their satanic master's bidding. More candles were brought. Scroggs tapped his throat. A goblet and jug of wine were brought, covered by a napkin. The Chief Justice filled the cup to the brim and quaffed it in one gulp. Then, burping noisily, he leaned back in his chair and gestured at the Attorney-General to continue his speech. It's a play, Maria Eleanora thought, staring desperately down at her beloved. These two men are playing a game, giving speeches like actors on a stage. She was aware of Samuel standing against the bar, Dolius whispering in his ear.

At last 'Bull-Face Jonas' finished. Scroggs glowered down at Samuel.

'Well, sir, it looks as if this court will rise. Do you have bail ready?'

Maria Eleanora was soaked with sweat. Scroggs was playing a spiteful game. A man accused of treason, of being accessory to murder, would never be granted bail.

'Well, sir?' Scroggs leaned forward. 'Do you have bail ready, or do you not?'

A deadly hush greeted his question.

'Are you going to answer, Mr Atkins?'

'Bull Face Jonas' was slumped in his chair, head down, sniggering softly to himself. Maria Eleanora caught a movement and noticed that the chairs behind the Attorney-General were empty. She counted three in all; these must be for the prosecution witnesses.

'My Lord.' Samuel spoke up. 'You know the charges levelled against me. I am prepared for my trial, if your lordship pleases, but not for bail.'

'Are you now? Are you now?'

Scroggs leaned back in his chair, resting his elbows on the arms, steepling his fingers. He lifted his white wig and scratched his balding head. He fluffed out his scarlet robe like a woman would do her dress on a hot summer's day.

'My Lord.' The Attorney-General was back on his feet. 'The business before this court is heavy and onerous. The burdens on your lordship are too great to be imagined.'

'What are they doing?' Maria Eleanora murmured. She dared not speak to Dolius who was now whispering rapidly to Atkins.

'They are trying to have the case referred,' Cecily replied. 'Not here but at the Sessions House. If that happens, Samuel could be back in prison till spring or early summer.'

'You, sir!' Scroggs bawled, pointing at Dolius. 'Who are you?'

'My Lord, I have business in other courts,' Dolius replied. 'My name is James Bartlett of Gore. This young man has begged me for my advice here in court. I have proper papers and warrants to show your lordship.'

Scroggs gestured at him to keep quiet.

'Master Atkins.' Scroggs's face was a mask of mock concern. 'The case against you is serious enough: if found guilty your troubles would soon be over.'

A chorus of laughter greeted his words. The Judge beamed round, accepting the plaudits at his witticisms.

'But you see, Mr Atkins,' Scroggs continued, 'we are approaching the end of the law term. Many people's livelihoods are at stake. We can't assume new business, just for your sake.'

'My Lord,' Samuel retorted, 'my life lies at stake. I have been under severe imprisonment a long time. I humbly pray that I may be tried. Besides, I have many witnesses who have remained in town to give evidence on my behalf. They have already tarried long enough.'

Maria Eleanora glanced quickly at 'Bull-Face Jonas' and his cronies. They seemed bemused by Samuel's reference to witnesses: their smiles disappeared and they sat, looking at each other, shaking their heads and whispering.

'Mr Atkins.' Scroggs decided to finish the argument. 'We cannot do this. You must be content. You shall be taken from here and tried at the Sessions House.'

'My Lord.' Samuel refused to give way. 'My witnesses are officers in His Majesty's ships. The country is in a parlous state, these men must put to sea. They cannot tarry around town for ever.'

His barbed remarks seemed to have an effect. Scroggs glanced sharply at 'Bull-Face Jonas' who shrugged and spread his hands. Dolius was whispering again.

'My Lord.' Samuel spoke up. 'As I have said, my witnesses are sea-faring men.'

Maria Eleanora closed her eyes. Oh God, she prayed, do not let our hard work be wasted!

'You've said that already,' Scroggs drawled, refilling the goblet. 'And I am aware of the dangers threatening His Majesty. That, sir, is why *you* are in court. But, the law is the law and the sea is the sea.'

'My Lord,' Atkins said, 'I merely wish to see justice done. I am a loyal subject of His Majesty. I am innocent of these charges. I, too, have business in hand.'

'What do you mean, sir? What do you mean?' Scroggs seemed to be enjoying the debate.

'I am not a wastrel, sir.'

'My Lord.' 'Bull-Face Jonas' sprang to his feet. 'Is this court in session or is it not? The prisoner is being allowed to speak and the jury hear his words.'

'True, true,' Scroggs agreed mournfully. 'Things have come to a pretty pass.' He glared at Atkins. 'You've had your say, sir.'

'No, my Lord, I haven't finished. The matters in hand are not the charges levelled against me but whether this court should try me now.'

'A fair point.' The Chief Justice hitched up his robe. 'So we finish and have done with it!'

'I am not one,' Samuel declared hotly and quickly, 'to roister in taverns such as the Sigh of Mourning or cavort with a young man in blue.'

The change in Scroggs's face was swift and remarkable. He lowered the half-raised goblet, placed it on the table and studied Samuel intently.

'What was that, sir?' The question came like a purr, a deep growl from Scroggs's fleshy throat. 'What are you talking about, sir?'

'My Lord.' Atkins leaned over the bar. 'I am simply saying some of my friends often visit the tavern known as the Sigh of Mourning. A few are captains in His Majesty's fleet. They have seen things which I would never talk about and certainly never practise. I am not such a wastrel: I do not yearn for the fleshpots, only for justice.'

Scroggs's lower lip came out as if considering some important point in law. Maria Eleanora clutched at Cecily. Dolius was blackmailing the Judge and Scroggs was carefully weighing the danger. The Chief Justice's popping eyes never strayed from Atkins. Only once did he glance at Dolius, as if speculating on the true source of the prisoner's hidden threats.

'My Lord, what is this?' 'Bull-Face Jonas' even forgot to rise: he stared anxious-faced at the bench.

'My Lord, I am simply making a point,' Atkins declared quietly, though his words rang through the court.

Everyone's interest was now provoked by this sharp exchange, though very few were aware of Samuel's hidden threat, it had been issued so swiftly. Scroggs got to his feet, so abruptly he surprised his own clerks.

'My Lord, will you not hear me?' Atkins cried out.

'I shall hear you!' Scroggs thundered back. 'But I must reflect.'

He left the dais and walked back down the stairs to his private chambers.

Commotion broke out. The clerks and ushers shouted for silence. The jury shifted uneasily on their benches. Maria Eleanora glanced at Samuel. He stared back, winked then turned away. Dolius remained cold and impassive. 'Bull-Face Jonas' sat back in his chair tapping his fingers against his lips, half-listening to one of his assistants whispering heatedly in his ear.

'What will happen?' Maria Eleanora turned to Cecily: her companion raised a finger to her lips. She felt Dolius's boot tap her ankle.

'Our Chief Justice,' Dolius whispered out of the corner of his mouth, 'knows he's caught and trapped. Scroggs has a reputation for being lewd and immoral. He's recognised the threat. If he doesn't try Samuel, certain complaints will be laid against him.'

'Oyez! Oyez!'

The clerk appeared at the top of the stairs: the rest of his words came gabbling out and he was almost pushed aside by Scroggs who came bounding up the steps, huffing and puffing, his face puce red. He returned to his chair, nodded at the court and sat down.

'My Lord,' 'Bull-Face Jonas' demanded. 'Have you decided?'

'I have,' Scroggs bawled back. 'If Atkins wishes to be tried before this court, then tried he shall be!'

'But my Lord?' 'Bull-Face Jonas' objected.

'Shut up!' Scroggs roared. 'And have the charges read!'

For a while commotion and chaos reigned. 'Bull-Face Jonas' was shuffling amongst his papers. Members of his group hurriedly left the court and came back. Maria Eleanora noticed they returned with Bedloe and two others who took the seats behind the Attorney-General. Dolius was whispering to Atkins. Samuel glanced at the witnesses prepared to swear away his life. Scroggs demanded silence and the charges be read out. 'Bull-Face Jonas' complied, declaring that on Monday, 14 October, late in the evening, Samuel Atkins, clerk, had been seen in Somerset Place standing over the murdered corpse of Justice Edmund Godfrey. They had chosen their date well!

'How do ye plead?' the clerk demanded.

'My Lord.' Atkins raised his hand. 'My Lord, I have one question.'

'How do ye plead?' the clerk screamed.

'My Lord, I have one question.'

'What is it?' Scroggs shouted.

'You, sir.' Samuel had now left the bar and pointed to the witnesses sitting between Captain Childs and Bedloe. 'What is your name?'

'Jeremy Prinkheart,' the fellow told him.

'And what is mine?'

Maria Eleanora could see that Prinkheart had been drinking. He was confused and dazed; he had not been informed of who was who amongst the throng at the bar. Bedloe tried to intervene.

'What is my name?' Samuel demanded.

'I don't know, sir.'

'And you've never seen me before?'

'Why no, sir, never.'

Even from where she stood, Maria Eleanora could see the consternation on Bedloe's face. 'Bull-Face Jonas' simply raised his hand to cover his eyes. Bedloe was tugging at Prinkheart's sleeve but the damage had been done.

'What is this?' Scroggs spoke up.

'Nothing, my Lord.' Samuel had now returned to the bar.

Maria Eleanora felt elated. In one bold stroke Dolius had destroyed the prosecution's chief witness.

'Well sir, you want to be tried!' Scroggs barked. 'Make your plea.'

'Not guilty, Your Honour.'

Scroggs gestured at 'Bull-Face Jonas' to begin. The Attorney-General had decided to do his best: Shaftesbury and his Green Ribboners had carefully honed the charges against Samuel. Godfrey had disappeared over a weekend but they ignored all this and tried to place Samuel in Somerset Place the following Monday evening, saying not that he had committed murder but that he must have been an accomplice to Green, Berry, Hill and the rest. They were hoping Samuel's confusion, his forgetfulness and lack of witnesses would make him vulnerable. The witnesses were called. Captain Childs, sharp-faced and shifty-eyed, approached the bar and described how Atkins had contacted him to hire an assassin to commit a murder on behalf of his master.

'How?' asked the Lord Chief Justice. 'Is Mr Atkins's master named?'

'Mr Pepys, Your Honour.'

'What! Mr Pepys of the Navy?'

'Yes, my Lord.'

'I find this hard to believe.'

'Bull-Face Jonas' leaned against the table. 'My Lord, we do have a witness before you who has taken an oath that this is so.'

'And what do you say to that, Mr Atkins?'

'I say it's a lie!' Atkins replied. He glanced along the bar to where Captain Childs stood all a-quiver. 'I find it difficult to believe that Captain Childs, a man who owes me money, who struck his colours to Algerian pirates, could lie so falsely about loyal subjects of the Crown such as myself and Mr Pepys.'

This cutting response was enough to set the court babbling. The clerk screamed for silence; Scroggs was not impressed.

'Is this the truth?' The Chief Justice turned to the witness.

'Yes, my Lord, unfortunately it is.'

'Aye, unfortunate indeed! You'd best stand down.' Scroggs smiled falsely. 'But we'll bear your evidence in mind.'

Maria Eleanora couldn't decide whether Scroggs felt so threatened he'd decided to change course and not be so hostile to Samuel, or whether he was genuinely vexed at how clumsy the prosecution's case had become.

'My Lord.' Samuel spoke up. 'I am a good, loyal, honest

Protestant. I have no business in Somerset Place, so why should I be there in the first place?'

'Sir William?' Scroggs stared hard at 'Bull-Face Jonas'. 'The prisoner has asked a pertinent question.'

'Yes, my Lord, he has. We have a witness who will demonstrate that Atkins often attended the Queen's Chapel and was a regular visitor to Her Majesty's household.'

Maria Eleanora held her breath. There was a grain of truth in the Attorney-General's string of lies. Samuel had often approached Somerset Place, hoping to have a glimpse of her.

'And you have a witness for all this?' Scroggs asked sweetly.

'Ah yes, my Lord.'

'And where is this witness?' Scroggs's voice dropped to a kindly whisper.

All in court seemed to hold their breath.

'I have a witness, my Lord.' 'Bull-Face Jonas' gestured towards where Prinkheart sat, head in hands.

'My Lord.' Samuel spoke up. 'If that man is their witness, he's already said he does not know my name nor seen me before.'

'I protest!' 'Bull-Face Jonas' squeaked.

'You can protest to your heart's content,' Scroggs bellowed. 'You can't have a man saying one thing, one moment in court, and the opposite the next. Is this all you have, Sir William?'

'Oh no, my Lord.' 'Bull-Face Jonas' became all bully-boy again. 'We have others and we wait, with great interest, to hear just where Master Atkins claims he really was that fateful night!'

Chapter Fifteen

Captain William Bedloe was next to take the stand. Despite 'Bull-Face Jonas's bravado, Bedloe seemed ill-at-ease. Cecily hid behind Maria Eleanora, who glared down at the bar at this perjurer prepared to swear away her beloved's life. Bedloe was greatly discomfited. The collapse of Prinkheart as a prime witness had clearly shaken him. He took the oath in a vibrant voice but Cecily could have laughed at how crestfallen and stumbling this perjurer became as his farrago of lies tumbled out. How, determined to betray the Plot, he had accepted the invitation of a priest to attend Somerset Place. How Green, Berry and Hill had committed murder. He was sure Samuel Atkins had been present. Or, at least, half-convinced that the prisoner at the bar, and the man he had seen, were one and the same person.

Dolius was whispering to Samuel and, when Bedloe finished his halting story, the young man attacked.

'Was the light as good as this, sir?'

'Oh no,' Bedloe replied.

'So, how can you be so sure that I was present?'

'A good question,' Scroggs intervened, tapping the tip of his quill against the bench. 'I mean, sir,' the Chief Justice pointed his quill at Atkins then back to Bedloe, 'can you make out every feature of the prisoner? Here, in this court?'

'No, my Lord.'

'Why was I there?' Atkins asked. 'What reason did I give?'

'The person I saw never spoke.'

'*The person you saw*,' Samuel repeated. 'Are you now saying, sir, that perhaps you were mistaken?'

'I think I may be.'

All chatter in the court died.

'Think?' Samuel cried. 'Sir, will you *think* my life away? Will you *think* me to Tyburn and onto the execution block?'

'Bull-Face Jonas' lumbered to his feet, trying to help his client but Bedloe's lack of confidence grew.

'You are a witness,' Scroggs reminded him, 'for the prosecution. This man's life is at stake! Did you see him or did you not?'

'I think I did.'

'Think!' Scroggs thundered, imitating the accused.

Maria Eleanora could have kissed the fleshy-jowled Judge.

'I am not interested in what you *think*, Captain Bedloe, but in what you *saw*. Now, I charge you, look upon the prisoner and answer. Is he the man or is he not?'

Bedloe stared across at Atkins who now boldly faced him.

'I cannot swear, my Lord. Indeed, on reflection, the man I saw had a more manly face, and a beard . . .'

Bedloe was finished. 'Bull-Face Jonas' sat head in hands.

'Your next witness!'

Atkins's old schoolmaster was summoned to the bar. A spindly-legged, grey-haired man, Master Edward Littlejohn had a jutting nose and short-sighted eyes. Maria Eleanora's heart sank. The fellow was what he appeared to be, an old busybody who, if he had really had any affection for Samuel, would have kept his mouth shut. 'Bull-Face Jonas' returned to the charge.

'Tell me, sir, on Friday the eleventh of October last, you had a longstanding invitation given to the prisoner to have dinner with you at Mount Horeb in Pudding Lane did you not?'

'Mount Horeb?' Scroggs intervened, licking his lips. 'What place is that?'

'An eating-house, my Lord,' the old schoolmaster squeaked. 'It serves good steaks and savoury pies.'

Scroggs nodded wisely.

'And did you go to Mount Horeb?' 'Bull-Face Jonas' asked.

'Of course.'

'And did the prisoner, Samuel Atkins?'

'No, he did not arrive.'

'Did he send you advance warning?'

'No, he did not!'

'Did he apologise the day after?'

'No, he did not!'

'Or since then?'

Again the denial.

'So, I ask myself,' 'Bull-Face Jonas' trumpeted, 'why should a young man, who has accepted an invitation to dinner, not keep that appointment or apologise for his absence? What was so pressing, so urgent as to keep him away?'

'A very good question.' Scroggs glared at Atkins. 'If I was invited to dine on fresh puddings and pies at Mount Horeb I would certainly attend, particularly with an old friend, a man to whom I owed so much.' Scroggs's voice became sweet and low. 'You do owe your old teacher a great deal, Master Atkins?'

'Oh yes, my Lord.'

'So why didn't you keep the appointment? Why didn't you apologise?'

319

'My Lord, I finished work on that Friday and made my way to a tavern.'

'Not the Sigh of Mourning?' Scroggs interrupted, a sneer on his face.

'No, sir, the Cat and Fiddle.'

'And?'

'My Lord, I became drunk that Friday and, God forgive me, I remained drunk until the following Tuesday morning.'

'So, you like your canary and sack?' Scroggs wheedled.

'Yes, my Lord.'

'Drink to the point of oblivion?'

'My Lord, I have remembered where I was on that particular Monday, or at least others have remembered for me.'

Samuel's reply provoked gasps from the court. 'Bull-Face Jonas' listened intently. Bedloe sat moodily staring before him. The seat between him and the Attorney-General was now empty: Prinkheart had been sent packing.

'We'll come to Monday in a while,' Scroggs replied. 'Do you often drink like this, Mr Atkins, deep in your cups? A drunken man is as capable of murder as a sober one.'

'My Lord, I have been in love. I *am* in love.'

'Ah!' Scroggs's sigh was sarcastic. 'And so you went to drown your sorrows?'

'Yes, my Lord.'

'Was he like this at school?' The Chief Justice turned to the old teacher.

'No, my Lord. A sober boy, industrious and studious.'

'A good Protestant?' Scroggs whispered.

'Aye, my Lord, and a loyal subject of the Crown.'

'That,' Scroggs replied, lifting his fingers, 'is for us to decide. Sir, you may stand down.'

Maria Eleanora, who had watched this pantomime, was jostled as Dolius turned and stared back at the entrance.

Maria Eleanora followed his gaze and whispered a prayer of thanksgiving. A sea captain stood just on the top of the steps leading into the court, resplendent in scarlet waistcoat, white stock and a canary-coloured frogged coat, his dark-red hair tied in a queue behind him. A look of disdain coloured his harsh, weather-beaten face; his blue eyes studied the court as if he believed everyone here, including Scroggs, was beneath him. To Maria Eleanora he appeared as an angel of light. She could see others standing behind him. Pepys had kept his word. Samuel's witnesses had been given permission to leave their duties and attend the court. 'Bull-Face Jonas', however, wasn't finished. He loudly declared that he had no further witnesses. He pointed out that Bedloe still half-believed Atkins was the man whilst the prisoner had not given a satisfactory explanation of where he had been that fateful weekend.

'We hear your case! We hear your case!' Scroggs nodded wisely. 'Now, Master Atkins, let us hear your defence: make it speedy.' He paused as a bell somewhere in Westminster Hall tolled the passing hours. 'My stomach is beginning to rumble. Let me remind you of the pertinent facts. I am now not interested, Mr Atkins, nor is the court, in where you were on Friday night, Saturday night or Sunday night but Monday, the fourteenth of October, is very important. If you can prove that you were elsewhere, and that proof is beyond doubt, then good. However, if you cannot, the finger of suspicion still rests upon you. I do not want any dancing round the Maypole or long, boring speeches. The jury have listened carefully. You have your trial by grace and favour. Do you understand me?'

'Yes, my Lord,' Atkins replied.

'In which case,' Scroggs boomed, 'call your first witness!'

'I do, my Lord. I call Captain Vittles!'

'Captain Vittles!' the usher of the court bawled. 'Present yourself for oath!'

321

The sea captain swaggered up to the bar. He thrust his hat into his hands, took the oath and stood before Scroggs as if he was on his own quarter-deck commanding a man-of-war.

'Is your name really Vittles?'

'Yes, Your Honour. Captain Henry Vittles, commander of the sloop *Catherine* now lying off Greenwich.'

'Vittles! Vittles!' Scroggs leaned back in his chair. 'You have your victuals, eh?' He laughed at the pun and glared round the court. The others joined in.

'A good English name!' the captain snapped.

'Of course! Of course!' the Chief Justice agreed. 'And a loyal officer of the Crown. Very well, Captain Vittles, tell me your tale.'

'It's not a tale, my Lord, it's the truth.'

'The truth?' Scroggs retorted. 'If it's the truth I look forward to hearing it.'

'Captain Vittles.' Samuel spoke up. 'Would you please tell the court about the events of Monday, the fourteenth of October?'

'Why, of course.' Vittles drew a deep breath. 'My Lord, at eight o'clock that morning I came up to London to see Mr Pepys and went immediately to Derby House. I arrived there at about nine o'clock in the morning but Mr Pepys was not present, being at Newmarket with His Majesty.'

'And the prisoner?'

'Master Atkins was also absent from his desk so I went to his lodgings. I found the young man in a distressing state.'

'Distressing?' Scroggs repeated.

'My Lord, he had been drinking deeply the night before and was in no fit condition to work. He did not seem very sharp or keen.'

'Is that his usual state?' Scroggs asked sternly.

'Oh no, my Lord. Master Atkins is a very good clerk, a

good seaman and an excellent companion. I tried to cheer him up but he seemed not interested. So I sat in his bedchamber and told him a few yarns, stories of the sea.'

'And what time did you leave?' Scroggs asked.

'Oh, my Lord, about noon but I took a solemn pledge from Atkins that he would join me on my sloop just after four in the afternoon. I said he could board my ship, broach a cask of claret and that I would have some merry company to cheer him up.'

'Did you now? Did you now?' Scroggs leered. 'Why, Captain Vittles, you are well named. I must visit your sloop myself.'

'My Lord, you would always be welcome.'

'Continue!'

'I returned to my sloop, the *Catherine*, my Lord, had the ship cleaned and my cabin prepared.'

'And who arrived first?' Scroggs asked. 'The merry company or Mr Atkins?'

'The merry company, my Lord. Four young ladies. Charming company indeed.'

'I am sure they were,' Scroggs breathed.

Samuel glanced despairingly at Maria Eleanora who had heard this story before; she smiled with her eyes. The thought of Samuel being with any other woman could hurt but, in the circumstances, she thanked God for Captain Vittles and his merry charmers.

'This is a delightful story,' Scroggs purred. 'Do continue.'

'Master Atkins arrived midway between four and five o'clock in the afternoon.'

'How do you know that?' Scroggs asked.

'My Lord, we are a ship, bells are rung, the watches are changed.'

'And how did Atkins come?'

'By barge, my Lord. He still looked miserable, downcast, very slurred in his speech. We had to help him over the side. He adjourned with me to my cabin where we drank some very good wine.'

Scroggs picked up his own goblet and slurped from it.

'And how long did this merry-making go on?'

'Oh sir, we were still drinking at seven.'

'And Atkins?'

'Deep in his cups, my Lord. He took to the wine like a fish to water.'

'Was he interested in the charming company?'

'He was polite enough but he kept getting their names mixed up. Sometimes he would begin to laugh.'

'And what time did Mr Atkins leave?'

'Oh, my Lord, it was dark, some time between ten and eleven o'clock at night. He was very much fuddled. I placed him in a barge with half a dozen bottles of claret and a large Dutch cheese but he forgot these.'

'So, so, so!' Scroggs tapped the table. 'Now here we have a true mystery.' He held up both hands. 'The prosecution claim that Mr Atkins was, all sober and murderous, at Somerset Place whilst we have this good captain saying he was very much fuddled on a sloop of war lying off Greenwich.'

'My Lord, if I may?' 'Bull-Face Jonas' clambered to his feet.

'Yes, Sir William, you may.'

Maria Eleanora held her breath: she hoped that the Attorney-General would stumble into the trap. He did so without a second thought.

'My Lord, members of the jury.' 'Bull-Face Jonas' swaggered forward beside Vittles. 'The accused works at Derby House. His superior is Master Pepys, Secretary of the Navy. For weeks Mr Atkins could not remember where he was or what he was doing and now, suddenly out of the mist, sails his saviour Captain Vittles.'

'My story is true!' the captain retorted.

'Is it?' 'Bull-Face Jonas' turned. He walked behind the captain to face the jury. 'I put it to you, Captain Vittles, that you are in command of a sloop. One day you wish to captain a man-of-war. I think you came along with this pretty story on the orders of your superior. Is that not so? I mean,' 'Bull-Face Jonas' lifted his hands as if in prayer. 'For weeks this young man has been trying to find out where he was. You must have heard of his imprisonment. Why didn't you come forward before?'

'My sloop has been in the Channel.'

'Your sloop has been in the Channel,' 'Bull-Face Jonas' mimicked. 'And that's a very good point, Captain Vittles.' He abruptly turned back. 'If your sloop was berthed at Greenwich, if you were entertaining young ladies, where are these doxies? Where is the bargeman who brought Atkins to your sloop? And isn't it strange that no one else saw him aboard?'

Vittles closed the trap. He gestured at Scroggs.

'But, my Lord, they did!'

'Bull-Face Jonas' stood, mouth gaping.

'My bosun, and four of my sailors, took Master Atkins back upriver,' Vittles explained. 'The tide was flowing so strongly they were unable to row the wherry under London Bridge, thus set him down near the Iron Gates at Billingsgate.'

'But, but . . .' 'Bull-Face Jonas' stuttered.

'Are these men in court?' Scroggs asked sweetly, openly enjoying the Attorney-General's embarrassment.

'Yes, my Lord, they are!'

Maria Eleanora looked over her shoulder: Bosun Tribblet and the four sailors Dickenson, Stephens, French and Holcock stood at the entrance to the court. Scroggs told Vittles to stand aside and all five sailors were called to the bar. They took the oath and faithfully described how they had loaded a very drunk and fuddled Master Atkins into their wherry. How they tried to row upriver but had turned round at London Bridge and eventually set him down at Billingsgate where one of them had escorted him back to his lodgings. Scroggs questioned them closely, as did 'Bull-Face Jonas' but the sailors' testimony couldn't be shaken. The seats behind the Attorney-General emptied: Bedloe and Childs had decided discretion was the better part of valour and fled. 'Bull-Face Jonas' gave up the fight and sat, surly-faced, staring at the floor.

Only then did Maria Eleanora realise that it was all over. She became suddenly aware of how heavy-limbed she felt. Her clothes seemed to swaddle and bathe her in sweat. The clamour in the court, the angry looks of 'Bull-Face Jonas' and the others, Scroggs enjoying another sip of wine, Cecily beside her – all these impressions filled her head, making her dizzy. When she looked up, Dolius had disappeared. Scroggs was shouting, asking if there was more evidence to be heard. Atkins replied that he had finished. Scroggs gave a pithy summation and the jury withdrew.

Maria Eleanora clung to the bar, staring at the shield above the Chief Justice's head. The jury were only gone a few minutes. She heard the usher tell the foreman to look upon the prisoner, and the words 'Not Guilty' echoed through that dreadful chamber. A cheer went up. Atkins thanked Scroggs, the ushers shouted for silence, followed by the patter of feet as people left the court eager to spread the news that, for the first time since this Plot had emerged, a 'Not Guilty' verdict had been returned.

Maria Eleanora tried to make her way across to Captain

Vittles to thank him. She wanted to clutch at Samuel but Dolius reappeared, this time dressed as an officer, and slipped his arm through hers.

'For God's sake, lass, we are not out of danger yet! Now is not the time nor the place.'

With that he steered her out of the court. Maria Eleanora was aware of walking quickly through Westminster Hall into the refreshing cold breeze outside. They pushed through stall-holders, lawyers and their clients, and at last they were out of the gateway. A sheriff's man, shouting about a horrible murder, recently committed, asked for any witnesses.

'There'll be no one,' Dolius whispered in her ear. 'But, Maria Eleanora, this is the last time you dress like this!'

She nodded absentmindedly. Only when they were through the gateway did she stop and look back over her shoulder.

'Samuel will be with you soon,' Dolius soothed.

They reached the waterfront and he steered her into a tavern; a garish sign above the doorway proclaimed it to be the Golden Griffin. Dolius took her down a stone-flagged passageway, up the staircase and along a gallery. He pushed open a door and gently guided her into a clean, sweet-smelling chamber.

'Stay here,' he instructed.

'Am I safe?'

'As long as you don't leave.'

Wearily, Maria Eleanora undid her cloak; she threw that and her hat on the bed and eased off the boots. Then she unbuckled her heavy swordbelt and let it fall to the floor. She seemed to wait an age; she realised how thirsty and hungry she had become, but she only wanted one thing. After an eternity she heard voices outside, footsteps along the gallery. The door swung open and Samuel, pale-faced, dishevelled, swept into the chamber. He stood, his back against the closed door, staring across at her, tears running down his cheeks.

'I love you, Maria Eleanora, I always have and I always will.'

'If you had died,' she replied, 'I would have died with you.'

Then they were in each other's arms. Maria Eleanora was aware of feverish kisses, his mouth hungry for hers. They embraced and caressed. She pulled him back towards the bed but he broke free, clutching her hands.

'It's so good to hold you in my arms,' he murmured hoarsely. 'Maria Eleanora, I thought I was going to die, that I'd never see you again.'

She would have responded but for a knock on the door. Dolius and Cecily stepped into the room. The King's most secret servant had now dispensed with any disguise, as had Cecily. She'd removed the grey wig and washed her face. Embraces and kisses were exchanged, then a servant brought in a welcome tray of food and wine.

'Come now.' Dolius made them sit round the table. He winked at Maria Eleanora. 'There's a time for kisses and a time for speaking. Now is the time for celebrating.' He filled four of the goblets to the brim. 'This is wine the King would pay gold for.' He lifted his cup. 'I give you Samuel Atkins: a brave and honest Englishman. I also toast one of the most beautiful, and bravest, women I have ever met, Maria Eleanora!'

The toast was accepted. Samuel responded. Maria Eleanora sipped the wine and, all of a sudden, found herself trembling, tears brimming in her eyes.

'Come now.' Dolius stretched across the table and covered her hand with his. 'It's only the shock which comes after battle. Even the bravest soldier experiences it.'

Cecily, sitting next to her, kissed her on the cheek. Maria Eleanora smelt the fragrant perfume she'd dabbed on her neck.

'It was so close.' Samuel shook his head. 'I really couldn't remember the details of that weekend. I acted like a callow youth deep in his cups – then all of a sudden I remembered Captain Vittles and his sloop off Greenwich. After that, I knew I was safe.'

'You caught gaol fever,' Dolius remarked. 'And everyone was all a-wonder why you kept talking about victuals, but now we know! It was good to see Bedloe discomfited whilst we took good care of Master Prinkheart.'

'Why did Chief Justice Scroggs become so alarmed about the boy in blue?' Samuel asked.

Dolius and his two companions laughed.

'It's a long story,' Cecily chuckled. 'But one worth the telling.' Her face grew serious. 'As with other matters.'

'But come.' Dolius gestured at the plate of cold meats, bread and pot of butter. 'We eat, we drink, we celebrate.'

'And then what?'

Dolius raised a finger to his lips.

'I must be honest, Maria Eleanora. You cannot stay in England. Shaftesbury and his gang have had one good bite at you.' He waved a hand at the alarm in her face. 'It's true, lass. They may try to bite again.'

'And Green, Berry and Hill?'

Dolius glanced sadly at her and shook his head.

'This is a war, Mistress. The King cannot do much, not for the moment.'

'And you?' Samuel asked. 'What will you do, Master Dolius?'

'Oh, I shall fight the good fight. I shall keep faith.'

'And Bedloe?'

Cecily raised her cup. 'Oh, leave Master Bedloe to me, and to God. Now, we must celebrate.'

Maria Eleanora ate as if she was in a dream. She was aware of her companions talking but she only had eyes for Samuel and he for her. The faint sounds of the tavern drifted up. The wine had its effect. There was a knock at the door, Dolius answered it and came back.

'Come now.' He clapped his hands. 'You must gather your possessions and go down.'

'Why?' Maria Eleanora asked, all alarmed.

'Someone wishes to see you.'

Maria Eleanora assumed her disguise. Samuel put his arm round her shoulders, drew her close and kissed her passionately on the cheek. Maria Eleanora glanced at Dolius's smiling face, broke free from Samuel's embrace and went up and kissed Dolius on the lips.

'Well, well, well!' Blood's eyes crinkled in amusement. 'That makes it all worthwhile. Maria Eleanora, I will remember that kiss and, when I'm an old man, I'll tell my grandchildren about it.'

Cecily stood silent, hands hanging down by her side. Her face, framed by the golden hair, seemed paler, thinner, those lustrous blue eyes larger, watchful and tense.

'Will I see you again?' Maria Eleanora asked.

Cecily shook her head. 'I do not think so. At least, not with the eye but, in my heart and soul, Maria Eleanora, I shall always remember you.'

'And I shall never forget you.'

They embraced and kissed. Cecily turned and walked away. Maria Eleanora could see she was crying. Dolius ushered them through the door and down the stairs. He took them out to the stableyard which lay behind the tavern. A black-painted coach pulled by four magnificent greys stood waiting, outriders, their faces hidden by broad-brimmed hats and heavy cloaks, grouped round it. One of them moved and Maria Eleanora glimpsed the holster of a heavy horse pistol fastened to his saddle.

'What is this?' she asked apprehensively.

Dolius beckoned them on. The yard was deserted. No ostler, grooms, nothing but this massive black coach with its golden lamps, the gleaming harness of the horses and those menacing outriders who guarded every approach. Dolius opened the door. Samuel and Maria Eleanora climbed into the coach and sat on the quilted seat opposite the King. Charles was swathed in a heavy robe; as they entered he took his hat off and placed it in his lap: he grasped the silver-topped walking-cane and beat a soft tattoo against the floor of the coach. Samuel realised who he was and became flustered and embarrassed.

'Oh, for pity's sake!' the King drawled. 'Sit back, Master Atkins, and make yourself comfortable.' He sketched a bow towards Maria Eleanora. 'Madam, you look most fetching.' His smile widened. 'But, there again, you would in anything or nothing.'

Maria Eleanora blushed. Charles grasped her hand, raised it to his lips and kissed it. He held it fast as his eyes studied her, cold and hard.

'But no more disguises, my dear! No more running about London for secret meetings.' He released her hand. 'You, Master Atkins, are most fortunate. It's not every day that someone appears before Chief Justice Scroggs and walks away an innocent, happy man.'

'Your Majesty, I am most grateful,' Samuel blustered. 'We are both grateful for all your help.'

'Nonsense! Nonsense!' Charles tapped the cane against his boot. 'It's the least I could do. I only wish I could help the others. But, I tell you this.' His voice became hard. 'As I've said before and I'll say again: in my time, in my place and at my own choosing I shall let my vengeance be known. Now you, Maria Eleanora, could be a danger to my Queen. The Green Ribbon Club already suspects you and, like rats at a cheese barrel, they'll gnaw and gnaw until they are successful.'

Maria Eleanora clutched her stomach.

'In three days' time, my man-of-war *The Invincible* will set sail from the Thames to pay a courtesy visit to my good cousin the Queen of Portugal. You shall be on board with all your possessions, baggage and impediments.'

Maria Eleanora's throat went dry. Charles's face broke into a smile.

'I am not banishing you, my pretty. I am protecting you and, above all, protecting my Queen.'

'But Your Majesty . . .' Maria Eleanora protested.

'I haven't finished,' Charles said. He moved the cane and tapped Samuel's boot. 'You, my fine fellow, shall be on board the same frigate. A time in the sun will do you the world of good. You can carry letters to my good cousins in Portugal and to the Queen's kinsmen. Your duties will be light and, what else you get up to,' he grinned, 'is a matter for you and Maria Eleanora to decide. No, no.' He gestured with his hand. 'Please don't thank me. I become embarrassed. So few people can thank me that, when they do, tears come to my eyes and it spoils my looks.' His face softened. 'Do you love each other?'

'Yes, Your Majesty!'

'Good,' Charles whispered. 'For I am a mighty Prince. I rule a great kingdom but, the older I get and the more sinful I become, I recognise one fact, one truth. There is nothing better under the sun than the deep love one person has for another.

Now,' he straightened in the seat. 'I left my lovely boys, my spaniels at the Queen's house. I must go back there. Maria Eleanora, when we do, you slip out with your love swain and prepare for Lisbon. Ah well.' He sighed. 'We must be going. My lovely boys will be waiting . . .'

Dolius and Cecily watched the carriage leave. Cecily dried her eyes.

'They are very fortunate,' she whispered.

Dolius put an arm round her shoulders.

'Because they have each other, yes!' he agreed.

'Do you think they'll marry?'

'Do you think the sun will rise tomorrow?' he chuckled. 'They'll be married before summer and Maria Eleanora will be carrying his child by Christmas.' His voice grew soft. 'They'll walk hand in hand through green, sweet-smelling vineyards and take the shade in cypress groves. Love like that will not be brooked. I suspect, Cecily, we are seeing the beginning of a fairy story. They'll live longer than we do and see their children's children dance in the sun.'

Cecily put her face in her hands and began to weep. Dolius hugged her closer and brushed her beautiful blonde hair with his lips.

'I know, I know. We shall miss them both but I have you and you have me, Cecily. I am not much. I was born a rogue. I have lived as a rogue and, unless God is good, I'll die as one.'

Cecily took her hands away; she turned and stared up into Dolius's eyes.

'Will this game ever be over?' she whispered.

Dolius leaned down and kissed her on the lips.

'As long as the music plays, my sweet, the dance goes on and dance we must!'

Cecily put her arms round his waist.

'Now, you are not going to say something stupid, are you?' Dolius breathed. 'You are not going to say you have fallen in love with my bright kind eyes?'

'I have loved once and I will never love again,' Cecily replied, 'but a small corner of my heart is yours, Captain Thomas Blood, to have and to hold.'

'You have all my heart,' he whispered back.

She stood on tiptoe and kissed him on the lips.

'You are a lying scoundrel. You say that to all the wenches.'

She went back into the chamber, picked up her goblet and sipped at the wine.

'We have business to do, Master Dolius. Accounts to settle. You have what I asked for?'

Dolius went to his cloak; he drew out a leather pouch and handed it to her.

'Drop by drop,' he whispered. 'Little by little. Don't hurry it. Don't let Master Bedloe go gently into the dark.'

Cecily took the leather pouch, her blue eyes hard as flint.

'I'll be missed.'

She drained the goblet, put it on the table and, picking up her cloak, left the chamber.

She found Bedloe drowning his sorrows in the taproom of the King's Head. The Judas man, the perjurer, was greatly discomfited; he sat by himself, an angry scowl on his face. This disappeared as Cecily approached carrying a fresh jug of ale and a clean goblet.

'You heard what happened in court?' he barked.

'Hush now, my sweet,' Cecily murmured. 'A minor setback. Atkins was only a minnow. You are Captain William Bedloe, Saviour of the Nation.'

She filled the fresh goblet to the brim and handed it over.

He lurched forward and tried to paw her. Cecily moved away and sat on a stool at the other side of the table.

'Well, Cecily, will I get what I want?'

'You will get what you deserve,' she teased back. 'Now, come, William, drink the ale. I broached a special cask.'

Bedloe lifted the cup and glowered round: the taproom was empty. Most of the Green Ribboners were still out in the city.

'I wonder what happened to Blue-skin?' he murmured. 'And they say Eastwell was murdered this morning.'

'Drink!' Cecily urged.

Bedloe did so. Aye, drink, Cecily thought. Drink the special poison Dolius has brought me! She watched her enemy drain the cup and demand more. Cecily obligingly poured it. Bedloe's head went down as the ale and the heat from the fire made itself felt. She got to her feet as if to move away.

'You'll come back, won't you?' Bedloe slurred. 'You'll come back and keep me company, Cecily?' He stared across at the fading light coming through the window. 'I don't like to be alone. At times like this I feel ghosts throng all around me.'

'Do you now?' Cecily came and stood over him. 'Which ghosts, Master Bedloe?' she whispered as she watched his head fall on his chest. 'Justice Godfrey? The souls of those you have murdered?'

Cecily moved away. What day of the week was it, she thought? Ah yes, 8 February. She cradled the jug. By summer, she thought, watching the sleeping Bedloe, you too will be a ghost. Cecily looked at the fire, the flames licking greedily at the scented pine logs. She drew comfort from another thought. In her mind's eye she saw Samuel and Maria Eleanora walking down a cypress-lined trackway, green fields on either side. The sunshine was warm and strong. She could hear their laughter, their words of love.

'For them too,' she whispered, 'the reckoning must be paid! You can drink, Master Bedloe, the cup of bitterness, whilst the loving cup will be theirs!'

Postscript

'*Dolius, King of Ithaca, to his good friends, Master Samuel and his beautiful wife Maria Eleanora, health and greetings.*

Two years have passed since you left the shores of Ithaca and travelled, like Ulysses, to more temperate climes. I talk in parables so that those, who may have unwarranted curiosity in my scribblings, do not fully comprehend what I say. Yet passion speaks and the heart cannot lie. I miss you, Maria Eleanora, I think of you and often meet you in my dreams. Now, Samuel, do not get jealous for your lady's heart is always yours whilst mine is always hers!

I miss both of you and listen very carefully to the news from abroad. God, in His infinite providence, has rewarded you. I hear of days and nights under warmer, sunnier skies, where the wine flows freely and danger does not lurk in the shadows of some filthy alleyway. You have children, twins I understand, a boy and a girl. I rejoiced when I heard that you had them baptised Thomas and Cecily. One day I hope to visit you and kiss these two sweet poppets.

The news from Ithaca is good. Plot and counter-plot is drawing to an end. More victims are being released and the kingdom grows tired of Master Oates and the machinations of my Lord S. The King will free himself from the traps which beset him and reign in his own subtle way, though God knows what will happen should his brother succeed! I still pursue my master's enemies: some have already gone into the dark and that includes the infamous Captain B. Taken ill suddenly he was, at the King's Head tavern in the summer of 1680. No one mourned him and he was hurried to a silent grave where his bones can rot and his soul can wander the fiery alleyways of Hell. As for sweet Cecily, Lord how I miss her! She is nearer to you than to me. She took a turn for religion and left the shores of Ithaca for a ladies' convent amidst the green woods and lush fields of the Bois de Vincennes outside Paris. No, she has not taken the veil or consecrated herself to God but retired from the world to think and reflect. As you can gather, her task is done. I shall mourn her for I miss her; in time I shall visit her. For the rest, I fight the good fight. I run the race, I keep the faith.

My love to you all.
Dolius, King of Ithaca.

Author's Note

The Great Plot of 1678–80 is one of the most fascinating mysteries of late seventeenth-century history. Sir Edmund Berry Godfrey's murder, the discovery of his corpse, his burial and the hysteria which ensued are accurately described in this novel. Historians have always debated the reason for Godfrey's murder, yet all the evidence points to Shaftesbury and his gang killing the Justice to whip up hysteria against Charles II and his pro-French leanings.

Shaftesbury was a most able politician, a diminutive Machiavelli who came within an inch of toppling Charles II from his throne. Many men died gruesomely because of the horrid lies of the likes of Oates and Bedloe. Both of these were most unsavoury individuals. Oates had been thrown out of a number of livings because of his sordid private life and, although hailed as a 'Hero of the Nation', when Charles II died and his brother James succeeded, Oates was given a public whipping through London. Captain William Bedloe also sent a number of good men to their Maker before joining them, rather mysteriously, in the summer of 1680 whilst in London.

The machinations of the Plot are faithfully reflected in *The Loving Cup*. The attack on the Queen, the searching of her palace, the arrest and unfortunate execution of Coleman, Hill, Berry and Green, not to mention others, really happened.

Samuel Atkins, Pepys's clerk, was taken up in a clever attack which was supposed to include his master, the Secretary of the Navy and, of course, James, Duke of York. Samuel Atkins, to his eternal credit, comes across as a man of great integrity, honesty and courage. He totally denied the charges and refused to implicate anyone else: his trial before Chief Justice Scroggs, as described in this novel, is based upon the historical record. Scroggs was about to adjourn the case when, for some unknown reason, he abruptly conceded and decided that Atkins could have his day. Scroggs was a bully-boy, a venal lecher whose private life had been openly criticised in the Commons. His conduct during the Great Plot would, today, certainly attract the attention of Amnesty International as Scroggs often assumed the roles of prosecutor *and* jury – as well as judge!

Atkins defended himself most ably. He demolished the prosecution's chief witness at the beginning of the trial by abruptly rounding on him and asking him if the witness had ever met him before. The perjurer Bedloe had brought immediately replied, 'No,' much to the consternation of those who wished to see Atkins hang. Samuel then completely routed the opposition by producing Captain Vittles and other seamen who took an oath that Atkins could never have been anywhere near Godfrey's corpse, for at the time he was dead drunk on the sloop *Catherine* anchored off Greenwich. Naturally Atkins walked free.

Captain Thomas Blood is not a figment of my imagination. One of the great rogues of seventeenth-century history, his exploits would fill a number of novels. Considerable evidence exists that Blood was very busy on the King's behalf in opposing and checking Shaftesbury and his Green Ribboners. One of the great mysteries of the Plot is, of course, Miles Prance. For some strange reason he never implicated Atkins though Shaftesbury would have loved this. It's a mystery which has never been solved, and *The Loving Cup* does offer one explanation. Prance may have been controlled by Shaftesbury but he was being secretly blackmailed by someone else. Rumours abounded that Miles Prance indulged in an alternative lifestyle which he would not have wished his wife and family to learn about.

King Charles II is accurately described in this novel: a monarch who wore a mask and acted the part of the merry rogue though this hid quicksilver wits and an astute brain. In many ways Charles was honourable. He never deserted his Queen and constantly begged for her forgiveness. Catherine of Braganza did not find this hard to grant. She adored Charles, despite his many infidelities.

I have no real evidence for the love affair between Samuel and Maria Eleanora except that Samuel did leave the country after his trial, returning some years later to rejoin Pepys's circle, becoming Secretary to Lord Dartmouth.

In the end all the actors have gone. The stage is clear but the passion and the fervour of those heady days in the late 1670s is still resonant in the historical records, the manuscripts and, above all, in the writings of Master Samuel Pepys.

Vanessa Alexander

Now you can buy any of these other bestselling
Headline books from your bookshop or
direct from the publisher.

FREE P&P AND UK DELIVERY
(Overseas and Ireland £3.50 per book)

Of Love and War	Vanessa Alexander	£5.99
Vale Valhalla	Joy Chambers	£5.99
The Journal of Mrs Pepys	Sara George	£6.99
Tales of Passion, Tales of Woe	Sandra Gulland	£6.99
Killigrew and the Golden Dragon	Jonathan Lunn	£5.99
The Queen's Bastard	Robin Maxwell	£6.99
The One Thing More	Anne Perry	£5.99
A History of Insects	Yvonne Roberts	£6.99
Under the Eagle	Simon Scarrow	£5.99
The Kindly Ones	Caroline Stickland	£5.99
Bone House	Betsy Tobin	£6.99
The Loveday Fortunes	Kate Tremayne	£5.99
Girl in Hyacinth Blue	Susan Vreeland	£6.99

TO ORDER SIMPLY CALL THIS NUMBER

01235 400 414

or e-mail orders@bookpoint.co.uk

Prices and availability subject to change without notice.

Of Love and War

Vanessa Alexander

In September 1921, Major Oscar Fairfax steps off a steam train at Caundon in County Durham and marches along the cobbled streets to the local pub, the Beaumont Arms, owned by Kitty Allerton and her widowed mother. A bloodhound of a man, Fairfax has scoured the country seeking out the crimes of those who, perhaps, did not do their best for king and country in the Great War. Now he has come to the mining town of Caundon, and Jack Allerton's name is at the top of his list.

Although the streets of her childhood are dirty and the terraced houses dominated by the pit, Kitty Allerton remembers only the delight of playing with her constant companions, Billy and Jack. The three were inseparable as they grew up, but Kitty finally married Billy. Before he left to fight in the Great War Billy asked for one strange promise: if he should die, she must marry his closest friend, Jack.

Some of the best, among them Billy, never returned from the mud and blood of Northern France. Kitty has kept her promise, but finds that the men who survived are tragically altered. Fairfax has come to exorcise their ghosts, but he brings new terrors with his desire for justice. Kitty watches in horror as he tears apart the lives of the men and women she has known, loved and respected, and slowly realises that he could hold a terrible secret concerning Billy's death.

Vanessa Alexander's powerful story of love, guilt, and retribution vividly captures the courage and tragedy of the Great War's survivors as they face a new and uncertain future.

0 7472 6464 3

headline